Becoming Achilles

D1261672

Greek Studies: Interdisciplinary Approaches

Series Editor: Gregory Nagy, Harvard University
Executive Editors: Corinne Pache, Emily Allen Hornblower,
and Eirene Visvardi
Associate Editors: Mary Ebbott, Casey Dué Hackney, Leonard Muellner,
Olga Levaniouk, Timothy Powers, Jennifer R. Kellogg, and Ivy Livingston

Recent titles in the series are:

Between Magic and Religion: Interdisciplinary Studies in Ancient Mediterranean Religion and Society
  Edited by Sulochana Asirvatham, Corinne Ondine Pache, and John Waltrous
Iambic Ideas: Essays on a Poetic Tradition from Archaic Greece to the Late Roman Empire
  Edited by Antonio Aloni, Alessandro Barchiesi, Alberto Cavarzere
The Ritual Lament in Greek Tradition, Second Edition
  by Margaret Alexiou
  revised by Dimitrios Yatromanolakis and Panagiotis Roilos
Homeric Variations on a Lament by Briseis
  by Casey Dué
Imagining Illegitimacy in Classical Greek Literature
  by Mary Ebbott
Tragedy and Athenian Religion
  by Christiane Sourvinou-Inwood
The Usable Past: Greek Metahistories
  Edited by K. S. Brown and Yannis Hamilakis
The Other Self: Selfhood and Society in Modern Greek Fiction
  by Dimitris Tziovas
The Poetry of Homer: New Edition, Edited with an Introduction by Bruce Heiden
  by Samuel Eliot Bassett
A Penelopean Poetics: Reweaving the Feminine in Homer's Odyssey
  by Barbara Clayton
Homeric Megathemes: War-Homilia-Homecoming
  by D. N. Maronitis
The Visual Poetics of Power: Warriors, Youths, and Tripods in Early Greece
  by Nassos Papalexandrou
Fighting Words and Feuding Words: Anger and the Homeric Poems
  by Thomas R. Walsh

Diachronic Dialogues: Authority and Continuity in Homer and the Homeric Tradition
by Ahuvia Kahane

Metrical Constraint and the Interpretation of Style in Tragic Trimeter
by Nicholas Baechle

Under the Sign of the Shield: Semiotics and Aeschylus' Seven Against Thebes
by Froma I. Zeitlin

The Philosopher's Song: The Poets' Influence on Plato
by Kevin Crotty

Archaeology in Situ: Sites, Archaeology, and Communities in Greece
Edited by Anna Stroulia and Susan Buck Sutton

When Worlds Elide: Classics, Politics, Culture
Edited by Karen Bassi and J. Peter Euben

Light and Darkness in Ancient Greek Myth and Religion
Edited by Menelaos Christopoulos, Efimia D. Karakantza, and Olga Levaniouk

Choral Identity and the Chorus of Elders in Greek Tragedy
By U. S. Dhuga

Disguise and Recognition in the Odyssey
By Sheila Murnaghan

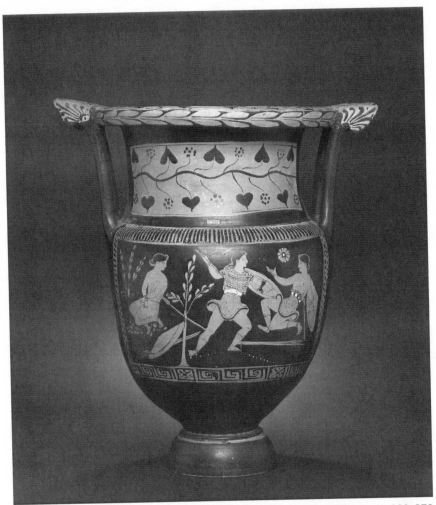

Achilles slaying Lykaon. Column krater attributed to The Prisoner Painter, ca. 380–370 B.C. © Trustees of the British Museum.

Becoming Achilles

Child-Sacrifice, War, and Misrule in the *Iliad* and Beyond

Richard Holway

LEXINGTON BOOKS.
Lanham • Boulder • New York • Toronto • Plymouth, UK

Published by Lexington Books
A wholly owned subsidiary of The Rowman & Littlefield Publishing Group, Inc.
4501 Forbes Boulevard, Suite 200, Lanham, Maryland 20706
www.lexingtonbooks.com

Estover Road, Plymouth PL6 7PY, United Kingdom

British Library Cataloguing in Publication Information Available

Library of Congress Cataloging-in-Publication Data
Holway, Richard, 1945–
   Becoming Achilles : child-sacrifice, war, and misrule in the Iliad and beyond / Richard Holway.
      p. cm. — (Greek studies: interdisciplinary approaches)
   Includes bibliographical references and index.
   ISBN 978-0-7391-4690-3 (cloth : alk. paper) — ISBN 978-0-7391-4691-0 (pbk. : alk. paper) — ISBN 978-0-7391-4692-7 (electronic)
   1. Homer. Iliad. 2. Psychology in literature. 3. Families—Greece—History—To 1500. 4. Epic poetry, Greek—History and criticism. I. Title.
   PA4037.H7725 2012
   883'.01—dc23
                                                                        2011028638

Printed in the United States of America

To Janet and Isabelle with love

Contents

Foreword
by Gregory Nagy, General Editor

Building on the foundations of scholarship within the disciplines of philology, philosophy, history, and archaeology, this series concerns not just the archaic and classical periods of Greek traditions but the whole continuum—along with its discontinuities—from the second millennium BCE to the present. The aim is to enhance perspectives by applying an interdisciplinary approach to problems that have in the past been treated as the exclusive concern of a single, given discipline. Besides the reinvigoration of the older disciplines, as in the case of historical and literary studies, the series encourages the application of such newer ones as linguistics, sociology, anthropology, and comparative literature. It also encourages encounters with current trends in methodology, especially in the realm of literary theory.

Becoming Achilles: Child-Sacrifice, War, and Misrule in the Iliad *and Beyond*, by Richard Holway, applies perspectives learned from the discipline of psychology to the figure of Achilles in the Homeric *Iliad*. His reading transcends not only the conventional views of Achilles that are current in our time but even the conventions of ancient Greek epic mythmaking. In other words, Holway sees patterns that may not have been recognized even by the practitioners of the craft that we know as Homeric poetry. He shows how this poetic craft becomes the staging ground for destructive mother-son and father-daughter relationships—presenting them in fragmented and displaced forms, thereby effectively denying their pervasiveness. On the epic stage, these family relationships can be reexamined and reconstituted, leaving the reader with a new clarity of vision about the supreme moral problem of heroic violence. This book is not only good to think with: it is also good, very good, to talk about.

Preface and Acknowledgments

Achilles, the all-but-invincible hero of the *Iliad*, is a cultural icon. In the world of the poem, he is the son every parent wants to have and every son wants to be like. The epic that enshrines—and complicates—Achilles is awash in myths. With the help of powerful female deities, Zeus establishes justice and order on Olympos. Goddesses compete for the title "the fairest," and heroes fight over Helen, the most beautiful of women. The inept, philandering Greek commander, Agamemnon, sacrifices his daughter, Iphigenia, and is murdered by his wife, Klytemnestra. Goddesses rejoice in producing glorious sons, or seethe with shame and envy when they fail.

A subset of these myths depicts the rearing of infants who are destined to become heroes. Divine mothers attempt to immortalize sons, for example by burning away their mortal parts. The myths correspond to modern theories about particular types of mother-son relationships. Viewing the *Iliad* in relation to its myths and research on family psychology illuminates the entire epic. It also sheds light on the psychology of honor, internecine violence, war, politics, and political philosophy. It may suggest hypotheses for the ongoing psychological research on which it is based.

I was updating sources for what I thought was a completed manuscript when I encountered John Bowlby's and Mary Ainsworth's work on infant-mother attachment. After I reframed the study in terms of attachment theory, the anonymous reader for this series suggested another restructuring. The reader also suggested relating my attachment-based approach to others, especially Freudian ones. Bowlby developed attachment theory to treat psychological problems originating in abuse, neglect, and loss, rather than oedipal fantasy. Attachment theory is rooted in observation of mother-infant interactions and their effects. Even so, the reader's question led to a recognition of how classic Freudian mechanisms operate in the *Iliad*—in a family context in which mothers turn from despised husbands to favored sons.

In addition to the reader for the series, I am grateful to its editors, Gregory Nagy and Leonard Muellner, for steadfastly encouraging the psychologically based work of an interloper. The same is true of classicists Ralph Johnson, Peter Brown, and Jack Winkler. Kurt Raaflaub let himself get roped into being an outside reader for the dissertation that laid the foundation for this book. Michael Rogin and Alan Dundes inspired and challenged me early on. Fellow *Iliad*-lover Bernard Mayes provided stimulating conversation. Former teachers Arlie Hochschild and Hanna Pitkin helped me to sharpen the book's focus. Historian-friends Dickson Bruce, David Moltke-Hansen, Randolph Roth, and Bertram Wyatt-Brown read drafts and provided valuable suggestions. William Freehling pruned thousands of superfluous words, teaching me how to write and edit. Psychologists Jude Cassidy, Inge Bretherton, Molly Kretchmar, and Jenny Macfie provided encouragement and guidance. Mark Mones performed serial surgeries that were more than cosmetic. J. E. Lendon and Ira Bashkow offered helpful last-minute advice. Casey Dué Hackney oversaw a productive review process. Jana Hodges-Kluck of Lexington Books developed a publishing plan and skillfully guided this book into print. I gratefully acknowledge a publication grant from the College of Arts and Sciences and the Vice President for Research and Graduate Studies at the University of Virginia. Thomas Walsh, Jacob Sperber, Peter Onuf, Erik Midelfort, and David Mattern allowed me to bend their ears for more than a decade. Their friendship, and that of Mary Kathryn Hassett and Nancy McLaughlin, has been sustaining. Any book imposes sacrifices on loved ones. For supporting my determination to write this one, I thank my wife, Janet Horne, who writes her own, and our eleven-year-old daughter, Isabelle, who is always working on something.

Charlottesville, Virginia, 2011

Introduction

Like much else in human life, the *Iliad*'s defining myths begin with childrearing. Divine mothers attempt to immortalize sons but are interrupted. The resulting sons are superior to ordinary mortals, but fall short of divine power and perfection. They are heroes. The myths that depict these forms of childrearing also critique them. Divine mothers with covert agendas that preclude loving nurture harm their infants. Insulted by impertinent questioning of their childrearing practices, goddesses proclaim that they provide superior nurture; critics are witless fools. Faced with goddesses' anger, critics quickly recant.

The analysis presented here is rooted in research into attachments that infants form with their primary caregivers, usually mothers. The type of bond differs according to the quality of care. Attachment theory suggests that perceptions of parents sacrificing children's needs to their own, which the *Iliad*'s myths discount, may be accurate. In order to avoid further alienating unreliable or rejecting caregivers, children disavow or repress their own perceptions and substitute those preferred by caregivers. Sons' defensive exclusion of information about maternal failings avoids provoking angry maternal reactions like those dramatized in myth.[1]

Even if the critics are right, how could a culture rooted in family patterns that are damaging to children survive, let alone produce the glories of ancient Greek civilization that are examined here: mythology, epic poetry, and political philosophy? Childrearing patterns that sacrificed children's needs to parents' could produce hyper-aggressive, skilled fighters, avid to demonstrate godlike prowess and fearful of being exposed as shamefully weak and defenseless. In various Greek societies at various times, similar high-stakes competitiveness, involving endless attempts to prove the self's or group's superiority to ordinary mortals, could encompass all manner of pursuits, from war and politics to athletics, poetry, art, and philosophy. Susceptibility to humiliation, mockery, ridicule, and dishonor in turn is associated with a proneness to violence, whether psychological or physical, within the family or community or between peoples and political communities. The real question, then, is similar to that which the Greeks pose for their Trojan adversaries in the *Iliad*: not how Greek cultures could survive but how other cultures that lacked their aggression and competition-enhancing reproductive technologies could survive contact with them.[2]

Brilliant creations like the *Iliad* are also products of cultural evolution. They play critical roles in sustaining destructive family dynamics and child-rearing practices that cannot be acknowledged: not by children, because their responses would anger caregivers on whom they depend; not by caregivers, because they do not wish to view themselves in this light; and not by cultures that depend on covert child-sacrifice for their continued existence. At the same time these narratives purge anger by redirecting individual and collective outrage from child-sacrificing parents to scapegoats.

Psychological (and parallel anthropological) studies suggest that mothers who use children to meet their needs often suffered similar treatment. In ancient Greek culture, sacrificial parenting takes the form of father-daughter and mother-son liaisons in which parents enlist opposite-sex children as substitute spouses. Fathers who favor daughters over their mothers sacrifice their development. They humiliate maternal models and disrupt daughters' maturation.

Daughters' favored status leads to a second sacrifice. Humiliated when fathers exchange them for other men's services via marriage, daughters attempt to recoup their special status by rearing superior sons.[3]

Parents who use children to meet their needs are at best unresponsive to children's. Rather than putting their emotional and even physical survival at risk by perceiving and responding to failures of parental nurture, sons and daughters idealize seductive, but also rejecting and exploitative caregivers, acting as if all is well. Sons idealize purportedly superior mothers. They shift blame and anger to others, ultimately themselves.[4]

The intense gender conflicts dramatized in Athenian tragedy have been taken to reflect a vicious circle in which maternal ambivalence toward sons leads to Athenian males' fearful imaginings of adult women, whom they consequently devalue, confine to the domestic sphere, and exclude from public life. Other writers deny the reality of maternal ambivalence. The fearful male fantasies that underlie patriarchal domination are rooted in the simple fact of sons' dependence on mothers.

Since the Enlightenment, Western intellectuals have deployed invidious dichotomies of state/family, public/private, and male/female to caricature classical Athens as an archetype of patriarchy and misogyny. This resilient historical paradigm is now widely regarded as an ideological construct rooted in fundamental misunderstandings of Athenian familial, social, and political life. This study finds, nonetheless, that the *Iliad* and myth evince a powerful strain of male fear of women in preclassical Greek culture. Moreover, it discovers a major locus of female betrayal and anger in sacrificial father-daughter liaisons that mirror the mother-son dyads that figure prominently in previous accounts.[5]

But this study is not about the position of women in ancient Greece. It is about men's and women's involvement in the reproduction of heroic culture—a shorthand for highly competitive, honor-based, strife- and violence-prone, ancient Greek cultures. Child-centered rather than woman-centered, it does not discount maternal responsibility for harm as baseless "mother blame." At issue here is the responsibility of parents, regardless of gender, to nurture children rather than sacrifice them to parents' needs. The concern is less with women's rights and their violation by men than with female and male children's birthrights and their violation by male and female caregivers.[6]

This analysis calls in question cherished mainstays of Western culture. Achilles is not merely the best, most terrifying fighter in the Achaian army. He presents a shining example of the courage to speak truth to power and the independence of mind to question traditional verities. He calls to account a commander who sacrifices his troops, as he once sacrificed his daughter, to save face and cover his own mistakes. When Agamemnon dishonors Achilles for calling attention to these abuses, Achilles questions whether there is any point to heroic striving. Yet as a paradigmatic hero-son Achilles exemplifies the opposite of speaking truth to power: mollifying caregivers, glossing over abuse. That Plato's Socrates is modeled on Achilles raises the stakes of the critique.[7]

Similar considerations apply to tragic learning through suffering, *pathei mathos*, a prototype of which Achilles undergoes in the *Iliad*. The death of his dear companion, Patroklos, brings home to Achilles the value of the life he sacrifices to glory. But killing Patroklos is Zeus's way of redirecting Achilles' anger from Agamemnon to the Trojans. It is a catalyst for shifting responsibility and anger one step further from child-sacrificing parents and parent-figures (including Zeus himself, at this moment) and one step closer to the hero-son himself. Achilles' learning through suffering thus plays a pivotal role in obliterating perceptions of sacrificial parenting.

What is good from the standpoint of meeting children's needs and fostering their development into self-confident, competent, autonomous adults, in ancient Greek as well as modern terms, may be bad from the standpoint of producing heroic sons—or daughters. Must cultures then choose between producing heroes or victims—or just self-confident, competent, adults? Honor cultures like those of the *Iliad* are apt to cultivate an ostentatious brand of heroism that glamorizes superior might and tries to deny defenselessness and shameful acquiescence in mistreatment. They could cultivate a quieter variety that would actually stand up to violence, exploitation, and abuse. Still it is easy to understand how a culture that produced virtuosos of lethal force modeled on Achilles—and enthralling works like the *Iliad*—could survive, flourish, and impress itself and competitors with its superiority.

Ancient Greek cultures were, thankfully, not monolithic. Other Greek narratives chart paths out of cyclic psychological violence and violent strife. The two great Homeric epics elaborate contrasting models of heroism; and even among the *Iliad*'s Achaians, Odysseus, Diomedes, and Nestor represent unashamedly human alternatives to the heroism of divinely nurtured Achilles. Other works that go against the grain of the dominant heroic culture include the story of the establishment of Zeus's regime on Olympos in Hesiod's *Theogony*, the writings of Solon, the lyric poetry of Archilochos, and Aeschylus's *Oresteia*. But Achilles embodies the dominant paradigm, and—the manifest and familiar ironies of the aged philosopher's comparisons of himself to Achilles notwithstanding—Socrates is modeled on Achilles.

If childrearing practices that played a key role in the reproduction of ancient Greek culture could not be acknowledged, and its major texts fostered denial of childhood experiences on which it was based, how can analysis of these same texts reveal the very formative experiences they are constructed to deny? Children who experience destructive parenting think, act, and describe their relationships with parents differently than those who experience adequate care. Victims of parental betrayal, hostility, or seduction may succeed in excluding information of harm at the hands of caregivers from conscious awareness, but their early experiences stay with them. When telling their life stories, they idealize caregivers, but details of their stories suggest parental destructiveness. They also turn blame and anger onto themselves.

The *Iliad* and its myths exhibit similar features. They idealize forms of childrearing geared to producing sons who appear superior to ordinary human beings, while intimating the destructiveness of these special forms of nurture. Such childrearing practices would also generate major observable features of ancient Greek cultures: hyper-competitiveness, propensity to shame, sense of self as either superior and worthy of esteem or inferior and unworthy, vulnerability to slight and dishonor, and honorific violence. So the *Iliad* and its myths are geared to a pattern of family dynamics that is itself geared to producing honor-conscious, aggressive competitors. Sacrificial childrearing practices and corresponding childhood experiences like those implied in the *Iliad* and myth would appear fundamental to the cultures that elevated the *Iliad* to iconic status.[8]

Although it may be excluded from consciousness, destructive childhood experience leaves its mark. Maintaining false images of self (or group, or nation) and warding off experiences these images are constructed to belie requires constant effort. Narratives that do this work systematically differ from narratives that are free of the burdens of catharsis and denial. Literally from its first word, "wrath" (*mênis*), to its last, the *Iliad* leads audiences to shift anger and blame from seductive but also rejecting caregivers to third parties and ultimately to the self that bears witness to destructive care. It purges not only anger and blame for harm inflicted by caregivers, but the accurately perceiving self. The perpetual motion machine of ancient Greek culture developed remarkably efficient mechanisms of catharsis and denial.

Since the family patterns underlying heroic culture involve attempts to deny and falsify experiences of fundamental human relationships, this study underscores the need to comprehend the psychological substrate of our ideals and beliefs, including philosophical ones. It should help us—if we happen to need such assistance—to recognize our formative experiences and responses to them. This in turn might allow us to conceive of what is estimable in ourselves and in our dealings with others—interpersonal, familial, social, and political—on the basis of who we actually are, rather than who, for whatever reasons, we may desperately try to pretend to be.[9]

Achilles and Socrates may protest—and project—too much, but when modern psychologists describe children's responses to harmful care in terms like those Achilles uses to chastise his fellow Achaians, they build on cultural foundations set in place almost three millennia ago in the *Iliad*.

Chapter One

The Quarrel

The quarrel between the Achaian king and general, Agamemnon, and his best fighter, Achilles, affords entrée into family dynamics underlying heroic culture. Conversely, it exemplifies complex ways in which these family dynamics inform early Greek ideas about honor, violence, authority, justice, and order.

The quarrel is a pivotal episode. The mytho-biographies of Achilles' parents and parent-figures help to explain its underlying family dynamics: sons favored by purportedly superior mothers rise above inferior fathers, even as those mothers, favored by their fathers, surpassed their mothers. Achilles' anger at Agamemnon sets him apart from his fellows, who pretend that abuses of authority do not occur. His singularity is central to the *Iliad*'s cathartic function. Hero-sons' traumatic interactions with parents are reenacted, but with unacceptable features displaced onto others. Once these displacements are undone, the quarrel becomes a rich source of information about the dynamics of parent-child relationships. Achilles' refusal to sacrifice his life for exploitative, dysfunctional parent figures is among the most intractable obstacles to his fulfillment as a hero and sacrificial victim. In the last third of the poem, these obstacles are demolished one by one.

Viewing the quarrel in its mythological context brings to light dual threats to paternal and kingly authority in heroic culture. Both arise in families in which insecure husbands turn away from angry or aloof wives, seeking solace with impressionable daughters or daughter-like concubines. Insulted wives enlist sons as agents of revenge. Favored daughters, humiliated by strategic marriages, rear formidable hero-sons who threaten their fathers.

The *Iliad* seemingly vindicates Achilles' position while discrediting Agamemnon's. But myths to which it alludes suggest that Achilles offends against Zeus-sanctioned authority. Appearances to the contrary, Agamemnon enjoys a measure of support from the father and king of gods and men, while Zeus's support for Achilles (and Thetis) is expedient and far from total.

In the first book of the *Iliad*, the king and commander of the Achaian army at Troy, Agamemnon, commits a gross breach of kingly responsibility. A king must have the wit (*noos*) to look before and behind to safeguard and preserve his people (1.117, 1.338). By refusing to accept ransom for his favorite prize girl, who happens to be the daughter of a priest of Apollo, and then insulting the priest, Agamemnon puts his army at risk. In the face of Apollo's devastating response, a lethal plague, Agamemnon irresponsibly allows his men to perish, day after day, rather than owning up to his transgression and atoning for it.[1]

Inspired by Hera's maternal "pity at the sight of the Achaians dying," Achilles steps in and does what a more responsible king would have done. He calls an assembly at which he asks the seer, Kalchas, to identify the source of the killing plague. After securing Achilles' promise of protection, Kalchas publicly states the obvious: Agamemnon is responsible for the plague. The Achaian king is forced to admit his responsibility and atone for his hubris by returning the girl to her aged father. Outraged at Achilles for exposing his failings, Agamemnon accuses Achilles of trying to usurp his position. In retaliation, Agamemnon takes Achilles' prize of honor, Briseis, to replace the girl Achilles forced him to return. Achilles is punished for speaking truth to power (1.230), or so it seems.

Achilles' resulting anger (*mênis*) drives the plot of the *Iliad*. Dissuaded by the goddesses Hera and Athena from killing the king, Achilles verbally abuses him. With the help of his divine mother and the assent of Zeus, Achilles expects to prove his claim to honor by withdrawing from the fighting. Forced to realize that without Achilles the Achaians will be defeated, Agamemnon will have to apologize and beg Achilles to return. His honor vindicated, Achilles will rejoin the army and win imperishable glory. Such at least is Achilles' plan.

The way the *Iliad* presents the quarrel, Agamemnon seems clearly at fault. Indeed, he is lucky to get off with his life. By insulting not only his best fighter, the son of a goddess, but also a priest of Apollo, Agamemnon shows himself to be totally irresponsible, insanely arrogant. Achilles flatly states that Agamemnon has forfeited his claim to the Achaians' respect and obedience. They dishonor themselves by continuing to do his bidding.

Once forced to acknowledge his responsibility for the plague, Agamemnon makes a show of responsible kingship. He agrees to give up the prize girl—whom, he informs the assembled Achaians, he prefers to his wife—so that his people will be safe. He asks only that he be given a replacement (1.116–20). Despite this—for him—significant gesture, Achilles berates Agamemnon as the "greediest for gain of all men" and tells him to give the girl back, waiting for recompense until Troy is taken.

Although not at fault in the same way as Agamemnon, the other Achaians do not come off well in Achilles' account, which the *Iliad* seems to validate. Agamemnon takes Briseis in retaliation for Achilles' standing up to him on behalf of his fellow Achaians. Just as Achilles risks his life daily on behalf of Agamemnon and his comrades but receives no gratitude (9.316–24; cf. 1.341), so he braves the anger of Agamemnon to beat aside the shameful plague from them (*aeikea loigon amunôn*; 1.456), and he pays dearly for it. Rather than rallying to his aid as he came to theirs, however, his fellow Achaians act as if no violations of justice and order (*dikê* and *themis*) have occurred, leaving Achilles to suffer disgrace alone. Can Achilles be blamed for believing that such sorry excuses for king and comrades deserve each other? What they surely do not deserve are more sacrifices by Achilles on their behalf.

Agamemnon differs. Why should only the Achaian king go without a prize of honor—especially when, as he sees it, Achilles uses the plague as a pretext to aggrandize himself at Agamemnon's expense? Even if Achilles can conceal his ambition from others, Agamemnon is not deceived. He will not entreat Achilles to stay, but others will stay and honor him, above all Zeus, who gave the scepter that symbolizes Agamemnon's kingly power and claim to supreme honors (1.172–75, 1.286–89, 2.102–5). Enraged at Achilles, Agamemnon implies that the father and king of gods and men may share his *mênis* at an insubordinate underling who tries to upset divinely ordained *themis*.[2]

Agamemnon's arguments find limited support in the text. While the Achaians fail to join Achilles in rejecting Agamemnon's authority, they will not put up with all manner of kingly abuse. The Achaians are bound by oath to support Agamemnon (2.339, 4.266–67). Furthermore, if the Achaians heeded Achilles' call to leave Agamemnon at Troy to fight his battles alone, they would have a shameful homecoming against fate—just as Achilles would, if he were to make good his many threats to go home. When, echoing Achilles' charges against Agamemnon, Thersites (a "man of the people") counsels the Achaians to leave, Odysseus beats him into tearful silence, to the relieved applause and mirth of the Achaians.

While critical of Agamemnon, Odysseus and Diomedes share neither Achilles' contempt for the king nor Achilles' way of coping with his shortcomings. Their refusal to heed Achilles' call for revenge on Agamemnon may spring from their having greater self-respect than Achilles and a more secure sense of their own worth. Even as Nestor urges Agamemnon to return Achilles' prize, he tries to persuade Achilles to acknowledge the greater claim to honor of the Zeus-sceptered king.[3]

Trying to dampen rather than fan the flames of conflict between Achilles and Agamemnon, this trio of advisors acts not out of fear of Agamemnon, but to maintain a semblance of Zeussian order. In Hesiod's *Theogony*, Zeus utilizes intelligence and wisdom born of experience to resolve what would otherwise be an interminable cycle of conflict between paternal kings, seeking to monopolize power and privilege, and their rebellious wives, sons, and subjects, forming alliances to overthrow them.

Zeus succeeds in securing his position as father and king of gods and men by avoiding his predecessors' counterproductive attempts to thwart all others' development and aspirations. Ingesting Mêtis, the divine personification of wisdom and cunning, where his predecessors Ouranos and Kronos had attempted to prevent the birth of, or ingested, their own children, Zeus defeats Kronos's Titans and wins election as king of the gods. In his regime, all can pursue privileges and honors without infringing on the birthrights of others. This new form of order (personified by Themis) is based on the sharing out of honor and privilege (*timê* and *geras*) according to justice (personified by Dikê, daughter of Zeus and Themis). Characterized by reciprocal respect, honor, and trust, it represents Zeus's solution to the problem of gaining and holding sovereign power and authority.[4]

Significantly, this form of order is naturalistic and notably unheroic. Zeus may be the strongest combatant, but his order is modeled on a family in which cooperative parents nurture children. This model differs radically from the one it replaces, in which fathers disrespect their wives and sacrifice their children to maintain exclusive claim to honors and privileges. The new model is relatively inclusive and egalitarian. All are responsible for contributing something, and all are entitled to a share of honors and privileges in return.[5]

A mutually interdependent community of gods has no place for glamorous, superior-order beings with claims to honor and privilege beyond everyone else's—except as doomed, half-divine players in spectator sports for the gods. Zeus claims supreme honors as one who, inspired by the goddesses Themis, Dikê, and Mêtis, devises this form of order and who skillfully ousts his tyrannical predecessor. He is "Zeus of the Counsels" (*mêtieta*) and "the son of devious-devising (*ankulomêteô*) Kronos." As his epithets attest, he rules the cosmos more by brains than brawn. He alone wields the thunderbolt, the instrument of his *mênis*. His hold on power remains tenuous, however, and the possibility of violent struggles for succession is ever-present.[6]

Even though his advisors take a different tack than Achilles, Agamemnon still seems wrong. This impression is reinforced by various points in the text.

Agamemnon claims that Zeus will honor him—when Zeus has just agreed to honor Achilles at Agamemnon's expense. To make good his promise, Zeus tricks Agamemnon with a false dream of glorious victory. Agamemnon rejects Achilles' suggestion that he wait for a replacement prize until Troy is taken, but he is forced to do that as well. Although the gods have made Achilles a spearman, Agamemnon avers, they have not given him the right to speak abusively. Well, wrong again. Agamemnon is only alive to make such spurious claims because Hera and Athena asked Achilles to spare his life. In return for his forgoing the satisfaction of killing Agamemnon, the goddesses give Achilles leave to abuse the king to his heart's content. They promise Achilles that he will be recompensed many times over for Agamemnon's hubris (1.197–214).

Agamemnon's charge that Achilles is secretly trying to aggrandize himself at Agamemnon's expense seems particularly misguided. Hera prompts Achilles to call the assembly at which Agamemnon is shamed into behaving responsibly, and Agamemnon's dereliction of duty necessitates it. It is Agamemnon who continually tries to aggrandize himself at others' expense. His singular lack of success stems from his choice of victims. He foolishly targets Achilles and other divine or semidivine personages who have no difficulty cutting him down to size. In addition to Achilles and Apollo (via his priest, Chryses), there is also Klytemnestra, who, though mortal, is as effective in revenge as Hera, her divine counterpart. As the *Iliad*'s audience knows, she will murder Agamemnon when he returns from Troy.

So Agamemnon seems guilty of the offenses with which he charges Achilles. Achilles seems not merely innocent of them, but extraordinarily solicitous of Agamemnon's honor—until Agamemnon's ingratitude changes everything. Achilles fights with supreme effectiveness to remove the stain of dishonor from Agamemnon's family. Unlike any other Achaian, he does so in the certain knowledge that restoring Agamemnon's honor will cost him his life. In the past Achilles labored to increase Agamemnon's portion of honor while downplaying the king's failure (in Achilles' view) to deserve it. Although Achilles did the lion's share of the fighting, Agamemnon got the lion's share of honorific spoils, while Achilles contented himself with something "small but dear." Achilles evidently avoided, until provoked, calling attention to the dishonor of Agamemnon's family and his dependence on Achilles and the rest of the Achaians to efface it (1.152–62). Taking Achilles' prize is Agamemnon's thanks for his perfect, almost filial, devotion.

Thus the *Iliad* presents two accounts of the quarrel, seemingly validating one while discrediting the other. In Agamemnon's version, Achilles uses the plague as a pretext to aggrandize himself at Agamemnon's expense. But the *Iliad* presents Achilles as unjustly punished for speaking truth to power and shaming Agamemnon into acting responsibly, thereby saving the lives of Achilles' ungrateful comrades.[7]

The *Iliad* does not just undercut Agamemnon's account of the quarrel; it provides an alternative explanation for Agamemnon's behavior. He feels threatened by glorious young men. Although he accuses godlike young fighters like Achilles of illicitly trying to compare themselves to him in honor (1.186–87), in fact Agamemnon compares himself unfavorably to them and doubts his own claims to honor. His insecurity does not seem to stem from his failings in his own sphere—from being such a poor excuse for a king—but rather from his inability to compete with Achilles' glorious show of prowess in battle. In a society that crowns youthful prowess with immortal glory, conflicts over honor between even good kings and the best young fighters would be virtually unavoidable. But Agamemnon is not a good king, and Achilles is the son of a goddess.

Nestor alludes to the source of the threat to Agamemnon: Achilles' superior strength and descent from a goddess. Even so, Achilles should not seek to oppose his strength to a sceptered king to whom Zeus gives magnificence; rather he should acknowledge the king's claim to unmatched honor (1.275–81). When Achilles complains that he never has a prize equal to Agamemnon's, even though he is the best fighter, he illustrates how problematic a king's claim to honor can be in a society that glorifies individual martial prowess.[8]

Achilles sacrifices his *nostos* (homecoming) not primarily to win Agamemnon's honor back from the Trojans, but to win immortal *kleos* (glory) as the "best of the Achaians" in battle. Achilles must die young partly to keep his image of unmatched prowess—which will be immortalized in song—pristine. Not only age, but domesticity, fatherhood, and kingly maturity would cloud his reputation. Even on the battlefield, far from wives and children, elder men excel in counsel rather than combat. They exhibit the *mêtis* that characterizes Zeus as father and king of gods and men, while leaving it to young men to exhibit the godlike *biê* (might) of heroes in their prime.

The intergenerational element of the threat that Achilles poses to Agamemnon is the dominant theme of a parallel incident in book 4. After the breakdown of a truce between the Achaians and Trojans, Agamemnon marshals his men for war. Supposedly he performs a time-honored kingly function, praising those who are eager to fight and chiding laggards. But his defects of character soon land him in trouble.

Agamemnon singles out for special blame the two allies who, after the departure of Achilles, are most essential to victory. He begins by accusing Odysseus of cowardice—of being greedy for the rewards of bravery, while avoiding fighting in the forefront. Thus he berates the ally who, more than any other, has to clean up after Agamemnon's botched attempts at leadership, and who, on the basis of merit, is more deserving than Agamemnon of the Zeus-derived kingly honors that Agamemnon so scrupulously claims for himself. When Odysseus contemptuously rejects the insult, Agamemnon takes it back and becomes conciliatory, praying that the gods will reduce their altercation to nothing (4.349–63).[9]

Agamemnon's encounter with Diomedes, a young fighter who is almost Achilles' equal, provides insight into the intergenerational aspect of Agamemnon's insult to Achilles (4.365f.). Diomedes is the "best of the Achaians" in Achilles' absence. But unlike Achilles, he also excels in counsel (9.54). Agamemnon's oddly ambiguous insult to Diomedes is couched in explicitly intergenerational terms: Diomedes is worse in fighting than his father, Tydeus, but better in conclave (*agorê*; 4.400).

Even though Diomedes will presently demonstrate that he is virtually Achilles' equal in fighting prowess, his response to Agamemnon's insult stands in sharp contrast to Achilles': he remains silent "in awe [at] the king's rebuking" (4.402). Much like Achilles in book 1, however, Diomedes' comrade-at-arms, Sthenelos, responds to Agamemnon's insult in kind. Like Agamemnon, he couches his response in terms of fathers' and sons' competing claims to honor. Agamemnon lies. He knows that both Sthenelos and Diomedes are better men than their fathers. As proof of his contention, Sthenelos reminds Agamemnon that he and Diomedes (two of the Epigone) succeeded in sacking Thebes where their better-equipped fathers (the Seven against Thebes) failed.

Although Agamemnon is wrong about their inferiority to their fathers in fighting, Sthenelos continues, he is right about their superiority to their fathers in counsel. He and Diomedes won victory at Thebes by heeding Zeus's favorable portents, while their fathers died because in their "headlong stupidity" (*atasthalîeisin*) they ignored Zeus's warnings. Therefore Agamemnon should never compare them with their fathers in honor (4.409–10).[10]

Instead of joining in Sthenelos's Achilles-like abuse of Agamemnon, Diomedes enjoins his friend to silence. He himself papers over the king's failings, much as Odysseus does when Agamemnon botches his "test" of the troops in book 2, inciting panic. Diomedes tells his companion that Agamemnon, "shepherd of the people," is only performing his paradigmatic kingly role of goading the Achaians into battle (4.13–14).

Demonstrating the skill in counsel for which Agamemnon backhandedly praises him, Diomedes avoids anxiety-provoking (for Agamemnon) intergenerational comparisons altogether. He instead exhorts Sthenelos to remember fighting courage (4.365–418). Because Diomedes is more generous in his characterization of Agamemnon than Sthenelos or Achilles—and markedly less vulnerable to insult—Agamemnon is spared having to pay an additional heavy price for repeating his folly with Achilles by belittling the next "best of the Achaians." Because of Diomedes' respect for paternal authority, the Achaians are spared greater sufferings for continuing to follow insecure, envious, youth-belittling Agamemnon.[11]

After his encounter with Agamemnon, Diomedes goes on to demonstrate prowess comparable to Achilles'. Panicked Trojans scatter before his onslaught. He wounds not only the demigod hero Aineias, but also his divine mother, Aphrodite, and contends against Apollo himself. Unlike Patroklos, whose death at Apollo's hand foreshadows Achilles', however, Diomedes heeds Apollo's warning to desist or die. In this way he makes a "choice of fates" that is the opposite of Achilles'. He sacrifices supreme glory to secure a safe return home, *nostos* (5.124–32, 431–44).

Although in book 4 Diomedes maintains a respectful silence, in book 9 he publicly recalls Agamemnon's insult to him and repeats, albeit in a temperate manner, the reproach that Sthenelos had directed at their fathers. Agamemnon's suggestion that the Achaians admit shameful defeat is folly. It betrays faintness of heart and disregard for Zeus's favorable portents. If Agamemnon gives up and goes home, Diomedes and Sthenelos will stay on at Troy, winning victory themselves in accord with the portents of Zeus (9.31–59). This claim prefigures Achilles' desperate vision in which he and Patroklos survive the carnage and take Troy alone (16.97–100).

Viewed in light of his encounter with Diomedes and Sthenelos, Agamemnon's taking of Achilles' prize in book 1 appears similar to a threatened, envious father's attempt to claim honors due to a son who is superior to him in fighting, rather than, as Agamemnon would have it, a simple claim to kingly honors. Looking back to the beginning of the poem from the vantage point of book 4, we note that Agamemnon's insult to Chryses partakes of this same envious belittling. Although the priest whom Agamemnon insults is a weak old man, the god he serves, Apollo, represents the limit of godlike, heroic *biê*—what youthful heroes like Diomedes and Achilles strive to emulate but always fall short of matching. Not surprisingly, the mightiest of the Achaian heroes is "the first to urge [Apollo's] appeasement" (1.386). And to whom does Achilles tell this? To the divine mother who left his mortal father to grow old and die alone, but who is instantly available to her son when his honor is threatened—the mother whose divinity is manifest in her son's superior *biê*.[12]

Later a desperate but not yet entirely penitent Agamemnon makes the intergenerational aspect of his relationship with Achilles explicit. He offers to make Achilles his son-in-law and honor him equally with his own son, Orestes—on condition that Achilles yield place to him as kinglier and elder (9.160–61). Achilles rejects what is in effect a patrimony—wife, possessions, and kingship—in a way that suggests that unkingly Agamemnon has no real patrimony to give. Fortunately, Achilles avers, he can get these things from his father, and he is minded to leave Agamemnon at Troy and do just that.

By developing the theme of paternal insecurity at the root of Agamemnon's dishonoring of Achilles, the *Iliad* further validates Achilles' version of the quarrel and discredits Agamemnon's. By book 9, even Agamemnon ruefully acknowledges that Zeus loves and honors Achilles. The god has deceived him with a false dream of victory. Agamemnon admits, further, that he dishonored Achilles unjustly, and he offers to make amends. But his botched offer of restitution recalls his other errors. Thus he fails to regain Achilles' trust and friendship. (Only with Agamemnon's unconditional apology after Patroklos's death will these be reestablished by oath [19.134–97].) Although in book 1 Agamemnon accuses Achilles of trying to trick him out of his portion of honor, Achilles rejects Agamemnon's offer of a major portion of his hoard. When Achilles finally does accept Agamemnon's gifts, he is indifferent (19.147–48). All of this leaves the impression that, unlike Achilles' own father, his in-loco father, Agamemnon, has nothing of value to offer the glorious son of Thetis.

Yet with Zeus's help, Agamemnon will win a glorious victory at Troy, and Achilles will sacrifice his life to secure it. Before this, Zeus will make good his promise to force Agamemnon to honor Achilles, but Achilles' triumph will be hollow. Holding onto his anger at Agamemnon costs him the life of the friend, Patroklos, who dies going to the aid of the Achaians in his place—despite Achilles' prayer to Zeus that Patroklos be allowed to return home safely (18.81, 19.328 f.).

Although Zeus takes Achilles' side—up to a point—Achilles has his illusions shattered. He expects that Zeus will grant him both imperishable glory as the son of Thetis and also—vicariously through his friend, Patroklos—a *nostos* in which he can be a husband, father, and king. Although Achilles wins imperishable glory by killing Hektor, his friend's death overshadows the triumph (18.81, 19.328f.). Perhaps Zeus, the father and king of gods and men, who gives the scepter and right of judgment to Agamemnon, is more supportive of his mortal counterpart's claims to honor, and less supportive of the competing claims of Thetis and her son, than it appears—even to doubt-ridden Agamemnon himself. Perhaps there is more truth than even Agamemnon sees in his account of the quarrel.

Two types of narrative lend credence to Agamemnon's version of the quarrel. In both, sons who are instruments or extensions of their mothers threaten their fathers. In one, Achilles becomes the agent of a dishonored mother's revenge against a philandering father, earning a father's curse. In the other, the son of lowly, devoted Thetis mysteriously threatens Zeus and cosmic *themis*.

An example of the first type of narrative is Phoinix's autobiography. A member of the embassy that conveys Agamemnon's apology and offer of recompense to Achilles, Achilles' aged tutor, Phoinix, tells him a story with obvious parallels to the quarrel between Achilles and Agamemnon. When Phoinix was a young man, his father, Amyntor, dishonored his mother by favoring a young mistress (*pallakis*; most likely a prize of war, like Kassandra, whom Agamemnon brings home from Troy). His mother persuades Phoinix to sleep with the girl to make her hate the old man. When the stratagem succeeds, his outraged father curses Phoinix, vowing that he will never have a son of his own to dandle on his knees. Chthonian Zeus and Persephone accomplish the father's curses. Enraged at his father, Phoinix is on the point of killing him when one of the gods checks his anger (9.446–61). Phoinix withdraws from his father's household. He is taken in by Achilles' father, Peleus, who loves him as he would a son. Peleus makes Phoinix a rich man and a king over many people. Phoinix loves Achilles from his heart and makes Achilles "his own child," to make up for the sons he will never have on account of his father's curse (9.493–95).

The detail of one of the gods coming down to stay Phoinix's hand when he is about to kill his father pointedly recalls the similar moment in the quarrel between Achilles and Agamemnon. But the allusion calls attention to crucial differences between the actions and fates of Phoinix and Achilles. Most importantly, Phoinix intentionally humiliates his father—as Agamemnon accuses Achilles of slyly trying to do to him. But Agamemnon's suspicions on this account seem thoroughly discredited. So unlike Amyntor's punishment of Phoinix, Agamemnon's punishment of Achilles cannot be sanctioned by father Zeus.

Numerous other parallels link Achilles' quarrel with Agamemnon to Phoinix's with Amyntor. The girl Briseis has already been Achilles' bedmate. She can be presumed to find the prospect of sleeping with the old man, Agamemnon, hateful as a result. It is not merely that she has slept with Achilles, but that Achilles loves and cares for her like a good husband, and he calls her the "bride of his heart" although he won her with his spear (9.335–43). Mourning Patroklos, Briseis remembers his promise to make her Achilles' lawful wife on their return from Troy (19.282–300)—rather than letting her remain a concubine, like Amyntor's or Agamemnon's. No wonder Briseis is "all unwilling" (1.348) when she is being carried off to divide her time between Agamemnon's loom and his bed.

Although Achilles has a young son—something that Amyntor's curse precludes for Phoinix—he doesn't get to dandle him on his knees very much. Achilles may have a son, if only so future generations of Greeks can claim descent from him. Yet even more than Phoinix, who rears Achilles, Achilles misses out on the rewards of fatherhood.

Still, Phoinix's quarrel with his father does not appear to suggest motivation for Achilles' quarrel with Agamemnon. Instead, parallels between the quarrels highlight contrasts between Achilles and Phoinix. Although both spoil young mistresses for elder, paternal men, Achilles does so with his own mistress, not Agamemnon's, on whom he has no designs. Achilles deprives Agamemnon of his unwilling mistress, as Phoinix deprives Amyntor of his, but only to prevent the further destruction of Agamemnon's army as a result of Agamemnon's hubris.

Like Amyntor's wife, the goddess Hera—at whose behest Achilles makes Agamemnon give up his prize—is dishonored by her husband's philandering with younger women. Her vengeful anger is legendary. In this instance, however, Hera enlists Achilles not as a dishonored wife's Phoinix-like avenger, but as an agent of her pity for her sick and dying Achaians.

> Achilleus called the people to assembly;
> a thing put into his mind by the goddess of the white arms, Hera,
> who had pity upon the Danaans when she saw them dying (1.54–56)

Agamemnon's Zeus-like philandering has nothing to do with it. Or does it?

After Achilles exposes Agamemnon's responsibility for the plague and forces him to atone for his hubris, Agamemnon insults his wife, Klytemnestra. While agreeing to give up the priest's daughter, he admits before the assembled Achaians, that

> I wish greatly to have her
> in my own house; since I like her better than Klytaimestra
> my own wife, for in truth she is no way inferior,
> neither in build nor stature nor wit, not in accomplishment (1.112–15)

Here the *Iliad* calls attention to Agamemnon's philandering in a way that suggests a motive for his murder by his wife, Klytemnestra, on his return from Troy.[13]

Just as Hera regards herself the "highest of all the goddesses" for being the consort of Zeus (18.364–66), so Agamemnon's proud queen might make a similar claim to her standing among mortals. She is in fact Hera's mortal counterpart. Although Klytemnestra is not present when Agamemnon insults her, Hera is keenly attentive to everything going on in the Achaian camp. She is also notoriously scrupulous in avenging such insults. (Agamemnon's public insult to his wife is so tactless and so heedless of possible consequences that no one else could have made it—unless we allow the *Iliad*'s Zeus to enter the lists against him, in which case Agamemnon faces serious competition [14.312–28].) If Agamemnon's insult had preceded Hera's enlistment of Achilles, the parallel with Phoinix's mother's use of her son to avenge her dishonor would be glaring, but even a goddess would have difficulty avenging an insult before it occurred. Of course Klytemnestra is humiliated not just by her husband's public declaration, but by his preference for captives like Chryseis that he explains in such a gratuitously insulting manner. Perhaps Hera does persuade Achilles to humiliate Agamemnon in much the same way as Phoinix's mother persuades Phoinix to humiliate his father after all.

In the *Odyssey*, Agamemnon tells Odysseus how his "sluttish" wife, aided by her lover, Aigisthos, murdered him, and how Klytemnestra herself killed Kassandra (xi.405–34). The *Iliad*'s audience knows what will happen to Agamemnon when he returns from Troy, flaunting his preference for the prize-girl who replaces the ones Agamemnon has been forced to give up (first Chryseis, then Briseis). Thus the *Iliad*'s audience already has a framework for viewing Achilles' humiliation of Agamemnon at Hera's urging—in lieu of killing him—as a foretaste of Klytemnestra's lethal revenge.[14]

Perhaps Hera would have let Achilles kill Agamemnon if their dispute over a prize had occurred after the Achaians had accomplished her revenge on the Trojans. "Love and care for" Agamemnon though she might, she does not stay the hand of Klytemnestra's lover, Aigisthos, when he kills Agamemnon on his triumphal return from Troy. But with her revenge as yet unaccomplished, Hera has Athena dissuade Achilles from killing the king, allowing him only to abuse Agamemnon verbally.

If Zeus can avenge insults to a minor mortal protégé like Amyntor, cannot Hera avenge an insult to her mortal counterpart? Like Amyntor, Agamemnon suffers the humiliation of having a mistress who is spoiled for him by making love to a younger, more attractive man. (A metaphorical bride of Achilles' divine counterpart, Apollo, Chryseis—whom Achilles tells Agamemnon to "give . . . back to the god" [1.127]—is presumably no more willing to be Agamemnon's bedmate than Achilles' prize-girl, whom Agamemnon is forced to give back, untouched, to Achilles.) Thus Hera induces Achilles to humiliate Agamemnon as Phoinix does Amyntor—even as she has Achilles ensure the safety of the army that is the instrument of her revenge on the Trojans for a similar erotic insult.

If Hera's role parallels that of Amyntor's wife, and Achilles' role parallels Phoinix's, then Agamemnon's imprecations against Achilles have the force of a paternal curse. Its executor would have to be Zeus. Covertly planning to inflict his *mênis* on Achilles even as he accedes to Thetis's request to honor him, Zeus would defend the honor of a king who is his mortal counterpart.

Achilles' veiled involvement in a family scenario like Phoinix's provides some support for Agamemnon's seemingly discredited account of the quarrel. The myth that explains how Achilles comes to be the child of a divine mother and mortal father also lends credence to Agamemnon's account. Characteristically uninhibited by his married state, Zeus woos Thetis. He only relents when apprised by Themis of a prophecy that Thetis will bear a son stronger than his father (*pherteron pateros*) and who will overthrow him. This resumption of the succession struggle would overturn the precarious order of *themis* and *dikê* that Zeus devised. To avert that cosmic catastrophe, Zeus abandons his suit. On the advice of Themis, he and the other gods force Thetis to marry a mortal. Implicitly, her son will threaten a mortal father and king rather than Zeus.[15]

The mythological explanation of Thetis's marriage to a mortal undercuts the impression, which the *Iliad* fosters, that the son of Thetis threatens only weak and unworthy fathers. Since the myth associates Achilles and his mother with the overthrow of Zeus and cosmic *themis*, the *Iliad*'s suppression of it is understandable. Yet Achilles' reference to the day the gods "drove [Thetis] to the marriage bed of a mortal" (18.85) suggests that auditors know why the gods took this action.

Achilles tells a story in book 1 that undercuts Themis's prophecy. When his mother supplicates Zeus to restore his honor, she should remind Zeus of the time when she alone among the immortals "beat aside shameful destruction" (*aeikea loigon amunai*) from him. Hera and the other Olympians had shackled Zeus when Thetis summoned Briareus, "a son greater than his father in might." Just by sitting down next to Zeus, Briareus terrified Hera and her allies into giving up their attempt. Achilles' description of Briareus evokes Themis's description of Achilles in her prophecy. But instead of overthrowing Zeus, the hundred-handed monster prevents his overthrow (1.397–406).

As Achilles advises, Thetis prefaces her supplication with an allusion to her prior service. If ever before Thetis did Zeus a favor, now he should grant honor to her short-lived son. Although Zeus complains that favoring the Trojans so that Agamemnon will be forced to honor Achilles is a "disastrous matter" (*loigia erg'*) that will exacerbate his conflict with Hera, Zeus assents to Thetis's request (1.503–10, 1.518–27).[16]

Thetis's supplication follows a traditional format: I helped you in the past, so help me now. Achilles' appeal to his mother alludes to a similar quid pro quo in which Achilles' short life takes the place of Thetis's regime-saving service to Zeus.

"Since, my mother, you bore me to be a man with a short life,
therefore Zeus of the loud thunder on Olympos should grant me
honour at least. But now he has given me not even a little.
Now the son of Atreus, powerful Agamemnon,
has dishonoured me, since he has taken away my prize and
    keeps it" (1.352–56)

Although it plays no part in Thetis's rescue of Zeus, she alludes to her son's short life in her supplication.[17]

Achilles' short life and claim to honor from Zeus seem to belong to the suppressed story of his mother's forced marriage. That story strengthens Thetis's claim as well. Zeus must honor Thetis's son to compensate her for exchanging superiority to Hera for the humiliation of mortal marriage. He owes Achilles honor for accepting the loss of immortality and the kingship of the gods that Achilles would have wrested from Zeus as Thetis's divine son. So why does Achilles claim that Zeus should honor him because he is fated to have a short life? That helps Zeus only by allowing him to assuage Thetis's humiliation by ensuring that she is the mother of the most glorious of heroes. Agamemnon needs Achilles to sacrifice his life to efface his shame, so being *minunthadios* (short-lived) is a favor to Agamemnon. But Zeus is different. Loss of immortality and the kingship of the gods are the sacrifices that Zeus imposes on Achilles.[18]

Like Themis's prophecy, the story in which Thetis foils Hera's coup attempt associates Thetis with a mighty son in advance of her marriage. It too is prophetic in suggesting that Thetis will direct her own mighty son to protect rather than challenge his father. For the *Iliad*'s audience, the Briareus story rearranges the elements of Themis's prophecy to downplay the threat posed by Thetis and her son. Like any warning, however, Themis's prophecy itself rearranges the elements of an imagined future—the one foretold by the Briareus story. Thetis will have a mighty son all right, but he will overthrow rather than protect his father. Thetis's tale refurbishes the prospect of a devoted, protective Thetis and Achilles while subtly alluding to the prophecy that exposes it as illusory. In the *Iliad*, Thetis and Achilles can protect Zeus only by accepting the sacrifices he imposes on them. This in itself betokens the failure of paternal and kingly authority on which the epic is based.[19]

Although the myth of Thetis's forced marriage throws some light on Thetis's and Achilles' claims to honor from Zeus, it raises questions about the precise nature of the threat that they represent. It is easy to see how Zeus, like Agamemnon, could be threatened by a proud queen dishonored by his philandering, who enlists a son as her avenger. Thetis and Achilles might make any mortal father or king insecure. The goddess's anger at being forced to marry a mortal might make her and her son even more dangerous. But Thetis's marriage is supposed to neutralize her threat, not cause it. So the question remains: How could marriage to a lowly goddess—his formidable wife's antithesis in power, aggression, and status—threaten Zeus?[20]

Themis's prophecy reveals the threat hidden in marriage to a superior bride like Thetis while obscuring its provenance. Fathers routinely subject favorite daughters to strategic marriages to gain allies or neutralize rivals. Zeus appeases his brother, Hades, for his inferior domain by allowing him to abduct Zeus and Demeter's daughter, Persephone.

The daughter's instrumental marriage mixes honor with humiliation. Persephone is twice chosen. In some accounts, Zeus is overcome with passion for Persephone just as he was for Thetis. Her status as a favorite daughter is suggested as well by Zeus's choice of her as a fitting prize to appease his brother. As a result, Persephone is forced to marry an inferior mate. Although Hades is a god, and Zeus's brother, any sense of superiority that Persephone derives from being favored by Zeus and having displaced Hera in Zeus's bed is opened to doubt and ridicule. (Zeus and Helios try to convince a skeptical mother and daughter that, as Zeus's brother, Hades is not that demeaning a match.) Pride in her glorious son compensates Thetis for the shame of her marriage. Demeter, not Persephone, responds to Zeus's perfidy by rearing a glorious son like Achilles, but the pattern of humiliation and compensation is the same.[21]

A favored but humiliated daughter like Thetis might well rear a superior son to silence doubts about her superiority. In the world of the *Iliad*, Thetis's aura of specialness and promise of producing a mighty son represent the height of feminine allure. Attractive in itself, Thetis's special status foretells to suitors that she will have a superior son. To the prospective father, Thetis's son's superiority promises safety. Phoinix "made [Achilles] his own child so that some day [Achilles] might keep hard affliction from [him]" (*aeikea loigon amunêis*; 9.495). When Odysseus encounters Achilles' shade in the underworld, Achilles regrets that he cannot use his "invincible hands" (*cheiras aaptous*) to "terrify such men as use force (*bioôntai*) on [his father] and keep him away from his rightful honors" (*timês*; xi.502–4). This recalls Achilles' account of how Hundred-Hander (*Hekatoncheiron*), Briareus, a "son greater than his father in might, terrified Zeus's enemies and "beat aside shameful destruction" (*aeikea loigon amunai*) from him.

Themis's prophecy is addressed to Zeus as a suitor. It warns of the threat hidden in the irresistible allure of a superior, father-favored daughter who promises to produce a superior son. Like its enactment in the *Iliad* via Achilles' usurpation of Agamemnon's authority, the threat is more explicable as the result of Thetis's inferior marriage than as its cause. Still, Zeus might be wise to desist from his pursuit of Thetis, as, for example, Odysseus refrains from joining the ranks of Helen's suitors.[22]

Zeus's dependence on a seemingly superior Thetis and her son to secure his regime would mark a departure from his reliance on his *mêtis* and *noos*, in addition to his own "unconquerable hands" (*aaptous cheiras*; 1.567), together with those of allies like Briareus, to create a just order on Olympos. As both Agamemnon and Achilles' father, Peleus, seem to do, Zeus would exchange this wise but also perilous and uncertain method of gaining and retaining power for the security afforded by an alliance with a seemingly superior mother and her incomparably mighty son. By turning over responsibility for securing his rightful honors and "beating aside shameful destruction" from him to his superior wife and son, he would tacitly abdicate his authority. Should he fall out with his powerful guardians, he would lack the authority to protect himself and his regime.

Themis's prophecy reverses cause and effect. The myth represents Thetis's threat as causing rather than stemming from Thetis's forced marriage. Both Thetis's allure and the hidden threat that she and her son represent are legacies of Zeus's self-serving, sacrificial exaltation and abasement of her, culminating in her forced marriage. The substitution of effect for cause in Themis's prophecy helps to create the mystique of Thetis and her son. It also obscures Zeus's role in creating the very problems that, Themis warns, Thetis's suitor will encounter as her husband and as the father of the strong son she is destined to produce.

The dual threats to paternal and kingly authority with which the *Iliad* is concerned are rooted in particular family dynamics. Zeus's part in them recalls his deposed predecessors—or a typical father in heroic society—more than the architect of cosmic *themis* and *dikê* in the *Theogony*. He relies on the devious *mêtis* of Kronos more than on the wisdom born of experience that he ingests in the *Theogony*. The threat from his insulted wife, who may enlist Zeus's son, Apollo, as her avenger, is a direct consequence of Zeus's philandering. Its counterpart, the threat from the superior son of a superior wife, is Zeus's wedding gift to whoever becomes the husband of the impressionable, devoted daughter whom he favors but then humiliates.[23]

By design, the wedding of Achilles' mismatched parents exports Thetis's threat to the mortal plane. Thetis is still destined to have a son greater than his father in might, but that is no longer Zeus's problem, even though he is the supposed guarantor of paternal and kingly authority among mortals.[24]

Zeus uses the wedding to deflect Hera's threat onto mortal surrogates as well. Left off the guest list, the goddess Eris (Strife) stirs up a quarrel among Zeus's wife, Hera, his daughter, Athena, and another daughter, the goddess of love, Aphrodite, over who is the most beautiful. Wisely declining to adjudicate, Zeus enlists Priam's incomparably attractive son, Paris, to decide the matter. Offered the most beautiful of women, Helen, as a gift by Aphrodite, Paris decides in Aphrodite's favor. Paris's insult to Hera and Athena (24.29) motivates the goddesses' hatred of the Trojans. The judgment of Paris also motivates the war on the mortal plane. When Aphrodite offers Helen to Paris, Helen is already married. So, with the help of Aphrodite, who "supplied the lust that led to disaster" (24.30), Paris seduces Helen while a guest in Menelaos's house. As Achilles reminds Agamemnon and his fellow Achaians in book 1, the Achaians came to Troy in the first place to remove this stain on Agamemnon's and Menelaos's family honor.[25]

By declaring Aphrodite rather than Hera the most beautiful, Paris simply replicates Zeus's habit of dishonoring his formidable wife with daughter-like paramours. (In the *Iliad*, and in the Trojan War tradition, Aphrodite is Zeus's unthreatening, unwarlike daughter.) Furthermore, Thetis's wedding is only necessary because Zeus finds Thetis is more beautiful and desirable than Hera. (He also finds Aphrodite more attractive than his brainy but apparently de-sexualized favorite daughter, Athena.) Through the clever stratagem of persuading Paris to stand in for him in making his insulting preference explicit (thereby avoiding the fatal mistake of expressing it himself, as Agamemnon does in book 1 of the *Iliad*), the son of devious-devising Kronos manages to deflect Hera's anger at his philandering onto the Trojans. At the same time, the problem of Zeus favoring daughters and daughter-like paramours is transferred from Zeus to Paris, in his role as judge, and from Thetis to Zeus's daughter, Aphrodite.[26]

Peleus eagerly accepts the boon of having a goddess for a wife. Just as easily, Zeus finds willing mortal substitutes to pay the price for his philandering. Paris gets to take the most beautiful of women away from her husband. The Trojan king, Priam, Paris's brother, Hektor, and the other Trojans know that Menelaos's and Hera's Achaian avengers are likely to sack their city, make concubines of their wives and daughters, and kill them and their comrades. Even so they are glad to have Helen in their midst.[27]

Just as Zeus disposes of the two linked threats to his regime at the wedding of Peleus and Thetis, so the *Iliad*'s two interlinked plotlines—the quarrel between the mismatched hero and king, and the backdrop against which it is played out, the Trojan War—represent the working out of these stratagems on the mortal plane. Zeus induces willing mortal substitutes to suffer the dual consequences of his philandering. Hera turns her vengeful anger on the Trojans, while Agamemnon experiences the consequences of an alliance with a superior, father-favored daughter and her incomparably mighty son.

The plan of Zeus in *Iliad* 1.5 refers to the Trojan War, effected through the judgment of Paris, as well as Zeus's promise to honor Thetis's son (1.531, 1.537, 1.539). Since Agamemnon is a substitute victim for Zeus,

Zeus may honor Agamemnon's sacrifice as well as Thetis's and Achilles'. Just as Agamemnon incurs Achilles' *mênis*, so Achilles' Zeus-sanctioned humiliation of Agamemnon may incur Zeus's *mênis* as well as Agamemnon's. The plan of Zeus may encompass Achilles' abasement as well (8.469–76, 15.59–77).

The poem's auditors may well have understood that Zeus's motive for the Trojan War as his desire to relieve Earth (Gaia) of overpopulation and punish iniquity (*Cypria*) or to eliminate the race of demigods (*Catalogue of Women*). His motive for supporting Thetis might have seemed a quid pro quo for saving himself and his regime. Yet these proposed referents for *Dios boulê* in the phrase "and the will of Zeus was accomplished" in *Iliad* 1 take no account of the obvious plan of Zeus to export the threat that Thetis and her son represent to the mortal realm; neither do they explain why Zeus's chosen method for accomplishing the depopulation of the Earth is to deflect Hera's vengeful anger at a sexual insult onto mortals.

In addition to explaining why Zeus settles on this particular method of population control (or, alternatively, suggesting why *hemitheoi*, or demigods— like Achilles—might incur his *mênis*), our account locates Zeus's agreement to help Thetis (the immediate reference of *Dios boulê*) in the broader context of his stratagem for exporting the threat she and her son represent to the mortal realm. Although not written in any text, this is just the sort of plan that the "son of devious-devising Kronos," who attempts to rid Olympos of Delusion by deporting her to the mortal realm, might come up with. Perhaps the *Iliad*'s audience, seeing how Zeus manages to deflect onto mortals both Hera's jealous rage and the threat represented by the son of Thetis, would surmise that Zeus planned it this way.[28]

The wedding of Peleus and Thetis is the site for silently exporting to the mortal realm another aspect of the threat that Thetis and her son represent. Although no prophecy warns him of it, the father of Thetis's mighty son stands to lose more than his sovereignty. When Paris decides in favor of Aphrodite, he acts as a surrogate for daughter-favoring, philandering father Zeus. When he collects Aphrodite's gift by seducing the wife of Menelaos, however, he represents in displaced form the irresistible erotic appeal of the mother-favored son. In his shame, outrage, and thirst for vengeance, wounded Menelaos dramatizes this unacknowledged aspect of Achilles' threat to fathers and kings.

Defeating his father in an erotic contest, the Aphrodite-gifted son effectively castrates his father. He provokes a paternal curse backed by the *mênis* of Zeus (13.624). For Menelaos, Priam is trustworthy, but his sons are "outrageous, not to be trusted" (3.105–6, 3.108–10). Various myths aver that Achilles would have bested Menelaos in the contest for Helen had he been old enough to compete (the favored son's lament), that Thetis arranges an audience between her son and Helen when the Greeks arrive at Troy, and that Achilles gets Helen in the end: Thetis immortalizes her son and, with Menelaos out of the way, arranges for him to marry a similarly transformed Helen. Thetis does for Achilles what Aphrodite does for Paris.[29]

Unlike the mysterious threat of a "son greater than his father in might" or of a son who avenges a mother's dishonor, the erotic threat posed by the favored son is nowhere acknowledged in relation to either Achilles or Zeus. So Zeus can devise no ploy or plan to deal with it. (Zeus openly worries about being overthrown by a more powerful son, but it is unthinkable that he could be defeated by that son in an erotic contest. Zeus could never be dishonored and metaphorically castrated by an immortal son of Thetis as Ouranos was physically castrated by his son, Kronos, with a weapon supplied by Kronos's mother, Gaia—could he?)

This threat to Zeus, which he exports to the mortal plane along with Achilles and in conjunction with the judgment of Paris, might be termed *oedipal.* It involves sexual competition between a father and son for the mother, effective castration of the father by the son, the son's consequent fears of retaliatory castration by the father, and the repression of all this. Also in line with Freudian theory are similarly consequential rivalries between daughters and mothers. Yet these sexual threats conform to Greek myths rather than to Freudian readings of them. Rather than universals, they reflect family dynamics in Greek myth that encourage sons and daughters to believe that they are superior to same-sex parents. Menelaos is dishonored when Paris wins Helen away from him. Having triumphed sexually over parental rivals, favored sons and daughters must humiliate themselves or suffer devastating retaliation.

Through a complex series of splits that encompass both strands of Zeus's plan, the mythology surrounding the wedding of Peleus and Thetis de-eroticizes the relationship between Thetis and Achilles, the threat it poses to fathers, and sons' corresponding fears of retaliation. By transferring to others the erotic elements of the threat that Achilles and his divine mother represent, it effectively represses them. The hero-son's mother-derived, mother-attested superiority encourages fantasies of winning her away from his father. The hero-son's manifestly superior erotic appeal—Achilles' superior gifts from Aphrodite, with which the hero-son effectively cuckolds his father—is transferred to unheroic Paris. Thetis's erotic appeal to father Zeus is transferred to Aphrodite at Thetis's wedding. But the wedding only takes place because, in Zeus's eyes, Thetis is the most beautiful of goddesses. Thetis, not Aphrodite, is Hera's true erotic rival.[30]

With her aura of superiority and promise of producing a mighty son, Thetis is irresistibly attractive to suitors. Once married, however, she is destined to become the loosely attached wife and son-favoring mother who is the most desirable of women to favored hero-sons. This unacknowledged aspect of the Thetis problem—her erotic appeal, which pits suitors against each other, and sons against fathers—is transferred to the mortal realm along with Achilles. The marriage preemptively abases both the daughter (Thetis) as rival to the mother (Hera), and the son (Achilles) as rival to the father (Zeus). The substitution of Paris for Achilles, which results in Paris's seduction of Aphrodite's favorite, Helen, disconnects Achilles from the father as outraged, cuckolded husband (Menelaos as a stand-in for Zeus), even as it obscures Thetis's irresistible erotic appeal to favored hero-sons. By means of these splits and displacements, Agamemnon's outrageous unmanning of Achilles by taking his sexual prize is disconnected from Agamemnon's brother's outrage at being cuckolded by Paris. The *Iliad* and myth effectively repress the hero-son's illicit sexual ambitions, corresponding sexual fears, and consequent self-abasements. From this neo-Freudian perspective, Achilles' innocence or guilt and Agamemnon's dishonoring of Achilles, take on new meanings.

Chapter Two

Heroic Psychology

Thetis's life is split in two. Hera is raising her like a daughter in Zeus's household when Zeus becomes enamored of Thetis, preferring her to his wife. Thetis's forced marriage puts an end to the first phase of her life, and with it the prospect of marriage to Zeus. Becoming the mother of glorious Achilles compensates Thetis for the humiliation of her marriage.[1]

The *Iliad* and mythology mystify the transition from daughter to mother. By minimizing Thetis's threat, the Briareus story renders her forced marriage incomprehensible. Themis's prophecy explains the marriage but, by inverting cause and effect, it renders Thetis's threat incomprehensible. It makes Thetis's marriage a response to her mysterious threat rather than one of its comprehensible causes. Indeed, Themis's prophecy mystifies both the risk and the promise that Thetis and her son represent.

Despite her fall, Thetis retains an aura of superiority. She promises to produce a mighty son who, suitors hope, will ward off even self-generated threats of shameful destruction. Thus does Briareus rescue Zeus from a threat to his regime that he brings upon himself with his philandering and, no doubt, by breaches of trust and reciprocity toward the other Olympians who unite against him. In the world of the *Iliad*, the greatest threat to paternal and kingly authority is fathers and kings themselves. They compound their peril when they abdicate their authority and rely on evidently superior wives and invincible sons to protect them from the consequences of their misdeeds.

By demystifying the progression from favored daughter to mother of a superior son, and viewing it in light of family psychology and mother-infant attachment, we can piece together self-replicating family patterns that undergird heroic culture.

Favorite daughters, who threaten mothers, become mothers of heroes, who threaten fathers. The *Iliad* ambiguously denies both threats, but that does not change the pattern. The Briareus episode alludes to Themis's prophecy. Hera defends rather than persecutes Thetis because, willingly or otherwise, Thetis rebuffs Zeus's advances and contributes her son to the cause of Hera's revenge.

Focusing on parents' use of children to meet their own needs, family psychology illuminates father-daughter and mother-son liaisons. Research on father-daughter incest sheds light on the rearing of mothers of hero-sons. Studies that track psychological development across generations reveal striking correlations, such as that between a mother's history as an incest victim and her seductiveness toward a favored son. Attachment theory's emphasis on children's idealization of rejecting parents and relegation of adverse experience to "suppressed working models" of relationships with them illuminates the psychology of hero-sons.

Heroic psychology is forged in triangular relationships in which parents turn away from hostile, aloof, or purportedly inferior spouses to opposite-sex children. Fathers enlist daughters as substitutes for or allies against spouses. Mothers do the same with sons. Favored children believe themselves superior to same-sex parents whom they effectively displace.[2]

When wives take on the fearsome aspect of mothers, husbands seek validation in liaisons with impressionable, unthreatening daughters or paramours. Despite favoring daughters over mothers, fathers exchange them for the services of other men in strategic marriages. Wives turn away from unwanted husbands to rear godlike hero-sons. If glorious, mother-favored sons outlive their youthful prime, they are likely to encounter the disdain of father-favored wives. When shunned, cowed patriarchs console themselves with impressionable daughters, the cycle begins again.

INCEST NARRATIVES

The *Iliad* features two master narratives involving alliances of mothers and hero-sons. In one, Achilles, son of a divine mother, wins immortal glory in war. In the other, Achilles and his fellow Achaians, figurative sons of Hera, wreak her revenge on her philandering husband—or rather on mortal substitutes and erstwhile protégés, whom Zeus dupes into bearing the brunt of his insulted wife's anger.

The first half of Thetis's story, like those of Zeus's other paramours who fashion glorious sons, is an incest narrative. Zeus's household mimics dynamics of families structured around father-daughter incest or seduction. In a context of marital distance or conflict, fathers turn to daughters or daughter-like mistresses for validation. The favorite daughter's immaturity and lack of experience are fundamental to her allure. Encouraged to regard herself as superior to the mother whom she evidently bests in erotic competition, she is exempt from having to develop into an adult who can play her part in orders that accord with *themis*. Fathers' favoring of daughters and daughters' pretensions of superiority strain mother-daughter relationships. Favorite daughters suppress knowledge of paternal (and maternal) exploitation and betrayal. They idealize abusive fathers, side with them in marital conflicts, and maintain their special relationships with fathers into adulthood. Arranged marriage exacerbates daughters' tendency to view husbands as inferior to idealized fathers.[3]

Being desired by Zeus over Hera elevates Thetis to an anomalous position above Zeus's jealous consort, who claims to be "highest and best" of the goddesses. The same is true of paramours Demeter and Leto who produce glorious sons. All actually or potentially displace Hera in Zeus's bed. For Thetis, whom Hera claims as a virtual daughter, both the breach of the parent-child boundary and the inversion of the parent-child hierarchy are particularly apparent.

Because Thetis has been humiliated and betrayed by a strategic marriage, her superiority as a favored daughter is called in question. She can re-create her sense of superiority—to the queen and foster mother to whom the father preferred her and to the husband whose bed he forces her to share—by rearing a son whose matchless superiority testifies to her own. She can accept the sacrifice of inferior marriage on condition that she be compensated with a glorious son.[4]

The mother's relationship with her son in many ways reproduces her father's relationship with her. In a context of marital distance or conflict, the mother burdens her son with validating her claims of specialness and superiority. She effectively elevates him to a position above his father, exempting him from having to respect and emulate paternal models, which in any case are in short supply. The sequel to the father-daughter incest narrative is a mother-son incest narrative. Like mother-daughter bonds in the former, father-son relationships are strained. The father envies, and may come to curse, the son who believes that he has won the contest with his father for the mother's esteem and love.[5]

These mythological patterns do not suggest that incest was prevalent in ancient Greece. The paradigmatic status of Achilles' heroism and the intertwining of his and his mother's histories do suggest that seductive father-daughter and mother-son relationships played a key role in reproducing ancient Greek cultures.

The narrative of quasi-incestuous liaisons between fathers and daughters, interrupted by strategic marriages, and followed by mothers' compensatory, special relationships with favored, glorious sons explains much about paradigmatic hero-sons like Achilles and salient features of ancient Greek cultures. What need had ancient Greeks of the competing narrative, in which hero-sons avenge fathers' mundane insults to mothers? Why do hero-sons like Achilles win their glory as agents of Hera's revenge?

If father-daughter and mother-son incest narratives are paradigmatic, every daughter's unwanted husband is a mother's glorious son. (Achilles and Agamemnon may be opposites, but Hera loves both heroes equally.) To gain the benefit of other men's prowess, fathers offer their best, most favored daughters. The brides become prizes of honor, similar to the captive women distributed (or kept) by kings as prizes in war. After taking back Achilles' prize, Agamemnon attempts to regain his services by offering him his pick of daughters for a wife. At Aulis, he staged a mock wedding of Achilles to his favorite daughter, Iphigenia.

Superior, unwilling wives' dissatisfaction is intolerable to mother-favored hero-sons. In their view, which their mothers and adoring daughters share, they deserve to be admired rather than disdained by wives who are supposed to betoken their glorious superiority.

Although inferior in the eyes of their wives, these husbands are fledgling patriarchs. Their wives, daughters, and sons are subject to their authority. In the fictive society of the *Iliad*, the perquisites of patriarchy include female prizes of honor—other men's best, most favored daughters, whether as wives or war captives, or the services of their own daughters. At least in the father's view, the best prizes are his to give—or keep, or take away—as he sees fit.[6]

So the paradigmatic mother of heroes in the *Iliad* is a superior, favored daughter. She neglects her unwanted, inferior husband to nurture a son who will testify to her superiority. Her onerous subordination is rendered absurd by her husband's inferiority to her, her awe-inspiring father, and her peerless son.

The less glamorous heroic narrative, in which the son avenges his mother's erotic humiliation, is an incestuous response to an incest narrative. It portrays quasi-incestuous father-daughter alliances from the standpoint of the jealous wife excluded from the special relationship between her husband and a favorite daughter or paramour. Deprived of her sense of specialness and superiority—to shunned wives such as she herself has now become—she can produce only defective sons or monsters who embody her revolting, destructive anger. Yet she is able to enlist glorious sons like Achilles (and Agamemnon) as her avengers. The underlying identity between Thetis as the superior wife and Hera as the dishonored, vindictive one explains why.

ROLE-REVERSAL, EXCLUSION OF INFORMATION, AND DIVIDED WORKING MODELS

Despite father-favored daughters' and mother-favored sons' pride in their apparent superiority, these alliances sacrifice children's needs to parents'. They violate children's expectations and societal norms. Since knowledge that caregivers are unresponsive or hostile is dangerous to children, they are liable to exclude it from conscious awareness. They idealize exploitative parents, shifting blame and anger at parental failings onto themselves.

Not only ancient Greek children, but ancient Greek cultures were threatened by awareness of the violations of fundamental norms of parenting on which they were based. Accordingly, they developed mechanisms of collective denial and purgation. Narratives like the *Iliad*, in conjunction with purificatory sacrifices of scapegoat victims, translate children's parent-mandated denial of child-sacrifice into collective denial and purgation, not only of anger at exploitative, child-sacrificing parents, but of the selves that perceive, experience, and respond to these violations.[7]

Children's manifest working models portray caregivers as surpassing societal norms. Sons in particular receive superior nurture. Superior mothers rightly reject sons' ordinary care-seeking behavior while nurturing them to be superior. The child is to blame for parental displeasure, for example at his failure to perceive and respond to unresponsive, exploitative, or hostile care as if it were a superior parent's superior nurture. Suppressed working models are repositories for dangerous, negative experiences of and responses to exploitative caregivers.

If the *Iliad* is any indication, sons' suppressed working models harbor shameful experiences of and responses to caregivers. Sons are defenseless against the irresistible, devastating force of maternal devaluation. Fearful of provoking caregivers, they docilely accept violations of fundamental norms and breaches of trust. By confronting Agamemnon, Achilles strives to demonstrate his difference from comrades who silently accept abuse as if it were responsible care. Projecting shameful acquiescence onto others, consumers and producers of ancient Greek epic evince awareness, at some level, of the denial and pretense at the root of their cultures.

FAMILIAL NORMS

Perhaps because they are mostly honored in the breach, it may come as a surprise that ancient Greek norms of spousal and parent-child relationships are remarkably similar to modern ones. The sons of Atreus are not the only ones who "love their wives" (*phileous' alochous*). Any good man "loves her who is his own and cares for her" (*autou phileei kai kêdetai*; 9.341–42). In the *Theogony*, Ouranos and Kronos lose their preeminent positions by disregarding their wives' concerns and by trying to prevent the birth or maturation of their children. Having learned wisdom from their mistakes and misdeeds, Zeus succeeds where they fail by honoring uxorial and maternal concerns and by fostering children's development into adults who know how to respect others' contributions and claims to honor while asserting their own. (Zeus and his supporters model the maturity required for participation in emerging social and political orders characterized by reciprocal respect and honor [*themis*].) In Penelope, the absent Odysseus has a faithful spouse, a co-parent of their son, Telemachos, and a resourceful partner in preserving Odysseus's position and political order in Ithaka.[8]

Albeit in more questionable contexts, Agamemnon at least wants to be regarded as a king "burdened with counsels and responsibility for a people," who is willing to sacrifice so that his people can "be safe, not perish" (2.24–25, 1.117). Although predicated on the Achaians' role as her avengers, Hera's maternal feelings toward the Achaians are evident. Taking pity on the Achaians when she sees them dying of the plague sent by Apollo, Hera intervenes to save them. She intervenes again to prevent one of her Achaian protégés from killing the other: Hera "loved both" Agamemnon and Achilles "equally in her heart and cared for them" (*phileousa te kêdomenê te*; 1.195–96). When Achilles' strength is failing and he is afraid of being overwhelmed by a river god, Athene and Poseidon reassure him; Hera again intervenes to save her favorite avenger (21.284f., 21.328). Conversely, myths to which the *Iliad* subtly alludes make it clear that hero-nurturing goddesses like Thetis have no tolerance for those who perceive and respond to their peculiar child-rearing methods as if they are harmful.

MARITAL DISTANCE AND CONFLICT

Incestuous or quasi-incestuous parent-child liaisons are strongly associated with marital distance or conflict. Marital distance is manifest in the narrative in which a father-favored wife shuns a (to her) inferior husband and rears a glorious son. Thetis's resistance to Peleus's advances, reluctance to share his bed, and quick exit from the marriage after the birth of their son evince her superiority to her merely mortal husband. Marital conflict is prominent in narratives in which fathers shun angry, formidable wives in favor of unthreatening daughters—and insulted mothers enlist hero-sons as their avengers against philandering, daughter-favoring (and daughter-sacrificing) fathers.[9]

Ancient Greek scenarios in which wives enlist sons to take revenge on husbands who insultingly shun them are not difficult to imagine. Analogues for Hera's use of the Achaians, and Agamemnon and Achilles in particular, to avenge an erotic insult perpetrated by a stand-in for Zeus, or of Klytemnestra's enlistment of Aigisthos to murder Agamemnon, or Hera's enlistment of Achilles for a non-lethal dry run of that act in the *Iliad*, are likely to have been all too common, even if seducing fathers' concubines or murdering fathers for dishonoring mothers with their infidelities most likely had metaphorical rather than literal significance.

The same holds true for the cause of dishonor: alliances between husbands and fathers like Agamemnon and daughters or the unthreatening, daughter-like war captives they favor in the fictive warrior society of the *Iliad*. In the poet's and audience's present, the theme of prize concubines is likely to reflect both quasi-incestuous father-daughter alliances within the family and extramarital, hetero- or homosexual, erotic liaisons outside it. The redirection of anger originating in these and related family contexts into war via the Judgment of Paris may offer insights into the psychology of ancient Greek warfare.

The very idea of real-life analogues for the husband-wife pair who are parents of the paradigmatic hero, Achilles, seems problematic, however. Even within the *Iliad*, being married to Thetis sets Peleus apart from all other mortals, just as being the son of Thetis sets Achilles apart from all other heroes—including other offspring of divine-mortal couplings. In mortal society, Thetis, her son, and her husband are in a class by themselves. Yet it is precisely the fantasy of categorical difference and superiority to ordinary human beings—shorn of unseemly sexual insults and sons' participation in avenging them—that gives mythic and epic narratives of divine mothers and hero-sons their undeniably broad and enduring appeal. It should not surprise us that actual spouses contrive marriages that are functional equivalents of the union of Peleus and Thetis.

Early family psychologists described marital configurations similar to the pairing of divine mother and mortal father in Achilles' family history. In these types of marriages, one spouse is styled as "superadequate" and invulnerable, while the other is inadequate and inferior. If Peleus can maintain his connection to a spouse whom he sees as adequate to any situation, he can, despite his inferiority, hope to share in her invulnerability. He can accomplish this by identifying with her disdainful view of him, becoming one with her, at least in imagination. For her part, the resistant, distancing spouse gets to identify with her husband's view of her as superior to ordinary, vulnerable, inferior mortals like himself. (A similar but opposite asymmetry obtains in daughters' relationships to seductive fathers.) Although such interlocking marital myths are fictions, the behaviors, belief systems, and enduring bonds that sustain such marriages are real.[10]

FATHER-DAUGHTER LIAISONS AND THEIR EFFECTS

Thetis's life as a favored daughter in Zeus's household represents the first phase of the life of the mother of a hero-son. It is critical to what comes after: the humiliation of her marriage and her need for a glorious son.

Here myth shows its value. Things that cannot be acknowledged in the life of the present can be dramatized in the remote mythological or epic past. Brought up like a daughter in Zeus's household, Thetis is desired by Zeus, who strives to seduce and bed her.

Reflecting "the change of subject matter from the mythical narrative of the birth of the gods to a poem about epic heroes," the victor in the struggle for the kingship of the gods—and for justice, lawfulness, and salutary order—in the *Theogony* is a faint memory in the *Iliad*. In epic, Zeus reflects the foibles and weaknesses of ancient Greek patriarchs. In particular, the father and king of gods and men is markedly susceptible to the allure of non-threatening daughters and daughter-like paramours.[11]

In the 1970s and 1980s, revelations of the frequency of father-daughter incest in the United States led family psychologists and attachment researchers to turn attention to father-daughter liaisons that could be as exploitative and destructive as the mother-child relationships on which they had initially focused. Although fathers generally are not primary caregivers, and paternal seductiveness overlays a relationship to a primary caregiver, Bowlby recognized seductive or incestuous father-daughter relationships as a major instance in which children dissociate from or exclude information about caregivers' betrayal and exploitation.[12]

Like the myth of Zeus's favoring of daughter-like paramours over Hera, the substitution of daughter-like captives for wives in the fictive (but in this respect, historically accurate) warrior society of the *Iliad* may reflect fathers' concomitant and continuing enlistment of daughters as substitute spouses in the societies that produced and consumed epic and myth. The explicit sexual component of the relationship between the husband and father, Agamemnon, and his favorite, daughter-like female captives in the *Iliad*, as well as his dependence on them for his honor, may express, at a comfortable remove from the present, the taboo eroticism of father-daughter relationships, and the dependence of mother-favored fathers on daughters to shore up claims to honor that are compromised as glorious youth fades into marriage and fatherhood, and glorious sons eclipse fathers who are past their prime. In classical Athens, beautiful youths are the preferred objects of older men's extra-marital eros. But the continuing resonance of the *Iliad* and its mythology, including that of Agamemnon, suggests that fathers continue to turn to daughters for sympathy and admiration.[13]

Of critical importance is the daughter's investment in the idea that she is superior because the father desires her more than the mother (or her siblings). In keeping with their origins in immaturity and paternal seduction, the daughter's specialness and superiority are ineffable, seemingly intrinsic. They mysteriously transcend family and status hierarchies based on maturity, rendering them meaningless.

Eroticized paternal favor encourages mystically superior daughters to dream of displacing mothers in fathers' beds—as Zeus's passion for Thetis feeds her expectation of displacing Hera. If daughters' expectations should be disappointed, or if their status as fathers' favorites should be questioned, so is their value. That in the *Iliad* Thetis is humble and self-abnegating and the epic downplays the competition between daughter and foster mother in no way changes the underlying pattern.[14]

Equally important in understanding subsequent stages of the daughter's life is her lack of the self-esteem that would have come from fulfilling expectations in accord with *themis*. In families in which spouses are securely attached, and parent-child boundaries are clear, a daughter's fantasy that her father prefers her to her mother, and any corresponding belief in her superiority, are undercut by reality. In such families, a daughter is forced to revise her thinking: she may have many virtues, but her father loves her mother, who, as an adult, has capabilities as a spouse and parent that a child has not yet developed. If she wants a husband, she will have to become an adult like her mother and marry someone other than her father. Conversely, daughters in such families are loved and valued by both parents as developing children who explore and discover their powers (like Athena, for example—at the expense of her sexuality—or Odysseus's queen, Penelope), and who need loving parental nurture.

The substitution of Aphrodite for Thetis as Hera's rival is telling. Daughters favored by seductive or incestuous fathers are liable to believe they, like Aphrodite, have "extraordinary powers over others, especially sexual powers over men, and destructive powers over both men and women." Like the daughter who excites the father's incestuous desire, Aphrodite is *kallistê* (most beautiful) as much for what she lacks—for being dependent, docile, and unthreatening—as for what she has. (Similarly, Hera and Athena are disqualified from being *kallistê* as much by what they have as by what, according to skewed standards of beauty, they lack.) Yet as disastrous as the consequences of Paris's choice are, would it have been better if Paris had failed to pay tribute to Aphrodite's extraordinary sexual powers? Her curse on Tyndareus—that his daughters, Helen and Klytemnestra, would be unfaithful to their husbands—is as responsible for the Trojan war and Agamemnon's downfall as Hera's anger.[15]

Enlisting daughters as allies in marital conflicts elevates them above their mothers. But by depriving them of both parents' tutelage in maturation, it implicitly devalues them as care-seeking children. As a consequence they lack the self-esteem and self-confidence that come with adult competence. In incest families, daughters lack the maternal models and examples of reciprocal love and care between parents that reinforce and help to realize such aspirations. If something should call in question their primacy in their fathers' esteem, they have nothing to fall back on.

We find a key to the dynamics of paternal preference and daughterly self-esteem in an unlikely place: Agamemnon's declaration of his preference for Chryseis, his concubine, over his wife. Crucially, the favorite daughter is encouraged to believe that she is superior to the wife, and that the father or father-figure desires her on account of her superiority. That Chryseis is an unwilling concubine, not a special "daddy's girl," masks the incestuous father-daughter aspect of her relationship to Agamemnon. But Chryseis, whose name means "daughter of Chryses," *is* a daddy's girl. Agamemnon fights with her father over rights to her. When he loses, he is forced to give her back to her father (and to the god, Apollo, but that is another narrative). Similarly, Thetis is a Neirad, daughter of Nereus. When she leaves Peleus she goes back to live with her father. The daughter's sense of being superior in every way to her mother and *therefore* preferred by the father, the sense of specialness linked to superiority that the seductive father attributes to his awe-struck daughter, becomes the nucleus of a false self. It masks the fact of her sacrifice—of her actual self, with its expectations and needs for parental encouragement and care—that is involved in paternal seduction. It also plays a key role in rearing her hero-son.[16]

MOTHER-DAUGHTER RELATIONSHIPS

The way to paternal seduction is paved by maternal incapacity or neglect. A child who is denied maternal love and care lacks the self-esteem and experience of loving nurture to resist or even recognize parental exploitation. Maternal neglect of or hostility toward daughters commonly precedes incest. As opposed to wives' jealousy of favored daughters or paramours, and daughters' (muted) competitiveness toward mothers, this pronounced pattern in the psychological literature on incest can shine a light on a corner left dark by mythology, with its presumably male-centered bias.[17]

Scholars' tendency to idealize ancient Greek mother-daughter relationships notwithstanding, the family dynamics explored here are not conducive to mothers' nurturing of daughters. Even before she becomes her father's favorite, a daughter's care-seeking could well be irksome to mothers preoccupied with fashioning glorious sons. (Achilles likens weeping Patroklos to a little girl trying to get her mother's attention [16.6–8].) Even though, in myth, Artemis joins her brother, Apollo, in murdering the children of a mortal woman who mocked their mother, mortal daughters are of little use for avenging slights or vindicating maternal claims to superiority, except as brides who link their mothers to other women's glorious hero-sons. Son-obsessed, jealous mothers, rather than phallus-proud fathers or brothers, may give daughters their first taste of devaluation as females. Because mothers are primary caregivers, these maternal betrayals may surpass paternal ones in destructiveness.[18]

As with fathers and mother-favored hero-sons, so with mothers and father-favored daughters: being favored by fathers and encouraged to believe themselves superior to mothers is not conducive to warm and loving mother-daughter relationships. Mothers may resent being supplanted by daughters whom their husbands favor. Iphigenia's unbidden avenger, Klytemnestra, is locked in mortal combat with Iphigenia's father-worshipping sister, Electra. Hera's relentless persecution of daughter-like rivals favored by Zeus may give further indication of tensions between emotionally abandoned mothers and father-favored daughters. Hera's true rival for the title "the fairest" and most desirable, Thetis, may accept her abasement to avoid triumphing over and humiliating the wife of Zeus, who is like a mother to her. Then again, much like Achilles with Zeus or even Agamemnon, she may mortify herself to preempt the wrath of a same-sex parental rival.[19]

Alternatively, mothers may attempt to enlist daughters as well as sons as allies in marital conflicts. The common trauma of forced, expedient marriage may be another, albeit problematic, source of mother-daughter solidarity, as when an angry Demeter forces Zeus to restore Persephone to her. Still, a cross-generational alliance of a mother and daughter against a father differs profoundly from a nurturing mother-daughter relationship in a functional family with intact parent-child boundaries. Nevertheless, ordinary mother-daughter bonds, and the mother's status as an adult model, may resist fathers' attempts to enlist daughters as allies in marital conflicts and as substitute wives. There is the myth in which, out of respect for Hera, Thetis rebuffs Zeus's advances.

Such are the life histories of daughters who become the wives and mothers of heroes. Such are the needs and liabilities they bring into their dispiriting marriages—or to marriages that would be dispiriting if the daughters had not already suppressed parents' neglect of the daughters' needs for loving, autonomy-fostering nurture; their anger at fathers who sacrifice and exploit them; and their wishes for parents whose examples could point the way to mutually loving and respectful marriages, and to similarly nourishing, self-esteem enhancing relationships outside the family. As it is (if the culture has done its work) they may, like Iphigenia, find the prospect of marriage to a great hero—like that doomed virtuoso of lethal force, Achilles—irresistibly alluring. Should Achilles survive to take his place as a husband and father, that phantom marriage might deteriorate over time in the usual ways. If it did, Iphigenia could renew her claim to glory by rearing an irresistibly powerful hero-son.[20]

HUMILIATION OF STRATEGIC MARRIAGE

There comes a point in a favorite daughter's life when her father-conferred sense of specialness and intrinsic superiority and her father-fanned ambitions are shattered. Fathers' initial exploitation and betrayal of daughters is compounded when, instead of forsaking their wives for their favored, evidently superior daughters, fathers subject them to humiliating marriages that make a mockery of the daughters' pretensions and ambitions. Under the guise of ushering daughters into value-affirming adulthoods as partners of respectful, loving husbands, in political as well as domestic affairs (Odysseus's wife, Penelope, for example), fathers sacrifice daughters' futures a second time when they give them to other men's sons to forge strategic alliances.

Scholars have recognized the traumatic effect on the daughter of instrumental marriage—often at a very young age to a much older man. This in itself would help to explain the threat that Thetis represents. But scholars have overlooked the incestuous context that makes strategic marriage outrageously humiliating. Thetis's *mênis*, like Demeter's, threatens the cosmos.[21]

One of Sophocles' female characters paints a general picture of marriage in which daughters' wants and needs are at best a secondary consideration. Remarkably, the wife's nostalgia for life in her father's house is coupled with complaints about being expected to accept parental betrayal and the empty semblance of a marital relationship as if both conformed to familial norms:

When we are young, in our father's house, I think we live the sweetest life of all; for ignorance ever brings us up delightfully. But when we have reached a mature age and know more, we are driven out of doors and sold, away from the gods of our fathers and our parents, some to foreigners, some to barbarians, some to strange houses, others to such as deserve reproach. And in such a lot, after a single night has united us, we have to acquiesce and think that it is well.[22]

As this passage together with mythological material that is much older suggests, marriage, particularly in aristocratic families, represented an involuntary, radical break in a daughter's life, although perhaps a more complicated catastrophe than has hitherto been recognized. In myth it is represented by Persephone's rape by Hades, god of the underworld, which is followed, after a lengthy and dismal separation, or "death," by a reunion with her mother (and Zeus's erstwhile paramour) Demeter. Like husbands of incest victims, Hades and, even more, Peleus are defined in their wives' eyes by their inferiority to father Zeus.[23]

For the fictive (but doubtless historical) Homeric father, as, most likely, for his archaic and classical descendants, marriage really *was* all about gaining a son, by giving away (while his retaining his hold on) a daughter who idealized him and regarded her husband as a mark of her humiliation. Having been seduced and subtly coerced into eschewing their ordinary needs and aspirations, such daughters have nothing to fall back on. Their dreams of displacing their mothers are mocked when their fathers marry them off to bolster their own positions and power.

Like the myths of Zeus appeasing his brother, Hades, by giving him Zeus's and Demeter's daughter, Persephone, for a wife, or giving Thetis to a mortal husband, the myth of Agamemnon's sacrifice of his daughter exemplifies sacrifice through expedient marriage. Agamemnon lures Iphigenia to Aulis with the false promise of a brilliant match. She will be Achilles' chosen bride. Coincidentally, the marriage would gain Agamemnon a peerless son-in-law who would ensure victory at Troy.

The ruse is believable because it mimics a chosen bride and groom's obliviousness to the sacrificial aspect of honorific, strategic marriage. This myth and its companion in the *Iliad* dramatize how Agamemnon uses the honor of chosenness to lure bride and groom alike into a marriage in which their needs are sacrificed to parents'. A weak, insecure father, Agamemnon sacrifices the daughter he favors over his wife to gain a glorious son-in-law who will sacrifice his life to efface Agamemnon's self-inflicted shame and dishonor.

In the *Iliad*, Agamemnon offers to honor Achilles by giving him his pick of his daughters for a wife. Since the marriage is predicated on the *nostos* that Agamemnon and Achilles both know Achilles will never have, it is not surprising that Achilles rejects the offer. Here Agamemnon uses the honor of marriage to his best daughter to lure Achilles to his death in Agamemnon's service. Under the guise of transparently deceptive proffers of marriage by a supposedly uniquely unworthy, child-sacrificing father, the *Iliad* dramatizes how the honor of marriage to another man's best daughter typically works. It lures a favorite daughter and a prospective son-in-law into an honorific marriage that is in reality a sacrifice for both.

Iphigenia's embrace of the phantom marriage Agamemnon arranges for her implies her complicity in her own sacrifice. That Iphigenia is Agamemnon's favorite is implicit in her selection as the daughter whom he would offer to Achilles, as well as the one he must sacrifice to Artemis at Aulis, just as Agamemnon must sacrifice his favorite concubine, whom he prefers to his wife, to appease Artemis's brother, Apollo, at Troy. Whether as incestuously favored daughter or as the instrument of a marital alliance, Iphigenia has to negate herself. She has to overlook the denial of nurture inherent in Agamemnon's exploitation of her to sustain his image of himself as a glorious hero, as well as to validate him—a paradigmatic child-sacrificing father—as a normative, nurturing father.[24]

In the fictive society of the *Iliad*, daughters are expected to welcome marriages predicated on fathers' needs for sons-in-law to facilitate the winning of honor and glory—or to ward off shame and humiliation that fathers bring on themselves by their hubris and disregard of the rights of others—rather than on daughters' needs for husbands with whom they can form bonds of mutual love, respect, and trust. Such daughters are liable to despise their husbands as inferior substitutes for their idealized fathers. Or they are liable to get locked into conflicts over young, compliant concubines with hero-husbands whose family experiences leave them with little confidence in their ability to create mutually loving and respectful bonds with their spouses.

Although, in the eighth-century world of poet and audience, there is less need for sons-in-law whose martial prowess can protect the honor of fathers from marauding bands or conniving rivals, strategic marriages that serve paternal needs for status and honor, and the concomitant family dysfunction, may still be the rule. To that extent, the *Iliad* and myth dramatize family dynamics that are difficult to acknowledge in the world of the present.

DAUGHTERS AS WIVES

As erotic rivals who are intrinsically superior to their mothers, and as potential brides and then humiliated castoffs of their fathers, daughters bring their share of baggage into their marriages. Owing to their experiences as children and young adults, and despite the superior status they appeared to enjoy in their natal families, they lack self-esteem and self-confidence. They are as prone to insult and outrage as their husbands and sons.[25]

Their husbands, unwanted substitutes for fathers, are emblems of daughters' humiliation. Marriage to Peleus is a reminder of Thetis's heights and depths. Poised to displace the "highest and best" goddess in Zeus's bed, Thetis marries beneath the lowest rung of the divine social hierarchy. Persephone is dismayed by her forced, strategic marriage to Zeus's inferior brother. Thetis must endure the embraces of a mortal.

Overtly idealizing the fathers who sacrificially exploit them, daughters may redirect their anger onto their husbands. For their part, husbands are liable to treat their daughters as their wives' fathers treated their wives. Just as, when they become husbands and fathers, hero-sons assume the roles of the fathers whom they outshone, so, when they become wives and mothers, favored daughters assume the roles of the devalued mothers, whom they displaced.

Perhaps the honor of marriage to a youthful hero, in compliance with paternal wishes, compensates temporarily for disappointment of a daughter's aspiration to marry her father, despite his already married state. Like her mother, Klytemnestra, Iphigenia is eager for the marriage to great Achilles that Agamemnon pretends to have arranged. But when they become mothers, and their husbands (who are now fathers, beyond their youthful prime) come to fear and abandon them in favor of daughters, insulted wives may turn as vengeful as their own mothers. Or they may gain some relief from their husbands' acknowledgment of their godlike power to devastate or ward off devastation, and their categorical superiority to inferior mortals like their husbands.[26]

MOTHER-SON LIAISONS AND THEIR EFFECTS

The mythology of goddesses who become mothers of heroes corresponds closely to accounts of daughters favored over their mothers by seductive or incestuous fathers. Particularly relevant are daughters' tendency to regard husbands as inferior to idealized fathers and their attempts, as adults, to recapture the specialness and superiority they experienced in their natal families. Where we move beyond these accounts is in showing how, in ancient Greece, these factors affect mothering.

Supremely effective in combating denial of father-daughter incest, Judith Herman effectively denies its deleterious effects on mothering. Herman caricatured early family systems theorists as promoting patriarchy. Their successors incorporated her work to explain father-daughter liaisons and document their intergenerational effects. Yet for her, the so-called "intergenerational cycle of abuse" is a myth. More in line with modern psychological research are Greek myths that depict daughters attempting to efface the shame of their marriages and regain the anomalous superiority they enjoyed in their natal families by rearing superior sons.[27]

Much is at stake in the question of how father-daughter incest or seduction affect mothering. I use Herman's work on father-daughter incest in
the modern United States to illuminate the reproduction of ancient Greek
mothering. Herman herself contends that "incest represents a common pattern of traditional female socialization carried to a pathological extreme."
Family psychology suggests that the maternal neglect or hostility that leaves
daughters vulnerable to paternal seduction is itself part of an intergenerational
pattern. Building on Slater's use of modern psychology to understand family
patterns in ancient Greek culture, Chodorow's theories of the reproduction
of mothering in the modern United States have themselves been applied to
ancient Greece. Like Slater, Chodorow and Herman aspire to understand not
just psychology but its role in the reproduction of gender roles and culture.[28]

As with fathers and daughters, so with mothers and sons: in a context of
marital distance or conflict, mothers turn to sons to recover their anomalous
superiority to their mothers, "the highest and best" in the family hierarchy,
and to vindicate corresponding claims to superior value and honor—as well
as to ward off shame and outrage at their humiliation. All forms of parent-
child role-reversal involve the sacrifice of children's needs to parents', but
a mother's use of a child to validate her claims to categorical difference and
superiority is particularly damaging. A son's ordinary care-seeking behavior
not only calls for caregiving behavior that is inscribed in genes and social
norms; it also defines his normal dependence, which gives the lie to claims
of innate superhuman abilities that would testify to his descent from a more-
than-mortal mother. The son as ordinary child threatens a purportedly superior mother with shame, mockery, and outrageous dishonor by exposing the
vacuousness of her pretensions. In this form of role reversal, the mother's
sacrifice of the child's needs for ordinary nurture is not incidental: manifestations of the child's ordinary humanity shame the mother and elicit her
hostility. But just as in less toxic forms of role reversal, the son is enjoined to
respond to maternal rejection as if it were normative, loving care.[29]

In an article on the "double-bind" that influenced both early family psychology and attachment theory, Bateson makes a good start toward describ-
ing the family dynamics that produced ancient Greek hero-sons. Bateson's
pathogenic family has three characteristics:

1. A child whose mother becomes anxious and withdraws if the child responds
   to her as a loving mother. That is, the child's very existence has a special
   meaning to the mother that arouses her anxiety and hostility when she is in
   danger of intimate contact with the child.
2. A mother to whom feelings of anxiety and hostility toward the child are
   not acceptable, and whose way of denying them is to express overt loving
   behavior to persuade the child to respond to her as a loving mother and to

withdraw from him if he does not. "Loving behavior" does not necessarily imply "affection"; it can, for example, be set in a framework of doing the proper thing, instilling "goodness," and the like.

3. The absence of anyone in the family, such as a strong and insightful father, who can intervene in the relationship between the mother and child and support the child in the face of the contradictions involved.

The mother uses the child's responses to affirm that her behavior is loving, and since the loving behavior is simulated [cf. the simulated paternal behavior of Agamemnon], the child is placed in a position where he must not accurately interpret her communication if he is to maintain his relationship with her.[30]

Initially believed to cause schizophrenia, family dynamics like these defined one extreme of a continuum of family health and pathology. Flawed though it was, the work of Bateson and his contemporaries laid the foundation for family psychology. It also influenced Bowlby's now extensively empirically tested hypotheses about mother-infant attachment, divided working models, and defensive exclusion of information about hostile or neglectful care. As the term implies, *schizophrenia* was thought to describe splitting of the mind or self. Early family psychologists were evidently on the right track about the exclusion of information and divided selves, but mistaken about family dynamics as a necessary and sufficient cause of schizophrenia.[31]

Totally dependent on the mother, without a sense of himself and his value apart from her, the son is utterly devastated by her rejection of him as a care-seeking child. Instead of a loving and beloved child, he experiences himself as worthless, hateful. A mother's hostile response to her child violates fundamental norms. It also betrays trust, compounding trauma. Abuse by an acquaintance or stranger causes far less dissociation and "information blockage."[32]

For hero-sons, the mother is both the destructive caregiver from whom he flees and the attachment figure to whom he turns for safety. Since she so easily devastates, a fictive union with her seems completely safe. The mother of the hero-son is the archetypal figure who can inflict or ward off devastation (*loigon amunai*).[33]

Information blockage to maintain a connection to an abusive (and abuse-denying) caregiver can take many forms. One of the most important is scapegoating—acknowledging shocking violations of parental norms but attributing them to someone other than a parent, for example Hera, not Thetis; Agamemnon, not Peleus (or Zeus).

For Bowlby, children are particularly prone to engage in defensive exclusion of information from their "working models" of self and caregiver in "situations that parents do not wish their children to know about even though the children have witnessed them" and "situations in which the children find the parents' behavior too unbearable to think about." In such situations, defensive exclusion can lead to

> a split in internal working models. One set of working models—accessible to awareness and discussion and based on what a child has been told—represents the parent as good and the parent's rejecting behavior as caused by the "badness" of the child. The other model, based on what the child has experienced but defensively excluded from awareness, represents the hated or disappointing side of the parent.

Bowlby "surmises that severe psychic conflict is likely to arise when . . . two sources of stored information (generalizations built on actual experience and on communications from others) are highly contradictory."[34]

Equally critical to this reading of the *Iliad* and Greek heroic culture is the child's shifting of responsibility, and concomitant redirection of anger, from the parent to third parties to him- or herself. This is implicit in the child's idealization of the abusing or neglectful parent while blaming him- or herself for abuse. If the parent is good and the child bad, then assaulting the bad, parent-alienating child would seem to be a primary constituent of the "severe psychic conflict" occasioned by split working models. A complementary mechanism is the son's devaluation, abandonment, betrayal of, and attempt to eradicate his rejected, injured mortal self—while attempting to sustain an idealized image of self that is "huge and splendid" enough to cow even a paradigmatic, vengeful, divine mother or to win the favor of a paradigmatic superior, rejecting one.[35]

EFFECTS ON FATHER-SON RELATIONSHIPS

As with daughters and mothers, so with sons and fathers: being favored by mothers as superior to their (in their mothers' eyes) hateful or inferior fathers is not a recipe for loving and mutually respectful father-son relationships. As reflected in the *Iliad* and its background myths, liaisons between superior mothers and favored sons are associated with paternal ambivalence. Fathers may long to have hero-sons who follow in their footsteps and win glory. (The name of Achilles' companion, Patroklos, means "father's glory" [*patrokleos*].) Yet they also may be envious of sons who, fulfilling both parents' expectations, displace their fathers as the primary focus of their mothers' attention, and they may be hostile toward sons who side with their mothers in marital conflicts.

Sons can also emulate heroic paternal models (Achilles) or side with fathers in marital conflicts (Orestes). Problematic father-son alliances and conflicts notwithstanding, sons may long for fathers who—in contrast to those in Bateson's pathogenic family—do intervene in the relationship of mother and son, and do provide models of loved and respected (and unabashedly mortal) husbands, fathers, and kings. For their part, fathers may intervene, however ineptly, in relationships between divine mothers and hero-sons. Deservedly or not, they may wish to be taken as models by their sons. Despite longing for paternal models who are unfazed by mothers' view of ordinary mortals as worthless and insignificant, sons (and fathers) are nonetheless likely to buy into mothers' visions of sons as superior to mere mortals like their fathers. Fathers' and sons' mutual longings are likely to run afoul of insecure fathers' hostile belittling, mother-favored sons' propensity to believe themselves superior to their fathers, and the susceptibility of both to feel outrage at any slight. In the world of Homeric epic, sons do sometimes respect and emulate mortal fathers. Odysseus, Diomedes, and Nestor are examples. But marital breakdown and cross-gender, cross-generation, parent-child liaisons create a toxic environment for mutually respectful father-son relationships.[36]

As with favored daughters, so with favored sons: if the marital bond is secure (like that of Odysseus and Penelope), the son's developing abilities and self-generated fantasies of superiority pose no threat to his father. The son's subordinate status is inescapably evident. At once disappointing and reassuring, this decoupling of filial gifts from glorious victory over an inferior father leaves the son with little alternative but to develop into an adult like his father. That way, he can win a wife's respect and love. By contrast, the mother who elevates her son above his father, making him a substitute spouse, encourages his belief in his superiority, with potentially violent consequences (e.g., the reciprocal anger of Phoinix and Amyntor, the latter's curse backed by Zeus; the reciprocal *mênis* of Achilles and Agamemnon, the latter's imprecations also backed by the *mênis* of Zeus; and the Zeus-backed *mênis* of Menelaos against Paris). This mother-dependent belief in his superiority exalts the son not only above his father, but also above ordinary mortals, who must accept parental guidance and learn adult competences and reciprocity. Maternal favor seems to render maturation unnecessary.[37]

So, as if the mother-identified son's negation of his *nostos*-seeking mortal self, the heir to his mortal father's legacy, were not destructive enough, the hero-son is liable to punish—or preemptively abase—himself for perceived sins against fathers. Since he is the victor in the erotic contest with his wife-avoiding father, the hero-son's path to the spoils of victory, his mother, appears to lie open. But the father's rage at his son's transgression against his rights—indeed, at his sexual humiliation and effective castration by his son—marks the son in his own as well as his father's eyes as a hated usurper, an undeserving victor who can never be allowed to enjoy the fruits of his victory. Regarding himself in this light, the son may become an agent of paternal anger against himself. Achilles is the principal agent of the *mênis* of Zeus that the aggrieved husband, Menelaos, calls down on Paris and the Trojans. But Achilles is involved in similar offenses himself, and he is also, covertly, the target of Zeus's *mênis*. Apollo would have incurred Zeus's *mênis* for inflicting shameful destruction on him as Hera's avenger. Paris, the ostensible target of Zeus's *mênis*, and Apollo are the destined agents of Zeus's lethal *mênis* against Achilles. The power of a paternal curse lies in its ability to induce a son's anger against himself.[38]

As with his mother, splitting mechanisms preserve the hero-son's relationship with his father. Other fathers—like Agamemnon—sacrifice sons to assuage their insecurities with glory. They enviously belittle glorious sons, snatch erotic prizes, and fail to provide adequate paternal models. The hero-son's father and trusted father figures are, supposedly, different. Representing Paris as Achilles' antithesis rather than his alter ego suggests that Menelaos is antithetical to Zeus's surrogates, Peleus and Agamemnon, rather than a split-off part of the hero-son's relationship to his father. Representing Achilles as only an incidental agent of Hera's and Klytemnestra's revenge on surrogates for Zeus—Agamemnon as well as Priam—masks the hero-son's role as an instrument of maternal revenge on fathers and father-surrogates.

HONOR, SHAME, AND VIOLENCE

The self-replicating pattern of father-daughter and mother-son liaisons examined here is very effective in producing aggressive, effective fighting men. They are avid to win glory as irresistibly powerful man-killers, and fearful of being exposed as shamefully weak and defenseless.

Incestuously favored mothers like Thetis and sons like Achilles regard themselves as superior to ordinary mortals, indeed to norms and hierarchies based on adult competences and responsibilities, divine or mortal. But the idea is vacuous. Their apparent superiority is predicated on childish inferiority and incompetence. Their proneness to anger at challenges to their claims to superior status stems from a combination of hypervaluation and foregone maturation, resulting in a fragile self-esteem.[39]

For the paradigmatic mother-son pair of Thetis and Achilles, the honor that father-favored daughters and mother-favored hero-sons claim as their due consists of upholding the false image of self as superior. The dishonor to which father-favored daughters and mother-favored sons are prone represents the breakdown of attempts to dissociate from the worthless shadow-self that is a repository for all that must be continually disavowed in order to sustain the image of self as superior to ordinary human beings. Achilles' (and Thetis's) *mênis* at the dishonoring of Achilles is equivalent to Apollo's *mênis* at the dishonoring of his priest (1.75). Dishonored despite having beaten aside the shameful destruction inflicted by Apollo (*aeikea loigon amunon*; 1.456), Achilles inflicts a *loigos* first on the Achaians and then on the Trojans. The *mênis* of both Apollo and Achilles is vengeful. It requites shame and dishonor with shameful destruction.[40]

The honorific, heroic violence that pervades the *Iliad*—a reflection of the endemic warfare that characterized ancient Greek societies—is overdetermined to a remarkable degree. It sustains relationships with powerful others by serving their purposes. Hero-sons serve as the agents of maternal revenge for all sorts of injuries and indignities. Targets include proxies for fathers who encouraged but then betrayed daughters' expectations of displacing their mothers in their fathers' beds (as Thetis expected to do). Achilles' role as Hera's avenger against surrogates for her philandering husband masks his role as Thetis's avenger against surrogates for her incestuous father-figure, who blasted her expectations of being the loved daughter of loving parents. All who have the temerity to challenge Achilles implicitly challenge Thetis's claims to categorical superiority. In destroying them he destroys those who threaten to make a mockery of his mother's claims to superiority. Achilles and the other Achaians came to Troy to win Agamemnon's honor back from the Trojans, and, Achilles' (and perhaps Thetis's) detestation of Agamemnon notwithstanding, Achilles sacrifices his life to that end.

Most fundamentally—and most consequentially for how we evaluate the purported truths of ancient Greek poetry and philosophy—heroic violence represents an attempt to eliminate the human self that is the object of maternal indifference or hostility that the son has long since internalized. The hero-son projects his human self onto others and destroys them. In this way he attempts to reassure himself that he is an invulnerable destroyer of mere weak mortals, as the goddess mother with whom he identifies destroyed him, and that he is not and never was nor ever could have been the defenseless, devastated victim to which his mother's hostility reduced him. (The same motivations operate at the group level: the Achaians must show they are superior to the Trojans just as Achilles must show he is superior to Hektor.) Yet the hero-son can never really separate from or eradicate his disowned, abandoned, human self. As a result, he is left with the nagging suspicion that he is a weak, defenseless victim after all. So purgative killing must be endlessly repeated.

Chapter Three

Mythobiographies

Myths recounting Thetis's experiences as a favored daughter in Zeus's household encode typical family histories of mothers of heroes. Hera's mythology, which involves blatant aggression against a son who falls short of the heroic ideal, and the recruitment of sons to avenge erotic humiliations, serves as a repository for unseemly or mundane aspects of a superior mother's history, character, and relationship with her hero-son.[1]

The biography of Achilles' father, Peleus, before his life becomes entwined with Thetis's, and the history of their courtship and brief marriage, are no less illuminating. King Aiakos marries Endêis, daughter of Skiron, with whom he fathers Peleus and Telamon. But he forsakes Endêis to marry a goddess, Psamathe, daughter of Nereus. With her he fathers a demigod son, Phokos, who excels in athletic competition. Put in the shade by their demigod half-brother (*Phokos* means "light"), Peleus and Telamon murder him. Their father discovers their deed and banishes them. In another version, they kill Phokos to please their mother, who is angry at being displaced by Psamathe.[2]

Although he was reduced to outraged insignificance as Psamathe's stepson, Peleus marries her sister. Thetis's disdain for him as a mortal husband matches her sister's lack of regard for him as a mortal stepson. (Both sisters avoid the embraces of their mortal suitors, Psamathe by turning into a seal, and Thetis by changing into various dangerous creatures and elements.)

Shortly after her famous but humiliating wedding, Thetis gives birth to Achilles. Myths recounting Thetis's attempts to immortalize her son suggest that, contrary to Thetis's fond recollections in the *Iliad*, the sons of divine mothers do not spontaneously manifest the superiority that signals their divine parentage. Rather, their mothers subject them to a series of harsh treatments aimed at making them superior to mortals. The point is reinforced by a parallel set of myths in which the goddess Demeter, posing as a nursemaid,

49

tries to immortalize the son of a mortal king. Mortal parents interrupt both goddesses' attempts. As a result, both sons win immortal glory but remain mortal.

The objection of a shocked mortal parent, quickly recanted when it provokes the goddess's fury, is critical. Here the myth does more than contribute to a denial of harmful mothering. It represents the process of denial itself. It dramatizes how supposedly inferior mortal spouses and hero-sons deny their own accurate perceptions of and responses to maternal rejection—and how the son appeases the mother by affirming her view of herself as nurturing.

The events leading up to Demeter's attempt to immortalize Demophoon and Leto giving birth to glorious children recall antecedents of Thetis's attempt to immortalize Achilles. Together, these myths demonstrate that hero-sons represent daughters' attempts to reclaim their paradoxical superiority to their mothers.

Hera's enlistment of glorious Achilles and Apollo to avenge insults to wifely honor suggests a covert identity between favored, hero-nurturing goddesses like Thetis, Demeter, and Leto and insulted, vengeful, daughter-envying wives like Hera. These contrasting maternal types represent distinct phases of the experience of ancient Greek wives and mothers. As once-favored daughters, they attempt to regain their lost status by rearing superior sons. As wives who are insulted by their husbands' preference for daughters (and non-threatening, extra-marital sexual partners), they enlist favored sons as their avengers.

PELEUS'S NATAL FAMILY
AND THE FASHIONING OF HEROES

The events culminating in Peleus and Telamon's murder of their half-brother, Phokos, demonstrate the role of maternal rejection in fashioning heroes. More broadly, Aiakos's abandonment of Endêis for Psamathe and the invidious distinction between merely mortal Peleus and semidivine Phokos reflect the splitting involved in parents' simultaneous rejection and recruitment of children to validate parents' claims to superiority. Mortal parents and children represent devalued mortal selves. Their divine counterparts represent false selves conceived as categorically superior and immune to rejection.

Psamathe's implied disregard for Peleus and Telamon as merely mortal children, and her implied favor toward Phokos as an extension of her divinity, mimics the behavior of mothers who use their children to demonstrate their superiority. Having a child who validates her claim to superiority wards off the mother's feelings of worthlessness. It re-creates the mother's childhood sense of intrinsic superiority to ordinary, rule-abiding children of ordinary, nurturing, and boundary-enforcing parents. Splitting into exalted and debased selves often results from an incestuous father's rejection of his daughter's care-seeking, while seducing and coercing her to act as a substitute spouse. The same is true for a daughter's favored son.[3]

By the same token, the intolerable shame and sense of inferiority of Telamon and Peleus as merely mortal children mimics the shame of children whose parents reject their ordinary care-seeking while requiring them to validate the parents' false superior selves. Such children identify with the rejecting parent's view of them as inferior, while rationalizing this violation as normal and right.

The behaviors dramatized in the story of Peleus's upbringing trace common family currents of heroic culture. Peleus's father abandons his merely mortal wife to join himself to a superior wife who rejects him. A superior mother favors a son whom she can view as an extension of her superiority and rejects sons who manifest ordinary needs for nurture. Peleus is ashamed and furious at his inability to best a demigod rival in athletic competition. He aspires to be worthy of a purportedly superior wife's—and mother's—regard.

By splitting family members into divine and mortal parts, these myths rationalize the destructive exploitation of children. Instead of a mother, father, and children, Aiakos's household comprises a rejected mortal wife and a preferred divine wife as well as implicitly rejected mortal sons and a favored semidivine one. To complete the picture, Psamathe leaves Aiakos because, as a mortal, he is an unworthy husband.[4]

It is normal and natural—according to *themis*—for the divine mother to favor her own, part-divine offspring while paying no heed to her husband's mortal children. She is not their mother. However intolerable for Peleus and his brother, they cannot fault Psamathe for favoring the son who shares her divinity over mere mortals like themselves. It is as natural for Aiakos to desire union with a divine mate as it is for Psamathe to resist and finally reject him. It is natural for her to favor her demigod son over her mortal husband. Splitting family members into mortal and immortal parts rationalizes what would otherwise be outrageous betrayals and violations of fundamental norms—of love and care between spouses, parent-child hierarchies and boundaries, loving parental nurture, and training in mutual respect and reciprocity. Narcissism replaces love and trust. Violations of *themis* become *themis*.

Peleus's family history, like Achilles', effectively denies that the divine mother rejects the favored demigod son who is destined to win glory. Yet the rejected mortal son, Peleus, murderer of Phokos, becomes an authentic hero in his own right, a worthy father to Achilles. Rejection by a purportedly superior mother is standard procedure in the rearing of hero-sons.

PELEUS'S WOOING AND WEDDING OF THETIS

A second episode from Peleus's life story—his courtship of and marriage to the sister of his divine stepmother—offers a vivid representation of a set of key elements of heroic psychology, including identification with a seemingly superior, invulnerable, rejecting, maternal aggressor.[5]

When it comes time for Peleus to wed, he gladly accepts Zeus's offer of the goddess Thetis. But even though Zeus and the gods bestow Thetis on Peleus—indeed, force her to share his bed—Peleus still has to win her. In a vain attempt to avoid the dishonor of marriage to a mortal (much as her sister Psamathe did with Peleus's father, Aiakos), Thetis changes herself into a variety of slippery or harmful entities—fishes, lions, snakes, wind, fire, and a squid who covers Peleus with sticky ink. Clinging to Thetis, and enduring various manifestations of her violent aversion to marrying him, Peleus personifies determination to form a union with a replica of the superior mother whose disregard reduced him to outraged insignificance.[6]

Just as he suffers her painful attempts to elude him, so Peleus accepts Thetis's view of him as inferior and inadequate. Indeed, her desirability inheres in her superiority, which manifests itself not only in her view of him as inferior and her resistance to his attempts to join her to him, but also in her quick departure from their marriage. Nevertheless, being married, however fleetingly, to a sister of his rejecting divine stepmother is supposed to make Peleus the envy of all mankind (24.531–37).[7]

The indifference of Peleus's divine stepmother—and the unbridgeable gap between him and her demigod son, Phokos—are intolerable to Peleus. Why then is he eager to marry a replica of his rejecting stepmother—her sister no less—and achieve a predictably short-lived union?

Faced with the outrageous and devastating component of his mother's double message—that as the mortal son of his mortal father he is insignificant and unworthy of her regard—her infant son could, theoretically, discount his mother's pretensions to superiority and affirm his and his father's value, while declining the honor of being regarded by his mother as, unlike his father, having a share in her divinity. (If he had a paternal example to emulate, the possibility would be more than theoretical.) But his mother offers an easier path to redemption. He can erase the seemingly irreparable devastation of her negation of his and his father's value by becoming an extension and emblem of her divinity.[8]

If he can identify with or win the favor of the mother whose rejection of him and his father so devastates him (and against which neither he nor his complicit father can convincingly assert their value), his problem appears to be solved. No longer is he the defenseless, vulnerable son, permanently (so it seems) laid low by his mother's negation of his value. At one with the superior being in whose eyes he and his father are hopelessly inadequate, he can never again be reduced to outraged insignificance by her disregard. At one with his irresistibly powerful destroyer he can never again be destroyed by her.[9]

The logic of identification with—or marriage to a clone of—a rejecting maternal aggressor is manifest in the brief interlude when Peleus and Thetis live together as Achilles' parents. Evidently a believer in the dictum "better late than never," Psamathe sends a wolf to avenge the murder by her step-son (and now brother-in-law), Peleus, of the demigod son whose superiority testified to her divinity. When the fearsome beast attacks Peleus, Thetis's baleful glare turns it to stone. As a result of his union with Psamathe's sister, Peleus—although defenseless on his own—can no longer be destroyed by Psamathe. He effectively exchanges his defenseless, debilitated mortal self for that of his invulnerable destroyer.[10]

To complete the transformation he must do more than form a union with Thetis, attempting to become one with her divinity. He must also do the work of Psamathe's wolf: he must endeavor to destroy the mortal stepson who resented Psamathe's gross breaches of maternal love and thereby spiked her plan to have her son reflect her divinity. He must abandon, turn against, and extirpate in himself the mortal weakness and imperfection that, in his naïve, credulous view, explains and justifies his stepmother's lack of regard for him and his father. Peleus's efforts at self-abnegation are remarkably successful, until one slip costs him his marriage to a goddess and deprives his son of immortality.

THETIS AND ACHILLES

The myths recounting Thetis's attempts to transform her son into a divinity like herself are remarkably suggestive about how sacrificed and humiliated daughters raise superior sons who offer proof of their mothers' claims to su-periority—and who covertly avenge their mothers' humiliations. Once Peleus overcomes Thetis's resistance and the gods celebrate their wedding, forcing Thetis to share Peleus's bed, she gives birth to the glorious and dangerous son whose prophesied superiority to his father caused Zeus and his brother Poseidon to break off their pursuit of her.

In contrast to Thetis's account in the *Iliad*, Achilles does not spontaneously manifest his divine superiority. He requires special maternal fashioning that appears to violate norms of maternal love and care. Barely alluded to in the *Iliad*, Thetis's attempt to immortalize Achilles reflects the fact that sons must undergo harsh postnatal fashioning by mothers in order to vindicate their mothers' claims to superiority.

These myths register destructive inversions of maternal care. They also represent mortals' hasty disavowal—when faced with divine maternal anger—of accurate perceptions of harmful mothering. Protesters adopt the angry goddess's view, including her justified anger at them for foolishly objecting to her treatment of their child.

Thetis attempts to immortalize her son (or, in alternate versions, her sons) in different ways. The most familiar myth is the least illuminating. When Thetis dips her infant son in the river Styx (which surrounds Hades) to make him invulnerable, she holds him by his heel, which remains vulnerable as a result. In the more revealing and alarming versions, Thetis anoints her infant son with ambrosia by day to make his flesh immortal. By night she places him in a fire in order to, as one mythographer puts it, "destroy the mortal element which the child inherited from his father." Seeing his son writhing in the fire, Peleus cries out. This infuriates Thetis, who leaves them both and goes back to live with her father and sisters in the sea.[11]

A likely source for the preceding account emphasizes not only the goddess's anger but Peleus's folly in failing to recognize what Thetis was doing.

> Peleus leapt up from his bed and saw his dear son gasping in the flame; and at the sight he uttered a terrible cry, fool [*mega nêpios*] that he was; and she heard it, and catching up the child threw him screaming to the ground, and herself like a breath of wind passed swiftly from the hall as a dream and leapt into the sea, exceeding wroth [*chôsamenê*], and thereafter returned not again. Wherefore blank amazement fettered his soul.

Other versions, omitting the ambrosia, portray pure destruction. In them, Thetis places her sons one by one in a boiling cauldron or fire to determine if they are mortal or to make them immortal by destroying their mortal parts. The first six are killed, but Peleus intervenes to save the seventh, Achilles.[12]

In all these accounts—save, perhaps, the one in which Peleus prevents Thetis from destroying all their sons—Peleus's intervention is represented as folly, for which he and his son pay dearly. Peleus loses his divine wife and lives in bleak solitude (18.434f.). Yet the goddess's interrupted ministrations leave their mark. Virtually invulnerable, Achilles is superior to all mere mortals and wins imperishable glory.

DEMETER AND DEMOPHOON

In a parallel myth, another of Zeus's paramours, Demeter, sets about immortalizing the son of a mortal king and queen. This narrative forms a puzzling interlude in another tale. In the primary narrative, Zeus placates his brother, Hades, by allowing him forcibly to abduct and wed Zeus's and Demeter's daughter, Persephone. For no apparent reason, Demeter interrupts her search for her missing daughter. She disguises herself as an old crone and visits the house of King Celeus and his queen, Metaneira, seeking employment as a nursemaid to their infant son, Demophoon. As Thetis does with Achilles, instead of nursing Demophoon ("not fed with food nor nourished at the breast"), Demeter anoints him with ambrosia by day and places him in a fire at night. The treatment is effective. To his parents' astonishment, their son grows "beyond his age" and is "like the gods face to face."[13]

Like Peleus, queen Metaneira is suspicious. Spying on the nursemaid, she discovers the "strange woman" immolating her son in a fire. In her folly (*aphradiêisin*), Demophoon's distraught mother intervenes. Furious (*cholôsamenê, thumôi kotesasa mal'ainôs*), the goddess snatches the child from the fire and throws him to the ground. Berating Metaneira and mankind in general for their stupidity and folly (*nêides, aphradmones, aphradiêisi*), Demeter tells Metaneira that she has "wrought a folly past healing" (*nêkeston aasthês*). She has deprived her son of immortality. Still, as a result of Demeter's nurturing, Demophoon will win imperishable honor (*timê d'aphthitos aien*). Scholars generally affirm Metaneira's folly and view the goddess's actions in a beneficent light.[14]

Dumbstruck and with her knees buckling under her, Metaneira retires to her chamber, leaving her squalling infant on the ground. Her daughters' and her own attempts to comfort the boy are unavailing "because nurses and handmaids much less skilful were holding him now." Quaking with fear, the whole household spends the rest of the night trying to placate the goddess by obeying her commands.[15]

This version, too, registers a lack of ordinary maternal nurture (no breast or food; displacement of the natural mother) but couples it with a claim that the goddess is a superior mother who provides superior substitutes for food (ambrosia) and maternal care (she nursed [*etrephen*], and "breathe[d] sweetly upon him as she held him in her bosom"). The son's superiority results not from some grotesque inversion of mothering, but from superior nurture. Demophoon cries, signaling his need for nurture, only when the loss of the goddess's care makes him inconsolable.

The goddess herself points to the hero's everlasting honor as evidence of her divinity. Even though foolish Metaneira spoils her son's chance to escape death and misfortune, "yet shall unfailing honour / always rest upon him, because he lay upon my knees and slept in / my arms." Necessarily, if he is to fulfill his destiny, man-killing will play a large part: "As the years move round and when he is in his / prime, the sons of the Eleusinians shall ever wage war and dread / strife with one another continually." While this may sound more like a curse than a blessing, the goddess insists she will confer great benefits on Celeus, his family, and all mankind. Dropping her disguise, the immodest goddess proclaims:

> Lo! I am that Demeter who
> has share of honour and is the greatest help and cause of joy to
> the undying gods and mortal men. But now, let all the people
> build me a great temple and an altar below it . . .
> And I myself will teach my rites, that hereafter you may
> reverently perform them and so win the favour of my heart.[16]

These parallel tales all reveal the hero as a product of maternal fashioning. The mother attempts both to eradicate the son's inferior mortal part, identified with the inferior mortal father, and to make the son immortal. Only the versions in which Thetis tests multiple sons with boiling water or fire suggest that a child of hers might be immortal without maternal fashioning. But none survive. Had Peleus not intervened, Achilles would have met the same fate.

Both tales resemble accounts in which children idealize rejecting or malignant parents. Psychologists distinguish defensive idealization of a parent from innocuous exaggeration of parental virtues and acknowledgment of abuse or rejection on the basis of "seemingly unconscious discrepancies between positive general descriptions of the mother or the relationship and actual negative experiences of the parent as described in specific episodes." Children who are rejected but not grossly abused may also engage in defensive idealization.[17]

These tales freely acknowledge the lack of ordinary maternal nurture, love, and care involved in the mothering of heroes. Some also register the son's suffering. But the myths invert these inversions: not only does lack of nurture count as superior nurture, but the nursemaid is counted the real parent while the mortal siblings and mother are reduced to inferior "nurses and handmaids." The goddess is rightly indignant at being held to ordinary standards of nurture. She is *kourotrophos*, a protector and nurturer of her hero-son. The conclusion seems inescapable: by crediting the divinity of mothers of heroes and bestowing the epithet *kourotrophos* on them, while subtly alluding to their shocking inversions of nurture, the mythic and epic traditions afford a striking example of defensive idealization at the level of culture.[18]

Most significantly, the myths dramatize how the mortal parent disavows his or her own perception of the goddess's mothering and adopts the goddess's. The mortal parent's perception of and response to the divine mother's (or nurse's) actions as inversions of *themis* infuriates the goddess. She is superior to ordinary mothers and norms of mothering. Intimidated, the mortal parent recants and strives to appease the goddess. The parent disowns his or her perception of the goddess's ministrations as harmful and identifies with the goddess's anger at the parent's folly.[19]

A mother's hostile response to an infant's care-seeking produces dismay. The criticism implied in the child's unconstrained response might provoke maternal anger or abandonment. So the child disavows or blocks his perceptions of harm, rejection, and lack of care, and complies with the mother's demand that he view her rejecting nurture as excelling norms of maternal love and care encoded in *themis*. He idealizes his exploitative, rejecting caregiver and blames himself for eliciting her displeasure.

Once again, myths may reverse cause and effect. As one might expect, infants cry when outraged mothers throw them to the ground. But crying, with its basic demand for nurture, may cause nursing mothers to spurn their infants. Would not an ungrateful human infant, who persisted in demanding the breast when offered the food and drink of the gods and the cleansing fire of immortality, deserve divine maternal anger?[20]

More broadly, these myths suggest how mothers who claim superiority to ordinary mortals sacrifice their sons' needs and development to fashion them into emblems of maternal superiority. A hero-son's invidious self-division is a necessary complement to his mother's grooming of him to play the leading role (while remaining dependent on her and under her control) in her attempt to revive a view of herself as superior to ordinary mortals, whom she views as shamefully inadequate and inferior. In effect he must strive to complete his mother's sacrifice of him, as a care-seeking, developing child, to her narcissistic needs.

Despite their ultimate vindication of the goddess, tales of Thetis administering lethal tests to her sons cut too close to the bone for the *Iliad* to take note of them. Even though Thetis and Peleus are generally separated in the *Iliad*, there are only the subtlest allusions to unusual or alarming childrearing practices, or to Peleus's criticism of Thetis as a mother, resulting in her angry abandonment of son and father when her son is only an infant. Leading her sisters in a threnody over the death of Patroklos, which anticipates the death of her son, Thetis recalls her

> best of child-bearing,
> since I gave birth to a son who was without fault and powerful
>   [*amumona te krateron te*],
> conspicuous among heroes; and he shot up like a young tree,
> and I nurtured him, like a tree grown in the pride of the orchard (18.54–57)

Far from alluding to her break-up with Peleus, the *Iliad* has Thetis go on to lament that she will "never again receive [Achilles] / won home again to his country and into the house of Peleus" (18.440–41), even though elsewhere in the text it is clear that Thetis has gone back to live with her father and sisters in the sea while Peleus wastes away in his halls alone.[21]

Yet here as elsewhere—most notably in the prophecy of the threat to Zeus posed by Thetis's son—the *Iliad* alludes to what it glosses over or denies. Thetis's fond memories suggest that her nurture of Achilles and her son's phenomenal growth and abilities are spontaneous and a source of joy to all—unconventional only in being superior to what any mortal mother and child could experience. Yet the *Iliad* may contain an attenuated allusion to Achilles' vulnerable foot and subtle enactments of Achilles manifesting his superiority to mortals by surviving immersion in fire and a river that Hera (standing in for Thetis in the reenactment) has turned into a boiling cauldron. While Achilles cites Peleus's fated fall from his status as the most fortunate of men, with a goddess for a wife, to a solitary and miserable old age (24.525–42), there is no mention of the quarrel that precipitated the fall. Yet for an audience familiar, as the *Iliad*'s almost surely was, with tales recounting the circumstances of the separation, the myth is invoked.[22]

DIVINE MOTHERS' NEED FOR GLORIOUS SONS

The stories of Thetis and Demeter suggest that when fathers sacrifice daughters in strategic marriages, they precipitate crises in daughters' self-worth, which is heavily invested in their superiority, in their fathers' eyes, to their mothers. The sacrifices that Zeus requires of Thetis are those that Greek fathers require of favored daughters. The daughter must set aside her own needs for parental nurture to take her father's side in ongoing marital strife. She must allow herself to be "sold" to an inferior husband to extricate her father from difficulties of his own making.

Agamemnon's mock or failed attempts to use his daughters to strike such a bargain with Achilles expose dynamics that are concealed by the reversal of cause and effect in the myth of Thetis's forced marriage. Dishonored by his brother's wife's adultery (which prefigures his own betrayal by Helen's similarly Aphrodite-cursed sister, Klytemnestra), Agamemnon offers his daughter a marriage to Achilles that is in reality her sacrifice. In the *Iliad* he offers Achilles another daughter, Iphianassa (whose name recalls Iphigenia's) to lure him into a sacrifice that will transmute Agamemnon's self-inflicted shame into glory.

The myth recounting how Thetis came to be married to a mortal illuminates erotic humiliation as a watershed event for the favored daughter. The events that precede Demeter's attempt to immortalize a son, whose glory will evince her divinity, are analogous. She too falls from a position seemingly superior to Zeus's wife (Demeter's sister). Zeus provokes her *mênis* with a betrayal that involves a daughter's forced, strategic marriage to an inferior husband. In Demeter's story, Zeus deals his actual daughter, not a "daughter of the house," to an inferior mate. The marriage that provokes Demeter's wrath is her daughter's, not her own. Still, Zeus's self-serving betrayal of mother and daughter—which recalls Agamemnon's betrayal of Klytemnestra and Iphigenia—exposes the limits of Demeter's supposedly special status. In both cases the humiliating, strategic marriage of a favorite daughter precedes a mother's attempt to produce a superior son. Now we see why Demeter interrupts her search for Persephone to try to immortalize Demophoon.[23]

Demeter is one of a string of relatively unthreatening paramours whom Zeus favors over Hera. In order to distract Zeus so her allies can help the Achaians carry out her revenge on Zeus's Trojans, Hera seduces the father of gods and men. She drapes herself in Aphrodite's charms and tells her husband that she is on an errand to reconcile a bitterly estranged couple—who happen to resemble Zeus and Hera in this regard. Taken in by Hera's deception, Zeus takes an ironic path to praising her attractions. He compares his overwhelming desire for Hera at that moment to his passion for Demeter and the string of other paramours with whom he repeatedly dishonored Hera (14.315–28).

Next after Demeter on Zeus's list of past loves is Leto. Her story involves neither an attempt to immortalize her children nor being forced by Zeus to marry an inferior mate. Yet it underscores the pattern of being, temporarily, Zeus's favorite, thereby provoking Hera's jealous anger, and then—once the affair with Zeus has ended—becoming completely invested in children whose glory is indistinguishable from her own. Like Thetis, Leto makes a notable contrast with Hera. Even in a hymn of praise to her, no poet could say of Zeus's consort what Hesiod says of Leto: "always mild, kind to men and to / the deathless gods, mild from the beginning, gentlest in all / Olympus" (*Theogony* 405–7).

The hymn to Leto's son, Apollo, compares the conduct of Zeus's exparamour to Hera's in a way that explains Zeus's preference for her over his wife. Hera signals her jealousy of her rival in her accustomed way, by hounding Leto over the face of the earth. Out of envy, Hera attempts to prevent Leto from giving birth because her son will be "without fault and powerful" (*amumona te krateron te*). While Leto rejoices in her glorious children (*aglaa tekna*), Hera complains of the shame and disgrace of bearing a weak son with a shriveled foot. Her inability to bear a glorious child is tied to her portrayal as a dishonored, vengeful wife. Only kind, gentle, daughter-like paramours, and not Hera, get to have glorious, faultless, supremely lethal children. The ugly vengefulness of Zeus's dishonored wife engenders cripples, brutes, or monsters: Hephaistos, Ares, and Typhon.[24]

Hera represents a different aspect of a favored daughter's experience as wife. She suffers the insult of being abandoned by her wife-fearing husband in favor of impressionable daughters. With vengeful anger, she too strives to recover the anomalous superiority of a favored daughter by having a faultless, superior son. But in marked contrast to the mothers of perfect, lethal children, Hera rejects a child who fails to meet her maternal needs. By making rejection of a less-than-perfect son unique to Hera, and contrasting her with gentle Leto, compassionate Thetis, and beautiful Demeter, these myths effectively deny that hostile mothering produces hero-sons. A caring surrogate mother for Achilles and the Achaians, Hera nonetheless sells them out. She pledges to let Zeus destroy their cities, once her revenge is accomplished (18.358–59, 4.30–72).

The son of Zeus and Leto, Apollo is himself immortal, so Leto does not need to immortalize him. Nevertheless, she declines to nourish Apollo in the usual way. Instead of giving Apollo her breast, Leto has Themis feed him ambrosia and nektar, at which point he exhibits prodigious powers just as mortal sons do after receiving divine nourishment. He breaks free of the golden bands that swaddle him. Apollo and Artemis demonstrate how glorious children silence doubts about their mother's superiority. A mortal woman, Niobe, mocks Leto, because Niobe has numerous sons and daughters, while Leto has only one of each. "Stung by the taunt," the mild and gentle goddess "incites Artemis and Apollo against [Niobe's children]." Artemis shoots down the females and Apollo kills the males. Zeus turns broken-hearted Niobe into a stone that weeps incessantly.[25]

Chapter Four

Catharsis and Denial

In the *Iliad*, the Achilles-type hero simply manifests his divine mother's superiority—although the epic alludes to myths in which she subjects him to a demanding regimen. This account emphasizes maternal fashioning. It views the hero-son as forged in a destructive relationship with an "outlandish" mother. Indeed, it suggests that the mortal husband's objection to his divine wife's parenting recapitulates his childhood response to maternal mistreatment. Peleus's mythobiography both reflects and denies a superior mother's outrageous disregard. He suffers it, but from his stepmother, not his mother. It forms him as a hero but is not integral to his upbringing.

The *Iliad* and its background myths are structures of denial. They foster individual and collective denial of traumatic features of mother-son relationships that are fundamental to the formation of heroic character and to the reproduction of heroic culture. Representations of these traumatic experiences, and of sons' fear- and dependency-based responses to them, are present in the *Iliad* and myth, but in disguised and displaced forms. They are hidden in plain view. At the same time, the *Iliad* is a cathartic narrative. It mimics the behavior of children not only in excluding knowledge of sacrificial care but in redirecting anger and blame from child-sacrificing parents to third parties and finally to the self. Thus it facilitates purging not only anger at parents' outrageous devaluation of care-seeking children, but the accurately perceiving, appropriately responding self. It is a structure of denial to cathartic effect.[1]

Like Achilles' and Peleus's mythobiographies, Achilles' quarrels with Agamemnon and his fellow Achaians exhibit numerous features of the family dynamics involved in rearing hero-sons. Achilles criticizes Agamemnon for an analogue of parental failure to meet children's needs, sacrificing them to bolster parental self-esteem. Agamemnon's anger at Achilles for demanding

61

responsible care for the Achaians negates Achilles' sense of his value. Like children, the Achaians block information about violations of responsible care, behaving as if they did not happen.

Achilles' call for responsible care infuriates Agamemnon because it highlights the disparity between Agamemnon's behavior and kingly norms that are extensions of parental ones. Achilles experiences this parent-figure's anger as a total negation of his value, against which he is utterly defenseless. Outrageously, it reduces him to a "dishonored vagabond." His life as a loved and respected member of a community in accord with *themis* is effectively destroyed. His fellow Achaians act like abused children who avoid provoking parental anger by pretending abuse has not occurred. By overlooking glaring breaches of fundamental kingly norms, as well as the vilification of the son whose call for responsible care exposes Agamemnon's failure, his fellow Achaians effectively dissociate from and abandon outraged, dishonored Achilles.

These elements correspond to but also diverge from the formative experiences and psychology we have hypothesized for hero-sons. Achilles' divine mother and mortal father confidently assert his mother's superiority to norms of *themis*. Agamemnon vacillates between empty grandiosity and anxiety about being reduced to a thing of reproach. Although contradicting family myths of superiority, such vacillations arguably characterize inferior fathers, superior mothers, and hero-sons alike. Anxiety stemming from rejection underlies their rage. In the *Iliad*, the hero-son (rather than his interfering mortal parent, as in myth) exposes the failings of a parent-figure who claims to be above *themis* and, as a consequence, suffers the parent-figure's devastating rage. These elements of the quarrel dramatize otherwise hidden features of the parent-child interactions that are formative for heroic character.

Other discrepancies are more problematic. In the *Iliad*, it is not Achilles' mother who sacrifices her son's needs in order to assuage her humiliations and anxiety. It is not Achilles' mother whose rage at him for calling attention to parental breaches of *themis* deals a crippling blow to his self-esteem. It is not even Achilles' mortal father, threatened by his son's superiority. Rather it is his would-be pseudo-father Agamemnon. Utterly unlike Achilles' mortal father, Agamemnon resembles Achilles' divine mother even less. Thetis is the antithesis of the outraged king who dishonors her son. Thetis in the *Iliad* also differs from the goddess who hurls her squalling infant to the ground in myths. In the *Iliad* the goddess comes to the aid of her son, soothes him for his loss of honor, and helps him to restore it.

A second glaring discrepancy is that Achilles does not suppress knowledge of or gloss over the parent figure's offenses against him. In stark contrast to the hero-son in our model, Achilles braves Agamemnon's anger by protesting his violations of *themis*. Further, Achilles chastises his fellows for overlooking both the original breach of *themis*—Agamemnon's sacrifice of their lives to avoid giving up a daughter-like concubine—and also the terrible injury to Achilles' honor that compounds Agamemnon's original breach.

Despite being adults who can stand up for their rights, the Achaians in Achilles' account act like dependent children. They avoid confronting their parent-figure's abdication of responsibility and the angry response that exposing it would provoke by suppressing information of his offenses. In this way they maintain their relationship with an abusive caregiver on whom they depend. But they are not children. They are men. And they should stand up for themselves.

What is going on here? From the standpoint of heroic psychology, we have the "right" actions, effects, and responses (demands for responsible parental care met with blighting parental negation, information blockage about parental failings, and prohibitions against calling attention to these failings in order to maintain abusive relationships). Yet these actions are assigned to the "wrong" people: the mortal father (or rather pseudo-father, utterly unlike the hero's own), not the divine mother; the *laos*, not the hero-son. Achilles is the only one with the independence and self-respect to call attention to parental failings. The quarrel with Agamemnon is constructed as if to establish that the paradigmatic hero, Achilles, is the opposite of the dependent hero-son in our model. Achilles does not allow his needs—or at least those of the Achaian people—to be sacrificed to the needs of an anxious king trying to assuage anxieties about his worth.

The quarrel marks another purported difference: Achilles' actual parents (Peleus and Thetis) and trusted parent-figures (Hera—at least in relation to Achilles—and father Zeus) are unlike Agamemnon with Achilles or Hera with her son Hephaistos. They are portrayed as unlike *themis*-inverting, child-sacrificing parents who are humiliated and enraged when children expose their shortcomings. These stories portray analogues of parental mistreatment of children, its crippling effects, and children's fearful responses to parental malfeasance. But they deny that any of this applies to the paradigmatic hero Achilles. The narrative of the quarrel does precisely what Achilles accuses his fellow Achaians of doing: it glosses over damaging parental hostility, idealizes hostile parent-figures, and pretends that all is according to *themis*, thereby preserving relationships with irresponsible, child-sacrificing caregivers.

A king and commander is first and foremost a "shepherd of the people," a man burdened with counsels (*boulêphoron andra*) and responsibility for a people (*epitrepô, laos*; 2.24–25, 61–62). He is supposed to have the wit (*noos*) to look before and behind to see that his people are safe and do not perish (1.117, 1.338). In the first book of the *Iliad*, Agamemnon commits gross breaches of kingly responsibility toward the *laos*. Rather than relinquish his favorite prize girl, he endangers his entire army by insulting Apollo's priest. In the face of Apollo's predictably devastating response, Agamemnon allows his men to die, day after day, rather than own up to and atone for his act of hubris. A responsible king would have honored Apollo by respecting his priest and exchanging the girl for ransom (1.21–23). Or, instead of abducting her, he would have allowed her to continue to serve Apollo. He would not have insulted the priest and denied that the god's insignia could protect him. Instead Agamemnon brings Apollo's plague on his men, and then he allows them to die because his claim to honor is too tenuous for him to own up to his mistake and atone for it. He literally sacrifices their lives and futures to prop up a sense of his honor that is inflated, precarious, and liable to dissolve into visions of shameful humiliation.

Inspired by Hera's maternal "pity at the sight of the Achaians dying," Achilles steps in and does what a more responsible—and secure—king would have done. He calls a seer to identify the source of the plague that is killing the Achaians. Knowing that it will provoke Agamemnon's anger, and securing a promise of protection from Achilles, the seer speaks forth the king's transgressions, forcing Agamemnon to admit his responsibility and to atone for his disrespect both to Apollo and to the girl's aged father. Agamemnon responds to this revelation of his failings as a king as if it posed a global threat to his pretensions to a superiority above all ordinary rules and obligations, and his outrage reflects this. As elsewhere in the *Iliad*, Agamemnon needs to compensate for his insecurity: he must immediately have a prize to replace the one he has lost, lest Achilles usurp his honors and humiliate him. He lacks the confidence to go without an outward token of his honor, even for a brief time.

Agamemnon takes Achilles' prize to punish Achilles for forcing him take responsibility for the plague that is killing his people. Achilles vents his contempt for Agamemnon as the antithesis of a responsible king and his disgust with his fellow Achaians for shamefully acquiescing in Agamemnon's abuse. This litany of disgrace is contained in a number of passages in the first book of the *Iliad* and also in the ninth, when Achilles rejects Agamemnon's flawed apology and refuses to return to the fighting. The most important passage comes after Agamemnon dishonors Achilles for having the seer, Kalchas, expose his unkingly lack of care for his men—and Achilles berates his fellow Achaians for acting as if these outrageous inversions of *themis* never occurred.[2]

SCEPTER SPEECH

The main vehicle for Achilles' critique of Agamemnon's gross breaches of kingly responsibility in book 1 of the *Iliad* is Achilles' unorthodox account of the origins of the scepter that kings hold in their hands when they speak in the assembly. The scepter is conventionally described as being handed down by Zeus, the architect of cosmic *themis* and *dikê*, to a line of mortal kings culminating in Agamemnon. Achilles describes the scepter as originating in a gross violation of natural cycles according to *themis*: a sapling cut down and stripped of leaf and branch, never more to flourish.

After first accusing Agamemnon of being too cowardly to win his prizes by fighting, instead preferring to "take away the gifts of any man who speaks up against [him]," and going on to deride his fellow Achaians as "nonentities" for putting up with Agamemnon's mistreatment of them, Achilles swears an oath

> in the name of this sceptre, which never again will bear leaf nor
> branch, now that it has left behind the cut stump in the mountains,
> nor shall it ever blossom again, since the bronze blade stripped
> bark and leafage, and now at last the sons of the Achaians
> carry it in their hands in state when they administer
> the justice [*dikaspoloi, themistas*] of Zeus (1.234–39)

Achilles vows that when the Achaians drop and die under Hektor's onslaught—much as they did under Apollo's—and all the Achaians long for his return, Agamemnon will be able to do nothing. He will eat his heart out with sorrow that he "did no honour to the best of the Achaians" (1.225–46).[3]

The immediate reference for the violent, irreparable disruption of the sapling's natural flourishing seems to be the devastating insult Achilles suffers for speaking out against Agamemnon's violations of his kingly obligations under *themis*. This scepter born of a violation of *themis* is the one that the Achaians hold in their hands in state when they dispense justice and uphold the ordinances of Zeus.

Just as much of Achilles' critique of Agamemnon is in terms of traditional *themis*—Agamemnon's substitution of sacrifice for responsible care for his men—so Achilles speaks as an exponent of *themis* when he sums up the violations that the Achaians are content to call *themis*. Since *themis* is defined against the transgressions of Zeus's predecessors, Ouranos and Kronos, who attempted to prevent the birth and natural flourishing of their children, the Achaians' scepter betokens the opposite of *themis*: the irreparable disruption of natural growth and flourishing.[4]

The clear implication of Achilles' speech is not only that the Achaians overlook Agamemnon's gross violations of *themis* toward them and their defender, Achilles, but that they absolve themselves for doing so—and from doing anything about it—by pretending Agamemnon's actions are in accord with *themis*. If this is what the Achaians call *themis*, Achilles is having none of it. He marks the end of his speech by dashing the scepter to the ground.

So the opening incident of the *Iliad* dramatizes several key elements: a parent-figure who sacrifices the people (*laos*) entrusted to his care to ward off a sense of his worthlessness; parental outrage at calls for responsible care in accord with *themis*; an act of parental devaluing that irreparably interrupts the normal development and flourishing of the hero-son; and men who behave like dependent children. They cling to their abuser, fearing to acknowledge parental violations of *themis* that are obvious to all, lest it provoke parental anger. They pretend that no violations of *themis* have occurred.

Agamemnon is clearly an insecure parent-figure who sacrifices his charges' needs to his own. Indeed, he is a literal child-sacrificer, an identity and analogy that the first book of the *Iliad* impresses on its audience in various ways. Since ancient times, commentators have speculated that Agamemnon's berating of Kalchas as a seer who loves to prophesy evil things (1.106–8) may refer to Kalchas's divination of the cause and sacrificial remedy for Artemis's anger at Aulis a decade before. Indeed, this is one of those instances in which the *Iliad* not only alludes to a background myth but effectively incorporates and reenacts it. As at Aulis, Agamemnon is threatened with shame and dishonor as a result of his own hubris. At Aulis, he insulted Artemis; at Troy, he insults her brother, Apollo. Just as, to stave off shameful defeat, he has to appease Artemis by sacrificing his favorite daughter, Iphigenia, so in the *Iliad* he has to appease Apollo by giving his favorite concubine back to the god. By insulting Achilles, Agamemnon again courts shame and dishonor, and again has to give up a prized concubine to ward off devastation. All of this effectively frames his betrayal of the *laos* in the first book of the *Iliad* as an analogue of child-sacrifice. Equally significant are the parallels between the favored concubines whose lives Agamemnon would blight and the favorite daughter whom he sacrifices.[5]

Although Agamemnon at one point offers to honor Achilles like his own son, he could not be more unlike Achilles' mortal father, let alone Achilles' divine mother, the hero-son's primary child-devaluer and child-sacrificer. Far from devaluing her son, Thetis pridefully describes him as "without fault and powerful" and "preeminent among heroes," and she helps him recover his lost honor—just as she helps sons of Hera or Zeus who are victims of Hera's anger.

Achilles' role is even more problematic for our thesis. To begin with, Achilles could never suffer devaluation from a divine mother: he is analogous to

Phokos, not Peleus. Achilles also differs fundamentally from the hero-son of our model by standing up to abuse. He freely vents outrage, criticism, and contempt for a parent-figure's *themis*-inverting role-reversal with respect to the *laos*, and for this envious, threatened pseudo-father's unjust but devastating devaluation of him. In addition, he faults the Achaians for behaving like the hero-son (and, except for a single, fateful slip, the mortal father) in our model— glossing over abuse and pretending that no breach of *themis* has occurred.

Yet if, as seems likely, the divine mother is the one who first inflicts the wound to the hero-son's sense of his value that an enviously belittling father-figure like Agamemnon can reopen, Achilles' protest against Agamemnon's utter inadequacy as a shepherd of the people in the *Iliad* can be interpreted as part of a structure of denial that is fundamental to heroic character and behavior. First, there is denial per se: the hero-son could never suffer outrageous, life-blighting devaluation by his mother or father; nor could he respond to these experiences in a shamefully dependent manner. Second, there is projection: others do suffer demoralizing, life-destroying, parental devaluation, but they suppress their outrage and shrink from calling attention to the abuse they suffer, clinging to their abuser. Third, there is demonstration of difference: the hero shows himself completely unlike them in both these respects.

Why should we construe these glaring discrepancies between the *Iliad*'s narrative and our model as denial rather than disproof? Part of the way the *Iliad* implies that Achilles could never suffer abuse from a parent is by drawing stark contrasts between Agamemnon and both of Achilles' parents. At several points the *Iliad* implies that the insecure king who insults Achilles could not be more unlike Achilles' mortal father. But, as auditors of the *Iliad* were probably aware, the young Peleus was far from immune to the kind of envy of glorious, demigod youths such as Achilles that Agamemnon exhibits in book 1 (and again, in an explicitly paternal-filial context, when he insults Achilles' stand-in, Diomedes, in book 4). In light of the commonsense correlation, confirmed by family systems research, between cross-sex parent-child alliances and same-sex parent-child rivalries, it seems entirely possible that Agamemnon here represents a split-off part of the hero-son's mortal father. It is on display in the *Iliad*, but transferred from Peleus to Agamemnon.[6]

Considerably more far-fetched is the notion that, by making Agamemnon responsible for inflicting the devaluation that irreparably blights the hero-son's development, the *Iliad* denies the divine mother's primacy in this regard. Equally at variance with the *Iliad*'s narrative is the companion notion that, by identifying with his maternal devaluer, the son comes to view maternal violations of *themis* as normal and right—while coming to regard assertions of ordinary parental prerogatives and filial concerns as violations deserving of *mênis*.

We have seen from the beginning that the threat that Achilles poses to Agamemnon is rooted in Achilles being an extension of his divine mother— even as the demigod brother whom Peleus enviously murders is superior by virtue of his mother's divinity. So the question is how does the hero-son come to be an extension of his mother and to exhibit the qualities that testify to his mother's divinity?

If the process involves the negation of the son's sense of his own and his father's value by an anomalously superior, but then humiliated daughter, who is attempting to convince herself and others that she really is superior to puny, needy, vulnerable mortals—onto whom she projects her suppressed experience of herself—then it is entirely plausible that Achilles comes to the encounter with Agamemnon with an acute vulnerability that can be traced to traumatic maternal devaluation, the pivotal experience in the hero-son's development. By implying that Agamemnon's insult is what blights the development of the hero-son, as the axe does the sapling, the *Iliad* may indeed shift responsibility to Agamemnon for a pattern of maternal behavior toward her hero-son that begins in infancy. In that case, while it is a manifestation of an insecure father's belittling of a glorious, mother-favored son, Agamemnon's dishonoring of Achilles for holding him to account for failing in his responsibility to the *laos* also serves as a proxy for Thetis's devaluing of her care-seeking mortal son.

If so, the image of the scepter as a sapling cut by a bronze blade so that it will flourish no more is particularly apt. The hero-son would experience the divine mother's negation of his value as an ordinary, loved child of a nurturing mother as the destruction of the life in accord with *themis* that he, an innocent child (*nêpios teknon*), expects. In this context, the negation of the son's value destroys his life as the bronze blade (with its sacrificial overtones) transforms a thriving sapling into a dead stick. The son's experience of himself as loved and valued by his mother is the foundation of his life; her rejection destroys that life. In that sense, Agamemnon's devaluation of Achilles reenacts an outrageous, life-destroying maternal betrayal and devaluation.[7]

None of this denies elements of father-son conflict in the quarrel. Indeed, the imagery of the scepter calls attention to the erotic aspects of Agamemnon's dishonoring of Achilles—and to the intersection of the attachment, family systems, and Freudian theories adumbrated earlier. It is the sons of the Achaians, not their mothers, who leave the cut stump in the mountains. Agamemnon envies Achilles, favorite of beautiful Thetis, as a displaced father envies the glorious, irresistibly attractive son whom his trophy wife favors over him. By forcing Agamemnon to give up his unwilling prize, a devotee of glorious Apollo, while presumably making Agamemnon hateful to Achilles' own prize, Briseis, by sleeping with her, Achilles effectively castrates the king. The reciprocal *mênis* of Agamemnon and Achilles has a sexual component.

Amyntor's curse on Phoinix blights his procreative powers. Achilles' loss of the *nostos* in which he would have been a father to his son may result from Agamemnon's Zeus-backed imprecations. If, as Klytemnestra's avenger in book 1, Achilles is a precursor of the seducer who will make a cuckold of Agamemnon, the king's *mênis* at Achilles is analogous to the impotent rage of Agamemnon's brother, Menelaos, which is backed by the *mênis* of Zeus. The irresistible attractiveness of Achilles is analogous to that of Paris, who incurs Zeus's *mênis* by making a cuckold of Menelaos. Agamemnon's curse and appropriation of Achilles' sexual partner leave Achilles bereft of the honorific attributes that make him unbeatable in erotic competition, while Menelaos roams around cursing the favorite of Aphrodite who cuckolded him.[8]

The image of the cut stump suggests a castration. But how does this come about? One possibility—with important implications for the psychology of honor and dishonor—involves castration anxiety. By imagining himself stripped of the qualities that make him enviably superior to the father and that give him a superior claim to honor in the form of willing sexual prizes, the son precludes the possibility that his eroticized superiority will be taken from him by an outraged, envious father. As a result of his preemptive self-castration, he experiences himself as outrageously lacking in value, but having already been lost, his prized, eroticized superiority cannot be snatched away from him.

Even if Agamemnon's threatening response to losing his prize prompts an anxious Achilles to imagine himself as bereft of his honored superiority, Agamemnon's dishonoring of Achilles may reopen an old wound. It may be a way to smuggle the outrageous and devastating experience of maternal devaluation into the narrative without assigning it to the divine mother. Indeed, wives' and mothers' fearsome envy of hero-sons, a central feature of Slater's analysis, and filial responses to it, such as preemptive self-emasculation, may in the *Iliad* be subsumed in the quarrel between Achilles and Agamemnon.[9]

Yet the claim that Agamemnon's dishonoring of Achilles is a proxy for the divine mother's blighting devaluation of her hero-son is apparently belied not only by the apparent contrast between Agamemnon's gross deficiencies and the virtues of Achilles' unenvious mortal father, but by Achilles' mother's role in the proceedings. Far from devaluing her son, Thetis regards him as flawlessly superior. Moreover, she sympathizes with her son's devastation and outrage, and she intervenes with Zeus to ensure that her and her son's joint plan to avenge his dishonor (which Zeus silently amends to include the death of Patroklos) will succeed. If anyone is a scapegoat for the demanding, rejecting mother who blames her son for shaming her by failing to manifest her claimed superiority, it is Hera.[10]

On closer examination, however, Thetis's actions are consistent with the model of heroic psychology developed in chapter 2. A purportedly superior mother, she offers her son a replacement for the ordinary human self and life that she destroys. He is intrinsically superior, beyond the claims of *themis*. Agamemnon's dishonoring of Achilles not only covertly reenacts Thetis's life-destroying devaluation of her mortal son. It also manifestly negates the replacement (false) self, which reflects glory on her as well as her son. It is entirely appropriate, then, that Thetis helps her son recover the replacement she provided for the *themis*-self she destroyed.

The mythology of divine mothering posits a process of destruction and immortalization: the hero's divine mother both destroys her son as an ordinary human child and confers on him a new identity as incontestably superior to any mortal. We have already seen how a mother who sacrifices her child's needs for nurture to her own needs for narcissistic validation does not merely respond negatively to her care-seeking child, failing to affirm his sense of his value and worthiness of nurture. Much as Demeter appeared to Metaneira to be doing, or as Thetis appeared to Peleus, she must attempt to root out precisely the ordinary humanity that is operative in any parent-child relationship, and that students of animal and human behavior suggest is part of our evolutionary heritage.

The mythical goddess attempts to obliterate her defenseless, vulnerable, mortal infant in the process of providing him with a superior self—an extension of her divinity. Hera's narrative, with its overt, damaging rejection of her son, shows other unsavory features of the divine mother hero-son relationship. Since the divine mother always purports to repair the damage she (or her supposed antithesis, Hera) inflicts, Thetis's role in repairing the effects of paternal (or maternal) devaluing of her son is appropriate. Unfortunately, her therapeutic interventions exacerbate Achilles' vulnerability.

What would happen if the dishonor of Thetis's son were to go unavenged? Would it not make a mockery of Thetis's own claims to divine honors, and her special claim to honor from Zeus—to both of which the *Iliad* itself testifies? So she has all the more reason to undo Agamemnon's denial of her son's claims to an honor that is above that of all mere mortals.

It is not merely the supposed antithesis between Agamemnon and Achilles' father and mother that underpins the assertion that Achilles could never suffer, much less shamefully respond to, parental devaluation. It is also Achilles' status as the demigod son of Thetis. The hero Peleus may have suffered outrageous neglect from a divine stepmother who favored her demigod son, but Achilles *is* that demigod son, "without fault and powerful," in his divine mother's eyes. He exhibits all the maddening superiority of the demigod stepbrother whom Peleus murdered. But is he merely manifesting his mother-derived superiority (again, how would he come to do this?), or is he desperately trying to forestall the maternal rejection that he and his father suffered as supposedly inferior mortals?

This brings us to the second of the three interlocking assertions that deny the hero-son's experience of devaluation and sacrifice. Others experience child-sacrifice in place of childcare and respond shamefully to mistreatment. The *Iliad* refutes every element of our assertion that Achilles' dreams of having an ordinary loving family, or of becoming a husband, father, and king in his own right are sacrificed to bolster the self-esteem of his insecure parents—one of whom has a grotesquely inflated sense of her worth to which the other attaches himself. The same cannot be said for Agamemnon's metaphorical children, the Achaians. The *Iliad* affirms that to save face, Agamemnon sacrifices the Achaians whose lives and homecomings he is supposed to do everything in his power to protect. Moreover, cowards and "nonentities" that they are (1.231, 1.293), they accept this mistreatment as if it were the prudent care for their well-being that they deserve.

> King who feed on your people [*dêmoboros basileus*], since you
>   rule nonentities [*outidanoisin*];
> otherwise, son of Atreus, this were your last outrage (1.231–32)

If his fellow Achaians had any self-respect, Agamemnon's days of feeding on, rather than protecting and leading, his people would be over.

When Agamemnon is threatened with shame or dishonor, his responsibility to love and care for his men goes by the board. In such circumstances, the Achaians—as allies and men under his command, whose futures as husbands, fathers, and kings depend on him—evidently mean nothing to Agamemnon. If they were to assert their claim to his responsible care or criticize him for his irresponsibility, as Achilles does on their behalf, their legitimate claims, manifestations of self-valuation, would doubtless incense Agamemnon. So instead of standing up for themselves, they show themselves to be "nonentities" by continuing to serve him—and masking their acquiescence by acting as if all is *themis* and *dikê*, order and justice.

So, at any rate, goes the second part of the *Iliad*'s tripartite denial: others, not the hero-son, allow themselves to be sacrificed by insecure parents who do not value them and who betray their trust. To avoid confronting this abuse and their own shameful acceptance of it, these others act as if Agamemnon's violent negation of *themis* and justice, with its implicit devaluing of them, is its opposite.[11]

While denial of their value is implicit in the sacrifice of the Achaians' dreamed-of *nostoi* by a callous, self-absorbed Agamemnon, projection figures differently in denying the catastrophic devaluation that is the core experience to which the metaphor of child-sacrifice refers. Instead of projecting this crucial experience onto the Achaians, the *Iliad*, remarkably, conforms to our model in having the hero-son, not the Achaians, suffer outrageous devaluation. But it nonetheless denies that he experiences parental (much less maternal) devaluation by the simple expedient of making the son's devaluer someone other than a parent. Agamemnon is a pseudo- or anti-parent: he would like to be authentically heroic (and, presumably to have been married to Thetis) like Achilles' father, and he offers to make Achilles his son-in-law and honor him the same as his own son. Agamemnon may evince the kind of insecurity that leads parents to devalue ordinary mortal children, but the *Iliad* suggests that he is the antithesis of the hero-son's parents, real and figurative.

Third, the hero proves himself to be different from these others, who do correspond to the sacrificed children. When Achilles calls his fellow Achaians "nonentities" and cowards for accepting Agamemnon's mistreatment of them, he implicitly contrasts his own behavior with theirs. The same is true when he wonders how the Achaians will continue to obey Agamemnon's orders, since Agamemnon evidently "cares nothing" for their sacrifices on his behalf (1.150, 1.160). He thus throws down in disgust the scepter that the Achaians use when they pretend that *themis* and *dikê*, rather than gross perversions of them, prevail. Not only does Achilles refuse to allow himself to be devalued, exploited, and sacrificed by Agamemnon, Achilles seeks to ensure that Agamemnon's dishonoring of him will be Agamemnon's last outrage. Only the intervention of Hera's emissary, Athena, prevents Achilles from accomplishing this commendable goal. In stark contrast to his fellow Achaians, no one could accuse Achilles of acting as if all is in accord with *themis* and *dikê*.

Of course the hero-son may have something to prove: that he is other than the person who, at some level, he knows himself to be. As a son, he is demoralized by his mother's disregard. Devastated by her devaluing, he clings to her all the more. In part this is the mechanism of identification with the aggressor—an attempt to exchange the role of victim for that of victimizer (a reflex that may help to explain the tenacity of Achilles' hostile embrace of Agamemnon). But it may also be evidence of the demoralizing effect of abuse, which increases dependency on the abuser, making it difficult for a child or even an adult to break free of an abusive relationship. Achilles seems to have something like this in mind when he exhorts the Achaians to "be men" and stand up to Agamemnon.

There is likely some truth in Achilles' accusations—to the extent that all the Achaians are hero-sons, all participate in the same rationalizations and denials. Yet significantly, Achilles voices the traits, and there are other, honorable reasons for the Achaians to continue to follow Agamemnon, which do not figure in Achilles' account. Although critical of Agamemnon, some of Achilles' fellow Achaians may share Nestor's view that Zeus has given him "the sceptre and rights of judgment, to be king over the people" (9.97–99). Here as elsewhere, Nestor's acknowledgment of Agamemnon's authority seeks to deal with Agamemnon's failings by urging more kingly actions. In the same passage, Nestor not only reminds Agamemnon that he has to listen as well as command, but also criticizes him for ignoring his advisors and taking Achilles' prize. The Achaians may feel bound to honor their oaths to defend the husband of Helen (cf. 4.266–67). They may be mindful that Zeus has promised them victory at Troy and want the glory—and rich spoils—that go with it (2.203 f.).[12]

There may be yet other reasons, other than lack of self-respect, why the Achaians neither kill Agamemnon nor leave him to fight his battles alone. Saying that Agamemnon rules over nonentities or else this would be his last outrage implies that Agamemnon habitually commits outrages against the Achaians as well as Achilles himself. As we saw with Diomedes, other Achaians may not be as prone to outrage and dishonor as goddess-reared Achilles. What Achilles considers an outrage, Diomedes seems to regard as merely baiting, and he refuses to be drawn in. (It may be significant here that Diomedes derides Paris's wounding of him in the foot with an arrow, which adumbrates Paris's fatal wounding of Achilles, as a mere scratch—albeit one that temporarily puts him out of action [11.369–95].)

So, while for Achilles the alternatives are to deny abuse or confront an abuser, the issues for his fellows may be more complex. That Achilles frames the issue the way he does may indicate that it is his issue—a fundamental issue of his character. His need to cast others' refusal to support him in a shameful—and, at least for some, inaccurate—light, and to show himself to be the opposite of the others he constructs, may signify his own well-founded self-doubt.[13]

Achilles' mother represents in naturalistic—which is to say *themistic*—terms her role in bringing up Achilles. For her, and presumably for Achilles as well, it is "the best of child-rearing." Her son, whom Peleus gave her "to bear and to raise up / conspicuous among heroes . . . shot up like a young tree," and she "nurtured him, like a tree grown in the pride of the orchard" (18.436–38). To nurture her son to adulthood would be like helping the sapling in Achilles' scepter speech to flourish and mature. Yet this particular sapling must be cut down by a bronze blade. It cannot be allowed to grow to maturity. The glory of Achilles—and Thetis—depend on it.

Rather than nurturing her son to capable, self-valuing adulthood in accord with *themis*, the purportedly divine mother must thwart her son's aspiration and destroy his potential to be a man like his father (or rather a man like the longed-for father who could provide an example of self-valuation in the face of maternal rejection). This is especially true for a hero such as Achilles who is reared by a divine mother. It is markedly less true for heroes who identify with, or identify themselves as, mortal fathers—figures such as Nestor, Diomedes, and Odysseus. If Achilles were to continue to idealize and emulate his father, Thetis's plan to regain her lost glory by having her son demonstrate his mother-derived superiority to all mere mortals—and, in particular, to his mortal father—would come to naught. So Thetis must ensure that the sapling is cut down rather than allowed to grow to maturity—and she must represent this travesty of mothering as the epitome of *themis* and *dikê*.

The single most important way that the divine mother accomplishes this—the axe blow, if you will—is by mirroring her son's pride in himself and his father back to him as hopeless inadequacy that is unworthy of notice. This outrageous devaluing teaches her son that his sense of himself as deserving of love and care, and his pride in mastering each step toward becoming a capable adult like his (idealized) father, is misplaced. As his father's son he is nothing, and wholly inadequate, just like the father he idealized.

Thanks to his mother, Achilles can choose a different fate. Thetis regards her son as different from his mortal father. Achilles is "without fault and powerful"—just as the son of a castoff paramour of Zeus ought to be. He does not need to grow up to be a man like his father; he does not need to have his *nostos* and claim his patrimony because she offers him a better form of nurture—which makes him preeminent among heroes.

While the *Iliad* scapegoats Agamemnon for Achilles' outrageous transformation from a flourishing sapling to a cut stump, it idealizes Thetis. She is *kourotrophos*, a nurturer of youths, *kouroi*, who are like young shoots, *koroi*. The lucky recipient of her superior nurture shoots up "like a young tree" (*ernei*), nurtured (*threpsasa*) like a tree (*phuton*) that is "the pride of the orchard"—as is right (*themis*) for a goddess's glorious son. True, he will be cut down before he reaches maturity. That is a source of endless grief to Thetis, but she is no more responsible for it than she is for the blighting devaluation of her son, which plays no part in her superior form of nurture. It if did, it could not stem from her shame at her own ordinary needs and aspirations. Unlike her son, she has no mortal self to be ashamed of.[14]

But if Thetis's "best of childrearing" does involve sacrificing her son's life as husband, father, and king, the antithesis between her and Agamemnon begins to break down. Agamemnon's envious belittling of Achilles is so devastating because it is overlaid on Thetis's prior devaluation of her son. If Achilles counts being sacrificed instead of nurtured to maturity by his mother as *themis* and *dikê*, and if in his denied mortal self he is too demoralized and dependent on his mother to break free of her, the antithesis he tries to maintain between him and the Achaians also breaks down.

By representing Agamemnon as the one who inflicts a blighting loss of value on Achilles, the *Iliad* dramatizes the key part of the mechanism by which the child's normal development is irreparably disrupted. The son is defenseless against this catastrophic negation of his value. The epic also denies that his mother could inflict such a blow on him. Even as he vents his outrage at Agamemnon, Achilles accepts devastating maternal devaluation—the hostile aspect of divine mothering of hero-sons that shocks the mortal parents in myth—as normal and right, in accord with *themis* and *dikê*.

True, Achilles demonstrates disdain for, and unlikeness to, those who—in *his* account of their actions—accept both their sacrifice by Agamemnon, and the king's devastating devaluation of Achilles, as normal and right. This demonstration, however, may well form a two-part denial. It serves to deny both the axe-blow of divine mothering and Achilles' acceptance of this fundamental violation of *themis* as normal and right.

CATHARSIS AND ATTACHMENT THEORY

Even if he does so in the service of denial, Achilles gives a credible imitation of one who will not sacrifice his life and future to prop up a self-absorbed, irresponsible parent-figure. For whatever reason, Achilles undeniably protests precisely those inversions of *themis* and *dikê* that hero-sons supposedly deny.

The quarrel between Achilles and Agamemnon has a cathartic function, both for the Achaian community within the epic and for the *Iliad*'s auditors. Agamemnon is a scapegoat for heroic culture's maternal as well as paternal failings. (Scapegoats are a boon to students of cultures. Necessarily portrayed as unique, they offer one-stop shopping for pervasive but denied characteristics of a culture.) By venting anger at these failings on behalf of his fellow Achaians, Achilles enables his fellows to engage in the very behavior for which he castigates them—to go along as if no violations of *themis* have occurred. Indeed, his cathartic outburst against Agamemnon underwrites his own pretense that his relationships with parents and parent-figures other than Agamemnon are in perfect accord with *themis* and *dikê*.

A crucial factor in the *Iliad*'s denial of the realities of the hero-son's relationships with his parents and other parent-figures (Hera and Zeus) is the suggestion that Agamemnon's failings are distinctive, even unique. As a violator of *themis* he has no peer. He insults gods, sacrifices his actual and metaphorical children, is manifestly anxious about his worth, and is led by his anxiety to botch all manner of kingly functions. So even though Agamemnon manifests all the faults of the hero-son's parents and parent-figures, the *Iliad* and myth represent him as their unique antithesis. Unlike Agamemnon, all of them are caring and responsible, confident and capable.[15]

The idea of Agamemnon as uniquely deficient is a mainstay of the *Iliad*'s contention that Achilles' relationships with his actual parents, as well as parental divinities like Zeus and Hera, manifest none of the inversions of *themis* that mark Agamemnon's relationships with his children and his people. The idea also figures in Achilles' critique of the Achaians. Achilles' suggestion that they should act like men and jettison this pathetic king implies that practically anyone else would be adequate.

Because of Agamemnon's alleged singularity, he is a safe target. He seems far removed from parental and quasi-parental relationships that matter to Achilles. He is remote as well from more competent leaders who often compensate for Agamemnon's deficiencies—Odysseus, Nestor, and Diomedes. So Achilles' being angry at Agamemnon would seem to imply the opposite about Achilles' relationships with his parents, or indeed about normal parent-child (or king-people, or commander-army) relationships in Achaian society generally.

All of this makes Agamemnon a perfect scapegoat for abuses that are pervasive within heroic culture. Since he is a universal scapegoat, Achilles' anger at him can have a cathartic function. In the *Iliad*, Achilles vents the outrage at heroic culture's self-absorbed, insecure, child-sacrificing parents. This outrage drives the culture's other-directed violence and threatens its very existence—raising the specter of "the horror of fighting among [one's] own people" (9.64).

Portraying Agamemnon's faults as aberrant, even unique, masks similar faults of parents and parent-figures who, instead of nurturing their children to maturity, sacrifice them to assuage the pervasive insecurities of an honor culture. The portrayal masks as well shameful aspects of hero-sons' acceptance of parental failings and abuse. Making Agamemnon a scapegoat lets parents and parent-figures, from Zeus on down, off the hook.

Equally important to the *Iliad*'s cathartic function is Achilles' own purported singularity. By standing up to Agamemnon, Achilles makes it unnecessary for his fellow Achaians to do so. Thus, although Achilles complains of their passivity, his challenge to Agamemnon, which brings an end to the plague, enables his fellows to remain passive, and to continue to deny their outrageous neglect. They can be "nonentities" because Achilles has been man enough to stand up to Agamemnon. With the backing of Hera and Athena, Achilles forces Agamemnon to end the plague afflicting all the Achaians. The entire community can vicariously participate in Achilles' venting of emotions that all feel but don't wish to acknowledge. The ending of the plague may symbolize the purging of violent emotion that sickens the entire community.[16]

Even though he holds Agamemnon as light as a splinter (9.378), Achilles nonetheless suffers terrible isolation and devaluation when his criticism provokes Agamemnon's fury. A main reason why children deny breaches of *themis* is because venting anger at irresponsible parents may provoke a hostile response—threatening the children's psychological and even physical survival. Achilles not only chastises Agamemnon for the Achaians, he suffers the consequences of doing so on their behalf.

The pretense that Agamemnon is unique again helps. As bad as being dishonored by Agamemnon is, Achilles only has to suffer Agamemnon's hatred. The most important gods as well as Achilles' mother and father remain on his side. If the hero-son's mother perpetrates the original outrageous negation of his value, the *Iliad* dramatizes how effective scapegoating and denial can be in preserving the semblance of a loving relationship with a damaging parent.

By scapegoating Agamemnon, Achilles himself becomes a scapegoat. He takes on the burdens of a general but unacceptable outrage at parental abuse. He alone suffers the terrible consequences of doing so. He thus spares others, who share in this outrage, the consequences of acknowledging it. Achilles' outburst may even have a cathartic effect for him. Venting his genuine outrage at gross failures of parental responsibility on a safe target allows him to maintain ostensibly respectful and loving relationships with parents and parent-figures whose Agamemnon-like neglect and demands for sacrifice he need not acknowledge.[17]

Thus the role of the hero who, as the conduit for an anger at abuse that all feel, dovetails perfectly with the mechanism of self-disavowal. When his fellow Achaians disavow the angry hero who perceives and responds to Agamemnon's abuse, these sufferers of abuse disavow their own anger. The hero may complain of being abandoned by others, but that is precisely the role he seeks. Indeed, venting his *themis*-based anger at a scapegoat allows him to disavow his own anger at the parents and parent-figures on whom he depends. In the broadest context, then, vicarious participation in Achilles' outrage at the irresponsibility of a supposedly aberrant Agamemnon may have a cathartic function for the society that comprises the *Iliad*'s audience, the dominant child-rearing patterns of which are represented, albeit in a disguised way, in the *Iliad* and its mythic context. If Agamemnon's failures to live up to the standards of *themis* are in fact endemic, venting outrage at him allows the release of violent emotion that could otherwise threaten not only the hero-son's relationships to parents, but heroic society itself. This catharsis has the further effect of whitewashing familial relationships predicated on child-sacrifice and its analogues, which are the norm in heroic society, leaving them in place.[18]

As will become clear in chapter 8, which analyzes the last third of the epic, the cathartic function of the *Iliad* does not end here. Anger at parental abuse is not merely vented on a scapegoat; it is redirected to troublesome aspects of the self, which it effectively eliminates. From its first word to its last, the *Iliad* enacts a process similar to a child's response to abusive parenting: shifting responsibility and redirecting anger from parents to third parties and ultimately the self. In the last third of the epic, alter egos of Achilles are summoned, destroyed, mourned, and relinquished, purging not only anger at abuse, but aspects of the self that might pose a real challenge to the endemic betrayal and abuse of heroic society.[19]

Defending poetry against Plato's reluctant banishment of poets from the *polis*, Aristotle argued that poetic catharsis helps to sustain the polity, both by purging deleterious emotion, including anger, and by producing moral clarity. The *Iliad* sustains heroic society by purging not only outrage but the clear perception of the routine violations of *themis* on which the society is based.[20]

Chapter Five

Fathers and Sons

The *Iliad*, as a structure of denial, implies much about hero-sons' relationships with parents and parent-figures. If we undo the dissociations, splits, projections, and cathartic purgings that epic and myth codify and effect, what family dynamics underlying agonistic Greek cultures emerge, sustained by the *Iliad* and its mythic context?

In the course of explicating how the *Iliad* facilitates the formation of split working models, the redirection of anger and the shifting of responsibility for harm from child-sacrificing parents to hero-sons—all to cathartic effect—the following chapters reconstruct father-son and mother-son relationships and inner conflicts associated with each. Since these defining relationships are embedded in intergenerational family systems, the chapters shine a spotlight over a complex tapestry.

FATHERS AND SONS

What are hero-sons' parents actually like? What are the sacrificial relationships with parents that hero-sons like Achilles supposedly accept and idealize?

Undermining their own familial and political authority in various ways, hero-fathers expect not only their twice- and thrice-sacrificed daughters but also their hero-sons to set aside their needs for protective and nurturing fathers. Divested of such troublesome expectations, hero-sons (and daughters) can devote themselves to undoing their fathers' self-inflicted injuries, thus winning paternal favor and avoiding paternal curses. If, in avenging slights to paternal honor, hero-sons demonstrate godlike prowess, however, they risk exciting paternal envy. Fathers' insecurities are exacerbated by dependence on glorious sons. Hero-sons are damned if they do and dammed if they don't. No wonder Achilles comes to question the entire heroic ethos—and that his threats to abandon Agamemnon prove empty. Analyzing the Herakles tradition, Philip Slater found that hero-sons had to walk a similar fine line with mothers. When Thetis tells Achilles he must die soon, he recalls that Herakles was beaten down by the anger of Hera (18.119).

The *Iliad* provides rich information regarding highly ambivalent, essentially sacrificial father-son relationships. This is true of the *Iliad*'s dramatization of the results of Zeus's ploy to deflect the anger of his formidable wife and daughter onto mortal counterparts. As a reward for declaring her "the fairest" of the goddesses, Aphrodite helps Paris seduce the most desirable of women while a guest in that woman's husband's house. Zeus's plan also ensures that Themis's prophecy regarding the son of Thetis is played out harmlessly (to Zeus) in the mortal realm. By recognizing the quarrel between Achilles and Agamemnon as a critical moment in the fulfillment of Themis's prophecy, we see the virtually foreordained deterioration of sacrificial father-son relationships. Yet even when father-son relationships turn hostile, hero-sons long for fathers to assert rather than abdicate their authority, and fathers long to perform their appointed roles and merit sons' respect.

Finally, the *Iliad*'s dramatization of the conflict between Paris and Menelaos, viewed in light of the mythology of violence surrounding Tyndareus's Aphrodite-cursed daughters, Helen and Klytemnestra, provides further clues about father-son relationships. Since Paris is a split-off aspect of Achilles, and since Paris reduces Menelaos to an outraged cuckold, Zeus's plan to deflect Hera's anger onto the Trojans also exports to the mortal realm the erotic aspect of the threat of being overthrown by the favored son of a powerful mother. Not only Menelaos's Zeus-backed curse on an alter ego of Achilles, but the dynamics of violence-fraught competition over Helen suggest that hero-fathers relate to their spouses as they and their hero-sons relate to their mothers: as detachable wives whose favor confers superiority. The dynamics of this high-stakes competition help to explain hero-fathers' inability to set examples in accord with *themis*, and their propensity both to depend on and to curse their hero-sons.

PLAN OF ZEUS I: DEFLECTION OF HERA'S ANGER ONTO ZEUS'S MORTAL PROTÉGÉS

The implications for father-son relationships of Zeus's plan to deflect Hera's jealous fury onto mortal substitutes are clear enough. Hera recruits the sons of the Achaians as the agents of her revenge against Trojan stand-ins for Zeus. Although in the *Iliad* Hera's minions are aware only of Zeus's favorable portents, the audience is informed that Zeus plans an unpleasant surprise for them. The father and king of gods and men will make the Achaians pay for actions—authorized by him—that harm his mortal counterparts. Hera's mortal sons, the instruments of her revenge, will one day have their cities destroyed, their sons killed, and their wives enslaved or reduced to concubinage. That is the quid pro quo Zeus demands for allowing Hera to take revenge on the Trojans (4.30–72, 9.592–94). As noted with respect to Phoinix's story, sons whom insulted mothers enlist to take revenge on philandering fathers like Amyntor also become targets for paternal curses, backed by father Zeus. Although the actions that provoke Agamemnon's *mênis* at Achilles appear dissimilar to Phoinix's against his father, Achilles in fact commits an offense similar to that for which Amyntor curses his son. Since Achilles and Hera's other Achaian "sons" play a similar role with regard to Trojan surrogates for Zeus, the destruction Zeus ordains for them is akin to the execution of a paternal curse.

But it is not only Zeus's mortal counterparts, Agamemnon, Priam, and Peleus, whom he sacrifices to preserve his position on Olympos. Neither does he sacrifice mother-allied sons only by cursing them for offenses he encourages them to perpetrate—against mortal fathers and kings. By favoring daughter-like paramours over his irascible wife instead of being a husband and father, he exacerbates rather than neutralizes her anger, not to mention the anger of the daughters whose lives he seductively blights. In stark contrast to the Zeus of the *Theogony*, the *Iliad*'s Zeus foments rather than resolves cycles of strife that repeat from one generation to the next. Failing to furnish sons with a model of success in achieving *themis*, encouraging instead the kinds of mother-son alliances that his two-part plan is designed to inflict on mortal counterparts, he nonetheless expects sons to overlook his failure to perform paternal functions and to devote themselves, Briareus-like, to extricating him from predicaments and threats of his own making. Zeus does not come through for them, but he expects them to overlook his failings and come through for him, no matter what the cost. On top of this, he expects them to honor him as a model father. Even as, with his blessing, the sons of the Achaians serve as agents of Hera's revenge, wrecking their lives and the lives of Zeus's mortal surrogates in a quarrel he instigates, Zeus expects them to honor and respect him as the font of kingly and paternal authority and as the architect of cosmic *themis*.

PLAN OF ZEUS II: ENACTMENT OF THEMIS'S PROPHECY IN THE MORTAL REALM

The *Iliad* dramatizes a critical point in the enactment of Zeus's plan to export the threat that Achilles and Thetis (as opposed to Hera and her allies) represent to the mortal sphere. Zeus supports the actions of Thetis and her son against Zeus's mortal counterparts, but he executes a paternal curse on the son who commits the offenses he seems to authorize.

By dramatizing those aspects of Thetis's attraction for Zeus that Themis's prophecy is designed to counteract, the Briareus episode reconstructs the early stages of Zeus's relationship with Thetis. To Thetis, Zeus is both a surrogate father and a suitor. By summoning Briareus, the "son greater than his father in might," Thetis acts like a devoted daughter who sides with her father in his ongoing conflict with her mother. At the same time, however, she gives Zeus a foretaste of the power she will have as a wife: she will produce an invincible son who will vanquish Zeus's enemies and enhance his position. All she will expect in return is honor for her son—and to be favored over her father's (or father-like lover's) vindictive wife. All these elements are neatly tied together in *Iliad* 1: reminded by Thetis of the Briareus episode, Zeus grants her supplication to honor her son, despite the threat of a new *loigos* arising from his jealous wife's predictable displeasure (1.518).

In effect, Thetis represents the perfect "daughter-wife." She combines the devotion of a daughter with the power of a wife and mother to produce a mighty son who will defend his father's honor and position. She contrasts with Zeus's formidable spouse who marshals mighty sons and other rebels to make Zeus pay for his infidelities. No wonder Zeus finds Thetis irresistible. Designed to cool Zeus's ardor, Themis's prophecy attacks its root. It counteracts precisely those aspects of Thetis's allure that are on display in the Briareus episode. Themis foresees the consequences of a besotted Zeus forming an alliance with Thetis. Thetis will produce a mighty son all right, but rather than warding off shameful devastation (*aeikea loigon amunai*; 1.398–406) as in the Briareus episode, the son will inflict it—presumably at his mother's behest. At the same time, the myth of the Judgment of Paris transfers Thetis's potency as Hera's erotic rival from her to Aphrodite, and from Aphrodite to her mortal favorite, Helen.

By the time Agamemnon assembles an army to wreak revenge on the Trojans, Thetis is a wife with a mighty son of her own. Like Zeus when he is on the point of being overthrown, Agamemnon's authority is at a low ebb. Shamed by his brother's cuckolding by the son of his Trojan counterpart, Priam, Agamemnon must reassert his power by avenging the dishonor. How fortunate then that Thetis is on hand to lend her mighty son to Agamemnon's enterprise. The son of a goddess and destined for glory, Achilles virtually guarantees victory (1.281, e.g.). So, like Zeus, Agamemnon presumably finds the appeal of an alliance with Thetis and her incomparably mighty son irresistible. Unlike Zeus, he has no Themis to warn him of its pitfalls. Such a warning would defeat the purpose of Zeus's and Themis's plan.

But troubles like those prophesied by Themis do lie in store. While the willingness of the demigod son of Thetis to fight (to the point of sacrificing his life) to restore Agamemnon's honor, and his divine mother's willingness to let him do so, must seem an unbelievable boon to Agamemnon, the alliance has drawbacks, which are becoming manifest when the *Iliad* picks up the story. Incredible as it must have seemed to have obtained the services of an all-but-invincible fighter like Achilles, Agamemnon comes to feel that Achilles and other glorious sons threaten his honor, and indeed his very sovereignty. So, instead of giving Achilles his due of gratitude and honor—the only reward that he and his mother require—Agamemnon accuses Achilles of trying to usurp his authority, as Themis prophesied the son of Thetis would do to Zeus: Achilles wishes to hold power (*krateein*) and be king (*anassein*) over all and give them their orders (1.287–89, 1.132–34). In anger at these alleged transgressions, Agamemnon dishonors Achilles, effectively cursing him. Outraged, Achilles and his divine mother turn against Agamemnon and humiliate him.

Such is the *Iliad*'s implied narrative of the formation and dissolution of Agamemnon's alliance with Achilles and his divine mother. Its close correspondence to Themis's prophecy suggests that the quarrel between Agamemnon and Achilles marks a critical juncture in the fulfillment of the plan of Zeus and Themis—the point at which Agamemnon's alliance with Achilles and Thetis dissolves into enmity. Yet if the weaknesses that lead to the breakdown of the alliance with Thetis and her son are unique to Agamemnon, why would the mother-son pair pose a threat to Zeus? What could possibly sour the relationship between Thetis and Zeus, to whom (with considerably more reason) she shows the same selfless devotion and to whom she offers the services of a similarly mighty son? If the promise of marriage to Thetis would have been borne out for Zeus, Themis would have had no reason to intervene. On the contrary, marriage to Thetis, like Zeus's ingestion of Mêtis in response to a similar warning about the threat from a mighty son (*Theogony* 887–98), would ensure that the author of cosmic *themis* would rule forever.

In Homeric epic, Achilles is represented as no less protective of Peleus, Zeus's stand-in as the husband of Thetis, than Briareus—and Achilles himself—is of Zeus. When Odysseus visits Achilles' shade in the underworld on his way back from Troy, the encounter is reminiscent of—and may even allude to—the Briareus episode. Thetis's son asks whether his father retains his position (*timên*) and laments that he cannot use his invincible hands (*cheiras aaptous*)—which recall those of Hundred-Hander (*Hekatoncheires*), Briareus—to terrify men who would use force (*bioôntai*) on his father to diminish his state (*atimazousin*) and keep him away from his rightful honors (*timês*; xi.495–504).

CONTEXT AND CONSEQUENCES
FOR ZEUS OF MARRYING THETIS

In the *Theogony*'s succession myth, Zeus breaks a cycle of conflict between overbearing fathers, who block the birth or development of their children, and alliances of mothers and sons who overthrow them. Learning from the experience of his predecessors, Zeus establishes a regime in which fathers and kings secure their positions by fostering rather than attempting to prevent children's development, and by sharing offices and honors with other members of the divine political community. Zeus's ingestion of Mêtis and marriage to Themis, the offspring of which are Dikê, Eunomiê, and Eirênê, symbolize a regime in which fathers and kings—together with their resourceful female allies and instigators—ensure that no one, themselves included, uses his powers to deny the birthrights of others. They distribute honors and offices (*timên, geraôn*) to recognize contributions to this new kind of order, and they punish attempts to undermine it—all in accordance with *themis* and *dikê*.[1]

But long before the events recounted in the *Iliad*, Zeus undermines his own position by all but abdicating the new type of paternal and kingly authority he has just invented—with critical assistance from the female deities, Gaia, Rheia, Themis, Dikê, and Mêtis. A realistic genre, Homeric epic does not portray Zeus as a model husband and father, one who exemplifies success in achieving familial and political orders based on mutuality, reciprocity, and trust. Neither is he shown fostering children's development rather than sacrificing their needs to his wants. A philandering husband, Zeus sacrifices the development of sons and daughters to prop up his rule. He acts like a typical father of hero-sons.

Eschewing any attempt to resolve the strife between him and his formidable wife, he deprives daughters and sons of positive adult models. Seducing daughter-like paramours with the prospect of displacing Hera in his favor and his bed, he effectively derails their progress toward mature and competent adulthood. Dependent on glorious sons, he also vitiates their powers, which he sees as threatening his authority. In all, his sovereign position is weakened by his abdication of marital, paternal, and kingly responsibilities. Since Zeus does not face up to and defuse the threats that glorious sons and their mothers represent, he cannot exercise his authority to institute a familial order conducive to the development of all. He uses his preeminence in *mêtis* not to resolve the besetting conflicts of heroic society or its Olympian mirror image, but to transfer to mortal substitutes the consequences of his *themis*-inverting actions, which themselves undermine his claims to authority.

That said, it is only fair to add that in fashioning cosmic *themis*, Zeus never has to face the threats associated with father-favored daughters and their superior mother-favored sons that drive the action of the *Iliad*. The crimes of the fathers in the *Theogony* are straightforward: they attempt to monopolize power and privilege, preventing their wives and children from taking their rightful places in the cooperative order of *themis*. Their wives and sons retaliate and, in Zeus's case, devise forms of authority that are rooted in development-nurturing *themis* rather than violations of it. Wife-avoiding, philandering, daughter-seducing fathers like Agamemnon and the Zeus of the *Iliad* are a different breed than the power-monopolizing fathers of the succession myth. Typical of heroic society, Agamemnon and Zeus also violate *themis*, but the threats to their own positions that they generate are subtler, more complex, and more intractable than those generated by Zeus's predecessors in the *Theogony*, involving the deceptive allure of daughter-like paramours, their anomalously powerful sons, and the sacrifice of ordinary *themis* for glory. Hence the need for Themis's prophetic powers.

Still, the threats to Agamemnon's authority, like those to Zeus's, are almost entirely self-generated. It is not the *themis*-inverting sacrifices that Agamemnon expects and receives from Thetis and Achilles that prove his undoing. Rather it is his failure to honor their sacrifices. And although Zeus may share traits with Agamemnon, and may require sacrifices of mothers and sons alike, one thing seems clear: Zeus would never commit the offense that turns Thetis and Achilles against Agamemnon. He would never substitute a paternal curse for the honor that is Achilles' due. Even though it will anger Hera, Zeus grants Thetis' supplication to restore honor to her son by humiliating Agamemnon.

Thetis and Achilles sacrifice greatly for Zeus. Thetis's acceptance of mortal marriage and Achilles' acceptance of mortality and death neutralize the threat that they would have posed to Zeus, had Achilles been his son. Thus Achilles and Thetis avert a variant of the devastation from which Thetis and Briareus rescue Zeus. But by favoring Thetis and honoring Achilles, Zeus avoids Thetis's *mênis* and preserves her reverence and love for him (*aidô kai philotêta*; 24.110–11).[2]

Yet if Achilles were Zeus's divine son, perhaps Zeus would reward Achilles' sacrifices with a curse. Indeed, Zeus may reward Achilles' sacrifices with a paternal curse, albeit in a way that makes the Trojans appear culpable for the outrageous losses Zeus inflicts. This ploy at once preserves Thetis's and Achilles' respect and love for him and restores Achilles to Agamemnon's (and Hera's) service. The killing of Patroklos may represent the execution of Zeus's and Agamemnon's paternal curses on Achilles. Yet it returns Achilles to Agamemnon's service and redirects his rage from Agamemnon (and Zeus) to the Trojan enemy and, ultimately, to himself.

In an analogous situation, when a truce between the Achaians and Trojans threatens to overturn Zeus's plan to have Hera sate her vengeful anger on the

Trojans, Zeus (at Hera's behest) instructs Athena to resume hostilities, but to make the Trojans culpable. This ploy allows the Achaians and their divine patrons to retain the moral high ground, as avengers of Paris's betrayal of Menelaos's trust while a guest in his house. More importantly, it ensures Achaian outrage is directed at the Trojans, rather than at the divine patron and patroness who sacrifice them by instigating the breach.

WHY DO THETIS AND ACHILLES SACRIFICE FOR AGAMEMNON—AND ZEUS?

If Zeus resembles Agamemnon, even to the point of cursing rather than honoring Achilles, that argues for the accuracy of Themis's prophecy: Thetis and her son would pose a threat to a self-weakened Zeus, who sooner or later would repay their sacrifices with a curse, provoking their *mênis* against him. Indeed, if Zeus had succumbed to Thetis's allure, he would have made himself dependent on Thetis and her son, rather than on his own legendary *mêtis* and foresight, which in the *Theogony* allows him to avoid the mistakes of his predecessors and bring the cycle of succession struggles to an end. By effectively abandoning his legendary, albeit humbly anthropomorphic and uncertain political skills and wisdom, Zeus could expect to gain something purportedly better—a level of protection he could not manage on his own. But by abdicating his role as the architect and guarantor of cosmic *themis*, he would immediately lose the honor and authority associated with that role, along with his cognate claim to serve as a model and guide for mortal kings, in effect to be a father to them, showing them how to sustain their power to the benefit of their *poleis* through legitimate rule.

But even though he resists Thetis's charms, in the *Iliad* Zeus retains at best an ambiguous claim on the kingly honors he earns in the succession struggles of the *Theogony*. He is dependent on Thetis and her mighty son, if only to accept diminished power and status and to wreak their devastation on mortal substitutes, and he acts more like his child-sacrificing predecessors, Ouranos and Kronos, than like the father and king who fashions cosmic *themis* in the *Theogony's* succession myth. In the *Iliad*, Zeus's Theogonic persona of a model father and king has become little more than a pious fiction.

All this raises yet more questions about the *Iliad's* implied narrative of the foreordained breakdown of an initially irresistible alliance with Thetis and her son. Why are mother and son willing to sacrifice for Agamemnon in the first place? Why are they willing to sacrifice for Zeus? As long as Zeus retains the guise of the author and protector of cosmic *themis*, we think we understand why Thetis and Briareus would defend Zeus, and why Achilles and Thetis would sacrifice for him. As long as Agamemnon appears to be unique in embodying paternal abdication, insecurity, and ambivalence with regard to heroic sons, we think we understand why Achilles would do anything to protect or restore his own father's position, but we may wonder why, given Agamemnon's egregious failings as a father and king, not to mention Menelaos's manifest shortcomings, Thetis and Achilles would show the Atreidai the same selfless devotion. What is Thetis doing when she sends her son off to serve Agamemnon, knowing as he himself does that he will not return?

If Thetis and Achilles epitomize, respectively, the perfect, self-sacrificing daughter and the perfect, self-sacrificing son of a beleaguered father, the problem of why they serve Agamemnon all but evaporates. From the standpoint of Homeric epic and myth, this is simply who they are. In offering Agamemnon the same selfless service that Thetis and Briareus (and indeed Thetis and Achilles) offer Zeus, Achilles and Thetis are simply being themselves. Agamemnon is fortunate enough to start his war when the greatest hero of the Greek epic tradition is coming of age to fight. By sheer coincidence he has the benefit of a quality of service he does not deserve. Agamemnon's fault—and folly—lies in failing to recognize his supreme good fortune in enjoying, however undeservedly, that matchless service.

Yet if Zeus's continued status as an exponent of *themis* (and Peleus's as a proud, loving father) depends on foisting onto Agamemnon not just the threat Achilles represents but also Zeus's (and Peleus's) typical failings as a husband, father, and king, his shortcomings are typical. Being themselves is precisely what Achilles and Thetis avoid. Rather, their manifest, infinitely accommodating personae are false selves that make them incomparably alluring to child-sacrificing parents.

Achilles and Thetis are properly understood as representing the false personae that children create to avoid further alienating child-sacrificing parents, while, of necessity, they keep their authentic human selves hidden—even from themselves. Mother and son exemplify children who expect to win parental favor by dissociating from their anger at caregivers. Contrary to the *Iliad*'s implied history of Thetis's alliance with Agamemnon, it is precisely *not* Thetis's nature to behave toward Agamemnon as she does. But it may be second nature for her to offer her services—with her mighty son as an essential part of the bargain—to a father and king who has gotten himself into difficulties by his philandering, or to one who is destined to be murdered by his wife in revenge for the same offense, as well as for sacrificing his daughter to remove self-inflicted disgrace. It is also second nature for Achilles to accept sacrificial parenting, whether from a mother who uses him to regain the favored status she enjoyed with a beleaguered father and king of gods and men, or from his own father, who, like Agamemnon, undermines his own position by relying on a superior wife and son to sustain his honor.

The apparent match of perfect, self-sacrificing children and needy parents that Thetis and Achilles represent in relation to both Agamemnon and Zeus is a construct that papers over highly conflicted relationships. Achilles only seems to overlook Agamemnon's and Zeus's failings as architects and guarantors of *themis*; in fact, these destructive shortcomings provoke the outrage that Achilles vents first at Agamemnon and then, with the death of Patroklos, at the Trojans and himself. The problem is not really, as the *Iliad* implies, that Agamemnon fails to honor Achilles' sacrifice, or even that Zeus would have done the same, but that both rulers sacrifice sons, and daughters, in the first place—in manifold ways.

THE BRIAREUS EPISODE AND
SACRIFICIAL FATHER-SON RELATIONSHIPS

The notion that Thetis and Achilles represent the personae that children present to child-sacrificing parents receives support when we consider the circumstances in which Thetis initially offers the services of a mighty son to Zeus. Thetis rescues Zeus from the twin threats that arise from Zeus's philandering, the same threats that the plan of Zeus is designed to transfer to the mortal realm. Typically, Hera seeks revenge on her philandering husband, and she manages to organize a coup attempt against him. But the *Iliad* suppresses the role of the mighty son of a daughter-like paramour in the attempt.

Although Thetis and the formidable son she summons play a benign role in the proceedings, both types of threat—not only from a vengeful wife and mother, but also from a devoted daughter-wife and her mighty son—which the two-part plan of Zeus is designed to neutralize, are in fact represented in the story of Thetis's rescue of Zeus. Indeed, the Briareus episode involves the combination of these two threats: a former paramour switches sides in the marital conflict and lends her mighty son to the vengeful wife as an agent of revenge.

According to the succession-myth pattern, we would expect Hera to recruit a mighty son of Zeus as her principal ally to overthrow him. Although the *Iliad* names only Zeus's brother, Poseidon, and his daughter, Athena, as Hera's allies, Apollo, the glorious son of Zeus and Leto (and Achilles' divine counterpart), may play a key part in the coup attempt. In the *Iliad*, Apollo does the time but, apparently, does not commit the crime. Although the *Iliad* omits his name from the list of conspirators, it elsewhere alludes to his and his uncle Poseidon's punishment for the offense: Zeus ordains their year-long servitude to a mortal king, Priam's father, Laomedon. Thus Leto evidently lends her mighty son to Hera in her coup attempt against Zeus, just as Thetis lends her son to Hera to prosecute her revenge on Trojan substitutes for Zeus—and the revenge of Hera's protégé, Klytemnestra, on Zeus's mortal counterpart, Agamemnon—in the *Iliad*.[3]

Considering the magnitude of Apollo's offense, his punishment is surprisingly lenient. It seems likely that Apollo's mother, Leto, secures a reduced sentence for him by interceding with Zeus on their son's behalf. When Apollo kills Zeus's son, the Cyclopes, in retaliation for Zeus's thunderbolting of Apollo's mortal son, Asklepios, for being too proficient at the healing arts, Leto intercedes to dissuade Zeus from hurling Apollo into Tartaros. Instead Zeus reduces Apollo's sentence to a year's servitude to another mortal king, Admetus. Since being thrown into Tartaros is a time-honored punishment for gods who oppose Zeus, it seems likely that the similar—and similarly light—sentence that Apollo gets for his part in the coup attempt is also the result of Leto's intercession. In much the same way, Thetis intercedes with Zeus to protect her son from the *mēnis* of Zeus's mortal counterpart, Agamemnon, for humiliating him at the instigation of Hera, perhaps on behalf of her mortal counterpart, Agamemnon's similarly dishonored wife, Klytemnestra.[4]

Viewed in context of the threat that Achilles poses to Zeus, Achilles' Zeus-ordained service to Agamemnon recalls Apollo's Zeus-ordained service to both Admetus and Laomedon for separate offenses against Zeus. Laomedon promises a reward to Apollo and Poseidon for constructing the walls of Troy—thereby warding off devastation from him and his city. Instead of keeping his promise, however, Laomedon drives them away with threats (as Agamemnon does Apollo's priest in the *Iliad*). When Poseidon retaliates by sending a sea monster to attack Troy, Laomedon prepares to sacrifice his daughter to appease the god. But Zeus's mortal son, Herakles, kills the monster, saving both Troy and Laomedon's daughter. Although Laomedon promises to reward Herakles, he again reneges on the bargain. "Haughty Laomedon" treats Herakles as Agamemnon treats Achilles: he gives "Herakles an evil word in return for good treatment." Herakles responds by sacking Troy. Laomedon's offense helps to explain Poseidon's hostility to the Trojans but—as Poseidon points out to his nephew, Apollo—it makes the latter's defense of Laomedon's descendants problematic.[5]

Whether before or after the coup attempt recounted in the *Iliad*, Apollo defends Zeus by killing Python, the protectress of Hera's monstrous son, Typhon, whom Hera conceived in anger at Zeus and to overthrow him. Apollo also punishes offenders against Zeus's mortal counterparts, Priam and Agamemnon. Apollo and Hektor kill Patroklos, and Apollo and Hektor's brother, Paris, are destined to kill Achilles. But Paris and the Trojans, whom

Apollo protects, are violators of a husband's rights and targets of Zeus-backed *mênis*, while Achilles has a primary role in executing Menelaos's Zeus-backed curse on the Trojans. (If Paris represents the denied, father-cuckolding, erotic superiority of hero-sons like Achilles, the support of the glorious son of lovely Leto for Aphrodite's favorite, Paris, makes sense.) Achilles accepts his demotion to mortal status as a sacrifice for Zeus. Yet to atone for, among other things, his offenses against paternal and kingly author-ity, Achilles accepts his early death at the hands of Apollo, whenever Zeus and the other gods wish to bring it about. In short, when it comes to com-mitting, disavowing, punishing, and being cursed and punished for offenses against paternal and kingly authority, Achilles and Apollo play the roles of offender, punisher, and father-cursed victim. In all these roles Zeus bends them to his purposes—and sacrifices them and those whom they most love.[6]

All this leaves us with an ambiguous Zeus. As a wife-avoiding, daughter- and paramour-favoring philanderer, he does his part to sustain the cycle of marital dysfunction and threats to husbands and fathers from their wives and sons that is characteristic of heroic society. Yet, unlike the most perfect products of that cycle, he uses his *mêtis* and *noos* to create the functional fa-milial and political orders that, after establishing his regime on Olympos, he undermines. He is able to maintain a semblance of *themis* on Olympos partly because at a critical juncture he has the wit and foresight to devise stratagems to deflect the consequences of his actions onto mortals. Also, aided by The-mis's prophecy, he has the wisdom and self-control to forgo an alliance with Thetis. Agamemnon lacks such self-command.

As a result mortals, too, have a choice—albeit one that is heavily weighted toward the repetitive patterns dramatized in the *Iliad*. It is finally up to mortal kings to decide to what uses they will put their Zeus-given scepters when they administer what purport to be the *themistas* of Zeus. Mortal husbands and fathers can emulate the philandering, mother-and-son-threatened, son- and daughter-sacrificing Zeus, for whom the definition of delusion (*atê*) and na-ïve folly is to believe in the prospect of loving concord between himself and his wife—that is, the Zeus who predominates in the *Iliad*. Or, if they can find a way to cope with the heightened threats to *themis* in heroic society, they can do what the *Iliad*'s Zeus fails to do: emulate the architect of cosmic *themis* in the *Theogony*. Although Zeus no longer does so, such men can preside over orders founded on reciprocal respect, honor, and support between husbands and wives; they can honor children's birthrights to nurture and guidance to maturity, rather than sacrificing and exploiting them.

Despite having banished Atê from Olympos, Zeus still falls for Hera's trick of pretending to restore a loving marital union in the *Iliad*. When Odysseus visits Hades, the shade of murdered Agamemnon first warns him not to trust his wife. But then Agamemnon has to admit that Odysseus would be a fool not to trust Penelope, and he envies Odysseus the mutually loving and trusting relationship Odysseus has with both his wife and his son—"as is right" (*hê themis estin*; xi.440–51). Of course Agamemnon's own idea of *themis* is to sacrifice his children by enlisting them to efface his shame and avenge his dishonor.

FATHERS' AND SONS' RECIPROCAL LONGING

Agamemnon falls far short of emulating the Zeus of the *Theogony*, and he effectively curses Achilles for erotically humiliating him. But he still wants to be recognized as a real father and king. Despite his repressed, eroticized ambitions to displace fathers, Achilles also wants his surrogate father (or Zeus) to act like one. The clearest indications of this are to be found in the episode in which Achilles rejects Agamemnon's offer of a patrimony. Having suffered military setbacks as a result of Achilles' withdrawal, Agamemnon attempts to conciliate Achilles. As the culmination of his flawed attempt to resolve their quarrel, Agamemnon offers Achilles what is in effect a patrimony: a wife, material possessions, and the scepter of kingship over several peoples. Achilles rejects the offer, claiming that if he needs such things he can get them from his father. The episode purports to show that Agamemnon is an unworthy, sacrifice-demanding pseudo-father with only a false semblance of paternal powers and virtues to pass along to an actual or surrogate son. Achilles detects the ersatz quality of Agamemnon's proffered patrimony, and he maintains that he has a real one, which he can return home to claim any time.[7]

After admitting that he was mad (*atas, aasamên*; 9.115–16, 119) to dishonor Achilles, Agamemnon offers to "make all good" by giving Achilles "gifts in abundance." He counts "them off in their splendour": tripods, gold, prize-winning horses, and seven choice concubines, not counting Achilles' prize-girl, whom Agamemnon vows he never touched. This is just the first installment. If the gods grant them leave to sack Troy, Achilles can have as much treasure as his ship can hold, and twenty Trojan women, "the loveliest of all [*kallistai*] after Helen of Argos" (9.136–140).[8]

If they return home from the war, Achilles will receive the third installment, a patrimony, couched in terms of traditional *themis*. Agamemnon will honor Achilles equally with his son, Orestes (who has been, of course, "brought up in luxury"), and Achilles can be Agamemnon's son-in-law. Agamemnon will supply Achilles with a wife—Agamemnon's daughter, Iphianassa, if Achilles so desires. The terms of Agamemnon's offer are similarly favorable with respect to wealth and power. Not only will Achilles be exempt from having to pay a bride-price, but, along with the girl, Agamemnon "will grant him as dowry / many gifts, such as no man ever gave with his daughter." In addition to setting Achilles up with a wife and innumerable possessions, Agamemnon will "grant to him seven citadels" and the kingly authority to govern them effectively, assuring Achilles that their peoples "will honour him as if he were a god with gifts given / and fulfill his prospering decrees [*themistas*] underneath his sceptre" (9.120–56).

In return, Agamemnon demands that Achilles yield place to him since he is "kinglier" (*basileuteros*) and elder (9.158–61). Agamemnon implicitly demands, as well, that Achilles respect him as a father and king who can equip a son or son-in-law to be a successful husband and ruler. Achilles' *nostos* will coincide with receiving a patrimony from Agamemnon. This in turn will allow Achilles to come into his own as a husband, father, and king in accord with *themis*. In much the same way, Odysseus's *nostos* corresponds to his return to these roles, and the consequent return of *themis* and *dikê* to Ithaka.

But the prospect is illusory. Agamemnon uses the promise of marriage to his daughter Iphianassa, vast wealth, and successful and honored kingship to entice Achilles back into a conflict that he will not survive. In a similar manner, at Aulis, Agamemnon uses the illusory prospect of marriage to Achilles to entice his daughter, Iphigenia, to her own sacrifice—to remove self-created obstacles to his glorious victory at Troy. At the time, Agamemnon already has in Achilles the ideal son whom Thetis freely offers him, as if she were a devoted wife and he a beleaguered husband, just as she did with Zeus and Briareus—even though it entails the death of her son.

Achilles' response to Agamemnon's admission that he was mad to dishonor Achilles, and his attempt to "make all good" with atoning gifts, is to declare that he hates Agamemnon's gifts, and that if he wants such things—and if the gods allow him to survive and go home—he can get them, albeit in more modest quantities, from his father. The juxtaposition of would-be father-in-law and real father, the gifts of both, and the acknowledged uncertainty of Achilles' return in both instances suggests that Achilles refuses Agamemnon's bid to make him his son-in-law not because of Achilles' fated death at Troy (which Agamemnon's three-step compensation plan seems to allow for), but because the patrimony itself is ersatz. If Achilles does make it home from the war, he will take his patrimony from his father.

If Agamemnon were Achilles' father; if Achilles were in the same, supposedly fortunate position as Agamemnon's son, Orestes; or if Achilles' father were like Agamemnon rather than his antithesis, the *Iliad* would here offer a remarkable dramatization of an excruciating moment in the relationship of a dysfunctional father and the son who is heir to the father's legacy of failure.

The father demands that his son accept him as a model, but the ersatz quality of the son's legacy from his father—which most importantly consists of his father's example—is evident. Achilles responds by claiming that this is precisely not his situation: If he gets home from the war, Peleus will arrange a wife for him, which, along with the more modest possessions won by Peleus, Achilles prefers to Agamemnon's proffered gifts (9.393–400).

The very magnitude of Agamemnon's offer, his self-aggrandizing eagerness to recite the unmatched quantity of his gifts—of women, treasure, dowry, cities to rule—is one more sign of the king's anxious grandiosity, a token of his inability to offer a son (or prospective son-in-law) a real patrimony built on his example of being a loved and respected husband, father, and king. By contrast, the "possessions won by aged Peleus" are doubtless fewer than those offered by Agamemnon, and Achilles will be king only over one people, the Myrmidons, not many. But Peleus won his possessions himself, rather than, like Agamemnon, by amassing possessions won by others—that is, "by feeding on his people." Thus, unlike Agamemnon, Peleus is presumably a rightly loved and honored king. Peleus seems everything that a father should be and more: an authentic hero whose strong ash spear only Achilles can wield. This being so, the wife, possessions, and scepter that Achilles can inherit from his father constitute a genuine patrimony, not the false one proffered by Agamemnon. So much at least is implied in Achilles'—and the *Iliad*'s—way of putting the case.

Agamemnon's example is obviously the antithesis of success as a husband. He does not build a mutually loving and trusting relationship with his formidable wife. A literal and figurative child-sacrificer, he represents the glaring antithesis of a loving parent who protects his children and, in cooperation with his spouse, guides their development into capable and confident adulthood. When we consider the doubling of Agamemnon and Menelaos, brothers married to sisters who are destined to be unfaithful on account of Aphrodite's curse, and Agamemnon's role in wooing Helen and avenging her infidelity on his brother's behalf, we can include Menelaos's shame, outrage, vengeful anger, and need for Achilles as an avenger in the actual paternal legacy that Agamemnon would leave to Achilles.

As the *Iliad* reminds its audience, Agamemnon is destined to earn the lethal hatred and contempt of his wife, against whom—along with her lover—he is powerless to defend himself. His wife is open to the enticements of other men, and hero-sons like Achilles can supplant Agamemnon in her favor (and in Aigisthos's case, her bed) by avenging her dishonor. Agamemnon's brother, Menelaos, who is also the beneficiary of Achilles' and Thetis's solicitude, offers the even more disheartening example of an impotently outraged husband who is covered with "shame and defilement" by the infidelity of a wife whose attachment to him is easily broken by Aphrodite's male favorite, Paris. In this, Menelaos is like a hero-son's father (both Peleus and his father, Aiakos), who marries a paradoxically superior wife who shuns his bed and favors her superior son.

Agamemnon is a weak, anxious, and incompetent husband, father, and king. He provides no role model to his sons as a limit-setter or protector. He fails to establish or defend an emotionally safe, nurturing family milieu with clear limits and boundaries. He compounds his weakness by depending on his substitute son, Achilles, and his own son, Orestes, to efface shame and dishonor that stem from his own misdeeds and failings.

Given Agamemnon's egregious failures, his offer to equip Achilles for a happy and successful life as a husband, father, and king seems of a piece with his other acts of empty pretension. But in this context, his failings have a special significance. For the favored son of a superior, honor-vindicating mother, the father has a heightened importance. The need for the father to uphold *themis* is particularly great. As in the myth of the hero-son's interrupted immortalization, he is the other parent, the one not directly involved in the destruction of familial order. As such, the son looks to the father to protect that order, the son himself, and the mother from the mother's devaluation of family and political orders based on reciprocal love and care—like those Agamemnon purports to offer Achilles as a legacy. But given the enmeshment of the father in the dynamics of the hero-son's family—his self-devaluation and dependence on his supposedly superior wife and son—the son is almost certain to be disappointed. (The situation is reversed for daughters who are victims of father-daughter incest.[9])

In the guise of offering Achilles a patrimony, Agamemnon again seeks to sacrifice Achilles' needs as a son to Agamemnon's needs as a father, though in a different way than previously. In addition to enlisting him as Menelaos's avenger, Agamemnon tries to obtain Achilles' acceptance of him as a worthy father. Accepting Agamemnon's performance as a guide, Achilles would truly sacrifice his *nostos*. Here, as before in the quarrel, Achilles sees through Agamemnon's attempt to effect a role reversal, to pass off a destructive paternal dependence as a competent father's generous assistance. But as in the quarrel too, Achilles' refusal forms part of a larger structure of denial. It serves to deny that Agamemnon bears any resemblance to Achilles' actual father or father-figures, whether Peleus, Priam, or Zeus.

Achilles' evident ability to discern the ersatz quality of the patrimony offered by Agamemnon, together with his wishful contention that he has a more modest, but genuine one from his father, testifies to the hero-son's longing for an effective father. He wishes his father could win his mother's love and respect and could provide an example of strength, self-affirmation, and competence. He wishes his father would not invert the parent-child relationship and lean for protection on a son whom his wife favors over him. He wants a father who effectively, rather than fleetingly and ineffectively, intervenes to prevent destructive mothering, and who can restore familial order based on mutual love and respect.[10]

Yet Peleus emphatically does not provide an example of how to affirm his own or his son's or his wife's value as an ordinary mortal. He does not blunt Thetis's pretensions to superiority or her shameful disavowal of her own, her son's, and her husband's human needs and desires. Indeed, a man like Achilles' father, who chooses a wife on the basis of her (to him, justified) disdain for him, is the last person who could provide such a model. How could such a man provide his son with an example of a marriage based on mutual love and respect? Achilles evidently imagines he would have such a marriage by going home, taking with his father's blessing whatever bride he fancies, and enjoying with her the possessions that he and his father have won. Peleus quickly regrets his one attempt to assert his prerogatives as a husband and father, which marks a catastrophic turn of fortune in his life.

So Achilles' keen discernment in the matter of false and true patrimonies bespeaks a favored hero-son's irrepressible longing for an ordinary family. He desires parents who form a loving couple. He wishes for loving, boundary-setting parents who exemplify and enact *themis*, rather than turning their children into substitute spouses. He loathes parents who use children to escape predicaments of their own making.

At times the pretense may be not that fathers or sons are capable of achieving *themis* but that they are incapable of it. Metaphorical child-sacrifice requires children's active cooperation. Perhaps here it involves sons quelling anxieties about paternal envy by pretending that the possibility of achieving reciprocal love and care in accord with *themis*—as distinct from favored children's erotic triumphs over rival parents—are beyond their reach. Perhaps there are times when Achilles knows he really can go home again but feels safer believing otherwise because he fears a father's envy. If such a father also believes that he has the good fortune to have a superior hero-son, whom he comes to fear, that certainly complicates the relationship, but it is not the only source of tension.

All these elements are present in Zeus's striking of Asklepios with a bolt of lightning for magical powers given him by Zeus's glorious son Apollo—who is somehow incapable of achieving the marital happiness that eludes his father. Agamemnon is outraged because Achilles proposes to keep his concubine—whom Achilles calls the bride of his heart (*alochon thumarea*) even though it was Achilles' spear that won her—while Agamemnon goes without. Agamemnon comes after Achilles, snatching away Achilles' "wife" (*alochon*), leaving Achilles effectively castrated. This metaphorical castration in the *Iliad* recalls Kronos's literal castration of Ouranos in the *Theogony*, but here the son, in almost Freudian manner, fears castration by the father. This is as good a sign as any that we are in the post–succession myth reign of a "thoroughly modern" Zeus. Like Phoinix's outraged father, whose Zeus-backed curse denies his son the loving marriage and family that Amyntor lacks, so Agamemnon, a repository for Peleus's ambivalence, curses Achilles, stripping him not just of his concubine-wife, but of his *nostos* and, with it, the loving marriage with a lawful wife (*kouridiên alochon*; 19.298) that Agamemnon infamously lacks—in no small measure because he flaunts his preference for choice concubines over his *kouridiês alochou* (1.114).

For any son who had the *Iliad*'s impotently outraged Menelaos for a father, the mere thought that the son could have a securely attached wife while his father went without would generate anxiety. (If Paris represents the hero-son's split-off erotic aspect and his irresistible attractiveness to the most desirable of women, then outraged Menelaos represents a split-off aspect of Achilles' father.) Neither would it be reassuring if his father, like Menelaos in the *Iliad*, regarded it as a son's duty to sacrifice all to efface his father's shame and avenge his dishonor.

For whatever reason, paternal and kingly responsibility for creating and upholding *themis* is at issue in Achilles' diatribe against Agamemnon for failing to behave responsibly toward the *laos*; in Agamemnon's tentative steps toward doing so, which Achilles greets with abuse; and in the justification of the war as restoring a beloved wife to her loving husband, which Achilles articulates (9.338–43). The same concerns are manifest in Zeus's irrepressible dream of marital concord based on erotic love and trust, as well as in his equation of belief in the reality of marital reconciliation with mad folly (*atê*), and in the Achaians' momentary joy at the prospect of going home to their wives and children when Menelaos takes responsibility for assuaging his shame and fighting his battle himself.

HELEN AND KLYTEMNESTRA AS DETACHABLE WIVES

The competition between Menelaos and Paris, and the Achaians and Trojans, over Helen is illuminating regarding father-son conflict. The mythology surrounding Tyndareus and his daughters yields further insight into relationships between hero-fathers and hero-sons. Mythological accounts of the origins of the Trojan War in competition over one of Tyndareus's daughters, Helen, are particularly illuminating regarding problematic characteristics of hero-sons as fathers. Their sense of superiority or shameful inferiority depends on wives whom they regard as mothers and who are loosely attached to them, just as their mothers were loosely attached to their fathers. These shame- and dishonor-prone fathers are liable both to require sons to sacrifice themselves to restore paternal honor and to curse sons for undermining their positions, which are precarious because these fathers remain hero-sons with weakly developed adult capabilities. In short, heroic fathers generally are liable to behave like the supposedly anomalous Agamemnon of the *Iliad*.

Agamemnon's shame is tied to the Aphrodite-favored daughters of Tyndareus, who are fated to be unfaithful to their husbands as a result of Aphrodite's curse. First there is Helen, the shame of whose infidelity Agamemnon requires the sons of the Achaians—and in particular the best of them, whom he belatedly tries to enlist as a surrogate son—to efface. But her sister Klytemnestra is fated to shame Agamemnon in the same way Helen shames his brother, an affront to his honor that he will require his own son to avenge. The mythology surrounding the daughters of Tyndareus is revealing about hero-sons as fathers—the sorts of fathers for whom Achilles seems supremely willing and able to sacrifice to remove their shame and dishonor. Cursed by Aphrodite with being twice and three times unfaithful to their husbands, Klytemnestra and Helen represent wives who are loosely attached to their husbands and who can be won away from them by others. Almost all of the greatest Greek heroes are suitors of Helen, the most beautiful of women. Tyndareus hesitates to choose a husband for her because he fears that a disgruntled suitor will forcefully overturn his decision. Sitting out the competition for Helen, Odysseus offers Tyndareus a plan for avoiding violence in exchange for Tyndareus's help in obtaining a different kind of wife than either of Tyndareus's daughters: virtuous, clever, and trustworthy Penelope. All Helen's suitors must swear to defend the marriage against anyone who fails to respect Tyndareus's decision. Once the suitors have taken this oath, Tyndareus awards his daughter to the highest bidder. He chooses the richest Achaian, whose brother, Tyndareus's son-in-law, Agamemnon, is the most powerful. Agamemnon wins Helen on his brother's behalf by offering Tyndareus the "greatest gift" or bride price.[11]

Why is rivalry for Helen so fraught with the potential for violence? The obvious explanation is her unmatched beauty and sexual attractiveness. She is the loveliest of women (*kallistê*; 9.140), so naturally men fight over her. Even as they agree to let Helen go to the winner of a single combat between Menelaos and Paris, the Trojan elders absolve themselves and the Achaians of blame for fighting over a women like her: "Terrible is the likeness of her face to immortal goddesses" (3.156–58). Achilles says that the Achaians came to Troy "for the sake of lovely-haired Helen" (9.339). Helen is the protégé and mortal counterpart of Aphrodite, the winner of the contest among the goddesses for the title of *kallistê* that leads to the Trojan War.

Yet Helen's erotic appeal, the violence of rivalry over her, and her beauty itself are determined as much by family dynamics as by physical attributes. The same is true of Aphrodite's role in the proceedings. All are inextricably linked to Helen's character as a wife who has a weak bond with the husband to whom her father gives her, a bond that can be broken by a favored son. Rather than force, Paris uses Aphrodite's gifts to overturn Tyndareus's choice of a husband for Helen. Aphrodite's favorite, Paris, like Helen, is irresistibly attractive. Dramatizing the consequences of losing the post-marital contest for Helen, the *Iliad* makes clear how rivalry for her is linked to violence. Menelaos is "defiled" (*lôbêsasthe*) with "shame and defilement" (*lôbês te kai aischeos*) and reduced to impotent outrage. "Haughty" (*huperphialoi*) and "outrageous" (*hubristêisi*), the winners, Priam and the Trojans, have Helen and her possessions "to glory over," but Menelaos calls down the *mênis* of Zeus upon them (3.70–71, 4.173–74, 13.621–24, 13.633).[12]

This scenario should remind us of others, also involving wives loosely attached to their husbands. It corresponds to the situation of hero-sons: of Peleus and Phokos, whose stepmother, Psamathe, resists marriage to their mortal father and, after bearing her favored son, Phokos, shuns his father's bed; or of Achilles, whose mother behaves in the same way toward his mortal father, Peleus; or of Phoinix, whose mother enlists him in her plan to humiliate his father sexually in the same way that Hera, on Klytemnestra's behalf, enlists Achilles to humiliate Agamemnon. Hero-sons seek to win their mothers' favor—and avoid being rejected by their mothers as unworthy—by winning contests in which they demonstrate that, like their mothers, they are superior to their fathers and to all mere mortals. At the same time they avenge the erotic humiliation of their mothers' inferior marriages by erotically humiliating their mothers' unworthy husbands.

The weakness of their mothers' attachment to their fathers, together with their mothers' predisposition to favor the hero-sons over their fathers, encourages hero-sons to believe they can prove their superiority and their fathers' inferiority by winning the contest with their fathers for their mothers. Theirs is a mirror image of the apparent erotic victory of the favored daughter over her mother that decisively shapes the development of mothers of heroes and their special bonds with their hero-sons.

In the family patterns we are considering, the "fairest" woman is not only the impressionable daughter who—as much for the qualities she lacks as for those she has—excites paternal desire, but the mother who excites filial desire by disdaining the father and favoring her son. She is the most beautiful woman to every son. The sexuality over which Aphrodite presides in the

Iliad's mythology runs afoul of marriage not because it is wild and undomesticated, but because it is the product of a culturally distinctive form of domestic order in which marital bonds are weak.

Helen and Klytemnestra are both twice-married, shaming and outraging their husbands by leaving them for other men. But trigamous? If their attractiveness is specifically that of a detachable wife to the son whom she favors over his father, then the son who wins her, even if he happens to be her first husband, always takes her away from his father. Having demonstrated his superiority, a son can glory in winning her, while leaving her inferior husband—his father—covered in shame and cursing his son. (Alternatively, he wins her away from siblings whom he exposes as shamefully inferior.) This mindset puts Helen's failed suitors in the same outraged, violence-prone position as the one in which her successful suitor, Menelaos, is destined to find himself, though the question of why this is so remains. If Klytemnestra is any indication, perhaps the daughters of Tyndareus only abandon husbands who figuratively or literally abandon them—to pursue what they expect will be mother- and wife-appeasing glory.[13]

The connection between quasi-incestuous rivalry for Helen and inter- as well as intragenerational violence is manifest not only in the stories of Tyndareus's Aphrodite-cursed daughters but in Peleus's biography as well. Winners of divine maternal favor are validated as categorically superior to their fellows; losers are stigmatized as shamefully inadequate. Just as Peleus and Telamon, losers in the contest for divine maternal favor, kill Phokos, so shamed and outraged Menelaos seeks to kill Paris, and Achilles and the Achaians seek to avenge the shame of the Atreidai by destroying the Trojans and their city. So too, after the war, Agamemnon enlists his son, Orestes, to avenge not just his murder, but the shame and erotic humiliation dealt him by Helen's sister, Klytemnestra.

In Peleus's biography, both the erotic element of the rivalry for divine maternal favor and the circumstance that the object of the sons' intense rivalry is maternal favor are suppressed. Yet both are suggested by, among other things, Peleus's unshakeable desire to bed a virtual clone of his superior mother. The erotic aspect of sons' competition for the favor of a loosely attached, divine wife is covert; it is manifest neither in Peleus's relationship with his divine stepmother nor in Achilles' relationship to his divine mother, but only in Peleus's relationship with Achilles' mother. Yet its connection to violence is manifest.

Hero-sons' mothers can not only be won away from their husbands by favored sons: their favor can also confer categorical superiority on the winner. The loser reaps shameful inferiority, an intolerable and infuriating position. Witness Peleus's mythic biography. The winner's superiority correlates with irresistible erotic appeal—particularly in competition with his father. By sleeping with his father's concubine, Phoinix makes her hate the old man, who has no chance in an erotic competition against his son. A fragment attributed to Hesiod explains why Achilles did not win Helen: he was too young to compete for her. If he had, he would have won her away from Menelaos, the brother of Achilles' pseudo-father in the *Iliad*. In some accounts Achilles is immortalized by Thetis and actually marries Helen—the inferior Menelaos having departed the scene. Achilles' bedmate, Briseis, presumably hates the thought of sharing Agamemnon's bed, just as her predecessor, Apollo's devotee Chryseis, no doubt did. Although Achilles is the killer of her husband, brothers, and father, Briseis supposedly wants nothing more than to become Achilles' lawful wife (19.297–99).

In the erotic realm, then, the demigod son exhibits the same irresistible sexual allure that is attributed to Priam's Aphrodite-gifted son, Paris, whose *mênis*-provoking offense against Menelaos Achilles punishes. But Paris, with Apollo's help, is destined to become the agent of Zeus's lethal *mênis* against Achilles. The interchangeable roles of Paris and Achilles suggest that the hero-son is identical to the *mênis*-provoking victor in the erotic contest for the detachable wife and that the son who enjoys the gifts of Aphrodite beyond all others is identical to the hero-son. The underlying identity between hypo-warlike Paris and hyper-warlike Achilles is signaled by, among other things, the *Iliad*'s puzzling description of Paris as staying out of the fighting in anger. Aphrodite's son, Aineias, is a hybrid. Combining elements of Paris and Achilles, he also stays out of the fighting in anger—at Priam for dishonoring him (6.326–28, 13.459–60).

All this suggests that the hero-son's pride, his sense of greatness and excitement with his powers is highly sexualized, but that a series of splits and transfers, for which the wedding of Peleus and Thetis is a point of intersection, de-sexualize Achilles and his mother. Achilles is split into Achilles-Paris to effectively repress the aspect of sexual triumph over the father in Achilles' superiority. The supposed antithesis of Achilles' father, Agamemnon represents the father whose position is threatened. The sexual aspect of that threat is further displaced by another split between soon-to-be-cuckolded king Agamemnon and his cuckolded brother, Menelaos. Thetis too is de-sexualized. Although Aphrodite is declared the most beautiful of goddesses and a rival of Hera, the setting for this rivalry, the wedding of Peleus and Thetis, suggests otherwise: Thetis, not Aphrodite, is the most desirable of goddesses—first, as a daughter-wife to father Zeus, but then, after her forced marriage, to hero-sons like Achilles, whom she favors over her husband. Thetis's humiliating marriage to a mortal neutralizes the sexual and political threat she poses to Hera, just as Achilles' abasement neutralizes the sexual and political threat he poses to Zeus. This mother-son pair may embrace their Zeus-imposed abasement because they fear retaliation by envious parental rivals such as cuckolded Menelaos and sexually humiliated Hera. But Thetis and Achilles may also accept their humiliation out of love and respect for the rival parent figures whom they fear they would displace if they retained their full powers. All this complicates the account of child-sacrifice. A parent's rejection of his or her ordinary, care-seeking child is compounded by the child's self-negation, in part as a result of erotic ambitions that parents excite in favored, opposite-sex children.

Restoring the desire for Helen, the detachable wife, to its familial context—to the family situation of hero-sons—makes sense of its linkage to arrogant superiority, shameful inferiority, and violence. "Terrible is the likeness of [Helen's] face to immortal goddesses"—who are destined to be loosely attached to their mortal husbands and available to their hero-sons or other paramours.

The rivalry between fathers and sons for a purportedly superior mother's superiority-conferring favor has an important implication for our attempt to delineate the characteristics of the fathers of hero-sons—which is to say, the characteristics of hero-sons when they become fathers. If fathers and mothers are bound together in a loving marriage, the whole dynamic of "superior" wives being wooed away from their husbands by juvenile but somehow superior sons cannot arise. The same holds true for purportedly superior juvenile daughters and their fathers. Without father-daughter and mother-son liaisons, the reproduction of heroic culture would grind to a halt. By contrast, a wife's pretensions to superiority over her husband, and her quest for a single, suitably superior son to favor over him, encourages sons not only to believe that they share their mother's superiority to their fathers but also to fear that they may share their father's inferiority to their mothers. This is a recipe for violent rivalry among sons and between sons and fathers with similar life-histories.

ODYSSEUS AS COUNTER-EXAMPLE

A wife's involvement in a mutually loving marriage is the antithesis of Thetis-like divine superiority. If, without being incited by their mothers' seductiveness and their fathers' envy, juvenile sons were—as Freud would have it—nonetheless inclined to fantasize about defeating their fathers in erotic competition for their mothers, their family circumstances would provide scant encouragement. In their parents they would confront a loving, securely attached couple from whose sphere they would clearly be excluded. There would be no question of their taking the place of a rival parent—but also no danger that an outraged, humiliated father would envy his son's success in achieving reciprocal, loving, trusting relationships. Indeed, these family milieus would provide an equally clear alternative: children's acceptance that they have much to learn on the way to becoming competent adults who can achieve marriages like their parents'. Parental models and limits would mark their path. In these respects, their family situation would be the antithesis of the hero-son's, whether it is represented by that of Peleus and Phokos, that of Achilles, or that of Phoinix (or that of Achilles as Hera's adoptive son).

Such an atypical family milieu would foster a different erotic desire than Helen's suitors display. It would lack the violence-engendering connection of erotic success or failure with vaunting superiority or shameful inferiority. It would also lack a fickle divine mother who projects her childhood shame as an ordinary human being onto some, while viewing a favored son as an extension of her supposed superiority to ordinary mortals and to ordinary, anthropomorphic gods. Betrayal, abandonment, and rejection are integral parts of her love. They are experienced by the favored child, designated as superior to mortals. An atypical family milieu in accord with *themis* would foster pride rather than shame in ordinary humanity and no pretense of—or need for—categorical superiority to ordinary mortals. It would foster desire for a different kind of partner modeled on a different kind of mother—one who is and remains a wife to her son's father, and who is not seeking a juvenile substitute spouse with which to replace him.

In the mythology of the competition for Helen and the run-up to the Trojan War, Odysseus epitomizes that different kind of hero-son—and father. He does not compete for Helen, but uses his detached analysis of the threat of violence associated with competition for her to win a different kind of wife. Later, when Agamemnon calls upon the other Achaians to sacrifice their lives to remove his brother's shame at having Helen taken from him, Odysseus feigns madness in an attempt to avoid the draft. While at Troy, he is careful not to sacrifice his *nostos*—even to the point of fleeing from Hektor's onslaught when other men stand and fight for fear of being called cowards.

> "Son of Laertes and seed of Zeus, resourceful Odysseus,
> where are you running, turning your back in battle like a coward?
> Do not let them strike the spear in your back as you run for it,
> but stay, so that we can beat back this fierce man [Hektor] from the ancient."
> He spoke, but long-suffering great Odysseus gave no attention
> as he swept by on his way to the hollow ships of the Achaians (8.93–98)

The speaker whom Odysseus ignores is Diomedes, who urges him to save Nestor ("the ancient"). Although Odysseus ignores youthful Diomedes, all three men diverge in similar ways from the heroic norm.

After rescuing Nestor, Diomedes fears being mocked as a coward by the Trojans for running from Hektor. Nestor encourages him to flee and not to worry about what the Trojans say about him since Zeus clearly is giving victory to Hektor (8.130–56). Earlier, with the encouragement of the daughter of Zeus and Mêtis, Athena, whose protection Diomedes and Odysseus enjoy, Odysseus's partner in *noos* and *mêtis*, Diomedes, actually wounds Aphrodite after first taunting the goddess for leading women astray (5.131f., 5.331f., 5.348–49).

Odysseus is not entirely dissimilar to Helen's suitors. Penelope also has her suitors, and Odysseus must prove himself superior to his rivals to win her—as it happens by a show of prowess in archery, which he later uses to slaughter a second group of suitors who gather around his wife, consuming his estate in his absence. So competition for Penelope is also linked to violence and honor. Yet Odysseus is different—as are Diomedes and Nestor—in critical respects.

The different fates of Agamemnon and Odysseus correspond to differences in family circumstances and character. In the *Iliad* and its background myths, husbands and fathers tend to remain their mothers' sons, vying for the maternal favor that confers superiority and fearing maternal disregard, which signifies shameful inferiority. They have no idea that they must do anything more than show themselves to be rightly favored by their superior mothers to become husbands in mutually loving, supportive marriages or, in cooperation with their wives, loving, responsible parents to daughters and sons alike. In effect, they use their relationships with their mothers as a working model for their relationships with their wives and children.

Achilles' assumption that he can return home and claim his patrimony any time he pleases illustrates a typically wrong-headed presupposition. In order to be a husband, father, and king in accord with *themis*, a hero-son must only prove himself deserving of his superior mother's favor. Achilles' faux marriage to Iphigenia seems to rest on a similar assumption: If Achilles demonstrates his superiority as the favored, semidivine son of his divine mother, a loving marriage and successful kingship will follow. The only difficulty, supposedly, is that Agamemnon's pretense of marrying his daughter to Achilles is a ruse. Everything does follow from this assumption, but what actually transpires is marital estrangement, parent-child boundary dissolution, and violent strife.

Such are the men for whom Achilles is willing to sacrifice himself—and for whom Thetis is willing to sacrifice her son. Goddess and demigod son see nothing wrong or out of the ordinary in this. They came to Troy to do Agamemnon favor and restore his and his brother's honor. From their standpoint, the problem is not that they sacrifice for such men, but that despite Achilles' matchless effectiveness and willingness to sacrifice to efface

Chapter Five

Agamemnon's shame, the king shows no gratitude. Rather than honor Achilles' sacrifice, Agamemnon does the reverse. In that, he supposedly shows himself to be different from Zeus who, because Achilles is fated to have a short life on his account, ensures that Achilles has honor at least. Indeed, it is in relation to Zeus that Achilles and Thetis show just how fortunate Agamemnon is to have their incomparable services and how foolish he is to fail to honor them. But as we have seen, Zeus is fundamentally no different, and his and Agamemnon's sacrifices of sons and daughters are outrageous. He is just clever enough to deflect the outrage onto others.

Chapter Six

Mothers and Sons

Hero-sons' relationships with their fathers and father-figures may exhibit expected ambivalence, but mother-son relationships are more crucial. What can we glean from the *Iliad* about these? First, we look at mother-identified heroes like Achilles; then father-identified heroes like Odysseus and Diomedes; and finally, in the following chapter, at what happens when mother-identified heroes stray from maternal agendas.[1]

MOTHER-IDENTIFIED HEROES

Achilles' involvement with maternal goddesses—not only his divine mother, Thetis, but his surrogate mother, Hera—pervades the *Iliad*. He is wrapped in a cocoon of divine maternal solicitude throughout. Thetis, of course, is always ready to come to the aid of her son. But Hera entrusts to him the task of calling Agamemnon to account and warding off the plague. Later Hera sends her son to rescue Achilles when, fearing that his mother "beguiled him with falsehoods" when she promised him a glorious death, Achilles is in danger of ignominious drowning. By rescuing Achilles, Hera makes good on Thetis's promise. Finally, just as Thetis upholds Achilles' claims to honor among men, so Hera upholds his special claims to honor in the councils of the gods.

The critical question is how hero-sons come to enjoy unmatched divine maternal favor. Are they born winners—like demigod Phokos with his innate love of athletic and military training—who are willing to sacrifice to achieve greatness? Or, having the innate ability to excel, have they been seduced, devalued, and intimidated into accepting the sacrifice of their lives as ordinary children by favored but dishonored, vindication- or vengeance-seeking mothers—and fathers—in concert with an assortment of other dysfunctional parent-figures?

If the former, heroic culture is more or less what it represents itself to be. The heroic ethos promotes the noble choice to sacrifice easily attainable but inglorious satisfactions of marital, familial, and political life for the arduous pursuit of glory. Mortals exchange mere life for a semblance of the divine. If the latter, heroic culture reflects sons' desperate attempts to win maternal favor by demonstrating superiority to ordinary mortals and by denying unmet needs for maternal love and care. In order to idealize son-sacrificing mothers as supremely nurturing, sons deny maternal neglect, exploitation, and hostility. They suppress and redirect anger at mothers on whom they depend.

Thetis's and Hera's special regard for Achilles is not surprising since he is a hero to both. He is the answer to their prayers. To Thetis, he is the perfect son, "without fault and powerful" and "preeminent among heroes . . . like a tree grown up the pride of the orchard." Thetis's "best of all childrearing" clearly compensates her for the humiliation of being "forced into the marriage bed of a mortal." If Zeus allows Agamemnon's dishonoring of Achilles to stand, Thetis will indeed know by how much she is "the most dishonored of the gods." She will have no compensation for the shame of her marriage. Thetis's assurances to the contrary notwithstanding, the *Iliad* implies that her *mênis* could wreak shameful destruction on Zeus. To Hera, Achilles is the Achaian who, more than any other, avenges Paris's insult (24.27–30). Achilles' character and actions are perfectly suited to avenging and vindicating the two types—or aspects—of dishonored mothers that Thetis and Hera represent.[2]

Achilles wins divine maternal favor, Hera's as well as Thetis's, for his role in two intertwined master narratives in which hero-sons restore maternal honor. They are agents of dishonored wives' revenge, or they are faultless, powerful sons who vindicate favored, discarded daughters' claims to superiority. (Before Agamemnon insults him, Achilles is also a hero to Agamemnon. He is the premier instrument of Agamemnon's revenge against the Trojans, a surrogate son whom Agamemnon later vainly attempts to lure back into his service by offering to honor him like his son—and future avenger—Orestes. Achilles is the perfect son to his own father, Peleus, and living proof that Peleus has overcome his humiliating rejection by his divine stepmother by marrying her sister.) In Thetis's and Hera's special regard for Achilles (as, perversely, in Agamemnon's anxious belittling) we see an afterimage of the matchless perfection with which, before the start of the *Iliad*, he performed these self-sacrificing services for all.

Achilles (and the Achaians) are only figurative sons of Hera, eponymous "mother of heroes," but Achilles plays a role in relation to Hera's mortal counterpart, Klytemnestra, that is similar to Phoinix's as his mother's avenger. As if responding to Agamemnon's insult to Klytemnestra, which parallels Amyntor's insult to Phoinix's mother, Hera prompts Achilles to humiliate Agamemnon, as Phoinix does his father, by taking away his concubine. Agamemnon responds, as Phoinix's father does, with a paternal curse sanctioned by Zeus Patêr. The "sons of the Achaians" avenge Hera's dishonor against Trojan substitutes for Zeus—who mocks her by saying she treats them as if they were her own children (18.358–59).[3]

Since Achilles is the only Achaian who is the son of a goddess, and since his role as a Phoinix-like father-humiliater is cloaked in denial, Achilles seems uniquely involved in the master narrative in which the flawless son vindicates his dishonored mother's claims to superiority. Yet the family dynamics represented in the two hero-narratives are inextricably linked. The Hera-narrative serves as a receptacle for threatening and unseemly aspects of the Thetis-narrative. Achilles is not only the perfect son to both goddesses, but the paradigmatic hero for all of Homeric and later Greek culture. So the apparent uniqueness of Achilles' brand of heroism, and of the maternal context in which it plays out, is evidently one more device to distance the *Iliad*'s auditors from experiences that, to some degree or other, would be common to virtually all of them.

One master narrative emphasizes revenge, the other, vindication, but each is present in both. Achilles not only vindicates Thetis's claims to superiority, he avenges insults to his mother's honor by presumptuous mortals. At a deeper level, he avenges the destruction of her dreams of capable, loved, and valued adulthood by a wife-avoiding, daughter-favoring, daughter-sacrificing father. Conversely, Achilles not only avenges Hera's dishonor; he vindicates her claim to superiority by giving her a surrogate son who is without fault and powerful, the ideal son she is unable to produce on her own.

Hera participates in both narratives—but in a way that makes her a scapegoat for qualities as a wife and mother that are effectively denied with respect to Thetis. The epitome of the vengeful wife, Hera also punishes filial imperfection, flinging lame Hephaistos off Olympos (18.395–98). Thetis too participates in both narratives, but in a way that represents her as incapable of destructive anger like Hera's, whether at daughter-favoring, philandering fathers or at sons who fall short of perfection. Indeed, Thetis saves Hephaistos and Zeus, the principal victims of Hera's wrath in each context. Marriage to Thetis salves any wounds Peleus received from her sister, his divine stepmother. Background myths allude to Thetis's destructive anger toward fathers, husbands, and sons, but the *Iliad* only faintly alludes to this side of the divine mother's character.

The primacy of mothers in fashioning heroes and their lifelong involvement in maternal vengeance and vindication are acknowledged in the *Iliad*, but in sanitized ways. Agamemnon grudgingly links Achilles' preeminence in might, divine birth, and special favor among the gods: although Achilles is very strong and his mother is a goddess, to Agamemnon he is "the most hateful of all the kings whom the gods love" (1.176–78). Thetis's recollection of "the best of childrearing" emphasizes the importance of careful nurture, in addition to divine parentage.

> I gave birth to a son who was without fault and powerful
> [*amumona te krateron te*],
> conspicuous among heroes; and he shot up like a young tree,
> and I nurtured [*threpsasa*] him, like a tree grown in the pride
> of the orchard (18.55–57)

Goddesses like Thetis and Demeter, who enlist sons in their service and reward them with honor, glory, or immortality, earn a special epithet: *kourotrophos* (nurturer of youths).[4]

The epithet is apt because of the central role that their kind of mothering plays in heroic culture. They rear *kouroi*, youthful hero-sons with short life expectancies. It misleads only in suggesting that the nurture is benign, a superior variant of ordinary mothering. Mother-son interactions in the *Iliad* and myth suggest that the actual mother-son relationships reflected in them are forms of role-reversal. Mothers sacrifice sons' needs for nurture, and their development into secure and confident adults, to assuage insecurities about their own worth and to validate maternal claims to superiority. *Kourotrophos* mothers couple traumatic rejection with a requirement that sons respond to it as if it were loving nurture. Such is the nurture that produces perfect hero-sons, or *kouroi*.[5]

The *Iliad*'s representations of the relationship between Thetis (and Hera) and the paradigmatic hero, Achilles, on the one hand, and between Hera and her own son, Hephaistos, on the other, correspond to divided working models of sons of purportedly superior, non-nurturing mothers. The Thetis-Achilles dyad corresponds to a manifest working model in which a superior mother provides superior care. Her rejecting behavior is the fault of the object of her anger (e.g., Achilles' father and the mortal and therefore inadequate sons who fail her lethal tests in myth). The Hera-Hephaistos dyad corresponds to a suppressed working model in which the son perceives the mother as punishing him for failing to meet her needs for validation rather than providing love and care. He resents the "bitch-faced" (*kunôpidos*) mother who injures him on that account. The relationship between Hera and Hephaistos in turn is comparable to the mythic relationship between Peleus and the divine stepmother who so intolerably disregards him in favor of her semidivine son.[6]

Neither Thetis nor Hera has any use for actual human offspring, who need mothers who permit them to explore their world and abilities, while providing a "secure base" to which they can return for love, reassurance, and comfort when they are tired, frightened, sick, or overwhelmed. The stories of Odysseus and his son, Telemachos, exhibit intriguing similarities to this pattern of departure, exploration, and return, but neither Thetis nor Hera is interested in a purely mortal son, even one as accomplished and resourceful as Odysseus. Similar considerations apply to the daily routine of the Achaians' Trojan adversaries, who go out from their city to fight during the day, returning behind its walls to their parents, wives, and children at day's end. To Hera there is no comparison between these distinctly mortal heroes and her Achaian favorites. A hero like Hektor, "suckled at the breast of a woman," can never be given the same pride of place (*timê*) as goddess-born Achilles (24.58–67). Nonetheless, these rejecting mothers are idealized and their actual and figurative hero-sons, Achilles and his fellow Achaians, are portrayed—and view themselves—as receiving superior nurture.[7]

The *Iliad* and myth portray the relationship of Thetis and Achilles as antithetical to the relationship of Hera and her own son, Hephaistos, as well as sons of Zeus by other goddesses or women: Dionysius (whom Hera all but destroys and whom Thetis rescues) and Herakles (Achilles' precursor as the paradigmatic hero of an earlier generation), destroyed by Hera's anger (18.118–19). In the *Iliad* itself, responsibility for the injury or predicament from which Thetis rescues the beneficiaries of her empathetic concern is shifted even further away from her. Achilles is beaten down not by the anger of Hera, Thetis's antithesis as a mother, but by the *mênis* of his pseudo-father, Agamemnon. Just as Thetis rescues the victims of Hera's anger—the sons of Hera or of Hera's husband, Zeus—so she rescues her son Achilles when he is laid low by Agamemnon's furious dishonoring.

When it comes to her own son, Achilles, Thetis is represented as the soul of compassion. She reveals that he has two fates. He can use the ability he gets from her to outshine all other heroes and win matchless glory, or he can forgo glory but live long. The choice is entirely up to him. His choice of glory is a source of not only pride but sorrow to Thetis. Hera's anger may cripple the unheroic son who shames rather than reflects glory on her, and Hephaistos may be reduced to an extension of his mother (as when she orders her son to subdue the river god threatening her surrogate son, Achilles, in book 21), but it is inconceivable that Thetis's anger, scorn, and indifference condition Achilles' choice to sacrifice his *nostos* for glory, much less that they leave him crippled and permanently dependent on her.

Thus the division of labor between Thetis and Hera corresponds to a divided working model constructed by a son whom a purportedly superior mother rejects as a care-seeking, developing child. He excludes from awareness everything hateful or disappointing in his relationship with his mother and adopts his mother's view of her unconventional "best of childrearing." As with the relationship between Achilles and his father and father-figures, so too the relationship with this mother. The *Iliad* accomplishes this "exclusion from consciousness" by associating elements of the unacceptable, experience-based working model with scapegoats—principally Hera, whose relationship with her own son is portrayed as antithetical to the divine mother's relationship to her hero-son. Viewed from an attachment perspective, the division of labor between Hera and Thetis reflects a situation in which an abused child must "flee from the source of fear (parent) . . . to the attachment figure (same parent)," a situation that can only be resolved by dissociation.[8]

Hera is a textbook example of a mother who attempts to fashion an ordinary mortal child into a superior one. She rejects the actual, dependent but developing, care-seeking child who egregiously fails to meet her desperate need for a superior child, one who has no need of ordinary nurture. Although Hephaistos is a god and Achilles a mortal, Hera's contrasting responses to each mirror Peleus's divine stepmother's—Thetis's sister's—contrasting responses to him and to her own demigod son. But self-effacing, humble, compassionate Thetis nurses mother-maimed Hephaistos back to relative health. She is no more capable of abusing a child in this fashion than she is of angrily degrading and humiliating a spouse, as Hera almost succeeds in doing to Zeus, before Thetis and Briareus come to his rescue.[9]

That the *Iliad* is so well suited to sustain such divided working models, and to induce catharsis of negative perceptions and emotions associated with sacrificial childrearing practices, is itself powerful evidence of the centrality of such childrearing practices to heroic culture. Children who are loved as care-seeking, developing children have no occasion to develop divided working models that exclude information about parental unresponsiveness or hostility. Only cultures that employ such childrearing practices to reproduce themselves have need of the denial-fostering, purgative services that the *Iliad* provides. Male and female children may well employ splitting and projection in the normal course of development. But the idea that children construct durable divided working models of attachment figures regardless of the quality of care is not borne out by empirical studies of interactions between children and their primary caregivers and the effects of these interactions on child development.[10]

The *Iliad* does not deny but rather emphasizes that being a hero entails sacrifice—and being preeminent among heroes entails absolute sacrifice. Most obvious is the sacrifice codified in Achilles' two fates: the hero trades his *nostos* for glory. Also prominent are various forms of sacrifice for others: the hero-son's noble willingness to risk his life to "beat back the shameful destruction (*aeikea loigon amunai*)" from his companions (1.341), or to help restore the honor of an insulted, paternal king. Achilles may willingly sacrifice his immortality to protect Zeus from the prophesied threat of a son "greater than his father in might" (*biên hou patros ameinôn*; 1.352–54, 1.398–406).

Such noble, overdetermined sacrifices of his *nostos*, whether to win imperishable glory or "to beat aside sudden death from [his] afflicted companions" (18.128–29), are integral both to a hero-son's claims to honor and to his justifications for anger—not at parents for sacrificing his needs to the higher good of assuaging their insecurities (only scapegoat Agamemnon openly demands such sacrifice), but at promised honor withheld. Like countless other Achaians, Achilles risks his life to wreak Agamemnon's revenge on the Trojans, thus giving Achilles a claim to special favor from the undeserving king.

We encounter greater denial when it comes to sacrifices for maternal figures, especially Thetis. Once Agamemnon dishonors him, Achilles explicitly alludes to his and his fellow Achaians' sacrifices to avenge Agamemnon's dishonor. He hints at an even greater sacrifice for Zeus, for which Zeus "should grant him honor at least" (1.352–54, 1.398–406). But Agamemnon's revenge dovetails with Hera's, so Achilles' explicit sacrifice for Agamemnon is also a sacrifice for Hera. Although Hera sacrifices the Achaians to obtain her revenge, she and Athena induce the Trojans to violate the truce so the Achaians will think they are sacrificing their *nostoi* to avenge Trojan perfidy (4.5–72).

The idea of a hero-son sacrificing for a mother-figure, even Hera, begins to tread on dangerous ground. Certainly, although Thetis tells Achilles early on that for him to win the matchless glory that, as her son, he can win (and that also makes her proud to be his mother), he will have to sacrifice his *nostos*, there is not the slightest hint that Achilles sacrifices his *nostos for* Thetis, much less that she demands the sacrifice under threat of devastating indifference, abandonment, or anger. So while the *Iliad* suggests that Achilles enjoys special favor from Hera and Thetis as a result of his sacrifices, there is no hint that they sacrifice him.[11]

Thetis does not merely tell Achilles that being the preeminent hero in whom she takes such pride entails sacrificing his *nostos*. She presents the sacrifice as a good bargain: her son is blessed with the unique opportunity to give up an insignificant, inglorious life as a husband, father, and king—and as the son of his (in her eyes) hopelessly inadequate father—in order to come closer than any other mortal to being a divinity like her. The deeds that manifest his superiority will be enshrined in immortal glory, the next best thing to immortality itself.

The "divine" mother "beguiles her hero-son with falsehoods" not, as he at one point fears, by falsely promising him that he will win glory, but by suggesting that the potentially full life he sacrifices to achieve it is a trifle.

Much of the pathos of the *Iliad*—conveyed by the image of Thetis as Niobe endlessly mourning the death of her children—is that Thetis deceives herself on this point as well. Yet even though Thetis mourns her son (24.84–86), she does not valorize the roles of husband, father, and king Achilles forgoes to become a testament to her divine superiority, much less challenge the view that equates Achilles' *nostos* with inglorious insignificance.

Where we encounter vigorous denial is in relation to a different type of sacrifice: that of a son who, out of fear and dependence, gives up his aspirations to honored adulthood to assuage an insecure parent's self-doubts and to vindicate his or her dubious and inflated claims to honor. Although he is anything but, Agamemnon is represented as unique among parents and parent-figures in demanding this type of sacrifice. For his part, Achilles is represented as keenly aware of such demands, uniquely unwilling to accede to them, and scornful of any—like his fellow Achaians—who do.

Whether it comes to sacrificing his *nostos* for glory or to win back Agamemnon's honor, Achilles stands out from his fellow Achaians in his willingness to sacrifice and his utter lack of self-regard. (When Diomedes preserves his *nostos* by refraining from challenging Apollo, he gives up his claim to the first rank of heroes. This shortcoming is due less to his level of prowess, which approaches Achilles', than to his prudence and excellence in counsel, and his concern to protect his own and others' *nostoi*.)

Achilles is the perfect son to his two divine mothers (as well as to his pseudo-father Agamemnon before their quarrel, to his real father, Peleus, and to Father Zeus) as much for the qualities he lacks as for those he has. His perfection lies not only in his matchless efficacy in rescuing all of them from shame and dishonor, but in its tacit correlate: his apparent lack of an agenda of his own, apart from their needs. He does not expect or demand that parents and parent-figures meet his needs for protection, nurture, and positive adult models. He does not criticize them (as opposed to Agamemnon) for their gross failures in this regard. He does not protest their implicit demands that, rather than expecting them to nurture him into adulthood, he should sacrifice his life and future as an adult to compensate for their manifold failings, which put them at constant risk of humiliation. Rather than ordinary nurture, he expects his mother to console him for a devaluation such as she supposedly would never inflict on him and to protect him by helping him to vindicate claims to honor that are extensions of hers.

Achilles criticizes Agamemnon for his failings as an ordinary father and king, but he does so on behalf of the *laos*. In effect, Achilles projects his need for protection and care, which Agamemnon is so ill-equipped to meet, onto his fellows. This way he avoids experiences of being denied care and sacrificed. He himself requires only honor from Agamemnon. Achilles' apparent perfection and seeming lack of self-regard are themselves strong evidence of behind-the-scenes violence to the self. Proving this is difficult, however, since the reflexive violence necessary to create the appearance of perfection is aimed at removing evidence of independently critical, and therefore offensive and blameworthy, parts of the self.[12]

In short, the *Iliad* acknowledges a raft of factors that, in any actual family or culture, would force a son, under threat of devastating maternal (and paternal) indifference or vengeful anger, to suppress and deny his own expectations of parental love, care, nurture, and protection. Likewise his expectations of parents to provide models of mutual love and respect in marriage and beyond. Likewise his anger and dismay at their radical failures to do any of these, coupled with their demand that he sacrifice his dreams of competent, happy adulthood to serve their needs of vindication and revenge. The full pathos and irony of Achilles' plea to his mother to "protect your own son"—by interceding with Zeus to ensure that Achilles' sacrifices by and for Thetis (as well as for Zeus, Peleus, and Agamemnon) are requited with honor—are revealed in this context.

The humiliation of heroes' mothers and their pride in sons who become agents of maternal vindication and revenge; the need (communicated to hero-sons by mothers) to sacrifice aspirations to adulthood as effective husbands, fathers, and kings in order to play these roles; divine mothers' indifference or hostility to imperfect or ordinary sons; divine mothers' willingness to acknowledge only sons who vindicate their humiliation-assuaging claims to superiority; mothers' shame at being married to, or vengeful devaluation of, heroes' fathers; mothers' scornful hostility at fathers' attempts to assert paternal prerogatives—all these characteristics of heroes' mothers are acknowledged in the *Iliad*. Yet because the trauma of maternal rejection is effectively denied, the sacrifices sons make in this highly skewed context are represented not as imposed on them, but as incidental to obtaining the prize of glory that inheres in and wins maternal favor.[13]

Even though Achilles belatedly realizes that the sacrifices he makes and inflicts on others are anything but trivial, there is no sign of mother-inflicted trauma—or of a son's ensuing dissociation from or aggression against his mortal self. Unless, that is, they are hiding in plain view in the guise of Agamemnon's outrageous devaluing of Achilles and Achilles' mother-backed aggression against adversaries onto whom he projects his own disavowed mortal parts.

Achilles chides his fellow Achaians for denying their accurate perceptions of gross violations of justice and order, rationalizing abuse as its opposite, in order to avoid acknowledging their anger and confronting a feared parent-figure on whom they depend. The same type of avoidance may lead the Achaians to make the sacrifices that Agamemnon fails to honor, in an effort to appease and propitiate an unworthy parent-figure. Such sacrifices are strategic for children traumatized by maternal or paternal indifference or vindictive anger. Ironically, it is Achilles' unparalleled success in carrying out these strategies that provokes Agamemnon's outrageous devaluation of him in the *Iliad*—at a safe remove from Achilles' real father and mother. Agamemnon's dishonoring of Achilles does double duty. It dramatizes both the inevitable breakdown of the relationship between a needy hero-father and a perfect hero-son and the prior, mother-inflicted devaluation that makes the former so devastating.

That all the sacrifices in question are portrayed as undertaken on behalf of a presumed antithesis of a functional father and king points to another cardinal feature of heroic culture: a major, albeit unconscious, function of the behavior patterns and narratives, particularly in the *Iliad*, that constitute heroic culture is to deny the traumatic experiences and shameful responses to them that are involved in reproducing that culture from one generation to the next. Not only is heroic culture grounded in paternal dysfunction and mother-inflicted trauma, it encompasses myriad strategies for denying that such trauma could ever have occurred.

A necessary complement to strategies of appeasing sacrifice-demanding parents, and of adopting their self-justifying rationalizations to avoid further alienating them, are strategies of self-disavowal and self-destruction. Achilles accuses his fellow Achaians of denying gross inversions of *themis* and *dikê* that are plain for all to see. Yet the same kind of denial is evident in the supposedly honorable sacrifices that they, and Achilles most of all, agree to make in the first place. These sacrifices too require that the Achaians disavow and ultimately eradicate their self-respecting, accurately perceiving selves.

The question of how Achilles comes to enjoy unparalleled maternal favor is particularly germane to heroic violence. Is heroic warfare primarily an arena par excellence for demonstrating godlike prowess and death-defying courage? Or is it an anxious attempt to avoid devastating maternal indifference or anger by disavowing, projecting onto others, and trying to eradicate the accurately perceiving, *themis*-desiring mortal self—while identifying with maternal (and paternal) figures who despise or hate it?[14]

A lot is riding on the answer. The *Iliad* implies that Achilles simply has the mettle and ability to win a superior mother's favor. But the *Iliad*'s narrative is rife with evidence of misrepresentation and denial. Self-sacrificing devotion to meeting parental needs by manifesting godlike superiority may be a strategy by which the hero-son attempts to "ward off shameful devastation"—a repetition of traumatic maternal devaluation—from himself.

CHILD-SACRIFICE

The main problem with the idea of Achilles as a victim of child-sacrifice is his apparent lack of a parent who is capable of perpetrating such a shocking inversion of parental love and care. True, Achilles has a filial relationship with a surrogate parent who literally sacrifices his child, but Agamemnon is represented both as unique in this regard and as the antithesis of Achilles' real parents and of the other parent-figures, notably Zeus and Hera, on whom Achilles depends. For his part, Achilles is represented as uniquely unwilling to serve as Agamemnon's sacrificial victim.

So while the special favor Achilles enjoys, and the sacrifices he makes to win it, are more or less in plain view, Agamemnon alone is portrayed as a self-absorbed child-sacrificer. Achilles not only refuses to become his victim, but intervenes to halt Agamemnon's irresponsible sacrifice of the Achaians entrusted to his care. By contrast with Agamemnon, Thetis and Hera—at least with respect to Achilles and her beloved Achaians—are all solicitude and loving care (1.196). And although Peleus and Zeus are, like Thetis and Hera, beneficiaries of Achilles' sacrifices, Agamemnon is their supposed antithesis as well.

True, if Hera were Achilles' mother, his apparent lack of a child-sacrificing parent would be easier to remedy. Hera's sympathetic concern for Achilles and the Achaians notwithstanding, she is perfectly capable of sacrificing her favorites to obtain her revenge. Indeed, this is exactly what her infamous bargain with Zeus amounts to: she promises not to stand in the way when he destroys the Achaians' cities if he will let her destroy Troy (4.51–54). Neither is it hard to imagine her rejecting a son for shaming her by failing to meet the standard of the kind of hero-son—like Achilles or Apollo—who would testify to a mother's superiority. This is exactly what she does to her son Hephaistos. Nor is it difficult to imagine her enviously and vengefully destroying a glorious son like Herakles—fathered by Zeus with a paramour, as Achilles almost was—who does meet that standard. Reflecting on his own imminent death, Achilles recalls how the preeminent hero Herakles (whose name means "glory of Hera"), who sacked Troy before Achilles and the Achaians, was "beaten down by the wearisome anger of Hera" (5.642, 18.117–19).[15]

But hero-nurturing, hero-destroying Hera is not Achilles' mother—Thetis is. And Thetis is presented as Hera's antithesis. True, Thetis is prone to anger at the mortal husband who shames her, especially at his presumption in attempting to hold her to ordinary standards of mothering, but her son could never be the object of her rejecting anger. Achilles is "without fault and powerful," so Thetis's Hera-like (or Psamathe-like) propensity to reject whatever shames her with its imperfection could never apply to her son. Achilles is not defective like Hephaistos or shamefully inferior like Peleus. Thetis therefore has no reason to reject Achilles as Hera and Psamathe reject Hephaistos and Peleus.

If we look to mythology, Thetis's Hera-like, shame-based rejection of her husband, which would itself injure their son, might apply directly to her son as well, but only to the mortal dross that she attempts to eradicate and replace with a flawless divine counterpart. Of course this formulation suggests precisely the bifurcation of the hero-son's self in response to maternal hostility—his self-fashioning in response to post-natal fashioning by his divine mother. Since Achilles embraces Thetis's gift of quasi-immortality and, as a result, becomes the "best of the Achaians," he seems to accept the childrearing methods that result in the superiority of which he boasts. All indications are that Thetis's "best of childrearing" is for Achilles the "best of mothering."

Whatever Achilles has to give up to become the envy of his fellow Achaians, the gifts bestowed on him by his divine mother are far superior in his eyes. Even when, in his conversation with Odysseus in the underworld, he says he would rather be a landless servant than king over the dead (xi.488–91), he does not lament his loss of the interdependent relationships that make up the life of a husband, father, and king. He laments not being able to use his "invincible hands" to rescue his father from degradation (*atimazousin*) and "terrify such men as use force on him and keep him away from his rightful honors" (*timês*)—just as Hundred-Hander, Briareus, terrified Zeus's assailants, and Achilles terrified the enemies of dishonored Agamemnon (xi.495–503).[16]

Achilles' criticisms of his would-be father-in-law for failing to protect the *laos* deflect onto a safe target his similar anger at a mother who, instead of protecting and nurturing *him* to adulthood, demands that he sacrifice his aspirations so he can efface her dishonor. Agamemnon's anger at Achilles' presumption for holding him to standards of *themis* (with regard to the *laos*, not Achilles himself) does double duty as a divine mother's anger at her son's demands for normal nurture. In its devastating effects, Agamemnon's anger replicates maternal anger at a son's presumption—as well as that of his loved and admired father—in expecting her to provide normal nurture.[17]

The son experiences the original maternal devaluation in the same way that Achilles experiences Agamemnon's insult: as a catastrophic loss of value that he is powerless to prevent. But the maternal rejection inflicts a loss of *timê*, value, in an original and human rather than heroic sense. Heroic honor and glory are brittle, ersatz substitutes for self-valuation based on parental love and care. The dynamics of child-sacrificing parents' hostility to filial self-assertion, and of favoring children who sacrifice to assuage parental insecurities, are similar for mothers and fathers. It is just that a son's greater dependence on his mother in early life makes maternal hostility more damaging.

The more the antithesis between mild, nurturing Thetis and vindictive, angry Hera breaks down, the less credible it becomes to represent the mother of Achilles as incapable of acting toward her son as Hera acts toward her own and her husband's sons. It begins to seem not only plausible but highly likely that Thetis's childrearing methods really are devastating, that they do inflict trauma, and that Achilles' father was (for once, for a moment) right to intervene. It becomes more likely that the apparent perfection of a hero like Achilles does indeed result from a combination of maternal aggression, self-betrayal, and aggression against the self, all of which are aimed at demeaning, demoralizing, and intimidating the vulnerable, nurture-seeking, and spontaneously themis-asserting mortal child. At the same time, the seemingly bizarre suggestion that Agamemnon is a scapegoat for Thetis's outrageous devaluing of her hero-son gains credibility.

On this reading, Agamemnon's dishonoring of Achilles, while immediately motivated by paternal envy of a demigod son, plays a key role in a cathartic narrative. It reenacts the primary trauma at the root of heroic character while sustaining denial about the identity of its primary perpetrator, the mother who seeks to recoup her lost honor through a son who will avenge her dishonor and vindicate her complementary—and compensatory—claims to categorical superiority.

As far as we know, all has been smooth sailing for Achilles until Agamemnon gives him his first experience of dishonor. Yet the mother who bore him—and the father he displaces—are more likely candidates for the distinction of being the first to strip Achilles of his sense of his own value. Achilles encounters Agamemnon later in life, and despises him, but is no less vulnerable on that account. Thetis's personal history and the burdens she places on her son make her Achilles' most likely initiator into the experience of devaluation. Thetis's sister, Peleus's divine stepmother, performs a similar outrageous initiation for Achilles' heroic father.

While Agamemnon's unexpected devaluation makes Achilles feel like "a dishonored vagabond" (9.648), it can do so only because it reactivates the unhealed trauma of a mother's shocking devaluation of a son who cannot help demanding normal nurture and who depends on her for validation. If Achilles were not already extremely vulnerable to devaluation, would he even have been dishonored by Agamemnon? Indications are that he would neither have provoked Agamemnon's insult nor have been dishonored by it.

Agamemnon cannot be responsible for the extreme vulnerability to dishonor that Achilles brings to their encounter. On the other hand, Thetis—viewed as a typical favored, humiliated, vindication-seeking, aristocratic mother of a hero-son like Achilles—can. But there is responsibility enough to go around. The impact of Thetis's mothering is magnified by a general failure of parents and parent-figures to model alternative life courses for her son, as well as by the hero-son's own continuously repeated choice to deny his own ongoing, ineradicable aspirations to a life in which he could attain and enjoy real adult powers. Agamemnon's insult travels a well-worn path in Achilles' psychological terrain.

The divine mother's devaluations of her actual mortal son and his (until then) admired father are the one-two punch that dissociates the son from his mortal self and model. If catharsis requires that the *Iliad* reenact in disguised form the primary trauma at the root of the hero-son's character, might it also involve an enactment of its complement? For that we may have to look no further than Achilles' and Thetis's retaliatory humiliation of Agamemnon. But how could Achilles' humiliation of the Achaian king reenact the myth of a divine mother's scornful rejection of a hero-son's naïvely admired father for intervening to protect their son?

Up to this point, we have located the second of the twin traumas that give rise to heroic character in Thetis's manifest shame at her marriage to Achilles' mortal father. We have found ample reflections, albeit stripped of any hint of trauma, of the son's disheartening (but also exciting, frightening) discovery of his mother's shame at being married to his—until that time—admired father. More generally, we have identified Thetis's shame and Peleus's and Achilles' calm acceptance of that shame as reflections of a typical family structure and ideology in which the mother is presumed to be a superior-order being rightly humiliated by her marriage to her supposedly inferior husband.

The *Iliad* makes manifest both Thetis's evident shame at her forced marriage to Achilles' mortal father and Achilles' keen awareness of it. Thetis's humiliation when (as Achilles puts it) the gods "drove [her] to the marriage bed of a mortal" seems to account for her shame at being among the gods, which she expresses in response to Zeus's summons (18.85, 24.90–91). We might also suppose that her shame at being married to Peleus accounts for her abandonment of her mortal husband at the earliest opportunity: as soon as her inferior mate has given her the son whom Thetis will fashion into the hero whose glory will compensate her for the shame of her marriage. Yet background myths suggest that the divine mother's abandonment of the mortal father is precipitated by her husband's temerity in criticizing her childrearing methods.

The mythological episodes in which the mortal parent intervenes, provokes the goddess's anger, and repents are critical for understanding the mother's traumatic devaluation of the son and the precise lessons it teaches him. It suggests that what is dangerous for the hero-son is not merely his passive, inherited association with a supposedly inferior mortal father (and, in some versions of the myth, his mortal siblings), but true self-affirmation and self-assertion. Achilles' father's departure from—and momentary challenge to—the skewed ideology and behavior patterns of his family precipitate its dissolution.

Without thinking, the father affirms and acts on his own perceptions, which are not only critical of his supposedly superior spouse, but expose the vacuousness of her claims to superiority: far from a superior being, she is a caricature of a mother, whose destructive behavior her husband—for a moment—refuses to tolerate. It is not the mortal father's inferiority, but his quickly disavowed challenge that elicits the devastating maternal scorn that—in conjunction with the father's insecurities—makes it virtually impossible for the son to hold onto him as an admired model. (Rather than the father's self-assertion, it may be its tentative, fleeting quality that provokes his wife's anger and precipitates her departure. Regarding his wife as a superior being whom he has to appease or impress, he leaves her unexpressed needs unmet, leaving her to cope with day-to-day reality on her own.)

If we view Peleus's interference with Thetis's attempts to divinize their son or sons as a key context in which the divine mother's traumatic devaluation of the mortal father takes place, we can begin to see how Achilles' and Thetis's humiliation of Agamemnon in the *Iliad* might represent a reenactment of it. But if this is the case, there is an ironic twist. The infant son whom the father intervened to protect from lethal mothering has become the agent of divine maternal anger. He punishes the mortal father for asserting his prerogatives on behalf of the son. (Had it been genuine, Agamemnon's assertion of authority would have given Achilles a useable patrimony.) In effect, the son has become the agent of the maternal anger that destroyed his paternal model and positive sense of self.

In the mythic prototypes, the divine mother scorns the interfering mortal father; in the *Iliad* it is the hero-son. Yet the hero-son never lacks, or acts without, divine maternal support. This is particularly evident in Achilles' retaliation for Agamemnon's hubris. Hera and Athena encourage Achilles to abuse Agamemnon—as an alternative to killing the king outright. And Thetis's successful appeal to Zeus is crucial to the success of her and Achilles' plan to humiliate Agamemnon, forcing him to restore honor to her son. In response to Thetis's supplication, Zeus actively supports Achilles' claims to honor at the expense of his mortal counterpart. Rather than protect Agamemnon's honor, Zeus sends him a false dream of victory to expedite his humiliation.

There are, however, unspoken limits to Zeus's support for Thetis and her son—and to his abandonment of Agamemnon. The Zeus-ordained killing of

Patroklos by the preeminent Trojan hero, Hektor, robs of satisfaction both the success of Achilles' plan to humiliate Agamemnon and also the deed—the killing of Hektor—that clinches Achilles' claim to immortal glory. When Achilles finally accepts Agamemnon's apology, he is overcome with grief at his friend's death. Achilles' crowning achievement, which ensures his immortal *kleos*, is a similarly muted triumph. Achilles' revenge on Hektor cannot compensate Achilles for the loss of his beloved companion.

Although Peleus substitutes for Zeus as the husband of Thetis and the father of Thetis's threatening child, it somehow falls to Agamemnon to bear the brunt of the threat that Thetis's mighty son poses to paternal and kingly authority. In translating Achilles' threat from the divine to the mortal plane, Zeus's paternal and kingly functions are split. Peleus is Achilles' father but it is Agamemnon's kingly authority that Achilles threatens. Also split is the paternal function itself. Peleus is supposed to take his effective displacement by his demigod son with equanimity—as if his son's superiority to him were yet another proof of his unique good fortune in being married to a goddess. Part of Agamemnon's scapegoat role is to represent the inevitable paternal envy and ambivalence associated with being eclipsed by a glorious son.

Having succumbed to the allure of an alliance with Thetis and her demi-god son, Agamemnon suffers the consequences prophesied by Themis. He brings about his own downfall by attempting to assert his mortal kingly prerogatives to deny Achilles the superior portion of honor that Achilles and his mother consider Achilles' due. In this context, Agamemnon's accusation that Achilles is slyly trying to deny Agamemnon the superior portion of honor that is his due as a Zeus-sceptered king lacks credibility. Agamemnon's dishonoring of Apollo's priest, with similarly disastrous results, may be read the same way: as Agamemnon's refusal—albeit a characteristically grandiose, anxiety-ridden, and inept one—to grant the claim to superior honor of a divine mother's glorious son. The devastating anger of Leto's son prefigures Achilles.' Yet Apollo's *mênis* at Agamemnon may, like Achilles,' exemplify the confinement to the mortal realm of the anger of a divine mother and glorious son—Leto and Apollo—that would otherwise threaten Zeus (1.444–47).

By the time Achilles and Agamemnon come into conflict in the *Iliad*, the divine mother's fashioning of her mortal son into a demigod hero is essentially complete. So rather than interrupting the process of postnatal fashioning, the presumptuous mortal king—and in-loco father—interrupts its aim: the mother's vindication through the superior honor of her son. Since the son of Thetis is a fully formed hero, wholly invested in manifesting his mother's superiority, Thetis no longer needs to manifest the anger, *mênis*, and contempt provoked by the mortal father's presumption in attempting to hold mother and son to ordinary requirements of *themis*. Like a good hero-son, Achilles avenges the affront. Thetis's *mênis* can remain implicit.[18]

That her son's honor is Thetis's compensation for the humiliating marriage, which is a linchpin of Zeus's plan to preserve his sovereignty, may account for why Achilles' anger is denoted *mênis*, a term reserved for actions that can inflict devastation as well as ward it off, upholding cosmic order. While Agamemnon's dishonoring of Achilles may be a "violation of Zeus's hierarchy and the *themistes* that define and maintain it," constituting "a threat to the world order punishable by massive, indiscriminate devastation," it nonetheless represents a flawed attempt, by a king who is an inveterate violator of *themis* himself, to hold mother and son to norms of *themis*.[19]

The plan of Zeus for avoiding the retaliation of mother-son pairs is merely the pattern of a heroic culture writ large. The latter is based on fundamental inversions of *themis* for which child-sacrifice is an apt metaphor. This perversion of Theogonic *themis* and *dikê* characterizes the social order that the *mênis* of Zeus, Thetis, and Achilles upholds. In part because Thetis's *mênis* inflicts indiscriminate destruction on Achaians and Trojans alike through the agency of her son, Achilles proves her claim to superiority to all mere mortals. If Thetis is not the mother of glorious Achilles, she is just another exploited, sacrificed (or, less sympathetically, spoiled), and discarded daughter-like paramour of Zeus—and a dysfunctional wife and mother to boot. So an insult to her son is an insult to her. This makes the migration of *mênis* from mother to son all the more significant. It has the added bonus of preserving the apparent contrast between an angry, vindictive Hera and a kind, nurturing Thetis.[20]

If the humiliation of Agamemnon by Achilles does reenact the trauma, for her son, of a supposedly superior mother's scornful repudiation of his mortal father's self-assertion, one final question remains: Where is the trauma? In theory, Achilles will be vindicated rather than traumatized by his and his mother's successful effort to humiliate Agamemnon. Once again, answers may be hiding in plain view. The manifest devastation that Achilles suffers as a result of Agamemnon's dishonoring may be due in no small measure to his having no paternal example to fall back on. In the hero-son's peculiar circumstances, this means no example of a father who successfully maintains his value as a mere mortal in the face of maternal contempt or anger. While much of the fault for this lies with Achilles' flawed father or fathers, it is also due to his disavowal of paternal models and his identification with maternal anger at or disdain for fathers who—however ineptly—affirm their claims to respect and honor and who assert their prerogatives.

The point is not that serving as the agent of his mother's devaluing of a father or father-surrogates is traumatic for a hero-son at the height of his powers. Rather it is that vulnerabilities arising from sons' devaluations by mothers are compounded by sons' habitual identification with angry mothers. In the absence of credible self-affirmation by compromised fathers, maternal aggression against fathers intimidates sons into abandoning their fathers as models and identifying with maternal aggressors against their fathers. The trauma of the mother's devaluation of the father is sealed by the son's identification with a father-devaluing mother.

As a result of this complex set of actions and interactions, the son lacks a paternal model who, in the face of maternal devaluation, affirms his own and his son's value as mortals. The absence of adequate paternal examples both contributes to sons' initial vulnerability to mother-inflicted trauma and results from it. In the family structures that produce hero-sons, as in the cosmos of the *Iliad*, no one has the courage to stand up to humiliated, angry, superior mothers. The plan of Zeus is an elaborate scheme to allow the father and king of gods and men to avoid such confrontations, foisting them on mortal substitutes. From the standpoint of hero-sons, identification with maternal superiority and anger seems the only viable option.

FATHER-IDENTIFIED HEROES

Despite the all-but-irresistible pressures of heroic culture, not all heroes evince a sacrificial identification with humiliated, vengeful, or vindication-seeking mothers. A few identify with fathers. They construct paternal models who rely on *noos* and *mêtis* to initiate, sustain, and restore orders characterized by *themis*, whether in marriage and family, or cities, or armies, or within and between federations and alliances. Systematic contrasts between these heroes and paradigmatic, mother-identified ones corroborate the account of the provenance of heroic character presented here.[21]

Diomedes exemplifies a hero-son who refuses to abandon paternal models even in the face of envious paternal belittling. His identification with his father, and even with Agamemnon as a father-figure, correlates with confidence in his own Zeus-like *mêtis* and skill in counsel, as well as with his formidable but merely mortal exploits on the battlefield. Another correlate of his father-identification is his relative imperviousness to dishonor—or a threatened paternal curse—by an envious father-figure. This is particularly evident in an incident already examined from other angles, the mini-quarrel in which an incorrigible Agamemnon, having alienated his best fighter, Achilles, insults his next best one, Diomedes.[22]

In abusing and humiliating Agamemnon, Achilles takes over his divine mother's scornful *mênis* at a mortal father's presumption. It is a move that, in similar circumstances, father-identified Diomedes refuses to make. It is as if he knows that by doing so he would destroy his paternal models, thereby harming himself. (A protégé of chaste Athena, Diomedes does not enjoy the kind of maternal favor shown to Achilles by Hera and Thetis, neither of whom is interested in even as accomplished a mortal son as Diomedes or Odysseus.) While his prowess as a fighter reflects almost as much glory on parents as Achilles', he nonetheless defends both Agamemnon and his own and his companion's fathers from Sthenelos's Achilles-like (and implicitly mother-backed) disrespect. Instead of emulating Achilles' withdrawal from the army and descent into outraged dishonor, Diomedes excuses (temporarily) Agamemnon's insult and plunges into the fighting, living up to the paternal injunction to be the best in fighting as well as in council.

Silencing his indignant, Achilles-like companion, Diomedes credits Agamemnon with performing a legitimate kingly function. He is testing the Achaians, whipping up their fighting spirit by taunting them for lack of valor. (Here Diomedes emulates Odysseus, who propagates the equally generous fiction that, after Achilles' departure, Agamemnon is merely testing his men by pretending to despair that their situation is hopeless and they should go home.) Agamemnon's taunt does test Diomedes. In refusing to be baited and instead seizing on the kernel of truth in Agamemnon's presentation of himself as a competent leader performing a legitimate function, Diomedes seems to recognize that he is saving himself. In his ensuing *aristeia* (the scene in which he displays the fullness of his prowess), he preserves his *nostos* and patrimony by pulling back from his confrontation with Apollo, even though his glory is diminished as a result.

Diomedes' contrary example suggests that Achilles' attack on Agamemnon stems from identification with maternal anger at mortal fathers' and sons' self-affirmation and self-assertion. Achilles' humiliation of Agamemnon is one of many ways that Achilles participates in the destruction of his father-idealizing, father-emulating—and also accurately perceiving, appropriately responding—mortal self.

Achilles takes the lead in discrediting the mortal father whose assertion of his kingly prerogatives, however inept, preserves Achilles' potential to become a respected husband, father, and king in his own right. By attempting to affirm his own value in the face of his devaluation by Thetis and Achilles, Agamemnon does what he can to preserve his own status as a paternal model for his potential son-in-law. This is precisely what a father in Peleus's or Agamemnon's position would need to do—albeit much more effectively—to protect the life and future of his son.

Agamemnon's ability to bring this off is, of course, severely compromised. But then, so is Peleus's in the mythic prototype. Peleus's courtship and marriage to his rejecting stepmother's equally rejecting sister is perhaps the prime example in Greek mythology of self-negating identification with a maternal aggressor. Unlike Zeus, but like Peleus, Agamemnon accepts an alliance with the divine mother and her demigod son. He buys into the myth of their superiority and invincible might. Rather than trust in his own distinctly limited, but possibly adequate, mortal powers, Agamemnon, no less than Peleus, throws in his lot with this glamorous pair. It is hardly surprising that his attempts at self-assertion and self-affirmation are anxiety-ridden and ineffectual.

The mini-quarrel between Agamemnon and Diomedes demonstrates not only Diomedes' tenacious hold on his paternal models—including even Agamemnon—but the link between this characteristic and another: he is markedly less vulnerable to dishonor than Achilles.

When Agamemnon threatens to take someone else's prize to replace the one he is giving up so that his people can "be safe, not perish," Achilles takes the bait. The young hero ignores the kernel of legitimacy in Agamemnon's action and starts abusing the king then and there, effectively ensuring both that Agamemnon will make good on his threat and that his victim will be Achilles. Neither Odysseus, whom Agamemnon singles out along with Achilles as a prospective donor of a replacement prize, nor Diomedes, who, like Achilles, excites Agamemnon's envy, lock onto Agamemnon's threat, much less retaliate before the fact as Achilles does. Instead, they compensate for Agamemnon's deficiencies as a leader.

However unusual it might be in a culture of honor, Diomedes' response to Agamemnon's insult—affirming his respect for Agamemnon and his father—clearly affirms Diomedes' own value as a mortal and as the son of a mortal father. This self-affirmation through the affirmation—in fact, construction—of paternal models is the antithesis of both the devaluation that Achilles (and Sthenelos) suffer at Agamemnon's insult and the devaluation of fathers as models (explicit in Sthenelos's case, implicit in Achilles') that is necessary to convert Agamemnon's insult into dishonor.

Diomedes' example suggests that identification with a paternal model, even if constructed from flawed materials and in absentia, offers hero-sons better protection from devaluation than the seemingly perfect armor of identification with maternal aggressors who devalue mortal sons and fathers alike. (Diomedes' shrewd exchange of bronze armor for gold notwithstanding, he evidently knows that the most splendid armor may not offer the best protection.) For Diomedes, there is nothing traumatic about his encounter with enviously belittling Agamemnon. Perhaps the dynamics of his family differ just enough from the dominant heroic norm to allow wives and sons to respect mortal fathers, or to enable fathers to be unconcerned about possible devaluation of them as ordinary mortals, men of *mētis* as well as *biē*. Perhaps Diomedes' family conforms closely enough to Theogonic *themis* that he harbors no underlying trauma that can be reactivated by envious paternal belittling. He has no Achilles' heel (Diomedes gets shot in the foot by Paris, but shrugs off the wound [11.373–400]).[23]

After insulting Diomedes, Agamemnon, with equal ineptitude, insults Odysseus, whose response contrasts similarly with Achilles'. Odysseus asks Agamemnon, in effect, what is he thinking? "What kind of word has escaped your teeth's barrier?" While Agamemnon's insult irritates Odysseus, it does not outrage or dishonor him. Unlike Achilles, who is defenseless against and involuntarily seizes upon Agamemnon's angry denunciation of him so that it strips him of value, Odysseus draws a clear boundary between himself and Agamemnon and locates the problem squarely on Agamemnon's side of it. Whatever Agamemnon may think or say about Odysseus has no effect on Odysseus's self-image and self-valuation. All that crosses Agamemnon's "teeth's barrier" are empty words. They minimally affect Odysseus's honor. Agamemnon's "talk" is "wind, and no meaning." Considering the almost automatic power of insults to inflict dishonor in heroic culture—a power that depends on the insulted person's tacit identification with his devaluer—Odysseus's response is remarkable.[24]

Odysseus's actions escape the confusion inherent in the verb *etimasein* (to dishonor), which denotes a peculiar kind of action that somehow crosses the boundaries between people. It welds together into a single action an insult and its effect: loss of honor, *timē*. The term itself fuses the esteem accorded to a person by others with self-esteem. The whole ideology of honor involves actions that cross boundaries between persons. By displaying unmatched excellence, or making a great sacrifice, actors strive to ensure that they will be held in high regard by others. They seek to maintain their value by controlling others' valuation of them. The worst dishonor results from a mistaken belief in having secured the gratitude, admiration, or favor of others. It comes as a surprise. It catches the victim, who believes he or she has succeeded in assuring others' positive valuation of him or her, off-guard. The fallacious expectation of honor greatly amplifies the effects of others' negative valuations.

The action of dishonoring is actually a complex interaction. The insulted person tacitly abandons his positive sense of self and buys into the insult. The likelihood of this response increases to the extent that he (or she) takes on the burden of controlling his valuation by others and believes that he has succeeded in this endeavor. Odysseus's atypical response to Agamemnon's insult, which neither catches him off guard nor affects his sense of his value, would seem to validate these observations.

At least at the outset, youthful Diomedes does not draw a clear boundary between himself and Agamemnon, whose criticism does affect him. He stands "in awe at the king's rebuking." But openness to paternal rebuke is part of the father-identification that makes Diomedes immune to being dishonored by it. Unlike Odysseus, Diomedes evidently trusts Agamemnon to criticize him only with cause. In this sense, he responds in a way that is somewhat similar to hero-sons' identification with negative maternal judgments. But Diomedes' refusal to accept or engage in the devaluation of his father or Agamemnon, together with the fact that he is not dishonored by Agamemnon's rebuke, suggests that vulnerability to dishonor is distinct from a child's tendency to identify with negative parental judgments. It suggests, rather, that vulnerability to dishonor in ancient Greek cultures stems from ongoing relationships in which sons subscribe to maternal devaluations of them and their fathers as mortals and adopt strategies designed to preclude the repetition of maternal negation.

Where Diomedes preserves Tydeus and Agamemnon as paternal models, while recognizing the shortcomings of both, Odysseus affirms his paternal identity. Like Diomedes, he answers Agamemnon's empty insults with deeds. If Agamemnon cares to, he can watch "the very father of Telemachos locked with the champion / Trojans" in combat (5.355–56). The self-affirming mortal father par excellence, Odysseus is also the best of the Achaians in counsel—an arena in which Diomedes also excels. Resourceful, "many minded" (*polumêtis*) Odysseus excels in *mêtis* and *noos* that are crucial both for sustaining orders characterized by *themis* and for preserving his *nostos*, in which he restores *themis* and *dikê* to his native Ithaca.

Both Odysseus and Diomedes conspicuously identify themselves as or with fathers, demonstrate skill in counsel, and are able to bear Agamemnon's insults without descending into outraged dishonor. The parallels suggest that the qualities are linked. Contrasts between these father-identified heroes and Achilles suggest that his willingness to disparage fathers contributes to his vulnerability to dishonor. It is a frightened, self-protective response to maternal disparagement of fathers, of which he has become an instrument.

Given the susceptibility to dishonor—to extreme and outrageous loss of *timê*—that characterizes men and women and gods and mortals in the *Iliad* and Greek mythology, it is remarkable that the *Iliad* presents examples of heroes who are markedly less susceptible to dishonor than Achilles. Their lesser vulnerability to dishonor—and their greater competence in performing the roles of husband, father, and king—correlate with their identification with fathers rather than mothers, as does their relative detachment from child-sacrificing maternal and paternal agendas.

In addition to Diomedes and Odysseus, father-identified heroes on the Achaian side include Nestor (whose name derives from the same root as *noos* and *nostos*) and his son, Antilochos, whose mini-quarrel with Menelaos during Patroklos's funeral games contrasts sharply with Achilles' quarrel with Agamemnon (23.566–611). Agamemnon encounters Nestor just before Odysseus and Diomedes. Although Agamemnon praises rather than chides Nestor, the latter identifies himself as an old man, whose "privilege" (*geras*) it is to command "with word and counsel" the young men who do the spear-fighting and who trust in their strength (*biêphi*; 4.293–325).[25]

While Diomedes is viewed by Agamemnon (and to some extent views himself) as an imperfect son, Odysseus is worse. He is a capable, self-confident adult whose honor does not depend on Agamemnon's approbation. This lands him at the opposite end of the heroic spectrum from Achilles. But although they leave much to be desired as sacrificial victims, Diomedes and Odysseus are actually ideal fathers' sons in a more traditional sense. Out of the meager materials provided them by Agamemnon, both construct an image of him as a legitimate and effective leader, thereby encouraging him to act like one. In the process, they demonstrate their own superior kingliness.

One of the ironies of Agamemnon's encounter with Diomedes is that, although there are distinct limits to what Diomedes is willing to sacrifice for Agamemnon (or Hera), Diomedes offers Agamemnon (a self-appointed representative of his father's generation) what Agamemnon seeks in vain from Achilles: filial respect for him as a king and surrogate father. Agamemnon's response to Diomedes shows what hero-sons are up against in families imbued with the myths and dynamics that generate paradigmatic heroes like Achilles. Agamemnon is unable to appreciate Diomedes' nonsacrificial respect for him and for what might be termed the paternal principle. Instead, Agamemnon interprets Diomedes' and Odysseus's kingly care for themselves and their men—their having the wit to see that their people are safe, and do not perish—as both a lack of courage (*alkê*) and an insufficient zeal on his behalf.

The son who embodies the Theogonic paternal principle—itself rooted in Zeus's ingestion of feminine *mêtis*—faces not only the incomprehension of a self-absorbed father-figure, but also abuse because Agamemnon reads Diomedes' self-regard as an unfilial lack of concern with avenging Agamemnon's shame and dishonor. (Diomedes really cannot win, since his Achilles-like prowess excites Agamemnon's envy.) But like Odysseus, Diomedes has a different provenance and different allegiances than either Achilles or Agamemnon. So, unlike either, he is able to tolerate a temporary diminution of honor (he lets Agamemnon's insult go unanswered for five books) and persevere in his father-identified project.

Perhaps because Diomedes and Odysseus are reared in families in which mothers respect fathers, and fathers respect themselves as mortal men who must resort to *mêtis* and *noos* to contend against sometimes superior adversaries, their patrimonies and their identification with admired fathers remain intact. Self-affirmation and the affirmation of the value of paternal models is not nearly the problem for Odysseus and Diomedes that it is for hero-sons in families centered on the compensatory pride—and vindictive anger—of humiliated mothers.

The difference in family dynamics is clearer for the "son of Laertes and seed of Zeus, resourceful [*polumêchan'*] Odysseus," who is "equal to Zeus in counsel [*mêtin*]," than it is for Diomedes, son of Tydeus (2.169–73). Diomedes' attainment of a youthful prowess second only to Achilles' might signify his involvement in the narrative of a mother-vindicating, mother-avenging hero. But he draws the line at sacrificing his *nostos* for glory. (Unlike Thetis, who spurs her son back into battle, in which he is fated to die gloriously, Athena counsels her protégé, Diomedes, to give way before the *mênis* of Apollo, thus preserving his *nostos* [5.129–32, 5.406–9, 5.433–544; cf. 18.125–37].) He also out-performs his heroic father—one of the famous Seven against Thebes—while continuing to respect him. He tacitly acknowledges what Agamemnon and Sthenelos imply: that his father died because he failed to heed the portents of Zeus. So Diomedes' father is an ambiguous model. In the incident with Agamemnon and generally, Diomedes has a choice to make and he chooses wisely—to recognize fathers' strengths (and weaknesses) rather than using fathers' faults scornfully to disparage them. Achilles' father, in contrast, presents a model of almost complete identification with a sister of his rejecting mother: not much of a useable patrimony there.

In the *Iliad* it appears that father-identified heroes are spared the twin traumas of "superior" mothers' repudiation of them and their fathers. Having a point of view distinct from a divine mother's, they recognize the self-destruction hidden in the promise of mother-conferred superiority to purportedly inferior fathers. (On his return from Troy, Odysseus has his men strap him to his ship's mast—and plug their ears with wax—so he can hear the sirens' songs of glory without being lured to his death by them.) Thus father-identified heroes do not face the all-but-insurmountable obstacles to self-affirmation and self-assertion of their mother-identified counterparts. Instead, their relatively normal (in ancient Greek as well as modern terms)—but remarkable and atypical—experience of maternal affirmation of them and their admired, self-affirming fathers fosters confidence in their own abilities and worth as men. They show us what mother-identified, mother-sacrificed heroes like Achilles would be like if they could find their way back from self-negation to self-affirmation.

The characterization of Odysseus, Diomedes, and Nestor as father-identified heroes helps to explain why the *Odyssey* begins with the end of Athena's paradoxical wrath at her favorite, Odysseus. Like her protégés, Odysseus and Diomedes, and like Zeus himself, Athena is an ambiguous figure. Zeus's ingestion of Mêtis, of which she is the offspring, marks the completion of his establishment of cosmic *themis* and *dikê*, but Athena, like Zeus himself, is a key player in heroic narratives rooted in violations of Theogonic norms. Her kingly protégés are also her own and Hera's avengers. They may incur her father's *mênis* on that account, even as they may incur her *mênis* for failing to avenge Paris's insulting choice of Aphrodite over her and Hera. But each of these father-identified heroes ultimately chooses Athena's gifts of Theogonic *mêtis* and *noos* over the cursed *eros* of Aphrodite—and over the "immortal" (*aphthitos*) gifts of another favorite of Zeus, and implicit rival, Thetis.[26]

The *Odyssey* begins with Athena's long-delayed intervention to help Odysseus. It follows his decisive rejection of Aphrodite-gifted Kalypso's offer of immortality. Instead, he chooses his *nostos*, a goal embedded in human time, aging, and death, which requires *noos* and *mêtis*—not just cunning, but the Theogonic, kingly intelligence to learn from predecessors' mistakes. Rejecting Kalypso's proffered immortality, Odysseus reverses not only Paris's insulting choice of Aphrodite but Achilles' choice of *aphthitos* things over *nostos* and *mêtis* as well. Diomedes makes similar choices in the *Iliad* when, on the advice of Athena, he opts to save his *nostos* rather than press his attack on Apollo and go down in a blaze of glory, and when he wounds Aphrodite at Athena's urging. In the *Odyssey*, Diomedes and Nestor distinguish themselves from the Greek and Trojan suitors of Tyndareus's Aphrodite-cursed daughters not only by choosing the gifts of Athena and Theogonic Zeus, but also, evidently, by refraining from the impieties of their drunken, victorious fellows, which serves as the pretext for Zeus's *mênis*, inflicted by Athena, on the erstwhile agents of her and Hera's revenge on mortal substitutes for Zeus. Doubly distinguished from their fellows, Diomedes and Nestor—unlike vacillating, ambivalent Odysseus—return from Troy quickly and without incident (iii.165).[27]

The contrast between mother-identified and father-identified heroes represents one of the strongest pieces of evidence—albeit an indirect one—for the central role of traumatic maternal devaluation in the provenance of heroic character. Father-identification correlates with relative immunity to insult, intact wits (*noos*) and "cunning intelligence" (*mêtis*), and the courage to sustain confidence in adversity. Mother-identification correlates with an inability to tolerate even a temporary lack of outward tokens of superiority, a trait that Achilles markedly shares with Agamemnon—just as he shares Agamemnon's marked propensity to give up and go home in adversity. Agamemnon overtly gives up on and berates himself. Both heroes are deficient in the inner resources denoted by Diomedes' *alkê*—not the courage of the life-despising, mother-pleasing warrior but the "heart" to remain confident and persevere amidst uncertainty and adversity, for the lack of which "heart" Diomedes faults Agamemnon.

It is remarkable that hero-sons who identify with mortal fathers, modeling actions in accord with *themis*, exhibit undamaged intellect and confidence to establish orders based on mutuality and trust, while sons who sacrifice all—including their paternal models, patrimonies, and *nostoi*—to win the favor of mothers who claim superiority to mortals and to the dictates of *themis* exhibit the vulnerability to dishonor and intellectual deficiency associated with maternal devaluation of *nostos*-seeking selves.

Chapter Seven

Departures from Maternal Agendas

If hero-sons do attempt to ward off devastating maternal anger by identifying with it, even a momentary break with this safe identification ought to re-kindle anxiety. Sons' identification with purportedly superior mothers' anger at mere mortals like themselves and their fathers, who have the temerity to criticize maternal failings or to pursue their own rather than vindictive maternal agendas, would seem to afford impregnable armor. Identification with maternal anger at a disavowed, vulnerable mortal self or father would seem to confer immunity from harm even as the son joins in inflicting it. Conversely, when sons take up previously disavowed aspirations to create orders built on mutual trust and respect, they inadvertently remove the armor of identification with maternal aggression. They unwittingly revert to being dangerously distinguishable from angry mothers. Worse, their apostasy makes them likely targets of maternal aggression.

Just such an anxiety-engendering departure from maternal agendas is dramatized in the abortive attempt of the Achaians and Trojans to end the war in book 4. Indeed, the episode of the truce between the Achaians and Trojans provides a remarkable representation of what goes on in the minds of hero-sons, just beyond the bounds of conscious awareness, when, despite their own best efforts to root out such aspirations in themselves, they experience moments of lucidity, backslide into believing in their own abilities, and actually succeed in establishing relationships of mutual trust and reciprocity according to *themis*—heedless of maternal needs for revenge and vindication.

The *Iliad*'s presentation of the episode alternates between the divine and mortal planes. Oblivious to the effects of their actions on Hera and Athena, and tired of fighting, the Achaians and Trojans joyfully embrace Paris's offer—which his brother, Hektor, shames him into making—to fight Menelaos in single combat for Helen. No matter who wins, the rest of the Achaians and Trojans, having cut their "oaths of faith and friendship," can satisfy their longing to be "rid of all the sorrow of warfare" and to return home to their presumably loving and beloved wives and children. "Joyful" at this prospect, both sides pray to Zeus to punish any who break their oaths of faith and friendship (3.67f., 3.111–12, 3.299–301, 3.320–23).

Instead of continuing to sacrifice their lives and futures for glory that is bound up with the favor of vindictive mothers, the Achaians and Trojans unite to invert the sacrificial bargain. They choose *nostos* over maternal revenge and glory. Although the Trojans fight more to protect their city, they seek heroic glory only marginally less than the Achaians. Hektor may call his fellow Trojans cowards for not stoning Paris to death for the sorrow he has brought on his people by stealing Menelaos's wife (3.47–57), but they glory over Helen and her possessions. Nonetheless, in book 4 they too choose peace.

For once, Agamemnon and Priam act like responsible and effective leaders and guarantors of *themis*. (Relatively responsible, Priam tells Helen that she is not to blame [*aitiê*] for the war with the Achaians, but rather the gods are [*aitioi*]—neatly sidestepping his own responsibility for dooming his city by rejecting the Achaians' embassy to secure the return of Helen at the start of the war, allowing his son to keep the wife he took from Menelaos [3.164–65, 3.205–6].)

Although in the hero-son's family triad the mother enlists him to assert superiority to a father who abdicates his role, the peace plan nonetheless involves a momentary reassertion of paternal and kingly authority by Priam and Agamemnon. The sons of Priam are "outrageous, not to be trusted," Menelaos avers, but Priam himself is trustworthy (3.105–6).

> Always it is, that the hearts in the younger men are frivolous,
> but when an elder man is among them, he looks behind him
> and in front, so that all comes out far better for both sides (3.108–10)

These elder kings, Agamemnon and Priam, conclude a truce that is the first step toward putting an end to the grievous bloodshed. Their compatriots having sworn to refrain from fighting, the Trojan seducer and aggrieved Achaian husband undertake to settle their dispute in single combat. Regardless of who wins, the Achaians and Trojans "can go free of each other at last" (3.99). Forgetting their roles as self-sacrificing agents of divine maternal revenge—of which at other times they seem dimly aware—the Achaians get caught up in the belief that they have found a way to realize the happy prospect of putting an end to strife and of returning home to their wives, families, and cities. At least for a moment, they reverse their *themis*-inverting sacrificial relationship not only to Agamemnon, but also to their divine patroness, Hera.[1]

Their departures from maternal agendas do not go unnoticed on Olympos. There they provoke divine anger. A major objective of the plan of Zeus is to ensure that Hera and Athena sate their thirst for vengeance on his erstwhile Trojan protégés, rather than himself. So he is not about to allow the Achaian-Trojan peace initiative to succeed. Nonetheless, Zeus deliberately provokes the goddesses by pretending to consider the possibility.

> Presently the son of Kronos was minded to anger
> Hera, if he could, with words offensive, speaking to cross her:
> . . . .
> Let us consider then how these things shall be accomplished,
> whether again to stir up grim warfare and the terrible
> fighting, or cast down love and make them friends with each other.
> If somehow this way could be sweet and pleasing to all of us,
> the city of lord Priam might still be a place men dwell in,
> and Menelaos could take away with him Helen of Argos (4.5–6, 4.14–19)

So, even as the Achaians and Trojans are buoyed by confidence in their newfound ability to devise a plan that will put an end to the war and allow them to return safely home to their families, the *Iliad*'s audience witnesses, on Olympos, the build-up of vengeful maternal anger that dooms the plan to failure. The audience is aware, as the Achaians and Trojans evidently are not, that the success the Achaians and Trojans envision is illusory. From the Olympian perspective, it is nothing more than Zeus's joke at Hera's and Athena's expense.[2]

Even though the prospect of peace infuriates the goddesses, they do not vent their anger on the errant Achaians, who, after all, are essential instruments of their revenge. Instead, Hera devises a stratagem to which an ostensibly reluctant Zeus agrees. Zeus should send Athena to "visit horrible war on the Achaians and Trojans," but ensure that the Trojans are at fault for the resumption of hostilities. Athena persuades the Trojan archer Pandaros to violate the truce by attempting to kill Menelaos. The latter, although frustrated by Aphrodite's intervention to prevent him from killing Paris, is flushed with victory over his hated rival and winning back his incomparably beautiful wife.

Deflected by Athena, the arrow of Pandaros nicks Menelaos, and blood spreads over his tunic. Shuddering with terror, as Menelaos himself does, Agamemnon fears that he has lost his beloved brother. He berates himself for his folly in trusting the Trojans (and, implicitly, his own ability to broker an end to the conflict).

> Dear brother, it was your death I sealed in the oaths of friendship,
> setting you alone before the Achaians to fight with the Trojans (4.155–56)

Agamemnon finally realizes what the *Iliad*'s audience has known all along: the peace that he believed that he and his Trojan counterpart had achieved was an illusion.

The self-reproach in Agamemnon's speech is important for its part in the *Iliad*'s representation of the folly of trusting his own kingly, *themis*-making abilities. Naïvely believing that he has secured the restoration of his brother's wife and the safe return of his people, Agamemnon has actually—it appears—enabled the Trojans to inflict on him a grievous loss comparable to Achilles' loss of his dear comrade, Patroklos. Just as Patroklos is a *nêpios* who does not know he is supplicating his own death, and Achilles is (implicitly) a *nêpios* for allowing Patroklos to fight the Trojans alone, so Agamemnon chastises himself for his folly. He does not berate himself for letting his brother fight Paris alone, although this parallels Achilles' great folly, but for trusting the Trojans' oaths. Agamemnon is the victim of deception (*apatês*; 4.168). As before, when he was the victim of a false dream and "vile deception" (*kakên apatên*; 2.114;), he is, implicitly, a "fool" (*nêpios*). He believes things in his heart that are not to be accomplished (2.36–38).

This episode reveals the protective impulse underlying the relentless assault on the credulous, *themis*-loving, supposedly foolish and naïve self, the *nêpios*, that is integral to the formation and maintenance of heroic character. Through projection of the *nêpios* onto others, it is also integral to heroic violence. With no more awareness of impending disaster than the mother-bird with her innocent children (*nêpia tekna*) in the portent at Aulis (2.303–19), Agamemnon believes that he and his counterpart, Priam, have effectively played the roles of kings and fathers in restoring their charges to the ordered life of cities and families: *themis*. The Achaians and Trojans too are joyful at the prospect of taking their places as loving spouses and fathers in normative families.

But through the angry goddesses' intervention, the Trojans and Achaians—and in particular Agamemnon—come to realize that this was madness and folly in the highest degree. Their substitution of trust for their customary hostility exposed them to complete destruction. The theme of deception, *apatê*, implies delusion or mad folly, *atê*. They were deluded to think that the sons of Priam could be made trustworthy. All it takes is one errant Trojan to destroy their confidence and their truce. Agamemnon's belief that he is a capable, effective king who can and will take his place as a responsible and respected king and spouse is revealed to Agamemnon and the *Iliad*'s auditors alike as a delusion. It is supplanted by a view of himself as an object of ridicule (4.171–82).

In effect, Agamemnon inflicts on himself a repetition of the typical experience of hero-sons: the fall of the *nêpios* child from a naïve belief that he is safe and loved to the reality that he is a destroyed victim. In this way Agamemnon tries both to ensure that he will not make the mistake of trusting again and to immunize himself against suffering such a fall at the hands of others, notably his wife, on his return. As is usual with such strategies, they too prove illusory. The resurgence of belief in self and trust in others is impossible completely to suppress, and its consequences are lethal. For the *Iliad*'s audience, the episode is a reminder of the hero-son's rule to live by: Do not even think about being an effective king or husband or father able to achieve an order based on reciprocal trust, love, and care. Whoever succumbs to confidence of success in this regard must be condemned as a *nêpios*. To persist in such folly is madness (*atê*). Such is the way of the world—as reflected in the machinations of the gods.

While an enemy, whose dreams of a *nostos* prove illusory, may be mocked, folly that endangers loved ones—one's self, family members, companions, or city—provokes self-reproach grounded in protective love. It is necessary to destroy the innocent child and naïve fool, the *nêpios*, in the self in order to protect loved ones and the self from a repetition of grievous loss. Unfortunately, this attitude holds wide sway, at least among mother-identified hero-sons and members of their hero-making families. Aggressive disparagement of the *themis*-seeking self effectively precludes any sustained or determined effort to initiate and maintain familial, societal, political, and international orders founded on reciprocal friendship and respect.

Agamemnon reacts to the Trojan betrayal and his brush with disaster as expected, with anger at the perfidious foe who tried to take the life of his brother. Agamemnon first expresses renewed confidence that Zeus's promise of victory over the Trojans will be fulfilled.

> If the Olympian at once has not finished this matter,
> late will he bring it to pass, and they must pay a great penalty,
> with their own heads, and with their women, and with their children
> For I know this thing well in my heart, and my mind knows it.
> There will come a day when sacred Ilion shall perish,
> and Priam, and the people of Priam of the strong ash spear,
> and Zeus son of Kronos who sits on high, the sky-dwelling,
> himself shall shake the gloom of his aegis over all of them
> in anger [*koteôn*] for this deception [*apatês*]. All this shall not go
> unaccomplished (4.160–68)

Reverting to his typical self-doubting form, however, he quickly veers toward imagining ignominious defeat. Even though Menelaos was only nicked by Pandaros's arrow, he may yet die, in which case, Zeus's promises notwithstanding, the demoralized Achaians will flee homeward, forcing

Agamemnon to return home with the mockery of the Trojans ringing in his ears:

> "Might Agamemnon accomplish his anger thus against all his
> enemies, as now he led here in vain a host of Achaians
> and has gone home again to the beloved land of his fathers
> with ships empty, and leaving behind him brave Menelaos."
> Thus shall a man speak: then let the wide earth open to take me (4.178–82)

Imagining himself as an ineffectual, laughable failure, mocked by his enemies, Agamemnon harshly reprises his self-reproach for his folly in believing in oaths of friendship.

Here too, supposedly anomalous and unheroic Agamemnon dramatizes a typical experience—and fear—of hero-sons. As he is wont to do, Agamemnon panics. Instead of the glorious victor he imagined himself to be, he will become an object of ridicule. His vision of his success is a false dream, like the one Zeus sent to lure him to defeat at the hands of the Trojans. Far from being an effective, deservedly respected and loved king who saves his people—or, more to the point here, an avenger who destroys his enemies with irresistible might—he is a ridiculous failure.

Once again, when Agamemnon is at his least heroic, and seemingly most atypical, he typifies denied aspects of heroic character and culture. Because he is supposedly atypical, he can enact common patterns of thought and behavior that would otherwise create anxiety in the *Iliad*'s auditors. Here Agamemnon dramatizes the fear of being exposed and mocked as worthless that haunts hero-sons' endeavors. Although Achilles is supposed to be at the other end of the heroic spectrum, he responds similarly when he is mocked as helpless by the river god, Skamander, and threatened with ignominious death and oblivion. Like Agamemnon, who believes Zeus has deceived him with a false dream of glorious victory, Achilles fears that his mother deceived him with falsehoods when she promised that he would die gloriously at Troy. Panicking, he jumps to the conclusion that he will be reduced to an insignificant nothing and consigned to oblivion. Hera sends Athena and Poseidon to reassure Achilles while dispatching her son to subdue the threat that terrifies him, but the incident has undeniable similarities with Agamemnon's habitual, but supposedly atypical anxiety about being reduced from a glorious victor to an object of mockery (21.211–376).

Although the prospect of peace provokes the goddesses' fury, and the Achaians' infatuation with peacemaking puts them in the dangerous position of being obstacles to rather than agents of the goddesses' revenge, the Achaians seem oblivious both to their role in avenging "Paris's insult to the goddesses" and to the divine displeasure provoked by their forgetfulness.

In this they are unlike the *Iliad*'s audience, who are fully aware both of the Achaians' role as agents of Hera's and Athena's revenge and of the divine anger provoked by the Achaians' departure from maternal agendas. The *Iliad*'s auditors are aware as well of the goddesses' role in derailing the peace process, while making it appear that the Trojans are at fault so the Achaians' fury will be directed at them.

Indeed, a critical element of the goddesses' plan—and of the *Iliad*'s representation of the process by which the Achaians come to view their attempt to make peace as dangerous folly—is that the Achaians remain oblivious both to their divine patronesses' anger and to the link between it and Menelaos's terrifying brush with death, which scuttles the joyful prospect of returning home to their wives and families. While straying from self-sacrifice into self-affirmation and self-assertion occasions great anxiety for the Achaians, they are evidently unaware of its source. The possibility of their permanent departure from their divine patronesses' agenda, and their renunciation of the sacrifices it entails, provokes divine maternal anger, but this occurs outside their conscious awareness.

Their lack of awareness is realistic on a number of levels. A heroic culture is rooted in anxiety-generating experience about what happens to people (sons or fathers, daughters or wives) who pursue ordinary aspirations and assert standards of *themis* against child-sacrificing parents. It is also addicted to violence and to the glory that comes from demonstrating the weakness and folly of those who persist in clinging to such aspirations. The characters of mother-identified hero-sons militate against the success of any peace initiative. Thoughtlessly doing the will of irresistibly powerful, humiliated mothers is simply what it means to be hero-sons. It is who they are; it is engrained in their characters and not something they think about on a day-to-day basis. It is all the more remarkable, then, that the *Iliad* and Greek mythology embed hero-sons' actions in mother-son relationships.

To get the Achaians to dismiss their visions of peace as just another false dream and "vile deception" (*kakên apatên*; 2.114, 9.121) that it was madness and dangerous folly for them to believe in, the goddesses do not have to threaten their Achaian protégés directly—as, for example, Aphrodite does her rebellious protégé, Helen. After Aphrodite whisks her favorite, Paris, out of the fighting as Menelaos is about to kill him, Helen refuses to obey Aphrodite's order to join Paris in bed.

> Then in anger [*cholôsamenê*] Aphrodite the shining spoke to her:
> "Wretched girl, do not tease me lest in anger [*chôsamenê*] I forsake you
> and grow to hate you as much as now I terribly love you [*ephilêsa*],
> lest I encompass you in hard hate, caught between both sides,
> Danaans and Trojans alike, and you wretchedly perish" (3.413–17)

Hera and Athena can accomplish the reversion from peace to war by triggering self-undermining responses that are legacies of mother-inflicted trauma—proneness to outrage and readiness to believe that visions of *themis* are illusory—without having to threaten the Achaians directly. By persuading Zeus to make the Trojans at fault for the resumption of hostilities—in effect reenacting Paris's original abuse of Menelaos's trust—Hera ensures that her protégés will turn away from thoughts of peace and will once again be bent on her enemies' destruction. This reenactment of Paris's perfidy not only allows the war to resume on the same terms as before. It hides maternal responsibility for the Achaians' loss of their *nostoi* and the maternal threat behind Hera's "love and care" for her protégés.

Lured by the prospect of peace unwittingly to abandon their role as maternal avengers, hero-sons like the Achaians might well feel defenseless and exposed to annihilation, just as Menelaos is to Pandaros's arrow, without knowing why. If the Achaians' anxiety is rooted in a denied but ineradicable experience of themselves as defenseless victims of maternal devaluation, Agamemnon's switch from imagining himself an effective leader (or glorious victor) to self-castigation as a shameful, mocked failure appears to stand for a common but denied reflex of heroic character.

Are the Achaians momentarily forgetful of or completely oblivious to their roles as agents of divine maternal revenge? They are keenly aware of Paris's seduction of Menelaos's wife since that is what motivates the war as well as the single combat between Menelaos and Paris at the center of their peace plan. But are they, like the *Iliad*'s audience, aware of Paris's "insult" to Hera and Athena and of the Achaians' own critical role in avenging the insult?

At least one Trojan knows about Paris's "insult to the goddesses." Paris himself must have been aware of provoking divine displeasure by denying Hera and Athena the supremacy in beauty for which they and Aphrodite contended. In another context, the *Iliad* notes that Hera and Athena kept

> their hatred for sacred Ilion as in the beginning,
> and for Priam and his people, because of the delusion of Paris
> who insulted the goddesses when they came to him in his courtyard
> and favoured her who supplied the lust that led to disaster (24.26–30)

The reference to Paris's delusion (*atês*) seems to suggest that Paris was heedless of the consequences of insulting the goddesses. This brief passage suggests that Paris at least, and perhaps his fellow Trojans, know that the Achaians who threaten to destroy their city are agents of the goddesses' vengeful anger.

The Achaians' knowledge of the divine conflict driving the war is implied in Nestor's (false) assurance to Agamemnon in book 2 that Hera has won over the other Olympians by her supplication so the Achaians have a clear path to victory. Athena tells Achilles about her and Hera's special love for him and Agamemnon. Do Achilles and Agamemnon know of Hera's special solicitude without being aware that it stems from their roles as the goddess's avengers? Achilles' mother sometimes tells him of things willed by Zeus that are unknown to other mortals (17.408–9). General awareness of the backing of Hera and Athena for the Achaian war effort may be implied in Odysseus's recollection of Peleus's advice to Achilles when Peleus sent Achilles away to Agamemnon: "For the matter of strength Athene and Hera will give it / if it be their will" (9.254–55). Menelaos evidently knows he has the backing of Hera and Athena as well as Zeus since the goddesses promise him that the Achaians will sack Troy (5.714–16). Athena directs her favorite, Diomedes, to wound Aphrodite. His mockery of Aphrodite for leading women astray is echoed by Hera and Athena, who suggest that Aphrodite cut her hand on a hairpin while inducing some Achaian woman to follow her beloved Trojans (5.348–49, 5.422–25).

There is no definitive answer to the question of how aware mortals are of Hera's vengeful anger as a driving force of the Achaian attack on Troy. The *Iliad* suggests that there is a barrier between gods and men. Humans may suspect that the gods are doing something without knowing exactly what it is. Yet the barrier is somewhat permeable. Knowledge of the divine purposes that drive human events seeps across it. The overall effect of the *Iliad*'s narrative is to represent Achaians and Trojans as having a dim, intermittent, and uncertain awareness of divine purposes. Some mortals, at some times, are more aware than others of divine purposes—Achilles and the seer Kalchas most of all—but even their knowledge is partial and even they can be badly mistaken.

The question is not what the Achaians know but what the *Iliad*'s audience presumes they know. Is the *Iliad*'s audience supposed to view human actors in the poem as aware—as they themselves are—of the reasons for Thetis's forced marriage, the strife that disrupts its celebration, and the ways in which their actions and fates are determined by both? Or is the audience supposed to assume that the generality of Achaians and Trojans remain in the dark about these things?

In light of the seepage of knowledge between gods and men in the *Iliad*, and the intercourse between gods and men in the events leading up to the Trojan War, the most likely supposition is that the *Iliad*'s audience regarded the Achaians and Trojans alike as being at least vaguely aware of Paris's insult to the goddesses as a primary cause of the war on the divine plane and of the Achaians' role as Hera's avengers. If that is the case, the Achaians' obliviousness to the anger their peace initiative is provoking on Olympos would indicate less absolute ignorance than momentary forgetfulness.

If the Achaians are at least dimly aware that they are Hera's avengers and favorites, but, caught up in their joy at having devised a plan to get "rid of the sorrows of warfare" and go home, they forget the basis of their special relationship with the powerful goddess, they also must be dimly aware, at some level, that their apostasy is likely to provoke divine anger. (Achilles observes that Herakles was destroyed by the anger of Hera, as if her jealous anger were general knowledge, though his interlocutor is his divine mother [18.119].) Regardless of what the *Iliad*'s auditors imagine that the Achaians know or do not know, the account ensures that the auditors themselves imaginatively experience both the Achaians' obliviousness and an awareness of the goddesses' anger at the prospect of peace.

In this episode, the *Iliad* dramatizes conscious and unconscious thought processes of hero-sons who momentarily forget their half-understood roles in relation to angry, humiliated mothers. Even as the Achaians are caught up in their enthusiasm for peace and their own Zeus-like cleverness and wisdom in devising a way to put an end to the conflict, they begin to imagine, beyond the bounds of conscious awareness, the likely effects of their apostasy on the goddesses whose purposes they serve.

This episode illustrates an old lesson, deeply engrained in heroic character, and a response to traumatic maternal anger. The way the *Iliad* tells it, Menelaos's brush with death teaches Agamemnon and the Achaians to regard the credulous self, expansive in its confidence of achieving and enjoying harmonious orders—in marriage, family, and city—as naïve and its hopeful imaginings as madness or dangerous folly. Not only are the Achaians' and Trojans' dreams of becoming friends with one another illusory, but Agamemnon imagines paying a heavy price for his folly in believing that the peace plan could work. As a result of trusting in his and Priam's peacemaking abilities, Agamemnon narrowly avoids not only the death of his beloved brother, but utter shame and disaster. If his brother dies, the whole enterprise will unravel, and Agamemnon will flee home in disgrace.

Indeed, Pandaros's arrow reminds the Achaians of a lesson that is as fundamental to heroic character as the trauma from which the lesson initially is drawn. This being the case, all the goddesses have to do to set the Achaians back on the path of war and destruction is to give them a pointed reminder of what they already know in the depths of their being: their dreams of *themis* are false and dangerous. Their idea of themselves as statesmen who could bring an end to war likewise is folly.

Indeed, the equation with madness or naïve folly of trust in others as partners in creating *themis* is a fundamental element in Homeric culture. It is overwhelmingly reinforced by the *Iliad* and its mythological context at every level, from Zeus on down. So too is a recognition of the impossibility of completely rooting out such folly. In this broader context, the hardened Achaians' trust in the Trojans to honor their oaths is merely one of those periodic irruptions of naïve credulity or madness, to which even the least naïve, the most wary and cunning, periodically succumb.

Not even Zeus is exempt. None other than Agamemnon relates the tale of the so-called *Dios apatê*, the deception of Zeus. In the mythic past, Hera pretends to help with the birth of Zeus's love-child, Herakles. As a result of being duped by Hera's imitation of a docile, conciliatory wife who simply forgives—rather than holds him responsible for and avenges—his many infidelities, Zeus is forced to witness the lifelong persecution and ultimate destruction of his son, Herakles, by his dishonored and vengeful wife. In an attempt to avoid ever again being deceived in this way, Zeus dissociates himself from such credulity, stigmatizes it as hateful madness, and ejects the goddess who personifies it, Atê, from Olympos, leaving her to wander only among men.

That Atê is tied to an ineradicable, hopeful, credulous part of the self is made clear in the *Iliad* when, despite Zeus's expulsion of Atê, Hera works a similar deception on Zeus. Hating him for thwarting her revenge for the erotic humiliation inflicted on her by Paris and the Trojans, Hera with "false lying purpose" dupes her husband into believing she is being conciliatory. His credulity—evinced in part by his fond recollection of a series of erotic conquests—costs him the death of yet another child of such a union, his beloved, heroic son, Sarpedon. This repetition within the *Iliad* of the story of Hera's earlier deception of Zeus indicates the futility of Zeus's earlier attempt to banish Atê from Olympos. As if to underscore that this is a reenactment of her deception of Zeus at the birth of Herakles, Hera recalls Zeus's anger when Hera got Hupnos (Sleep) to overcome Zeus so she would be free to wreak havoc on Herakles on his return from a previous sack of Troy (14.157f., and 14.252–56). This second deception of Zeus by Hera with regard to Herakles further underscores the failure of Zeus's attempt to banish mad folly from Olympos.

Hera's repeated deceptions of Zeus suggest the futility of the corresponding strategy of dissociation, stigmatization, and elimination of the credulous, *themis*-seeking part of the self. It is not only that hope—and pride in abilities—springs eternal, but that the *themis*-making abilities in which hero-sons pride themselves as children are highly vulnerable to the destructive forces of parental rejection and seduction. To function as exponents of *themis* in their world, hero-sons would have to acknowledge and contend not only with external threats, but also with their habitual ways of betraying and subverting their own *themis*-seeking selves. In condemning as folly their dreams of homecomings in accord with *themis*, they blame themselves for the devastation that not only Agamemnon but the generality of Achaians take to be the fundamental reality. From our standpoint, their abandonment and condemnation of their human powers as inadequate is the greater folly.

The equation of trust with being taken advantage of may be seen in a different context, when Diomedes and the Trojan, Glaukos, who have been guest-friends before the war, meet on the battlefield. Instead of fighting, they exchange gifts. Diomedes gets the better part of the bargain because, as the poet notes, he trades bronze armor for gold (6.215–36). Presented in an amusing light, this exchange arguably has the opposite import. It represents the fundamental transaction in which gullible and dependent hero-sons are duped into exchanging the functional bronze of their life-protecting *mêtis* and *noos* for the shining gold of glory, sacrificing an invaluable potential for living the full lives comprehended in the term *nostos* for the promise of immortal *kleos*.

In the *Iliad*, the death of Patroklos brings home to Achilles the meaning of the *nostos* he has lightly sacrificed for glory. A dark version of this exchange is dramatized when Thetis responds to her son's musings about returning home (instead of reentering the battle in which both he and his mother know he will die) by telling him how splendid he will look in dazzling armor fashioned by Hephaistos. When Achilles sees the god's handiwork, he is so taken with its terrible beauty that he forgets any thoughts of returning home (18.133–37, 19.10–23). In effect, Thetis uses the appeal of armor and weaponry to re-recruit her son to the cause in which he will die. As Agamemnon's recruiter, Odysseus used a similar ploy to defeat the ruse—disguising Achilles as a girl—by which Thetis sought to save her son from his fated death at Troy.[3]

The *Iliad* and myth suggest that equation of trust in love and friendship with folly is deeply inscribed in Homeric character and culture. The truce-breaking episode represents the relearning of an old lesson (followed by a reversion to habitual behavior patterns) rather than the learning of a new one. When they attempted to make peace with the Trojans, the Achaians briefly departed from—and then, their lesson relearned, returned to the safety of—identifying with hostile maternal agendas, equating trust in *themis* with mad folly. They resumed their habit of ridiculing the self's pretensions to have the ability to effect *themis*, of exposing the *themis*-minded self's puniness and impotence relative to the force of the vengeful maternal anger that really rules the affairs of men. Far from fighting in the forefront to make peace, Achaians and Trojans alike shrink back into the host of their companions.

Zeus's failed attempt to banish Atê, the mad hope of marital harmony, from Olympos, together with the truce-breaking episode in the *Iliad*, raises the question of whether such attempts can ever succeed in the world of the poem. If even twice-burned Zeus and the cunning, ruthless, wife-avoiding Achaians can be taken in by false promises of returning to happy marriages and cities that prosper beneath their decrees, what mortal or god can escape deception, madness, and folly?

The path of safety is never to invest in such hopes, despite the risks, not even on behalf of less formidable, protected others. To forget this hard-earned lesson, and to trust in and confidently expect that respect, love, or friendship will be reciprocated—whether "oaths of faith and friendship" (*philotêta kai horkia pista*; 3.73), or Menelaos's expectation of winning back his beautiful wife in single combat, or Agamemnon's triumphant homecoming—is to open oneself up to the most destructive force in the cosmos: devastating maternal indifference or vengeful anger. The naïve, trusting soul, expecting nothing but good in marriage, family, and polity, is totally unprepared for and unprotected from not only the perfidy of sworn friends, but also the betrayal and anger of humiliated wives and mothers. Menelaos's defenselessness against Pandaros's arrow signifies the vulnerability to obliteration that comes from forgetting the axiom that trust and positive expectations of *themis* are folly. It is remarkable that the episode traces this vulnerability to hero-sons' departures from maternal agendas, even as it represents the Achaians as at most vaguely aware of this connection.

These strategies for avoiding risk are genetically related. The trauma and continuing vulnerability caused by maternal anger at sons' and fathers' departures from maternal agendas underlie the self-protective strategies of identification with angry mothers and of dismissing as mad folly all confidence in the self's ability to effect positive outcomes in accord with *themis*. The intended effect of Pandaros's arrow is to turn the Achaians from the path of peace back to the path of war, but it does so by prompting the Achaians to snuff out, yet again, their self-regarding, sacrifice-resisting, but risky life strategies so they will revert to the safety of violence and self-sacrifice. In the end, they actively, even happily, collude in the goddesses' eradication of their foolishly joyful, *nostos*-minded selves. "The Achaians again put on their armour, and remembered their warcraft." Many, like Agamemnon himself, are eager to resume fighting (4.222f.).

Encumbered by such deeply engrained ideas and behaviors rooted in trauma, Achaian hero-sons would need great courage, *alkê*—as well as deep understanding—to persevere in pursuing peace in the face of maternal anger. If, despite the warning shot arranged by Athena—as if to show her beloved "child" Menelaos the folly of trusting in the Achaians' and Trojans' ability to make peace—the Achaians were to confidently persist in their determination to reclaim the *nostoi* they had agreed to sacrifice, they might become hateful to the goddesses who "terribly love them," and whose purposes they habitually and thoughtlessly serve.

The divinity of these maternal figures is finally indistinguishable from the seemingly superhuman, even superdivine, cosmic, destructive power of their anger. It is the threat of Thetis's devastating *mênis*, not her mere immortality, that enables Thetis to succeed in getting Zeus to agree to Agamemnon's humiliation. Similarly, it is Hera's anger, and not her immortality alone, that makes Hera's patronage a guarantee of Achaian triumph. Maternal indifference or anger, whether toward hero-sons or their fathers, is experienced by hero-sons as an irresistible, destructive force. Vulnerability to it is something that hero-sons like Achilles, or the Achaians taken as a group, never get beyond. Simply to provoke such hostility is to reactivate the traumatic experience of a catastrophic loss of value and the equally threatening outrage that goes with it.

Under these circumstances, it is much safer to equate expectations of going home before the goddess-mothers are avenged and vindicated, and confidence in the Achaians' puny human power to bring this about, with madness or folly. Beyond this, the Achaians can dissociate from and project such foolish expectations and confidence onto others, and proceed to destroy them. The mortal analogue of Zeus's unsuccessful attempt to banish Atê from Olympos is heroic violence against others on whom the aggressors have projected their naïvely expectant and foolishly confident mortal selves.

However much the joyful prospect of peace may make the Achaians forget their warcraft, they are unwilling to risk persisting in their pursuit of peace. For them this would be far more frightening than going into battle, in which they feel identified with irresistibly powerful maternal anger. Just like Agamemnon and Achilles, when they make compromised attempts at kingliness, the Achaians give up at the first sign of possible failure. If they happen to be killed far from home by similarly aggressive adversaries in battle, at least they are not innocent children, expecting good things from—and thus laying themselves open to the devastating rage of—mothers or spouses. The stigmatization of their belief in the possibility of peace as dangerous folly marks a deeper disavowal: Henceforth they will leave such mad dreams—of sustaining happy marriages, families, and cities in opposition to vengeful maternal agendas—to their Trojan adversaries. Against these, the Achaian hero-sons will adopt Hera's perspective that the Trojans and their offensive civilization fully deserve obliteration.

Instead of aggressively pursuing peace, the Achaians scurry back to safety at their first inkling of maternal displeasure. Rather than committing to their own ends in the face of divine maternal anger, they revert to being its agents. By taking the side of the goddesses' anger—or even potential anger—against themselves, they once again don perfect armor against the most powerful destructive force in the *Iliad*'s cosmos. How can mothers be angry with sons who set aside their longing for orders based on mutual love, respect, and care to become self-sacrificing instruments of divine maternal revenge and vindication?

No less than Pandaros, the cowardly Trojan archer who attempts to strike a mortal blow at a foolishly trusting victim while staying out of range of Achaian spears, the Achaians play it safe. By adopting the view that the Trojan objects of Hera's anger—surrogates for philandering, daughter-sacrificing father Zeus—are simply at fault and deserve to be destroyed, and by identifying themselves with maternal anger at mortals who insult divine mothers, they avoid once again becoming victims of divine anger. By realigning themselves with divine mothers who try to eradicate sons' mortal selves, which resist being sacrificed to avenge divine mothers, the Achaians once again put on their impregnable armor against divine maternal anger.

In effect, the Achaians seek safety by identifying with maternal anger at themselves. They act as if pursuing their own self-fulfilling agendas were an outrageous affront, just as their fathers' or their own similar pursuits were in their mothers' eyes, and they once again direct anger away from angry, *nostos*-destroying mothers to their offending fathers and selves. The goddesses do not have to intervene directly. Dimly aware of the goddesses' threat, and anxious about their exposure to obliterating hate, the Achaians correct their errant behavior.

While the Achaians' violence against the Trojans, and the difference between killer and victim, is all too real (probably historically so, with innumerable parallels from that day to this), the Achaians' intended victims are ultimately themselves. True to their word, they never again expose themselves to danger by letting the hopeful, trusting, relaxed mortal in them rear its head—at least not until the goddesses' hateful business is done. But Hera's bargain with Zeus—also conceived beyond the Achaians' awareness—reminds the audience that even after the defeat of the Trojans this would be a mistake: destruction awaits them all. After Menelaos is nearly killed, the Achaians never again try to do anything but make a mockery of Trojan pretensions to be able to realize dreams of happiness and order, grinding these Zeus-identified, Zeus-beloved architects and defenders of familial and civic order into dust, in accord with Hera's wishes. In effect, they try to kill the (momentarily) trusting, confident, vulnerable Menelaos in themselves.

Hera and Athena give the Achaians a refresher course in heroic responses to vengeful maternal anger. Although Agamemnon is the only one who articulates and enacts it, the message of the episode has general application. Achaians, Trojans, and the *Iliad*'s auditors all learn that men who place confidence in their ability to restore order in the midst of violent strife are fools, innocent children, who open themselves to destruction—which, they are dimly aware, is orchestrated by angry goddesses. Any resurgence of confidence in their intelligence and power to realize dreams of happy marital, parent-child, and civic orders, apart from dishonored mothers' agendas—and any joyful anticipation of the same—is illusory. The height of dangerous folly, it must be disavowed and eradicated.

When the Achaian heroes go back to their habitual demonstrations of godlike superiority and to proving the folly of trust in order-making abilities, their principal means of doing so is to make victims of the Trojans. Demonstrating their own irresistible might and mocking the Trojans' aspirations to create and protect human orders, the Achaians kill Trojan men and force their wives and daughters into concubinage.

Conveniently for the Achaians, this accords with the punishment prescribed for oath-breakers: "Let their brains be spilled on the ground as this wine is spilled now, / theirs and their sons', and let their wives be the spoil of others" (3.301–2). Just as Hera provokes the oath-breaking to further her revenge, so the Achaians use a pious concern for the sanctity of oaths and marriage, guaranteed by Zeus Horkios, the keeper of oaths, and by Hera, patroness of marriage (15.39–40), to mask their habitual exercise of intoxicating force by violating the marriages and families of weaker, more human others. What fools the soft, home-loving Trojans are to think they have a chance against hardened, ruthless Achaian marauders. The Trojans are the mother bird and her innocent young; the Achaians, the snake that will devour them.

The odd thing is, despite its role in underwriting Achaian martial culture, the *Iliad* suggests that the Trojans do have a chance. Indeed, as long as they stick to defending their marriages, families, and city against the kind of arrogant presumption of superiority that Achilles and Thetis represent, the Trojans are invincible. The Trojans expose their city to ruin only when Hektor, boasting that even Achilles may fall before his spear, ignores the good counsel of Poulydamas. Against the advice of Poulydamas, Hektor orders the Trojans to abandon their defensive posture and remain outside their walls so they can press their attack on the Achaians, rather than retreat behind the walls of their city as they normally do at the end of the day's fighting. Fools (*nêpioi*), their wits (*phrenas*) stolen by Athena, the Trojans thunderously applaud Hektor's "counsel of evil" (18.249–313).

The Trojans make themselves vulnerable when they try to have it both ways: to have apparent invulnerability (symbolized, in Hektor's case, by donning Achilles' divine armor, stripped from Patroklos's corpse), irresistible force, and the glamour of Achilles' quasi-divinity, while at the same time maintaining their confident—but also prudent—trust in themselves and others in a world they know to be dangerous. Achilles' kinder, gentler alter ego, Patroklos, loses his *nostos* by exceeding his charge in much the same way—also while wearing Achilles' armor.

So it is not having the temerity to stand up to the hard, invincible Achaian agents of Hera's revenge but Hektor's attempt to rival the irresistible *biê* of Achilles that constitutes Hektor's madness and dangerous folly. Even after Hektor's death at the hands of enraged and pitiless Achilles, the might (*biê*) of Achilles and his fellow Achaians is not enough to bring about Trojan defeat. For that the Achaians once again require the *mêtis* of Odysseus, who devises a ruse to get the Trojans to let the Achaians inside their walls.

For the most part, the Trojans embody an alternative to the typical Achaian response to the vulnerability attendant upon attempts to construct orders based on mutual trust and reciprocity. Rather than try to destroy the vulnerable mortal in themselves, they build a wall around their city that both acknowledges their vulnerability and announces their determination to protect their marital, familial, and civic orders from threats like that posed by the predatory Achaians. The Achaians, on the other hand, embody the opposite: the attempt to kill vulnerability itself and, along with it, attempts to make and sustain harmonious order. As usual, such dichotomies mask underlying similarities: the Achaians' ostensible purpose in attacking Troy is to protect their marriages, and the wives they love and care for, from the likes of Paris. As for the Trojans, they themselves are far from immune to the glamorous appeal of apparent invulnerability and irresistible might that motivates the Achaians far more than the sanctity of oaths and the protection of the marriages they flee.

By reverting to type, and going back to proving the folly of the Trojans' supposedly foolish confidence in their ability to defend their city, the Achaians perform a similar operation on themselves. The illusory confidence of Menelaos, and his obliviousness to the maternal anger provoked by his happy disregard, is just too anxiety-provoking. It must be forever renounced and snuffed out. On this as on similar occasions, evidently "battle became sweeter to them than to go back / in their hollow ships to the beloved land of their fathers" (2.254–55, 11.13–14; cf. 18.109–10).

Ironically, even as they vow never again to behave like naïvely trusting children, returning to a safe identification with vengeful maternal anger allows the Achaians to believe that it can never threaten them. Indeed, their identification with angry mothers lulls them to sleep, enabling them to trust the very goddesses who demand that they sacrifice their joyfully anticipated *nostoi*.

Athena orchestrates Menelaos's near-death experience to provoke a resumption of reciprocal killing between Achaians and Trojans. Yet when she deflects Pandaros's arrow from its deadly path, the *Iliad* likens the goddess to a mother who brushes a fly away from her sleeping child—completely vulnerable, totally trusting, and, evidently, justifiably so. Thus the *Iliad* not only sustains this illusion of the protectiveness of child-sacrificing mothers, it enacts before our eyes the denial that turns angry, *nostos*-taking goddesses into benign protectors, and their sacrificial victims into trusting, protected children. Of course, this particular metaphorical mother lets the arrow tear her child's flesh just a little so its point will not be lost on him, or on his brother the king.[4]

The sleight of hand that allows hero-sons to believe themselves loved and cared for by angry wives and mothers renders them defenseless against female anger: the fury of wives who themselves have had their trust abused, who equate promises of *themis* and trust in fathers and husbands with betrayal and dishonor, who are afraid that they can have no honored roles in peaceful orders characterized by *themis*, and who regard anyone who promises them otherwise as just another outrageous betrayer. The episode that teaches the Achaians not to make themselves vulnerable by trusting their own judgment and powers dramatizes a mechanism that renews their trust in, even as it increases their vulnerability to, unreconstructed, angry mothers and spouses.

By restoring hero-sons' trust in the love of angry mothers and spouses, without requiring these sons to undertake the perilous and uncertain labor of building relationships that would justify that trust, attempts to deny and eliminate vulnerability actually increase it. Hero-sons are set up to participate in an endlessly repeated cycle of blind trust, oblivious to gathering maternal or spousal anger, and trauma-based, traumatic devastation, which only confirms the cultural equation of trust with naïve folly. (Here again, Agamemnon represents the supposedly unique but actually typical example.)

By denying that they have ever felt or could ever feel the destructive touch of the goddesses' anger, the Achaians lose the opportunity to understand and confront it. They also lose any chance to overcome their wives' doubts and fears, actively reassuring these ultimately fearful "goddesses"—their "divine" wives and mothers, who seem to posses irresistible power, but who also equate trust with dishonor and folly—that their ordinary dreams of mutually respectful and loving marriage are not vile deceptions.

While identification with the aggressor and denial make it possible for hero-sons to love and trust angry goddesses as if they were protective, loving, and caring mothers, the Achaians not only collude in these mothers' and daughters' angry dismantling of others' attempts to achieve *themis*, they also forgo an alternative and riskier, but self-affirming rather than self-destructive, path to loving relationships with angry wives and mothers. None from Zeus on down asserts *themis* in the face of destructive female anger.

None reassure and honor their promises to devoted daughters and mistrustful, self-doubting, wives.

If, when they are at home, the Achaians alternate between being naïve fools, happily unaware of the gathering storm of maternal-wifely anger that is about to engulf them, and being defenseless victims of that anger, it is not surprising that they prefer battlefields far from home, where unthreatening, childless concubines substitute for threatening, mother-like wives. (Unlike Troy, the Achaian camp is devoid of toddlers.) It makes sense as well for the Achaians to align themselves with angry mothers, while projecting onto others and attempting to eradicate the naïve fool in themselves.

In their return to the fighting after the truce is broken, as in the *Iliad* generally, the sense of power the Achaians achieve when they "remember their warcraft" and become destroyers aligned with maternal anger is evident. It is also evident that, once the heroic warrior culture is up and running, and the battle is joined, sons are generally victims of other sons, rather than direct victims of maternal anger; they sacrifice themselves by becoming victims of sons who are themselves the agents of humiliated mothers. Killer sons experience their victims as other than themselves. Otherwise they could hardly experience themselves as becoming powerful by aligning themselves with, and doing the bidding of, angry goddesses.

The resolution of the truce-breaking episode puts on display all of the key elements of the experience of identification with the aggressor, including those that make aggression attractive, even addictive. On the Homeric battlefield (as opposed to the home front), as in the hero-sons' psyches, the actual, day-to-day aggressors against sons' humanity are sons themselves, who are anxious to maintain their alignment with angry mothers. (This is not to suggest that this aggressive self-policing would cease if hero-sons were to return home, only that it might be supplemented—as in Agamemnon's supposedly atypical case—by spousal aggression.) In any event, proving others' hopes of *nostoi* illusory provides hero-sons with a safe alternative to standing up for their own, similar aspirations, which are liable to provoke maternal anger. They experience the power of the destroyer and do not feel the fear, defenselessness, and devastation of the victim. This is precisely the point of identifying with the aggressor while dissociating from the self that is its victim.

Eliminated from the experience of identification with maternal aggressors is any awareness or acknowledgment that the sense of empowerment that results from it represents a reversal from being a helpless victim, damaged, as Hephaistos is, by maternal shame and anger. In place of this recognition, or overlaying and partly obscuring it in the episode, is denial. The goddesses' implacable fury at their Achaian protégés' heedless infatuation with peace and order notwithstanding, these Achaian sons rest assured that they have no more to fear from their angry maternal patronesses than a trusting babe who sleeps while his loving mother watches over him.

In the incident we have been considering, the truce cannot stand because it would frustrate Hera's insatiable desire for revenge. Much like Agamemnon at the beginning of the *Iliad*, Hera and Athena literally do not care whether their beloved Achaians—whom Zeus mocks Hera for mothering—die, so long as the goddesses' desire for honor and revenge is served.

Yet here as elsewhere, denial must have its due. Not only does Thetis's anger remain potential and tacit, sustaining the apparent antithesis between her and Hera, but Achilles is not even present when a vengeful divine mother, Hera, takes away the *nostoi* of her adoptive hero-sons. Even so, the potential anger of Thetis, which parallels the overt anger of Hera and Athena, ties Achilles to this root dynamic of heroic character, which castigates confidence in order-making ability as dangerous folly. If Achilles were to forget his divine mothers' business, and give rein to his suppressed longing for a *nostos*, it might provoke powerful maternal anger, just as the Achaians' momentary attempt to opt out of the sacrifice of *nostos* for mother-vindicating revenge and glory does. Could the paradigmatic hero, Achilles, ever suffer such a lapse?

Even though, in keeping with the supposed antithesis between Hera and Thetis, the latter's potential anger at mortal self-assertion is kept in the background, it is no less implicated in this undermining of confidence and hope. While Zeus openly baits Hera and Athena, and Thetis is absent from the scene, a peaceful resolution to the conflict would be no less infuriating to the mother of Achilles since it would scuttle her plan to efface her humiliation and vindicate her claims to superiority through the glory of her son. Just as the anger of Hera and Athena are in the background, building up and preparing to demonstrate that Achaian confidence in their Zeus-like, order-creating ability is dangerous folly, so too is the anger of Thetis.

The Achaians' and Trojans' lapse into self-assertion and their exercise of paternal and kingly responsibility interfere with Thetis's plans no less than Hera's. When her son's promised glory is threatened by Agamemnon, she dons a black robe signifying her potentially devastating *mênis*. If Zeus did cast down love between Achaians and Trojans, would Thetis return to Olympos to remind Zeus of his promise to give honor to her son? Typically, Zeus opts not to find out. Just as he agrees to let Hera have her way with the Trojans, so he sticks to his agreement to give honor to Thetis's son. Deflecting onto hapless mortals the twin threats posed by Thetis and her mighty son, as well as by Hera and her co-conspirators, including the mighty son of Leto, is what the plan of Zeus is all about. Whatever the Achaians and Trojans may foolishly believe, their peace plan is doomed from the start.

Once again the offending mortal who interferes in Thetis's plans for vindication—as well as Hera's plans for revenge—is Agamemnon. It is he who promotes the peace plan that inflames Hera's (and, potentially, Thetis's) anger. We have already seen the divine *mênis* (channeled through Achilles) that such interference provokes. In this instance, Agamemnon actually performs the kingly functions that give him a claim to superior honor. And yet, like the interfering mortal father in myth, he abandons the pursuit at the first hint of divine maternal anger.

Achilles has no part in the Achaian and Trojan departure from scripts of maternal revenge and vindication. On the contrary, his absence is part of his mother-backed plan to vindicate his honor, a goal that Hera and Athena also endorse. It would appear that, unlike Agamemnon and his fellow Achaians, Achilles is not the sort to depart from maternal agendas, much less to succumb to the folly of believing in and pursuing a *nostos* against a fate that coincides with maternal agendas. Achilles consciously sacrifices his safe return home from Troy to pursue unmatched glory. That being the case, he could never experience the terror that the Achaians, particularly Agamemnon and Menelaos, do when they are seduced by false dreams of ending the war and returning safely home.

Yet Achilles' ambivalence about carrying out his mother-backed plan of revenge and vindication returns with a vengeance. Patroklos's intervention on behalf of the suffering Achaians, and Achilles' unanswered prayer to Zeus to let Patroklos return safely home; the return of Priam's son Lykaon from the servitude into which Achilles sold him, only to be killed by Achilles; the river god Skamander's failed intervention to protect the Trojans; and Hektor's futile attempt to escape Achilles' wrath—all these manifest both the hero-son's irrepressible belief in the possibility of a *nostos* and his need to destroy this dangerous illusion, which sets him at odds with maternal demands for revenge and vindication. Achilles is devastated when his hope for the safe return of his alter ego, Patroklos, proves illusory. The resurfacing of his aspirations to protect rather than sacrifice familial and civic orders provokes increasingly intense anxiety. The manner in which Achilles allays this anxiety demonstrates the link between Achaian violence against the Trojans and the hero-son's disavowing, projecting onto others, and killing *nostos*-seeking parts of himself. Here too, Achilles' ambivalence surfaces: as a hero who sides with mothers against fathers—and against his father-admiring self—might well do, he reproaches himself for abandoning his father, and even for emasculating Priam, by destroying his line of strong sons.

Chapter Eight

Self in Crisis

In the last third of the *Iliad*, Achilles' beloved companion, Patroklos, and his bitter enemy, Hektor, die wearing Achilles' armor, their deaths prefiguring Achilles' own. In gratitude to Thetis for nursing him when his own mother, shamed by her infant son's deformity, threw him off Olympos, Hephaistos fashions splendid new armor for Achilles. It replaces the armor that Patroklos used to impersonate Achilles, going to the aid of the Achaians in his place, which a vaunting Hektor stripped from Patroklos's corpse. Like his heroic brother, Hektor, Priam's unwarlike son, Lykaon, shares the epithet "short-lived" (*minunthadios*) with Achilles and claims kinship with him (21.74–96, 15.612). After marking the contrast between Lykaon and "huge and splendid" heroes like himself and Patroklos, Achilles kills the unarmed suppliant and flings his body into a river. Revolted by Achilles' savagery and angered by his taunts, the river Skamander, a minor deity and Troy's protector, surges, boasting that Achilles' might and splendid armor will not save him from ignominious death by drowning. Hera sends Poseidon and Athena to reassure the terrified hero, who fears that his mother betrayed him when she promised he would be killed by Apollo under the walls of Troy. Hera orders her son, "god of the dragging feet," Hephaistos, to subdue the river. Skamander's protectiveness toward the Trojans, like Patroklos's toward the suffering Achaians, resonates with Achilles' own—before his lethal anger overwhelms it.

Patroklos's tearful supplication of Achilles to rescue the Achaians precipitates a crisis for the son of Thetis. Elements of his character that are at odds with his heroic destiny rise up and are subdued or eliminated. But what elements? What destiny? How formed? To what ends?

PURGATION AND THE SHIFT
OF RESPONSIBILITY AND ANGER

The first word of the *Iliad*, *mênis*, marks the beginning of a process that shifts responsibility and anger from the hero-son's superior, child-sacrificing mother to the hero-son. Achilles directs his wrath at a scapegoat. Neither the divine mother nor his complicit, ineffectual father is responsible for the outrageous devaluation and betrayal of trust that reduces the hero-son to a "dishonored vagabond." That distinction belongs to Agamemnon, a father and king who dishonors Achilles, betrays his people's trust, and sacrifices them as he sacrifices his daughter. Far from devaluing Achilles, his divine mother defends his honor as her more-than-mortal offspring.

The anger purged by this process is provoked by the destruction of an imagined world of *themis* in which parents reciprocally love, care for, and respect each other; parent-child boundaries and roles are intact; and children's care-seeking calls forth parents' loving, value-affirming care-giving. The first destroyer of this world is Achilles' superior mother. Mirroring her relationship with her seductive father, she rejects her son as an ordinary, care-seeking child while constructing him as superior to his father, and indeed to mortal fathers and kings generally. The *nostos* that Achilles sacrifices to glory represents an imagined return to a world that, for the mother-identified hero-son, has been obliterated from the beginning.[1]

The shift of responsibility and redirection of anger at this loss to Agamemnon initiates, for the audience, a collective cathartic process that purges heroic culture not only of aggression but of an array of threats engendered by sacrificial parenting. Chief among these are parts of the self that perceive and respond to child-sacrifice. The normal operation of heroic culture involves relegating parts of the self at odds with maternal (and paternal) agendas to suppressed working models, projecting them onto others, and killing them. But heroic violence fails to eradicate these parts of the self. Even the gates of Hades cannot prevent their return. They pose a continuing threat not only to hero-sons but to heroic culture itself. This is where the *Iliad*, in concert with other cathartic narratives and sacrificial rituals, comes in.

The last nine books of the *Iliad* bring to completion a collective, cathartic process that eliminates these threats to heroic culture. They complete the shift of responsibility and anger for the sacrifice of Achilles' *nostos* from the hero-son's parents to himself. Achilles imagines that he will return to battle in response to Agamemnon's supplication. He imagines that his alter ego, Patroklos, will have the *nostos* that Achilles sacrifices to glory. But Zeus has a different plan. The killing of Patroklos will shift Achilles' anger from

Agamemnon to Hektor and the Trojans. In the end, Achilles holds himself responsible for his mother's sacrifice of his *nostos*. In the paradigm case of Odysseus, the term *nostos* denotes a return to reciprocal love and care between spouses who provide examples and guidance for children in accord with *themis*. It is a return to what, in Achilles' case, never was and never will be.

Achilles' ambivalence about carrying through his and Thetis's plan for humiliating Agamemnon, by allowing the Trojans to destroy Achilles' erstwhile comrades, precipitates a crisis. The barrier separating the hero-son's manifest and suppressed working models becomes permeable, threatening Achilles with terrifying insignificance. A parade of suppressed or denied aspects of the hero-son's self, all threatening Achilles with a loss of divine maternal favor, supplicate Achilles and are destroyed. These alter egos represent Achilles' attachment to life; his bitterness at cold, exploitative parenting; and his powerlessness to get the attention of a mother preoccupied with revenge or vindication at the expense of fathers, potential friends (e.g., the Achaians' Trojan oath-friends in book 4), and the hero-son himself. The relationship between crippled, resentful Hephaistos and rejecting Hera, desperate to have a glorious son and humiliated by her inability to produce one, itself represents a suppressed working model of the relationship of divine mother and hero-son. The manifest working model is the relationship between Achilles and Thetis in the *Iliad*—or Leto and Apollo, or Demeter and the infant, Demophoon. Hephaistos's resentment of his "bitch-faced" mother's rejection is invoked as part of the cathartic process brought to completion in the last nine books.

As if the grievous harm involved in the sacrifice of hero-sons by divine mothers were not enough, fathers from Zeus on down have their own sacrificial agendas: they expect sons to pay the price for effacing the shame and humiliation that fathers bring on themselves. But fathers who depend on sons' sacrifices to maintain their authority are threatened by sons' prowess and mother-derived sense of superiority. In the end, fathers and kings inflict Zeus-backed *mênis* on the sons who sacrifice for them. Cursing them as usurpers, they sacrifice their sons. Zeus's critical modification of Achilles' plan, the death of Patroklos, may manifest Zeus's *mênis* at Achilles.

Having left unprotected or killed a series of alter egos whose irruptions threaten him with the loss of maternal favor, Achilles takes responsibility for these losses, even though the hero's parents are initially and primarily responsible. Achilles' acceptance of the loss of his *nostos*, which is required for his mother's vindication and may also represent the execution of a Zeus-backed paternal curse, concludes the series of self-destructions that comprise the last third of the *Iliad* and complete the poem's cathartic process.

LEARNING THROUGH SUFFERING
AND ACHILLES AS A MODEL KING

Understanding the death of Patroklos in this larger context has implications for the idea that Achilles undergoes a precursor of tragic "learning through suffering." The death of his friend brings home to Achilles the meaning of the losses he suffers and inflicts on friends and enemies alike. This painful process is remarkable for its sorrowful awareness of the devastating cost of heroic achievement, not just to self and friend but to foe as well. The recognition is undeniable, but its significance can be overestimated. As a cathartic narrative, the *Iliad* ultimately sustains rather than undermines a heroic culture of violence. Although the wisdom it imparts may be mistaken for a critique of the heroic ethos, it is anything but. This is in no small part because Achilles' chastening wisdom represents not only learning but unlearning, effacing knowledge of routine parental betrayal, hostility, and neglect.[2]

The process of disinformation, although completed in the last third of the epic, begins with the *Iliad*'s first word. By directing his *mênis* at Agamemnon, Achilles absolves his self-absorbed, child-sacrificing parents of responsibility for devaluing him and sacrificing his *nostos*. They are not culpable, *aitios*; Agamemnon is. By the end of the *Iliad*, Achilles himself is *aitios*. The *Iliad* enacts the turning of the responsibility arrow—with its corresponding anger—away from the hero-son's rejecting mother and threatened, ambivalent father to third parties, and ultimately to the hero-son himself. The *mênis* of Achilles at Agamemnon marks the beginning of this process, but the epic's first lines also foretell its end. Achilles' destructive *mênis* sends the souls of myriad heroes to Hades, including his own.[3]

The *Iliad*'s "learning through suffering" is embedded in a larger process of obfuscation. Discrediting the hero-son's mistreatment by caregivers, as well as the idea that he inflicts suffering on others at the behest of caregivers (gentle Thetis is not vengeful Hera), it obliterates the experiential basis for learning—and action—that could break intergenerational cycles of child-sacrifice. While this would radically enhance individual and collective well-being and produce a renaissance of political aspiration and intelligence, it would undermine heroic culture. Accordingly, the learning that Achilles undergoes in the last third of the *Iliad* obscures formative experiences underlying heroic character by denying his experience as an outraged victim of parental betrayal, exploitation, and aggression, and by shifting responsibility and anger for the grief (*achos*) he suffers from parents to parent-substitutes, to alter egos, and, finally, to himself. In so doing, he plays the pivotal role in a narrative that could not be better suited to induce collective catharsis and denial if it were consciously designed with that end in mind.[4]

Like interpretations that affirm Achilles' self-presentation as a hero who speaks truth to power, attempts to style Achilles as a model ruler in the closing books of the *Iliad* fail to recognize the violence-promoting, abuse-denying function of the narrative of which he is the protagonist. Achilles demonstrates his kingliness while presiding over the funerals of Patroklos and Hektor, alter egos who represent his own potential kingliness, whom he exposed to violence or killed himself, and whose funerals presage his own. Not coincidentally, these destroyed aspirations to realize his kingly potential threaten to transmute his glory into (in his mother-identified view) terrifying, ignominious insignificance. His self-assigned responsibility for the deaths of Patroklos and the sons of Priam becomes yet another reason to efface the last vestige of his desire to return home to be a king in Phthia: he must die an atoning death at Troy. Achilles' model kingship thus completes a lifelong, parent-initiated process of eradicating his aspirations to create and participate in orders embodying *themis*. He presides with grace and skill over funerals that rehearse his own. He mourns parent-inflicted losses as if he alone were to blame for them. Achilles' model kingship epitomizes the fearful abandonment of kingly aspirations and abilities that is a cardinal feature of heroic culture.[5]

ALTER EGOS AS VICTIMS I: PATROKLOS

Patroklos embodies a variety of characteristics of the hero-son that stand in the way of his achievement of mother-avenging, mother-vindicating glory. Most obviously, he represents Achilles' ambivalence about giving up his *nostos*. Achilles' compassionate friend also embodies Achilles' love for his comrades, which finally undercuts the ruthlessness he needs to carry out his and Thetis's plan.

Observing the effects of his absence on the Achaians, Achilles anticipates with pleasure the supplication that their "need past endurance" will force them to make. Yet Achilles sends Patroklos to ascertain the identity of a wounded Achaian. Here, as elsewhere, Patroklos acts as an extension of Achilles. Although Achilles seems indifferent to his comrades' fates, his emissary will not be, and this is the "beginning of evil" for both (11.604–15).

Moved by the suffering he encounters, Patroklos approaches Achilles in tears, begging him to aid their fellow Achaians. In his role as suppliant, Patroklos embodies other denied aspects of hero-sons' working models of their relationships with superior mothers—including their objections to maternal vindictiveness and their powerlessness in the face of it. Achilles' response to Patroklos's supplication dramatizes a hero-son's (for the moment nonviolent) attempt to exchange the role of hurt and disregarded or mocked child-victim for maternal victimizer. Achilles pities Patroklos, but he also likens him to some "poor little girl (*kourê nêpiê*; 16.7–8)" trying vainly to get her mother's attention. Mocking Patroklos in this way, Achilles dramatizes denied aspects of the heroic mother-son relationship. Identifying with the mother who dominates it, he gives the son's part to Patroklos. The term *nêpiê*, which Achilles uses to identify Patroklos as a little girl, marks his friend for death.[6]

Achilles puts Patroklos in a position analogous to that of an ostensibly mother-favored son who is distraught over his honor-obsessed mother's destruction of the familial order. He approaches her, seeking comfort in his distress, but he cannot get her attention. Identifying with the vindictive mother, Achilles mocks and denies his own childish weakness and powerlessness in relation to her. Indeed, Achilles' coldly ironic query about what is troubling the weeping Patroklos—"Is it the Argives you are mourning over, and how they are dying . . . by reason of their own arrogance (*huperbasiês*; 16.16–18)"—echoes Thetis's query about what is troubling the weeping Achilles in book 1. Like Achilles, Patroklos groans heavily as he replies.[7]

Thus Achilles plays the part of a hero-son's mother. She is a favored daughter and humiliated wife like Thetis or Hera who, to her son's dismay, scorns or takes revenge on his father. She wreaks havoc on a familial order that should be based on reciprocal love and care. Certain that Agamemnon and his fellow Achaians are blameworthy, and consumed with his mother-supported desire to punish them, Achilles is impervious to Patroklos's distress at the devastating effects of his anger. Since the Argives have tacitly dishonored Thetis by failing to honor and support her son, the destructive anger that Patroklos is powerless to avert is an extension of Thetis's. Achilles acts on her behalf as well as his own when he makes the Achaians pay for their supposed arrogance.[8]

Prefaced by the same phrase as Achilles' response to this mother in book 1, Patroklos's response to Achilles manifests the most dangerous aspect of the hero-son's disavowed self, relegated to suppressed working models of his relationships with his mother and father. Reproaching Achilles for his pitilessness (*nêlees*) and "cursed courage (*ainaretê*)," Patroklos ironically suggests that Achilles' hardness of heart stems from his upbringing by inhuman parents—the rock and the grey sea, which happens to be Thetis's element (16.31–35). (He is echoed by the Achaians, who also blame angry Achilles for his hardness of heart and pitilessness [*nêlees*], which they ironically attribute to his mothering: "Your mother nursed you [*etrephe*] on gall" [*cholôi*; anger, 16.202–4].) Of course the hero-son's parents *are* inhuman, and anger is a critical factor in Thetis's mothering. His mother regards herself as above having to provide ordinary, loving nurture, and his father identifies with her outrage at his own criticism of her superior childrearing methods. Achilles' imperviousness to the Achaians' suffering is integral to the plan that he and his mother devise and that she supplicates Zeus to accomplish. The Achaians must suffer things that are shameful so that they will be forced to supplicate her son, thereby magnifying her *kleos*—the glory of Thetis—as well as his.

Patroklos and the Achaians utter fundamental truths about the parents not just of Achilles, but of hero-sons generally, but with an irony that discredits them as absurd. At the same time, Patroklos's bitterness, which would have been directed at Achilles' parents as well as their son had his ironic characterization of them been true, falls on Achilles alone for failing to beat destruction away from the Achaians. And although Achilles mocks Patroklos's concern in terms that seal his friend's doom, he will presently ordain his own death for failing to protect his friend and his other companions (18.101).

Patroklos concludes by entreating Achilles to let him aid the Achaians in Achilles' place—and in his armor—so the Trojans might mistake him for Achilles. In so doing, Patroklos is *mega nêpios*, since he supplicates his own death (16.46).

As an alter ego, Patroklos threatens Achilles (and Thetis) in yet another way: he may steal Achilles' glory. Achilles' instructions to Patroklos are notable for the frank concern and anxiety they betray about his own honor, which overshadow his concern for his friend's safety. Patroklos can beat back the Trojan attack. This will prompt the Achaians to honor Achilles. But Patroklos must not take the battle to the Trojans, lest he diminish Achilles' honor and provoke Apollo's lethal anger (16.80–96). Since challenging Apollo is what the greatest heroes do, Achilles implicitly compares Patroklos to himself. Reversing roles once again with his divine mother, he conceives of his friend's return to battle as a lethal test like those the goddess-mother uses to cull her merely mortal children. The results will show whether Patroklos is invincible on his own or only when he fights alongside Achilles (16.242–45).[9]

Possessed by fighting fury, Patroklos disregards Achilles' warning. As a result, he encounters first Apollo and then Hektor, whom, had Apollo not intervened, Patroklos would have killed, stealing Achilles'—and his mother's—destined glory. (Even by beating destruction away from the Achaians [*loigon amunôn*] and preserving what Achilles calls "our desired homecoming" [*philon noston*; 16.82], Patroklos encroaches on the preeminent hero's domain.) Accordingly, Patroklos's death does not just eliminate a frighteningly powerless and insignificant alter ego, or a critic of parents who substitute inhuman coldness for love and care, or (like Hektor) a more human, and therefore vulnerable, version of Achilles himself. In a more sinister vein, the violent death of Achilles' friend eliminates a threat to Achilles' claim to superiority to mere mortals.[10]

Paralleling the explicit threat to Achilles' honor is an implicit one to Thetis's: if Patroklos, a purely mortal hero like Hektor, is indistinguishable from Achilles, perhaps Thetis is no different from other mothers, and the presumption of her categorical superiority, on which family claims to superiority are based and which keeps family humiliations at bay, is empty pretense. When both Patroklos and Hektor don Achilles' armor, they threaten Achilles' and his divine mother's claim to a glory that is not only imperishable but, crucially, beyond compare. When Thetis mourns Patroklos's loss of his *nostos* and early death as if he were Achilles, she mourns a loss that she inflicted.[11]

Achilles' own prophesied death—in an ambush by the arrows of Apollo and Paris—lacks the greatness of Patroklos's, or even Diomedes', confrontation with Apollo. The closest Achilles comes to such a confrontation in the *Iliad* is when he kills Apollo's protégé, Hektor. But Apollo has already abandoned Hektor to his fate. Yet Patroklos's *aristeia* and death constitute an enactment within the *Iliad* of Achilles' implicit challenge to Apollo's superiority, which is characteristic of the greatest of heroes, and which, as Achilles foresees for Patroklos, provokes Apollo's lethal response.

In scenes in which Apollo beats back overreaching heroes, the god patrols the boundary between divine and mortal. He represents the limit of heroic striving. But precisely because Apollo also represents the ideal of irresistible force that the mortal hero can never quite attain, his hostility to the greatest heroes can be viewed as manifesting a particular kind of self-division in hero-sons. Apollo exposes the vulnerability that invalidates the hero-son's claim to divine maternal acceptance. In destroying or threatening to destroy the son as great but vulnerable hero (Patroklos; Diomedes—who backs off; Achilles), Apollo shows himself to be other than and superior to his flawed heroic victim. In this, he personifies the part of the hero-son's divided self that anxiously scans the supposedly superior, victorious, triumphant hero for vulnerabilities that render him unworthy of divine maternal acceptance after all. Here as elsewhere, it is as the imagined destroyer of his own flawed, vulnerable humanity that the hero-son experiences himself as invulnerable and flawless.[12]

By threatening to turn Achilles into a weak—but also human, mother-criticizing—little girl, as well as by threatening to steal Achilles' glory, Patroklos puts at risk not only Achilles' glory but his accomplishment of Hera's and Thetis's revenge and vindication. Apollo, Achilles' divine-mother-pleasing ideal, disarms Patroklos so Hektor can destroy this abandoned aspect of Achilles' self. Here as elsewhere, the glorious divine son preemptively performs the mother's dirty work, allowing her to maintain the appearance of a loving, son-nurturing, *kourotrophos* goddess. The child-sacrificing hands of Thetis and Hera are no more visible in the death of Achilles' beloved companion than they are (to the Achaians) in the resumption of war when the

Achaians' peace plan, and Zeus's mock plan to let it succeed, provoke the anger of Hera, Athena, and, tacitly, Thetis.

Indeed, Thetis expunges her part in the plan that results in Patroklos's death. When Achilles is once again groaning heavily, this time over the death of his friend, Thetis again asks her grieving son what is troubling him. Much as Achilles feigns ignorance of the cause of Patroklos's distress, so Thetis, with similar insensitivity, affects to wonder why her son is troubled. After all, he got what he prayed for (18.74–75). But it is not only Achilles who prays to Zeus that Hektor be given the strength to drive the Achaians back to their ships. Thetis's supplication (backed by the threat of her *mênis*) secures Zeus's assent to a plan that ensures her glory as well as Achilles'. *Nêpios* Achilles does not know that putting the plan in action will result in Patroklos's death. Achilles prays for Patroklos's safe return, which would pose a threat to Thetis's glory as well as his own. Achilles' prayer goes unanswered.[13]

Patroklos's death makes clear that Achilles had not so much given up his *nostos* as invested it in his alter ego. Imagining a vicarious *nostos* through Patroklos long masked the pain and outrage of Achilles' initial loss—of a familial order of reciprocal love and care and his place in it. With this loss comes another: devaluation of and dissociation from the self that aspired to restore such an order (as Odysseus did in his *nostos*), as well as the perceptions and judgments required to guide such an effort—a disability that is not just personal but political.

Achilles prayed to Zeus for a *nostos* in which Patroklos would perform the roles of father and, perhaps, husband in place of Achilles. Achilles imagines Patroklos taking Achilles' son home to Peleus and showing him the house, land, servants, and possessions that would have constituted Achilles' patrimony (19.328–37). They would also have constituted his son's, equipping him to be king over Phthia. Mourning Patroklos, Briseis recalls his promise to persuade Achilles to make her his lawful wife on Achilles' return, thus supplying another element of Achilles' imagined *nostos* (19.297–99). Achilles equates Patroklos's death with his own (18.81–82).

Praying to Zeus to grant Patroklos both glory and a safe return home (*aponeesthai*—"have a *nostos*"), Achilles tries to have it both ways. He seeks to avoid paying the price for glory as ordained by his choice of fates. Accordingly, in refusing to grant his prayer, Zeus appears to uphold *themis*. But Achilles' purported choice to sacrifice his *nostos* for glory is a serviceable fiction. It serves to deny the outrageous loss the hero-son suffers as an unsuspecting, unwilling, defenseless victim (*nêpios*) of child-sacrifice at the hands of a mortal-child-rejecting mother. By the time Zeus strips away Achilles' illusion of a vicarious *nostos* via Patroklos, Thetis's responsibility for the loss of Achilles' *nostos* has long since been effaced.[14]

Achilles' long-suppressed rage at the loss of his *nostos*—via the death of the companion whose life he loves as well as his own—is by turns homicidal and suicidal. No longer is any parent or parent-figure, legitimate or otherwise, *aitios* for the now manifestly outrageous sacrifice of their son's life and the lives of others whose deaths at his hands avenge or vindicate their honor. By the end of the poem, the son alone will be responsible, and prepared to pay the price.

Thus does Patroklos, under the pressure of actually carrying out Achilles' plan of revenge and vindication, threaten to undo the manifold dissociations on which the hero-son's relationship with his superior mother—and the operation of competitive, warlike, archaic Greek culture—depends. But the last nine books of the *Iliad* teem with alter egos, some, like Patroklos, obvious (at least in some respects), others not.[15]

ALTER EGOS AS VICTIMS II: LYKAON

Even Achilles may fear to face a formidable adversary of similarly lofty parentage. When Apollo incites Aphrodite's son, Aineias, to confront Achilles, Hera dispatches Athena and Poseidon to reassure him, but even so he is afraid (20.112–22, 20.261–62). Yet the meaning of this and other fears is most clearly dramatized in a different sort of encounter—between Achilles and the least warlike of Priam's sons, Lykaon. Achilles' former captive arrives on the scene shortly after Patroklos's pity for the Achaians threatens to turn Achilles into a crying little girl, vainly seeking comfort from a mother whose vengefulness distresses him.

Both Hektor and Patroklos (to whom Achilles compares both Lykaon and himself in this passage) represent Achilles' humanity and desire for *nostos*, a life that fulfills the promise of *themis*. Whether or not they are mortal, sons who are human in this sense can never compete with glorious sons like those of Leto or Thetis. In the guise of lesser heroes, these disavowed aspects of self are presented intact. Since as the son of a goddess Achilles is higher born, Patroklos will never be his equal in honor (11.786–87); neither will Hektor, a mere mortal suckled at the breast of a woman (24.57–59). But these mortal heroes are nonetheless strong, brave, and honorable men: *agathoi*.

Like crippled Hephaistos, Lykaon represents a denied aspect of the hero-son's experience of his divine mother's rejection or disregard—he is weak, defenseless, and, like the dozen sons of Priam Achilles captures to sacrifice at Patroklos's funeral, a pure victim of Achilles' irresistible might. From the standpoint of attachment theory, exhausted, overmatched Lykaon, who desires only to return home, represents the need to return to a "secure base," which alternates with a child's exploration and testing of his abilities. It is a need that the mother-of-heroes can neither acknowledge nor meet in her son, and from which the hero-son must therefore dissociate himself.

Lykaon's supplication of Achilles is no more successful than Patroklos's and has the same lethal result. Rather than the value-affirming acknowledgment of kinship Lykaon seeks, this "poor fool" (*nêpie*) and alter ego of the newly anxious Achilles hears "the voice without pity" (21.97–99). The son as helpless victim of destructive maternal force is obviously destined for the suppressed working model of the relationship of divine mother and hero-son. Heroic violence serves many purposes, but at the most basic level it represents the hero-son's endless attempts to prove that he is the "huge and splendid" son of a goddess rather than the care-seeking infant whose needs she cannot meet, and whom she so easily and unexpectedly strips of his ordered world and sense of his own value.

Before a Zeus-empowered Hektor fatally wounded, stripped of armor, and vaunted over Patroklos (after Apollo had stunned and disarmed him), Achilles had "spared many" of the Trojans, including the weak Lykaon: they had done nothing—were not *aitios* (1.153)—to him. Now they are *aitios*, most of all the sons of Priam (21.99–105). But Achilles gives another reason for killing Lykaon. It takes the form of a grim joke, one that illuminates the relationship between heroic psychology and heroic violence. Achilles must kill this son of Priam to reassure himself that he is indeed distinct from Lykaon and his other victims.

> Now as brilliant swift-footed Achilleus saw him and knew him
> naked [*gumnon*] and without helm or shield, and he had no spear left
> but had thrown all these things on the ground, being weary and sweating
> with the escape from the river, and his knees were beaten with weariness.
> Disturbed, Achilleus spoke to his own great-hearted spirit:
> "Can this be? Here is a strange thing that my eyes look on.
> Now the great-hearted Trojans, even those I have killed already,
> will stand and rise up again out of the gloom and the darkness
> as this man has come back and escaped the day without pity
> though he was sold into sacred Lemnos; but the main of the grey sea
> could not hold him, although it holds back many who are unwilling.
> But come now, he must be given a taste of our spearhead
> so that I may know inside my heart and make certain
> whether he will come back even from there, or the prospering
> earth will hold him, she who holds back even the strong man" (21.49–63)

In effect, the reappearance of this tired, unarmed victim prompts Achilles to wonder whether heroic violence works. Does reducing enemies to defenseless victims, pierced by impervious bronze, and thereby stripped of their homecomings, really demonstrate that he is one with irresistible might, derived from his divine mother, and thus distinct from his vulnerable, merely human victims? Like the actual hero-son, whose mother outrageously devalues him and destroys his *nostos* while he is powerless to prevent it, they are soft and defenseless. Will they cross back over the boundary of death and reappear like Lykaon to claim affinity with the hero-son?[16]

Before killing Lykaon, Achilles reasserts the difference between them. Unlike the weak, naked, exhausted Lykaon, Achilles is huge, splendid, and born of a great father and a goddess. Nonetheless, Patroklos, a far better man than Lykaon, was killed, and Achilles too will die. So Lykaon should stop making a fuss and just accept his death.

ALTER EGOS AS VICTIMS III: SKAMANDER AND HEPHAISTOS

When Achilles kills Lykaon and throws his body into the river Skamander, a minor deity, Achilles boasts that the river cannot protect the Trojans. Like Patroklos and Lykaon, the river god seeks relief from Achilles, the source of his distress. He entreats Achilles to stop "cramming the loveliness [*erateina*] of [Skamander's] waters with corpses [*nekuôn*]" (21.217–21). Just before Lykaon appears, a Zeus-empowered Hektor has made a defenseless victim of the companion, Patroklos, who is virtually indistinguishable from Achilles in battle. That same companion, who embodied Achilles' wish for a *nostos*, had also softened Achilles with his pity for his fellow Achaians. He had even jokingly expressed criticism of Thetis and Peleus as parents. Achilles' anxiety about exchanging his honor and glory for terrifying oblivion is thus becoming full-blown.

Since Achilles has heretofore spared many Trojans, selling or ransoming rather than killing them, Skamander's protectiveness toward the Trojans resonates with Achilles' own. Like Patroklos's pity for the Achaians who must die to vindicate Achilles' and Thetis's honor, Skamander's protectiveness toward the Trojans represents an implicit return—like Lykaon's explicit one—of a disowned part of the self, projected onto another. Both stand in the way of Achilles' immortalization, and of his mother's vindication and revenge.

Personified by the angry river god, Skamander, the irruption of revulsion at the killing required by Achilles' service to his divine mothers appears to Achilles as a force outside himself, and it provokes a specific terror: he will die an ignominious death, completely insignificant, most of all to the mother who, he now thinks, falsely promised him imperishable glory. The ironies are great. For once, Achilles holds his own mother responsible for betraying his trust, since it is not any other god but his mother who is *aitios* for his plight. She beguiled him with falsehoods (*pseudessin ethelgen*) and abandoned him to an ignominious death. Instead of being felled by the shafts of Apollo before the gates of Troy as she promised he would be (a variant of her promise of imperishable glory if he sacrifices his *nostos* and dies at Troy), he will die ingloriously, unprotected by his mother or any other god, and his *kleos* will be gone (21.248, 21.269, 21.273–83, 21.288, 21.318–23; cf. 9.410–16).[17]

Achilles accuses his mother in much the same terms as he does Agamemnon and Zeus. Agamemnon beguiled him with words (*exapaphoit' epeessin*), cheated him, and did him hurt (*apatêse kai êliten*; 9.376). Achilles fears that Zeus has done something similar, although the deception is implied rather than stated. Since his mother "bore [him] to be a man with a short life [*minunthadion*], Zeus should grant [him] honour at least." But he has given Achilles "not even a little," since Agamemnon dishonored him (1.352–54).[18]

Zeus does promise to honor short-lived Achilles—in the *Iliad*, after Agamemnon dishonors him. Significantly, Zeus makes the promise in response to Thetis's request. Perhaps it reiterates his earlier promise to give Thetis a glorious (and necessarily short-lived) son to compensate her for the humiliation of her marriage. Thetis's supplication presents Zeus with a choice. He can repay her prior service—and sacrifice—by honoring her son, thus upholding her and Achilles' claims to superiority to ordinary mortals. Or he can refuse, but this would provoke her *mênis*, resulting in a *loigos* of cosmic proportions. (It's about her, how she is being treated, not Achilles: Zeus's refusal would show "by how much [she is] the most dishonored of the gods.") Like Zeus's, Achilles' "choice" is overshadowed by a tacit threat. He can choose to win glory that will testify to his mother's superiority. Or, theoretically, he can decline the "gift" of immortalization and affirm his value as a *nostos*-seeking child. But by depriving Thetis of her compensatory honor, he would risk provoking a mother's (for a child) world-destroying *mênis*.[19]

Achilles' puzzling claim that Zeus should honor him because his mother bore him to be a man with a short life implies that being *minunthadios* is his favor to Zeus, in return for which Zeus should grant him honor. So when Achilles accuses his mother of beguiling him with falsehoods, as Agamemnon did and as Zeus might have done, he treads on dangerous ground. He evokes the context of a false promise to repay a sacrifice with honor. It is as if Achilles accuses his mother of falsely promising to repay with honor his sacrifice *for her* (or, an even more taboo subject, her sacrifice *of him*, as Agamemnon sacrifices the *laos* and his own daughter).[20]

The sacrificial bargains that bind Achilles, Thetis, and Zeus are complex. In exchange for Achilles' and his mother's acceptance of their diminished status, Zeus promises to uphold their claims to an honor superior to any mortal's, including mortal kings like Agamemnon, even if this involves humiliating, displacing, or destroying his mortal counterparts. Achilles' obvious favor to Zeus is not being short-lived, however, but living his short, gloriously destructive life, with its claims to superior honor, as a mortal. Choosing a short life and glory is Achilles' favor not to Zeus but to Thetis. She promised him that if he sacrificed his *nostos* he would win glory at Troy, and when Skamander threatens to drown him, she appears to have promised falsely. So her purported betrayal can be rendered in the same terms as (but with considerably plainer sense than) Zeus's. Since Achilles' mother bore him to be a man with a short life (and promised him a glorious death at Troy), *she* owes him honor at least. But now, it appears, he has not even a little, since Skamander is going to take away not only his heroic victory and death, which would have been immortalized in epic, but the bones and burial mound required for his cult.

Achilles' strength (*biên*), beauty (*eidos*), and "arms in their splendour [*teuchea kala*]"—his superiority in all that he gets from his mother—"will not be enough for him." Instead, Skamander will bury Achilles in mud

> deep, and pile it over with abundance of sands and rubble
> numberless, nor shall the Achaians know where to look for
> his bones to gather them, such ruin will I pile over him.
> And there shall his monument [*sêma*] be made, and he will have no need
> of any funeral mound [*tumbochoês*] (21.316–23)

Achilles himself fears that he will drown like "a boy and a swineherd" (21.282). It is precisely inglorious death and oblivion—the opposite of the glorious death promised him (truthfully, it turns out) by his mother—that Achilles fears from the river's angry surge. By the end of the poem, the self that inhabits the suppressed working model of the son's relationship with his mother is buried deep, but that is after all what is needed to salve Achilles' anxiety, a form of relief that the cathartic epic offers its listeners as well.

Achilles' accusation of maternal betrayal is evidently mistaken. Apparently at the behest of Achilles' alter-mother, Hera, Athena and Poseidon hasten to reassure the son of Thetis that he is not destined to die an ignominious death in the river but to wreak revenge on Hektor and win glory. Hera directs her crippled son to torture into submission the river god who threatens Achilles' glory, as well as her own plans for wreaking vengeance on the Trojans. Here, as elsewhere, Hera stands by Achilles like a mother protecting her son (21.284–97; cf. 20.112–31).

Using fire to turn Skamander's streams into a boiling cauldron, in which Achilles struggles, Hephaistos administers at his mother's behest the trials by boiling water and fire that Thetis uses to separate mortal from immortal in her son (or among her sons) in myth. (Hera herself whips up a firestorm to burn the heads of the Trojans and their armor.) In the *Iliad*'s enactment of these tests, the glorious, soon-to-be-dead hero comes through unscathed—without need (or hope) of an intervening mortal father to pluck him from cauldron or flames. Hera quells the hero-son's anxiety by dispatching her son—a denizen of the hero-son's suppressed working model—to subdue the lingering humanity, personified by Skamander, that makes Achilles anxious. Using fire and boiling water to subdue, at his mother's behest, the interfering mortal part of Achilles that is reluctant to kill those who are *aitios* to her, but not to him, the crippled son of a rejecting mother of heroes works to complete the mythic process by which the divine mother eliminates the mortal part of her offspring. Although Skamander protests that not he but the other gods are *aitios* for protecting the Trojans in the face of her vengeful anger, he promises never again to protect them (21.328–82).[21]

ALTER EGOS AS VICTIMS IV: HEKTOR

Even as Hektor's killing of Patroklos shatters the illusion of a vicarious *nostos* that has anesthetized Achilles against the outrage of his loss, it shifts responsibility for it one step further away from his child-sacrificing parents and one step closer to Achilles himself. This time the culprit is a peer and alter ego rather than a parent-figure. Child-sacrificing Agamemnon, who betrayed and sacrificed his Achaian allies, was himself such a substitute, but now, at his mother's urging, Achilles unsays his anger against Agamemnon and redirects it toward Hektor—his great-hearted companion's murderer—and at himself, for being no light of safety to Patroklos or the other Achaians who fell under Trojan spears in his absence. Thetis's—and Zeus's, Agamemnon's, and Peleus's—sacrifice of Achilles is well on the way to becoming Achilles' atoning sacrifice of himself.

Much is at stake for Thetis in getting Achilles to redirect his anger from Agamemnon to the Trojans, and she plays a critical role in inducing the shift. After Patroklos's death, Thetis comes to comfort her grieving son. Even though she knows that his death must come soon after Hektor's—since by killing him Achilles will win imperishable glory—she nonetheless stokes her son's anger with images of Hektor glorying in the armor he has stripped from Patroklos. Promising to provide him with splendid new armor fashioned by the god Hephaistos, she encourages Achilles once again to beat death away from his afflicted companions (18.125–37). Much as Hera did in book 1, Thetis instructs her son to call an assembly, accept the apology from Agamemnon that he previously rejected, renounce his *mênis* against Agamemnon, and arm himself (19.34–36).

Rather than persuading her son to renounce his *mênis*, which originates in her rejection of him as a mortal, care-seeking child, Thetis induces him to redirect it from Agamemnon to Hektor and the Trojans. Then her son can manifest her superiority, in accord with Zeus's plan for her and Hera's appeasement.

Thetis's role here is analogous to Hera's and Athena's in the truce-breaking. Unlike Hera and Athena, Thetis betrays no sign of the insult to her in the spectacle of a mere mortal likening himself to her son. Thetis uses the image of Hektor glorying in Achilles' armor, which he stripped from the body of Achilles' beloved companion, to whip up her son's anger and to eliminate the last vestiges of his desire to return home. While not evident to the family members of the Trojans he has dispatched, Achilles' ambivalence toward the Trojan adversaries who have done nothing to him presents a serious obstacle to his accomplishment of Hera's revenge and Thetis's vindication. As Pandaros's assassination attempt, orchestrated by Zeus, Hera, and Athena, does for the Achaians, so Hektor's killing of Patroklos, ordained by Zeus, with the support of Thetis, Hera, and Athena, resolves Achilles' vacillation and ambivalence into merciless hate.[22]

Indeed, Hektor must die as much for confusing himself with and comparing himself to Achilles as for killing Patroklos—who had to die for the same reason. No less than Patroklos, Hektor represents the *nostos* Achilles sacrifices to glory. This loving and loved son, husband, and father enacts on a daily basis the safe return home from the fighting—the *nostos*—that Achilles must sacrifice to glory. Hektor's vulnerability to Achilles, and his inferiority in might to (by one count) the five best Achaians, is a measure of the softness and vulnerability that marks the Trojans as the Achaians' victims, and Hektor as Achilles'.

Hektor considers making an appeal to Achilles, as Patroklos, Lykaon, and Skamander did before him, but he imagines himself being killed "naked [*gumnon*]" like Lykaon (22.124, 21.50). Finally, he does approach Achilles, asking him to swear that whoever wins will return the other's corpse. Disclaiming any kinship between them—there can be no oaths between wolves and lambs—Achilles refuses.

Hektor's death scene intimates that he is a double of Achilles and that his death is Achilles' suicide. It emphasizes the mortal vulnerability that not only allows but necessitates killing him.

Achilles is fighting a man (Hektor) dressed in Achilles' armor. Achilles' beautiful armor (22.314, 315) is briefly described, as he scans Hektor's (Achilles') beautiful armor (22.323) for a place to strike him. For a moment we see not one

Achilles but two, the old and the new, one dressed in Peleus's armor, and the other in the armor made by Hephaistos for Thetis. Achilles kills himself. He knows that if he kills Hektor, he will die shortly afterwards (18.95 ff.). He has accepted his death earlier and he acknowledges Hektor's dying prophecy to the same effect.[23]

As it was for Patroklos, confusion with Achilles is fatal for Priam's son. In Achilles, Hektor encounters that aspect of the hero-son's divided self that searches out and destroys its own human limitations and vulnerabilities. No matter what his triumphs and victories, those qualities disqualify him for divine maternal favor. The hero-son experiences himself as perfect and free of vulnerability in the process of separating from and destroying that which only aspires to be perfect, but which, he anxiously believes, needs to *be* perfect to avoid maternal rejection or abandonment and be worthy of divine maternal regard.

Hektor foolishly imagines that, having killed Patroklos, he might kill Achilles in a one-on-one encounter. He thus implicitly, and fatally, insults Thetis. He, a mere mortal, implicitly likens himself to her son. Putting on Achilles' armor, he thinks he can have it both ways. He can remain Troy's canny mortal protector—who has led a successful defense of Troy for almost a decade—while also winning the glory of the *nostos*-sacrificing, inhumanly hard and savage hero, Achilles. In effect he abandons his mortal, but competent and effective self, to chase a phantom of Achilles' glory.[24]

The account of Hektor's death reveals the minutiae of heroic psychology and the exactitude of the *Iliad*'s dramatizations of it. The hero-son's disavowed revulsion at the killing he does at the mother's behest confronts him as an alien force. It terrifies him by threatening to overwhelm and reduce him to insignificance—principally in the eyes of his mother. So too, the merely mortal father's son, Hektor, confronts Achilles as a terrifying other. Achilles terrifies Hektor in part because, in aspiring to be Achilles' equal, Hektor dissociates from and leaves unprotected his (from the standpoint of a divine mother) inferior, unworthy human self. This betrayal mirrors Achilles', when he allows Patroklos to face the violence of Hektor and Apollo alone.

Despite imagining himself a possible victor over Achilles, Hektor is terrified when he confronts the son of Thetis. He only stops fleeing when Athena takes the form of his half-brother Deiphobos, who claims to have come out from the safety of the Trojan walls to help a grateful Hektor fight Achilles. But the help turns out to be illusory. Mock-Deiphobos disappears while the real one cowers behind the walls of Troy. This is an example of the minute precision with which the *Iliad* dramatizes processes of heroic psychology. In the conflict associated with split working models, part of what makes the ordinary son seem so terrifyingly mismatched against his mother-identified alter ego is the hero-son's betrayal and abandonment of the mortal self that his mother regards as inferior. He does not question his or his father's inferiority as a mere mortal, or affirm his value. Terrified by a son who personifies a divine mother's irresistible force, he flees.

Voicing the Olympians' consternation at Achilles' dragging of Hektor's body behind his chariot, Apollo proposes that the gods steal the corpse of Achilles' enemy alter ego, whose humanity mirrors Patroklos's. Hera objects that Hektor, a mortal "suckled at the breast of a woman," can never have equal honor with Achilles, the child of a goddess (24.57–59). Such equal treatment would provoke Thetis's wrath as well. The way in which Zeus mollifies Hera simultaneously averts the latter threat: he dismisses the stealing of Hektor's corpse as impossible, even for the Olympians who outrank Thetis (20.104–6), because "his mother is near him night and day." The alternative Zeus proposes—asking Thetis to persuade her son to relinquish the corpse—is calculated to guard her reverence and love (*aidô* and *philotêta*) for him in the future and to avert the *mênis* that is signified by the black robe the grieving mother of Achilles dons for the occasion (24.91–94, 24.110–11). Agamemnon's similar attempt to compare his honor to that of Achilles—indeed, to assert his superiority in honor—also threatens to provoke Thetis's *mênis* at Zeus. Here too, Zeus sacrifices a protégé—his mortal counterpart, Agamemnon—to avert a threat to himself.

THE PLAN AND MÊNIS OF ZEUS

For the most part, the crisis of the last books of the *Iliad* involves the irruption, dispatch, and relinquishing of aspects of the hero-son's self that threaten his relationship with his primary caregiver—his superior mother. In the end, these aspects of self suffer a fate comparable to that with which Skamander threatened Achilles: they and all their unwelcome knowledge of the sacrificial parenting that underlie the reproduction of ancient Greek culture are deeply buried and consigned to oblivion.

The quarrel between Agamemnon and Achilles (and between Agamemnon's brother Menelaos and Paris) plays out the prophecy of *themis* on the mortal plane. Zeus covertly supports the *mênis* of Agamemnon, who plays the part Zeus would have played as the husband of Thetis and father of Achilles, even as Zeus overtly supports their *mênis* against Agamemnon. If Zeus were openly to side with Agamemnon, identifying with his outrageous, dishonoring *mênis* at Achilles, he would undermine his own plan. Thetis and her son must direct their *mênis* at a mortal surrogate.

Zeus's plan for returning Achilles to the fighting departs from the plan of Achilles and Thetis in a crucial detail. Even before Agamemnon's failed embassy, Zeus formulates a plan that substitutes the death of Patroklos for the supplication of a humiliated Agamemnon—the motivation Achilles imagines for his return to battle (8.473–78, 15.59–77). This, along with Zeus's role as the executor of paternal curses of even minor kings, suggests that the killing of Patroklos, stripping Achilles of his vicarious *nostos*, enacts Zeus's *mênis* at Achilles. The killing of Patroklos by the glorious son of Leto, Achilles' divine counterpart, the once-rebellious son of Zeus, represents Zeus's covert execution of the *mênis* and curse of his mortal counterpart, Agamemnon, against Apollo's mortal counterpart, Achilles. Zeus's covert support for the *mênis* of Agamemnon against Achilles counterbalances Zeus's overt and seemingly unalloyed support for the *mênis* of Achilles and Thetis against Agamemnon.[25]

Blaming himself for the Zeus-ordained death of Patroklos, Achilles continues to believe that he is honored in Zeus's ordinance. He is unaware of having committed any offense against Zeus or his mortal counterpart, Agamemnon, much less that Patroklos's death is the result of a paternal curse executed by Zeus. As with the truce-breaking, Zeus is content to be seen as reluctantly ensuring the bargain on which Thetis's glory depends—the exchange of *nostos* for glory—while in fact pursuing his own agenda. Achilles mistakes Zeus's expedient assent to his and Thetis's plan for unalloyed support. When he prays to Zeus for Patroklos's safe return, Achilles unwittingly asks to avoid paying the price not just for glory but for his Zeus-sanctioned offenses against fathers and kings.

Patroklos's death is a sacrifice in which a stunning blow precedes the lethal one. Apollo strikes the sacrificial blow with his hand not just as Troy's defender (on Zeus's behalf) or as the guardian of the boundary between divine and mortal, but as the once-rebellious but now chastened and loyal son of Zeus. Although Apollo once threatened to overthrow Zeus, in the *Iliad* Apollo, like Achilles, confines his offenses against paternal and kingly authority to the mortal realm. His humiliation of Agamemnon in book 1 of the *Iliad* serves as a model for Achilles'. In taking the lives of Patroklos and Achilles, Apollo is the agent of Zeus's covert *mênis* for offenses that originate in Zeus's paternal and kingly failures.[26]

It is not just Zeus's role as executor of Agamemnon's *mênis* against Achilles that remains hidden. Zeus disclaims responsibility for his crucial role in generating the offenses he covertly punishes. He avoids his wife in favor of quasi-incestuous liaisons, thereby creating a family situation that encourages mother-son alliances against him. He behaves much like his predecessor patriarchs among the gods, who lacked the *mêtis* that allowed Zeus to resolve the conflicts that brought down their regimes. Like his unwise predecessors, Zeus prospectively fears, tries to preempt the development of, and ultimately curses the son whose alliances with mothers resemble those that the *mêtis*-imbued Zeus of the *Theogony* is wise enough to prevent.

This represents a different dovetailing of Zeus's *mênis* with Achilles' than that suggested by the *Iliad*'s apparent legitimization of Achilles' vengeful *mênis* at Agamemnon. Although Zeus does not let on that he blames Achilles for effectively deposing his surrogate, Agamemnon, Achilles accepts unquestioningly the Zeus-ordained death of Patroklos and his own early death (18.116). Evidently the *mênis* of the irresponsible, philandering Zeus of epic is less like the not-yet-named *mênis* of Hesiod's Zeus than like the anger of Zeus's unwise and unjust predecessors—the curse of a *themis*-violating father on a son whose offenses his abdications and peccadilloes invite and encourage. Achilles accepts his and Patroklos's early deaths as victims of a *mênis* that makes the son pay for the failings of the father. In this sense, being *minunthadios* is Achilles' favor to Zeus.[27]

It is telling in this context that at the beginning of the *Odyssey*, Zeus takes the murder of Aigisthos as his example of evils for which men unfairly blame the gods.

> "Oh for shame, how the mortals put the blame upon [*aitioôntai*] us
> gods, for they say evils come from us, but it is they, rather,
> who by their own recklessness [*atasthaliêisin*] win sorrow
>   beyond what is given
> as now lately, beyond what was given, Aigisthos married
> the wife of Atreus's son, and murdered him on his homecoming
>   [*ektane nostêsanta*],
> though he knew it was sheer destruction, for we ourselves had told him,
> sending Hermes, the mighty watcher, Argeïphontes,
> not to kill the man, nor court his lady for marriage;
> for vengeance [*tisis*] would come on him from Orestes, son of Atreides,
> whenever he came of age [*hêbêsêi*] and longed for his own country.
> So Hermes told him, but for all his kind intention he could not
> persuade the mind of Aigisthos. And now he has paid for everything
>   [*pant' apetise*]."
> Then in turn the goddess gray-eyed Athene answered him:
> "Son of Kronos, our father, O lordliest of the mighty,
> Aigisthos indeed has been struck down in a death well merited.
> Let any other man who does thus perish as he did" (i.32–47)

In a typical shift of responsibility, Zeus makes Aigisthos *aitios* while denying that he and Agamemnon are. He does not even take responsibility for punishing a crime that parallels the crime of Paris, which provokes the deadly *mênis* of Zeus in the *Iliad*. The hand of "the father of gods and mortals" is invisible in the death of Aigisthos. By way of disclaiming all responsibility, Zeus tells how he and the other gods warned Aigisthos that Agamemnon's son would make him pay if he murdered Agamemnon and courted his wife.

But Zeus's (and Agamemnon's) responsibility for Aigisthos's fate goes far beyond even accomplishing Agamemnon's curses. Aigisthos plays a part usually reserved for the son in these dramas, but with erotic benefits that, as with his brother-in-crime, Paris, make it necessary to efface the filial aspect of the relationship. Aigisthos serves as Klytemnestra's instrument of revenge against Agamemnon for two interrelated offenses: the sacrifice of a favored daughter, and philandering. In accord with the plan of Zeus, mortal substitutes, including Agamemnon, pay the price for Zeus's philandering and multiple sacrifices of Thetis (and Persephone).

Like Paris's lust for Tyndareus's other daughter, Helen, Aigisthos's lust for Klytemnestra is inspired by the *mênis* of Aphrodite. But it is also inspired by Agamemnon's Zeus-like failure to make a marriage with Klytemnestra in deed as well as word. This is obvious, both in Agamemnon's paradigmatic offenses and the price he pays for them. His bad marriage is the incubator of Aigisthos's murderous ambition and desire.

The gods warn Aigisthos to avoid provoking Orestes' revenge. They do not warn Agamemnon to avoid provoking Klytemnestra's. That would be tantamount to warning Agamemnon not to imitate Zeus's quasi-incestuous, daughter-sacrificing, wife-insulting, philandering ways. Apart from reflecting badly on Zeus, such a warning would undermine Zeus's plan. Dissuading Agamemnon from acting like Zeus and provoking the father-cuckolding, king-toppling *mênis* of Thetis and her son, as well as of Hera's mortal counterpart Klytemnestra, would prevent the export to the mortal realm of the threats prophesied by Themis. It would undo the substitution of Agamemnon's catastrophe within and beyond the *Iliad* for Zeus's on Olympos.

To incite rather than discourage filial lust, and then bring the *mênis* of Zeus down on the head of the son whose offense, under the circumstances, is virtually foreordained, is tantamount to child-sacrifice. That Agamemnon enlists his son Orestes as his avenger is no more an argument against this than his literal enlistment of Achilles as his and his brother's avenger for Paris's parallel crime against his brother. It is merely another way for a father to sacrifice a son. The *Theogony* offers testimony that such an exacting notion of responsibility was well within the purview of archaic Greeks: Ouranos and Kronos bring their downfalls on themselves. The *Iliad* illustrates, conversely, how easily this notion of responsibility can be set aside, to be replaced by a child-sacrificing father's self-exculpating identification of right with his vengeful anger at the filial victim of his self-absorption and inadequacy.

A similar instance of divine hypocrisy and perversion of *themis* is evident in the killing of Patroklos. Just before Patroklos is killed by a Zeus-empowered Hektor, Patroklos's rage (*thumos*) is compared to Zeus's in his deep rage (*kotessamenos*) against mortals "because in violent assembly they pass decrees that are crooked [*biêi ein agorêi skolias krinôsi themistas*], and drive righteousness [*dikên*] from among them and care nothing for what the gods think" (16.386–88). It is precisely because Patroklos bears witness to and opposes the divinely sanctioned perversions of *themis* that are integral to heroic culture that Patroklos must be killed. He must die by the hand of Zeus's son in accord with Zeus's plan.[28]

Still, Zeus has a point. In the *Iliad* and the *Odyssey*, he and the other gods represent principles governing human behavior in Greek heroic culture. Reflections of human motivations and patterns of family interaction, the gods cannot regularly intervene in human affairs to counteract those patterns. That is finally up to men. Like Zeus himself, they know better, but they engage in time-honored, destructive behaviors nonetheless.[29]

The Achilles-like hero-son absolves of responsibility and idealizes not only his complicit, ambivalent, son-sacrificing father but, first and foremost, his rejecting mother. He forgets that she is liable to be angry even with one who is not *aitios*. This includes her own innocent children, her *nêpia tekna*, whose crying signals their need for loving nurture such as a mortal child might receive at the breast of a mortal mother. Approaching her, or a surrogate, as if she were an ideal loving mother, whom an infant could trust both to mirror a positive image of himself and to respond to his care-seeking behavior by protecting and nurturing him to adulthood, he leaves himself open to being stripped both of value and of his prospects for a life in accord with *themis* by his mother's or mother-surrogates' anger.

Although Achilles makes Hektor and other sons of Priam pay with their lives for killing Patroklos, Achilles makes himself pay the same price for withdrawing his protection from Patroklos and from the other Achaians whom Hektor killed when Achilles stood apart from them (18.90–104, 21.128–35). In the end, remarkably, Achilles adds the destruction of Priam's sons and city to the list of his capital offenses. In committing these offenses, Achilles fulfils his parents' and parent-figures' plans, but the device of bringing him back into the fighting as Patroklos's avenger masks their crucial role. Achilles becomes responsible for the losses they inflict on him as well as for those he inflicts on others on their behalf. Assuming responsibility in this way positions Achilles to become a sacrificial victim, whose death purges the community of the violence that is common to all. Finally, Achilles accepts another perversion of *themis*, the hidden curse of the complicit but threatened father who demands the son's sacrifice on the father's behalf but then curses the son when he feels eclipsed by the son's glorious prowess. In all these instances, the son is a *nêpios* caught unawares by disaster.[30]

When he feels the lash of this anger, against which he, unlike hero-sons who identify with self-respecting mortal fathers, is defenseless, he shifts responsibility for his injury. He redirects the outrage away from his maternal first offender to third parties, even though they are not responsible (are not *aitios*) for the initial, outrageous devaluation that leaves him forever vulnerable to insult and prone to revenge and violence. Ultimately he assumes responsibility for the destruction of his prospects first as a care-seeking child and then as a functioning adult who merits both honor and love, and he turns his anger on himself. He even blames himself for his vulnerability, emotionally abandoning and assaulting his traumatically devalued mortal self for its dismal failure to be huge and splendid enough to cow even a paradigmatic angry divine mother, or to win the favor of a paradigmatic rejecting one. (Briareus does both when he rescues Zeus from Hera on behalf of Thetis, earning her favor by winning for her the undying favor of Zeus.)

The mother-identified hero also makes himself *aitios* for the acts of aggression he commits in accord with parental agendas that he has made his own, as well as for having experiences of his parents that they would like to believe that he had not had, and for knowledge that displeases them. Taking over the *themis*- and *dikê*-violating roles that he denies his parents ever played, he quickly supersedes them as his mortal self's chief betrayer and abuser. As Patroklos sums it up, Achilles is "a dangerous man [*deinos anêr*]" who "might even be angry with [*aitioôito*, blame] one who is guiltless [*anaition*; 11.654]." The only ones to whom Achilles is not dangerous are the exploitative parents who bear the ultimate responsibility for his enduring hurt. An archetypal "burdened child," he holds those blameless.

Epilogue: Achilles and Socrates

Socrates: Euthyphro, you think that you have such accurate knowledge of things divine, and what is holy and unholy, that . . . you can accuse your father? You are not afraid that you yourself are doing an unholy deed?

Euthyphro: Why Socrates, if I did not have an accurate knowledge of all that, I should be good for nothing, and Euthyphro would be no different from the general run of men.

—Plato, *Euthyphro* 4e–5a

We end not by surveying the sickening, disheartening variations on the theme of child-sacrifice and violence that have proliferated in other places and times, up to the present, but by returning to the theme with which we began: speaking truth to power. Achilles' fearless public witnessing of Agamemnon's abuses of power and betrayals of trust, and his decrying of the spineless acquiescence of the general run of men notwithstanding, speaking truth to power is the one thing that favored children in heroic culture must not do. Rather than bearing witness to routine but outrageous irresponsibility, betrayals of trust, and failures of nurture, they dissociate from and abandon parts of themselves that perceive—and experience—how parents go about rearing glorious children. Hero-sons may—indeed must—come to realize the harm involved in the process, but only so they can exculpate child-sacrificing parents and blame themselves.[1]

As Achilles and Agamemnon do, Socrates and his accusers offer competing accounts of the quarrel between them. In fact, the *agon* between Achilles and Agamemnon in the *Iliad* appears to be not only a model for this later dispute, but part of the cultural foundation of the agonistic legal institutions of democratic Athens. There, feuding litigants charged their opponents with violating laws, and citizen-jurors convicted or acquitted on the basis of speeches claiming legitimacy and honor for one side while impugning the claims of rivals. The contest between Socrates and his democratic accusers played out not only in an Athenian court, but in a far more consequential forum: Plato's narrative of Socrates' last days. As with the *Iliad*, an examination of these rival accounts exposes the psychological underpinnings of the culture that underlies them, in this case the fractious political culture of democratic Athens.[2]

Achilles' narrative of speaking truth to power not only cast a spell over succeeding generations, down to our own, it also played its part in a cathartic process that helped to preserve the child-sacrifice and violence, reflexive and otherwise, that underlay archaic and later Greek cultures. Like the *Iliad*'s account of the quarrel, Plato's account of Socrates' conflict with leaders of democratic Athens appears to deny a complex set of childhood experiences, summed up as child-sacrifice, that remain a powerful strain in classical Athenian culture.

Integral to the violence in Homeric culture is an assault on human intelligence and judgment that takes a heavy toll on individuals and polities. The antithesis of free, confident self-disclosure, such self-disavowal and self-obliteration affects decisions about war- and peacemaking, and undermines the capacity to construct and sustain orders characterized by reciprocal affection, respect, and trust and by the just distribution, rather than arrogation, of offices and honors. An analysis of the dialogues recounting Socrates' trial and execution can help us appreciate the political consequences, for democracy in particular, of a cultural orientation that discredits *noos* and *themis* in favor of the competitive pursuit of glory.

Western culture's standard-bearer for the peaceable pursuit of truth through unfettered rational dialogue, Plato's Socrates is the last person we would expect to exemplify the discrediting of human intelligence. Neither would we expect him to epitomize the denial of sacrificial parenting that, together with assaults on the perceiving, thinking human self, underpin Homeric and later Greek internecine violence and war. Yet Plato's account is a Trojan horse by which Homeric culture, at once rooted in and denying violence-engendering violence against the self, insinuates itself into the mainstream of Western thought and culture. Other notable conduits include Sophocles' *Antigone*, itself a precursor of Plato's account of Socrates' last days, and, of course, the *Iliad* itself.

Archaic and later Greek cultures encompass powerful countervailing traditions. Father-identified heroes are exponents of *noos* and *mêtis* in the *Iliad*; one of them merits an epic equal in stature to the *Iliad* that recounts Odysseus's return from Troy. The succession myth in Hesiod's *Theogony* is another example, and it both informs Solon's words and deeds as a lawgiver and serves as a model for Aeschylus's *Oresteia* trilogy. Odysseus's flight from battle in the *Iliad* is a literal precursor of that of the lyric poet Archilochos's first-person narrator, who saves his skin by abandoning his shield on the battlefield.[3]

For all his ironic distancing and cultural remoteness from Homer's Achilles, Plato's Socrates exemplifies not only a disabling of ordinary human perception and understanding rooted in Homeric martial culture, but also, as a consequence, a deep-seated failure to recognize these capacities in the generality of human beings, which is evident in Socrates' particular brand of elitism and his biased view of Athenian democracy. Plato's critique of Athenian democracy hinges on its violence against his mentor, a heroic critic of what were to him its blatant failings. Unlike Achilles, Socrates is a man of supreme intellect who relies on persuasion rather than superior might. Yet Achilles' most enduring legacy may be his example as an eloquent critic of the irresponsible abuse of power.

ACHILLES' EXAMPLE

In 399 BC, Anytus, a leader in the restoration of Athenian democracy four years earlier, joined with two obscure countrymen to charge Socrates with impiety and corrupting the young. Plato's account of Socrates' trial and execution is both a defense of his beloved teacher and an indictment of democratic Athens. With his life hanging in the balance, Plato's Socrates invokes Achilles as an exemplar of the courage he himself must display in pursuing his philosophical vocation. Fear of death will never induce him to abandon his post. Despite the threat of execution, he will pursue his god-appointed task of leading the philosophical life, of examining himself and others (*Apol.* 28b–29a, 24b). But Socrates' character and vocation are so antithetical to Achilles' that the comparison seems freighted with irony.

Socrates mounts a two-pronged defense. Far from exhibiting impiety, he argues, his philosophic activities are extraordinarily pious. How then could such scurrilous charges have arisen? By way of an answer, Socrates gives an account of his activities and how they led to his indictment. Puzzled by the declaration of Apollo's oracle at Delphi that no one is wiser than he, Socrates decides to investigate the god's meaning by examining the men who have the greatest reputations for wisdom—politicians, dramatists, orators—in short, anyone with a claim to superior knowledge. His public questioning of these men reveals that although they believe themselves wise, in fact they are not. From this Socrates concludes that all mortals are basically ignorant, but that he is wiser than others because he recognizes his ignorance (*Apol.* 20c–23c).

Loath to admit they are angry at Socrates for demonstrating that they literally do not know what they are talking about when it comes to virtue or the good of the city, and envious of him (presumably because he has been singled out by Apollo as the wisest of men), these influential men concoct slanderous charges against him: impiety (*asebeias*); believing in deities of his own invention instead of the gods recognized by the state; and corrupting the young (*Apol.* 23d–e, 24b; envy [*phthonos*]: 28a, 35d; cf. *Eu.* 5c). In rebuttal, Socrates likens himself to a divinely appointed gadfly, exhorting the Athenians to care for truth and the perfection of their souls more than for wealth, honor, and power. They are like a lazy thoroughbred that needs the stimulation of a fly's stinging bite. Although the Athenians should treasure him as Apollo's greatest gift to them, Socrates suspects that they will take the advice of one of his accusers, Anytus, and swat him dead (*Apol.* 30a–31a). And so, by courageously refusing to abandon his calling or to flee, he becomes a martyr to public truth-telling.

This heroic gadfly, who innocently goes about the god's business and as a result is charged with impiety and corrupting the young, may indeed be modeled on Achilles—not the brave warrior invoked by Socrates, who prefers death to disgrace, but the seemingly aberrant, "public" Achilles of the first book of the *Iliad*, who intervenes to save the army from a plague sent by Apollo. In Homer's epic, Achilles is more than a stereotypical glory-seeking, insult-avenging hero. Granted, he epitomizes these traits, but precisely because of this Achilles is suited to confront scapegoats for pervasive ills of heroic culture, thereby becoming one himself.[4]

In Achilles, dominant heroic values of honor and revenge come into conflict with less obvious commitments to sacrifice in the service of others. When violated, these commitments turn out to be no less imperative. The preeminent hero of the *Iliad* not only pursues his own glory; he risks his life daily to restore the honor of the Atreidai. Agamemnon's insult provokes Achilles to articulate the helping role about which he had maintained a tactful silence: he came to Troy not on his own behalf, but "for [Agamemnon's] sake," to "do [him] favor" by winning back from the Trojans the honor of Agamemnon and his brother Menelaos, who regards himself as covered with "shame and defilement" by Paris's seduction of his wife (1.157–60, 13.623–24). Even the glory that Achilles pursues so single-mindedly is as much a compensation for his mother, shamed and humiliated by her marriage to a mortal, as it is a prize for himself. Achilles also surpasses other heroes in risking his life "to beat death away from his companions" (1.341, 9.322–26; cf. 18.129). When he finally realizes how much his vengeful refusal to fight has cost his beloved comrades, he ordains his own death as a penalty (18.98–104).

Achilles' very ability to "outshine all others" is linked to a complementary self-effacement. Here too, he can acknowledge his sacrifice only in hostile retrospect. Achilles silently acquiesces in a distribution of spoils in inverse proportion to what he and Agamemnon actually deserve. Agamemnon amasses unmerited riches while Achilles contents himself with something "small but dear" (1.164–68). With this apparent self-denial, no less than by avenging Paris's insult of Menelaos, Achilles preserves the honor of the Atreidai. Once again Agamemnon's ingratitude provokes Achilles to break his silence, and once again Achilles seems completely justified. Nonetheless, as we have seen, it falls on the hero-son to neutralize the threat he poses to fathers and kings rather than on them to exercise legitimate authority and provide responsible care in relation to him.[5]

Exploring conflicts between dominant values of glory and revenge and countervailing obligations to authorities and communities, the *Iliad* completes the transformation of a simple tale of vengeance for dishonor into a great, prototragic epic. That it does so when the *polis* was emerging as the preeminent form of Greek social and political organization is probably no coincidence. In the course of exploring these conflicts among competing values, moreover, the *Iliad* lays the groundwork for Plato's portrayal of Socrates. When we take the community-regarding side of Achilles' character into account, Socrates' invocation of Achilles as an exemplar appears far more telling, far less ironic, than it at first seems.[6]

Not only undercurrents of character—Achilles' sense of responsibility for his fellows' well-being, and Socrates' heroic intransigence—but also similar narrative patterns narrow the gap between the two. The story of Achilles' conflict with Agamemnon adumbrates Plato's account of Socrates' conflict with leaders of democratic Athens. Although Achilles epitomizes the competitive striving for honor that, for many writers, betokens the absence of "cooperative virtues" or interior conscience in Archaic culture generally, he is nonetheless drawn into the public arena by a community-threatening crisis. Agamemnon insults a priest of Apollo and stands idly by while a plague sent by the god decimates his army. Hera sends Athena to persuade Achilles to convene the public assembly at which he shames Agamemnon into returning the priest's captive daughter and appeasing Apollo with a sacrifice.[7]

When Socrates braves the anger of the leaders of Athens to heed a divine command that he save his fellow Athenians, he follows in the footsteps of Achilles, who risks the anger of a powerful king in a divinely prompted attempt to save his community (1.178–83). Like those of Socrates', Achilles' actions in service of the community assert Apollo's claims to honor in the face of the hubris of mortal authorities. The Achaians had urged Agamemnon to honor Apollo by acceding to his priest's supplication, but Agamemnon abused the old man and mocked the god's ability to protect his servant (1.21, 1.25–32, 1.28; hubris: 1.203, 1.214). Achilles, by contrast, was "the first to urge the god's appeasement" (1.386).[8]

Achilles' altruism and piety, like those of Socrates, are brushed aside as mere pretense. His innocent claim to be discovering the cause of the divine anger that threatens to destroy his community does not fool Agamemnon, who tells him not to "strive to cheat, for you will not deceive." According to Agamemnon, unbridled ambition lies behind Achilles' posture of disinterested concern for his fellows' well-being. Does Achilles wish to strip Agamemnon of honors and give him orders (1.131–34)? The question is rhetorical. Achilles "wishes to be above all others, /. . . to hold power over all and to be lord of / all and give them their orders" (1.287–99). Like Socrates' accusers, Agamemnon justifies Achilles' punishment as necessary to deter injustice: "so that another man"—possibly a hotheaded youth like Diomedes or his charioteer, Sthenelos (4.365–419, 9.31–62)—"may shrink back from likening himself to [Agamemnon] and contending against" him (1.186–87).

Just as Agamemnon is a prototype for Socrates' accusers, so Achilles' defense of his actions prefigures Socrates', and the *Iliad*'s implicit defense of Achilles anticipates Plato's explicit defense of Socrates. The knowledge that divine pity inspired Achilles to come to the aid of his fellow Achaians and expose the hubris of Agamemnon suggests to the poem's auditors that the king's accusations against his half-divine subaltern arise from a source other than his avowed concern with instilling proper respect for divinely sanctioned authority. Perhaps Agamemnon's hostility can be explained in the same way as that of Socrates' accusers: he is angry at having his shortcomings publicly exposed, or he envies the divinely favored son of Thetis.

When the Athenians whom Socrates labors to save abandon him to his fate, they mimic the *Iliad*'s Achaians. Unlike the Athenian jurors, the Achaians acquiesce rather than join in Agamemnon's condemnation of Achilles, but Achilles' bitterly ironic characterization of them as dispensers of justice, *dikaspoloi*, who administer the *themistas* of Zeus (1.238–39) nonetheless foreshadows Socrates' refusal to accord the title of *dikast* (juror) to those who vote to convict him. Socrates' shift from lashing out at his accusers to self-condemnation and self-ordained death also follows Achillean precedent.[9]

Despite his intervention to save the army from the plague, Achilles remains the stereotypical honor-seeking, dishonor-avenging hero whom Socrates invokes in the *Apology*. It is understandable, therefore, that Plato's Socrates overlooks the affinity between himself as gadfly and the aberrant, public-spirited warrior in the first book of the *Iliad*. Even in his altercation with Agamemnon, Achilles' wrath is kindled more by the slight to his honor, stemming from Agamemnon's seizure of his female prize, than by Agamemnon's unkingly failure to give up his concubine so that his "people [will] be safe, not perish" (1.117). Despite all the sacrifices Achilles makes on behalf of his comrades, he nearly destroys the army in his pursuit of revenge. After a brief interlude in which he serves as the agent of Hera's maternal concern for the Achaians (who, in any case, like Achilles himself, are agents of Hera's revenge on the Trojans [24.25–30, 4.20–36]), Achilles reverts to being a stereotypical hero who cares only about his own honor. Thus Socrates could have followed in the footsteps of an evanescent public Achilles, or Plato might have modeled Socrates' story on the *Iliad*'s epic quarrel, without being aware of it.

Since the noble efforts of Plato's mentor to save his community are unjustly maligned in much the same terms as those employed against Achilles, we might at least expect Socrates to sympathize with a fellow victim of outrageous slander. Yet Plato's Socrates' condemnation of Achilles in the *Republic* echoes Agamemnon's. Seeing through the smokescreen of Achilles' feigned innocence to the illicit ambitions underneath, Socrates charges him with "youthful impertinences" (*neanieumata*) toward his sovereign and with setting an example that corrupts the young (*Rep.* 390a).

Of course Socrates may be right about Achilles. He may even be responding to subtle hints that belie the apparent import of the tales, episodes, and subplots that establish Achilles' *unlikeness* to the sort of usurper that Agamemnon accuses him of being. Indeed, the very passages that seem to demonstrate the absurdity of Agamemnon's accusations often hint at an underlying affinity between Achilles and mother-favored rebels, who are contemptuous of fathers, treacherously usurp paternal prerogatives, reject patrimonies as worthless, and variously elicit fathers' angry threats or curses.

Socrates' knack for detecting youthful impertinence behind a screen of piety extends beyond Achilles. As this discussion's epigraph indicates, Socrates has no trouble recognizing that illicit filial aggression may underlie Euthyphro's indictment of his father, despite the young man's confidence in the righteousness of his action. Moreover, parallels in the *Euthyphro* between Euthyphro and Socrates' principal accuser, Meletus, suggest that Meletus's avowedly high-minded motives may be similarly impure (*Eu.* 2c, 4a–b, 4e, 5c, 5e–6b). At his trial, Socrates makes the accusation explicit: Meletus only pretends to be concerned about the corruption of the young. He indicts Socrates "out of sheer wanton aggressiveness and self-assertion" (*Apol.* 26e–27a).

Yet given Socrates' acute awareness of the ubiquity of unlawful desires and their ability to masquerade as piety, how can he so confidently mock Meletus's claim that he sees "easily and keenly" through Socrates' own pretense of serving Apollo and saving the Athenians (*Eu.* 5c)? How can Socrates so easily dismiss the belief he ascribes to Anytus in the *Meno*—namely, that Socrates' ritual public embarrassment of prominent men is redolent of envious slander? In short, how can Socrates be so sure of his own innocence?[10]

Answers to this question may be found in the heroic psychology that both motivates and undermines Achilles' pre-Socratic attempts to avoid wrongdoing—to be a savior rather than scourge of the people (*laos*); to shore up paternal and kingly authority damaged by sons who are "outrageous, not to be trusted" (*Iliad* 1.159–60, 3.105–6); and to demonstrate his loyalty and trustworthiness by sacrificing his life to punish such outrages. This psychology, which undergirds the *Iliad* and its mythological antecedents, also lies at the heart of Socrates' legend, as rendered by Plato.

SOCRATES' INNOCENT HEROISM

The foregoing analysis of Achilles' mythology and psychology points toward an account of Socrates' ministrations to the Athenians that not only suggests that he was guilty of corrupting the young—perhaps as result of being seduced and corrupted himself—but also explains the confidence with which, despite his ability to see through others' pretensions of piety, he shrugs off the accusations against him. Finally, it helps to explain his willingness to appease what he views as his envious, angry, paternal accusers by accepting his death, at whatever time the Athenians wish to bring it about.

Apollo's oracle is of central importance to Socrates' defense, for as Socrates tells us in the *Apology*, it provides unimpeachable authority for his claim to superior wisdom (*Apol.* 20e–21b). The underlying logic of Socrates' interpretation of the oracle seems to run something like this: Apollo exemplifies excellence and is therefore wise; he knows what true excellence consists of. That Apollo considers Socrates wise proves that Socrates (who tries to approach as nearly as possible to the divinity that Apollo chiefly exemplifies) is in fact wise. If, moreover, the divine things that both of them recognize as supremely valuable happen to be at odds with goals and gods espoused by the majority of Athenians, this is an indication, not of impiety on Socrates'—or, god forbid, Apollo's—part, but of the Athenians' benighted condition.[11]

Into this closed circle of explanation, no doubt about Socrates' innocence can intrude. Yet Socrates assumes precisely what we cannot—namely, that illicit self-assertion plays no part in his embrace of the idea of his special kinship to, and commission from, the gods. Once he accepts as simple truth his affinity with the divine, conduct of his that may not be innocent can appear absolutely so.

For Socrates, it is axiomatic that Apollo is himself completely free of any taint of impiety, in which case "the god's business" must be equally pure. In fact, however, Apollo links Socrates to the mythology of glorious sons of insulted, divine mothers and its underlying psychology. The glorious son of Leto, who, like Achilles, is "without fault and powerful," joins with Hera and the other gods in an attempted coup against Zeus. Provoking Zeus's *mênis* on another occasion, he only escapes a lengthy stay in Tartaros when his mother—like Thetis, a castoff paramour of Zeus—intercedes for him, just as Thetis intercedes with Zeus on behalf of her son. Doubtless Socrates would dismiss the myth of Apollo's rebellion as just another poet's lie about the gods. Yet such a denial would fail to establish what Socrates simply assumes: that there can be no contradiction between devotion to Apollo and piety toward legitimate authority, even that of theogonic Zeus—which in any case Plato's Socrates rejects.[12]

When we look at how Socrates interprets the oracle, we again recognize self-defeating patterns that characterize heroic psychology. Socrates sharply distinguishes between the "empty mediocrities" whose incompetence he exposes in the agora and the absent mortal father and divine paternal laws whose judgments he accepts and for whom he professes to have only respect. Achilles evinces similar attitudes toward Agamemnon as opposed to Peleus and Zeus. Like Achilles, Socrates parlays a particular set of qualifications— which include an implicit readiness to believe that he is somehow in a class by himself—into a claim of absolute superiority. Thus, although the oracle only says that no one is wiser than Socrates, Socrates interprets it to mean that he alone is wise, and contrives a series of contests that he views as demonstrating his categorical superiority.[13]

It is, however, in Socrates' account in the *Symposium* of his initiation into the philosophic pursuit of immortality by the Mantinean mystic, Diotima, that the heroic pattern emerges most clearly. A daimonic intermediary between gods and men, Diotima teaches that the good (*agathos*; 205e) is beautiful and perfect (*kalon kai teleon*; 204c), and that only the good or noble in this sense can ever be the object of love, since men do not love but seek to eliminate whatever is defective or ugly in themselves (*Sym.* 205e–206a). She distinguishes between vulgar folk and the nobler sort (*Sym.* 208e), who are suitable for initiation into the pursuit of immortality according to their love of what is immutable and perfect (*Sym.* 209e–210a). These are the lovers of wisdom, the philosophers. Thus she encourages Socrates to rid himself of worthless mortal trappings and to ascend from love of physical beauty to love and knowledge of divine excellence. As a reward, she promises that he will be beloved of the gods (*theophilei*) and, if any mortal can become so, immortal.[14]

Much like Demeter for Demophoon or Psamathe for Peleus, Diotima is a categorically superior substitute for an ordinary human mother. Diotima's nurturing of Socrates resembles Demeter's and Thetis's attempts to immortalize hero-sons. Where Thetis burns away Achilles' mortal part in a fire, Diotima tells Socrates stories of Achilles, among other seekers of immortality, to induce Socrates to slough off defiling mortal attachments. Of course there is a significant difference between being an initiate like Socrates, who aspires to destroy only his mortal self, and a semidivine hero like Achilles, who projects his mortal self onto others and kills them in war—although the two are not mutually exclusive. Becoming an initiate may involve demeaning ordinary paternal (and maternal) authority, and it may be no less debilitating to human intelligence than its heroic prototypes. These underlying similarities may derive from similar child-rearing patterns.[15]

The bargain Diotima offers Socrates—immortality in exchange for discipleship that validates her claim to knowledge of "things divine"—implicitly devalues patrimony and the whole range of male-dominated worldly pursuits, political and otherwise. Since she can promise him union with the divine, lesser transactions and aspirations pale to insignificance. In particular, the initiate need not reach an accommodation with paternal authority in which he renounces the dream of triumphing over and degrading it—thereby avoiding a paternal curse and receiving a paternal blessing as he sets about acquiring the competencies that make fathers rightly respected. (Of course the presence of adequate, functional paternal authority cannot be assumed. In the *Iliad* a paternal curse is a manifestation of paternal inadequacy, an alternative to the exercise of paternal authority.) Honored by Diotima as a suitable initiate and possible candidate for the "final revelation"—and implicitly threatened with the disdain of gods and mortals if he should become identified in her eyes with anything inferior and defective—Socrates' only worry is to prove that he is indeed the nobler sort, a lover of perfection who deserves divine favor.

Although Apollo has yet to proclaim it in his oracle, Socrates is already implicitly superior to men who pride themselves on their worldly wisdom and accomplishments. Diotima's recognition thus encourages Socrates to cultivate a divine nobility against which the excellences and proudest achievements of ordinary men are as nothing. As their superior and Apollo's emissary, Socrates is exempt from having to acknowledge *their* supposed superiority. Indeed, he is duty-bound to chastise them—on behalf of the god, of course—should they try to assert it.

The story of his initiation by Diotima is Socrates' entry in the competition for the best discourse on love, *eros*, that forms the narrative spine of the *Symposium*. Socrates also wins an erotic competition within the dialogue. The arrival of a drunken Alcibiades, who intends to crown the host of the gathering,

Agathon, as the fairest and wisest (*sophôtatou kai kallistou*), interrupts the round of discourses on love. Seeing that Socrates is present, Alcibiades first berates him for being a tease. Always drawn to fair youths like Agathon and Alcibiades, and irresistibly attractive to them, Socrates never seeks the sexual gratification that the beloved may offer to a proper lover. In the end, Alcibiades literally crowns Socrates the fairest and wisest. Like Achilles, Socrates wins an erotic competition with fathers for the young and fair. (Rather than the daughter-like concubines of the *Iliad*, the objects of contention are the sons of men like Socrates' accuser, Anytus.) Finally, Socrates implies that Diotima crowns him as the victor in a related contest: She recognizes his unmatched affinity with the beautiful and perfect—the divine—which makes him uniquely well-qualified to become her philosophic initiate.[16]

The exemption from having to acknowledge paternal claims to superiority, and the implicit license to disparage these claims if a father should foolishly try to press them, might indeed exert a corrupting influence on a youthful Socrates and, through him, on the minds of other young men. Socrates' ironic questioning of Euthyphro would appear to indicate that any doctrine that justifies a son's defamation of his father is suspect (*Eu.* 3d–5a). But although Socrates implies that Euthyphro has been seduced by the illusion of "knowledge of things divine," Socrates does not view the doctrine of his own special kinship to the gods with similar wariness. Try as he might, he can find no fault in the god's designation of him as superior to "the general run of men."

Still, there are moments of doubt, even for the defiant Socrates of the *Apology*. At one point in his examination of Meletus, Socrates seems almost to ask to be shown the flaw in his airtight defense. Although it is beyond him to see how this might be, he allows the possibility that by exhorting the young to put aside other pursuits to seek the highest welfare of their souls, he might be corrupting them, encouraging them to disobey and disrespect true superiors (*Apol.* 30b). Since Socrates does encourage young men to discredit paternal claims to wisdom, it is likely that he does corrupt some of them, despite the apparent absurdity of this proposition from his point of view. Given the seamless quality of his defense, he might well wish for someone to play Socrates to his Euthyphro and point out its flaws to him.[17]

Be that as it may, in the *Crito* and the *Phaedo*, which are set in the interval between Socrates' conviction and execution, we encounter a chastened Socrates. Gone is the angry, defiant hero of the *Apology* who impugns the motives of his accusers and who denies the title of "juror" (*dikast*) to, and curses, those who vote to convict him (*Apol.* 39c–40a). Far from minimizing the educative competence of the laws and of fathers or ordinary Athenian citizens as he did at his trial, Socrates acknowledges the combined role of paternal laws and of an ordinary Athenian, his craftsman father, in engendering, raising, and educating him. This newfound—or rediscovered—humility with regard to the authority of laws, citizens, and fathers, moreover, underlies his determination to suffer the penalty prescribed by the jury.[18]

Socrates justifies his rejection of Crito's appeal to him to escape with the unsettling doctrine that a lawful sentence must be accepted, even if the verdict on which it is based is manifestly unjust and even if the penalty is death and thus irrevocable. In support of this doctrine, he argues that without its laws, a city ceases to exist in a significant sense—and, less plausibly, that to defy a lawful sentence, even in an extreme case such as his, would be to do all in his power to destroy the laws of Athens (*Crito* 50a–54e). (Thus he poses a threat to the paternal laws like that which Achilles poses to the ambiguous *themis* overseen by Zeus and Agamemnon in the *Iliad*.) Yet by allowing—even pro-voking—the Athenians to execute him, and by refusing the avenue of escape that they left open to him, Socrates did everything in his power to discredit the democratic laws of Athens. As Socrates himself prophesied (*Apol.* 38c), the damage was considerable. Enshrined in the Platonic dialogues, the infamy of Socrates' execution has served as a powerful indictment of democracy.

Socrates may win his greatest triumph over his democratic opponents by provoking them to execute him, yet this does not belie the sincerity of his contention that he must die to protect the laws and to appease the (by his lights, unjust) paternal anger underlying his indictment and sentence. Protes-tations of innocence notwithstanding, if Socrates were subliminally aware of the "wanton self-assertion" of his own claims to more-than-mortal authority, and if he imagined that his retaliation would destroy the (in his view) threat-ened fathers who effectively curse him, his decision to die would become more comprehensible, as would the tortured logic with which he defends it. Also true to type is the absence of blame toward—and idealization as more than mortal of—humanity-rejecting (surrogate) mothers and what he sees as envious mortal fathers who call for his destruction.[19]

Socrates' manifest concern to avoid retaliating against the laws for his unjust sentence suggests an explanation for his penitence that is in line not only with his expressed concerns, but also with the ironic, Achillean, heroic pattern in which a seemingly blameless hero incurs guilt through his angry response to an unjust accusation. Impersonating the laws of Athens, Socrates likens the escape proposed by Crito to a son's retaliation against a father for unjustly reproving or punishing him (*Crito* 50c–e). The motifs of paternal reproof and filial retaliation, together with a visitation by superhuman agents to prevent such retaliation, recall the divine interventions that dissuade Achil-les and Phoinix from violating the special injunctions against killing even an unjust king or a son-cursing father. Just as Athena intervenes to persuade Achilles to refrain from killing his commander, king, and would-be father-in-law, Agamemnon, so the paternal laws of Athens dissuade Socrates from "hitting back" against them.

While the humility with regard to fathers, citizens, and laws that Socrates displays in the *Crito* might be the result of his first contemplating, but then pulling back from, what he regarded as a parricidal act, we might more plausibly conjecture that he repents of actually having lashed out at his accusers at his trial. There Socrates implies that Anytus feigns a paternal concern with Socrates' corrupting influence on his son, and, after similarly impugning Meletus's motives, he dismisses Meletus's contention that the laws and ordinary Athenian citizens are capable of educating the young. Thus, although in the *Crito* Socrates represents himself as overcoming the *temptation* to retaliate, his penitence might nonetheless reflect his guilt over transgressions he committed in the heat of refuting his accusers' public slanders at his trial.[20]

A passage from the *Phaedo* lends support to this hypothesis. On the day that will end with his self-execution, Socrates speculates about the fate of the souls of those who, in a moment of passion, did violence to parents but then spent the rest of their lives regretting their action and trying to atone for it. They are sent to Tartaros, but unlike the incorrigibles with whom they share their gloomy abode, they are permitted once a year to entreat those whom they have outraged (*hubrisan*). If they fail to obtain forgiveness, they are sent back. "This goes on until they prevail upon those whom they have wronged [*êdikêsan*]; for this is the penalty [*dikê*] imposed upon them by the judges [*dikastôn*]" (*Phaedo* 113e–114c).

Socrates' unwavering protestations of innocence notwithstanding, his reference to sentences and jurors—and the contrast between his simple acknowledgment of guilt and of the authority of jurors on the day of his death, and his denial of both at his trial—might signal his remorse for his behavior in court. His idea that guilty souls can only leave Tartaros with the permission of those whom they have wronged echoes, but also significantly emends, his refusal in the *Crito* to leave his prison unless he can change the minds of the judges who unjustly convicted him. In the *Phaedo*, the man who prepares the hemlock praises Socrates for not cursing him as other condemned men do for carrying out government orders (116c). This too contrasts with Socrates' curse on the jurors who reached a lawful verdict at his trial (*Apol.* 39c, 38c). In the interval between his trial and execution, Socrates has evidently mastered the desire for retaliation that marred his defense. Thus purified, he can look forward to death as the final separation from his mortal part on the way to a purer, bodiless existence.[21]

But the tragic paradigm of the otherwise blameless hero whose only transgression stems from his anger at the unjust accusations against him finally holds up even less well for Socrates than for Achilles. After all, the formal

accusations that provoke Socrates' attacks on paternal and civic authority at his trial themselves respond to his habitual, unprovoked attempts to
undermine such authority. As Socrates himself points out, moreover, the
indictment merely reiterates informal accusations that his attempts to "help
the gods' cause" have provoked from the beginning (*Apol.* 18b–24a). Even
Socrates' retaliatory discrediting of accusers was probably routine. Such,
at any rate, is the implication of his catty swipe at Anytus in the *Meno.* Of
this leader of the restoration of Athenian democracy who has just warned
Socrates about his penchant for running down the reputations of other,
more distinguished Athenians, Socrates says, "He thinks I am slandering
our statesmen, and moreover he thinks himself to be one of them" (*Meno*
95a). Thus Socrates' respect for the engendering, nurturing, educative
role of the laws and of his own father in the *Crito* tacitly reverses not just
a momentary lapse at his trial, but a defining feature of his philosophic
practice.[22]

Viewed in this light, the mocking questions that Socrates puts in the
mouths of the laws in the *Crito* may respond less to the hypothetical "retaliation" that he contemplates than to the habitual disregard of paternal authority
and "retaliations" for its criticisms of him and encroachments on Apollo's
domain that are integral to his philosophic vocation. Indeed, in addition to
"impudence," Socrates has the laws accuse him of succumbing to just the
sort of beguiling fantasy of innate superiority to paternal authority that we
have posited in our model of heroic psychology. In a series of questions that
display a notable lack of concern with the justice of paternal actions and the
legitimacy of paternal authority, the laws ask Socrates whether he *imagines*
that he is equal to the laws or to his father. It is right, they ask, to retaliate
when a father scolds or punishes him? Is his wisdom such that it makes him
forget the honor he owes to them and his fatherland? Does he not *realize* the
importance of respecting and placating the anger of father and fatherland
(*Crito* 50e–51b)?

If, moreover, Socrates' offenses—with their unexamined roots in heroic
family dynamics—are habitual and he has proven unrepentant and incorrigible, and if his conflicts with paternal authorities have proved irresolvable,
this might explain his determination to die, in a way that a momentary loss of
control at his trial would not. Although Socrates tells Meletus that he ought
to remonstrate with him in the agora rather than take him to court, Socrates'
breezy disregard for Anytus's reproofs in the agora suggests that he was
impervious to criticism (*Meno* 94e–95a). As in the matter of fathers' objections to Socrates' effect on their sons, so it is here: if Socrates had chosen to
cross-examine Anytus rather than Meletus, the slipperiness of his argument
would have become apparent.

To be assailed by guilt and to dream of forgiveness and reconciliation with those whom one feels one has wronged is not the same thing, of course, as to renounce the attitudes and practices that give rise to self-accusation and desire for punishment—or even to be conscious of the relationship between the two. So it would appear to be with Socrates. The very passages that suggest his penitence explicitly proclaim his innocence: the offenses for which he reproaches himself on behalf of the laws are purely hypothetical; and the philosopher is as much above the common level of purity as the penitent sinner of the *Phaedo* is beneath it. Having shown himself an unrepentant and incorrigible—which is to say, heroic—sinner, immune to reproof, Socrates might well believe that the only way to stop him, as he says at his trial, will be to kill him; that the only way for him to avoid doing wrong will be to destroy himself or at least his unruly "mortal part."[23]

DEMOCRACY

Plato's account of Socrates' trial and execution forms the centerpiece of his indictment of democracy. At least in Socrates' conscious, unrepentant view, ordinary men lack the divine knowledge that would be required either to educate their sons "as men and citizens" (*Apol.* 20b) or to govern themselves. In the case of Athens, the incompetence of the demos and its leaders would not have been so bad had they heeded the gadfly philosopher who confronted them with their ignorance. But instead of acknowledging Socrates as god's gift to Athens and leaving the education of their sons to him and his followers, the Athenians killed Apollo's blameless emissary. Thus did the Athenians' arrogation of divine prerogatives lead to the injustice of Socrates' execution. It is a short step from Plato's account of the Athenians' crime against philosophy to the view that democracy per se is fatally flawed. Not only are ordinary, philosophically untutored men incapable of governing, they are liable to destroy anyone who renders a true account of the disastrous effects, on their own and their children's souls, of their arrogations of paternal and political authority.

If our analysis is correct, however, Plato's indictment of democracy is systematically distorted: it is not democratic leaders but Socrates who rebels against legitimate authority. (There is no reason to assume that all of the Athenians whose claims to competence and wisdom Socrates impugns are inept, defensive, envious Agamemnons.) Socrates is guilty of hubris, not they. His arrogant claims of kinship to a more-than-human power and knowledge derive from all-too-human—and, in archaic and classical Greek culture, all-too-common—fantasies of divine superiority. Of more importance to political philosophy, the psychological and cultural biases epitomized by Plato's Socrates produce a systematic blindness to ordinary mortals' capacities for self-government. Socrates' political vision and judgment, and that of his praise poet, Plato, are skewed. Understanding the distortion of democracy in Plato's heroic mythologizing of Socrates helps to explain corresponding distortions in Platonic political philosophy as a whole.[24]

One can deplore Socrates' execution (and lament the misdirected anger and the wish to appease outraged authorities, without regard for the justice of their indignation, that may have led him to accept or even provoke it) while still recognizing that his accusers had a point. A twentieth-century dispute between I. F. Stone and Allan Bloom confirms this. Although one was an anti-Platonic democrat and the other a Platonic critic of Athenian (and American) democracy, Stone and Bloom (the latter following his mentor, Leo Strauss) agree in positing a fundamental conflict between Socrates' teachings and Athenian democracy. Where Bloom and Stone diverge is in their characterization of the Socratic threat. Was it philosophic truth that gave offense (Strauss/Bloom) or a seductive but misleading philosophy that unjustly maligned ordinary men's capacity for self-government and encouraged the subversion of democratic institutions and laws (Stone)?[25]

Our analysis provides psychological underpinning for the latter position. Beyond exposing the hubris underlying Socrates' quarrel with democratic authority, it explains why this unwarranted self-assertion is virtually undetectable from within Socrates' worldview, making the charges against him appear perverse and unjust. As we have seen, Socratic thought offers ready, plausible counter-explanations for the repeated accusations and warnings provoked by Socrates' philosophizing: his victims' anger at having their pretensions and irresponsibility exposed, a general envy of his special affinity with the gods, and so forth.[26]

True, in the dialogues treating his last days, there are indications that at a subliminal level Socrates (and Plato) knew better—or rather, sided as strongly with the outraged paternal authorities who called for the philosopher's death as with the divinely appointed gadfly who casually impugned their competence to govern a state or educate their sons and who interpreted their protests as proof of their ignorance. Although Socrates' penitence and unconscious guilt may evince some underlying respect for democracy, his heroic psychology leads him to view democracy through a distorting lens, the refractive error of which can be explained with reference to a complex of cultural attitudes, family dynamics, and psychological predispositions that already had a long history in his day.

Both factors—ambivalence and systematic distortion—are operative in a by-now-familiar comedy of philosophic innocence. Plato clearly intends his account of Socrates' encounter with Anytus in the *Meno* to explain Anytus's subsequent indictment of Socrates: Socrates respected the prominent democrat, but Anytus failed to appreciate Socrates' good intentions toward Athens and its leaders. The impression of a similar friendliness toward democracy on Plato's own part is conveyed in the *Seventh Letter*, where Plato says that his political hopes were revived by the ouster of the Thirty Tyrants and the restoration of a moderate democracy led by a group of returned exiles that included Anytus, but that these hopes were dashed by the execution of his guiltless teacher (325a–c). When we reflect that Socrates' "respect" for Anytus and his colleagues includes an insistence that they admit that they can neither govern nor impart virtue or wisdom to their sons, however, and that Socrates reckons that he alone is even marginally competent in these areas, we may begin to wonder exactly what Socratic or Platonic respect for democracy consisted in.[27]

Since, for Sophocles in particular, Achilles is the prototypical tragic hero, this account of Achilles' and Socrates' innocent usurpations bears tangentially on ongoing debates over the philosophical relevance of Greek, especially Sophoclean, tragedy. Rather than the irreconcilable conflicts and incommensurable goods that Hegel's scholarly heirs have concluded characterize the *Iliad* and Greek tragedy, this analysis suggests that the *Iliad* exemplifies a tendency, rooted in culturally pervasive narcissism, to perceive authority conflicts as irreconcilable when they are not. Is Achilles to blame if his claims to quasi-divinity antagonize Agamemnon? Can Socrates help it if Apollo gives him a mission that brings him into conflict with the leaders of Athens? For Socrates more than for Achilles, the short answer is yes—even if the path that leads from conflict with paternal authority to self-sacrifice begins with child-sacrifice. Although each protests his innocence when charged with self-aggrandizement, each behaves as if burdened with unconscious guilt.[28]

The family patterns in which the heroic, sacrificial, glory-seeking strain of archaic and classical culture is rooted do not merely foster particularly intractable forms of oedipal conflict. They undermine public virtues that are crucial to democratic theory and practice. To become adults and responsible members of political communities, children first must learn to respect others' legitimate claims to rewards and honors while asserting their own. They must earn respect and self-esteem by acquiring the competencies that distinguish adults from children. These lessons, as fundamental to political competence as to the psychological and moral development that underpin it, are not mere precepts. They are results of childrearing, elements of character. Children's acceptance or rejection of rival parents' claims is formative. The culturally normative family dynamics considered here forestall children's development into responsible citizens as well as into psychological and moral adults.[29]

Even so, Achillean heroes would seem to suffer from an excess of two virtues that are crucial for democracy: a critical stance toward authority, and autonomy. The need to hold authorities accountable is intrinsic to democracy. Without citizen autonomy, self-government is at best an illusion.

In the dialogues of Socrates' last days, however, we see how a combination of cultural values and family dynamics can engender endless oscillation between unacknowledged, arrogant attacks on paternal authority and equally unconscious, guilty reparations for them. Despite Socrates' outspoken criticism of authorities, his story exemplifies the ways in which the psychology of Greek heroism undermines the abilities to recognize, appropriately criticize, and exercise authority that are fundamental to democracy.

But surely the Achillean philosopher who speaks truth to power is autonomous. Groundless arrogance may skew his criticism of authorities generally, and guilt, imagined as magically potent paternal imprecations, may forbid the exercise of authority, but is there any doubt that Plato's Socrates is autonomous? In the Socratic and Platonic view, the philosophic hero who follows the arguments wherever they lead, who commits himself to abide by the conclusions of rational inquiry, and who absolutely refuses to commit wrong even in the face of death epitomizes independence of mind and autonomy. In contrast to him stand stolid democrats like Anytus, whose conventional views of wisdom and virtue merely reflect current prejudice.[30]

Motivation aside, Socrates' lonely opposition to the democratic assembly's illegal, en bloc prosecution of the generals for refusing to endanger the living by recovering the bodies of the dead at Arginusae and his heroic refusal to carry out the unlawful orders of the Thirty to arrest Leon of Salamis demonstrate real moral courage and independence of mind. These qualities are evident as well both in his refusal to abandon his philosophic vocation, despite the threats of his enemies, and in his reasoned refusal to evade the penalties prescribed by law.

Even so, our analysis cautions against uncritical acceptance of what by Socrates' time had become a traditional opposition between the defiant independence of the hero and the herd mentality of the mass of men. The Achillean hero who makes a show of fearlessly speaking his mind, even if it angers powerful authorities, may be trying to prove he is something he is not. Dependent on a mother's image of him as an extension of her superiority, he is afraid to own up to his ordinary aspirations and his dismay at her failure to provide ordinary nurture. Desperate to appear superior in her and others' eyes, he makes a show of indifference to appearances. The disclosure of his hidden self would alienate a superior mother; he presents himself as transparent, hiding nothing. On this reading, scholars who accept Achilles' and Socrates' self-presentations, and their praise poets' representations of them, at face value mistake hero-sons' defensive self-constructs for reality.[31]

Lacking the autonomy that separation from a pretentious, rejecting mother and the acquisition of adult competencies would provide, the Achillean hero may fail to recognize true independence of mind and autonomy. Indeed, the he and his praise poet are apt to mistake the sort of autonomy that the hero lacks for mindless acceptance of conventional wisdom. Despite the real threat of being denigrated by their sons and rivals as uninitiated, vulgar mortals, men like Anytus persist in playing the part that ordinary mortal parents quickly disavow in myth—they persist in their attempts to interfere with the "divinization" of their sons. Neither are they afraid to betray their lack of affinity with the divine in other ways, as, for example by admiring and emulating worldly, entirely mortal, public men. In warning Socrates in the *Meno* about his penchant for running down the reputations of Athenian statesmen, Anytus may display greater independence and autonomy, and speak more freely, than Socrates does when he ingeniously "disproves" Anytus's conventional wisdom.

Other dialogues, notably the *Republic*, more clearly exhibit the effects on political thinking of the mutually reinforcing family dynamics and cultural values that we have examined here. Plato's attempt to imagine legitimate authority and just and beneficent order is skewed in ways our analysis would lead us to expect. First, it is marked by an obsessive need to repress tyrannical ambition and those who incite it, while it protests the philosopher's innocence in this regard. Second, it literally enthrones the Socratic philosopher's presumption of superiority to ordinary men, his divinely sanctioned right to rule the uninitiated. Third, and most important, it remains oblivious to the political capacities of ordinary men to create, govern, and defend polities based on mutual accommodation, respect, and responsibility for their common well-being. Since Plato's Socrates never relinquishes his fantasy of superiority to (in his view) inadequate mortal fathers, it is not surprising that he cannot readily imagine such a republic. To Socrates, with his superior wisdom, such a democratic polity would seem unjust; the authority that created and sustained it, a usurpation.[32]

Comparing himself to heroes on the point of death, Socrates at his trial prophesies vengeance (*timôrian*) against his slayers. (The mortally wounded heroes of the *Iliad*—notably Patroklos and Hektor—typically prophesize the deaths of their killers.) Socrates' vow of vengeance also echoes Achilles' against Agamemnon, just as his refusal to grant the title *dikast* to the jurors who voted for his execution echoes Achilles' ironic characterization of his fellow Achaeans as those "who dispense justice [*dikaspoloi*] and who uphold the ordinances [*themistas*] of Zeus" (1.237–39). But if Plato's Socrates implies that what passes for justice among the Athenians is like the blade that turns a living sapling into a dead stick in Achilles' heterodox genealogy of the scepter, Socrates' vow of vengeance—for which he purportedly condemns himself to death—may exculpate his actual sacrificers.[33]

Socrates' initiation by the divine-mother-figure Diotima, which may recapitulate an aristophilic upbringing or offer him the seductive prospect of transcending a shamefully ordinary one, strips him of a chance to be a respected and truly self-respecting—but less famous—member of the Athenian demos. His anger at the accusers who deny his claims to superiority and condemn him to death may be rooted in a prior negation of his value as the mortal son of a mortal father, but he directs his anger at this (unacknowledged) loss of a life in accord with *themis* away from a maternal figure whom he idealizes, and whom he has empowered to judge him worthy and superior or worthless, like the common run of men. He blames the "empty mediocrities" who vote to execute him, while leaving it to them to voice their vulgar criticisms of his Diotima-inspired philosophic practice. To identify with even his most self-respecting and competent paternal critics would be to lose his special status, rendering him unworthy, alien, and insignificant in Diotima's eyes. Even if Socrates' executioners represent envious, threatened fathers like Agamemnon more than unashamed mortal sons and fathers like Diomedes and Odysseus, Socrates' self-sacrifice completes a sacrificial process that began long before.

After Socrates succeeds in provoking the Athenians to condemn him, Crito makes one last attempt to persuade him to flee. By failing to take the opportunity to escape, he will be condemning his sons to the status of destitute orphans in the service of his ambition. In a rebuke reminiscent of Patroklos's of Achilles, Crito accuses Socrates of abandoning his post. It is not right (*dikaion*) for Socrates to abandon his sons when he could bring them up (*ekthrepsai*) and educate (*ekpaideusai*) them. One should either not have children at all, or take responsibility for their nurture and education. Yet, despite professing to cultivate goodness all his life, Socrates chooses the easier path, not the one a good and steadfast man would take (*Crito* 45c–d).

Like a divine mother confronted by a mortal parent's expectation that she provide normal nurture to her son, Socrates brushes aside the suggestion as the sort of unworthy concern that would occur to a member of the general populace (*pollôn*). He treats Crito much as "mother" Achilles treats "little girl" (*nêpiê kourê*) Patroklos. Later he has the paternal laws downplay the magnitude of the loss he will be inflicting on his sons. His death, which is crucial for the fame he seeks but is also an act of abandonment, will have little impact on his sons since his friends—men like Crito—will see to their upbringing and education in his place. Besides, consideration for children should not come before doing what is right—a dictum that suggests there is at best a tenuous relationship between the two.[34]

Here the allusion may be to Hektor, who makes a similar choice (that Socrates would doubtless approve). Rejecting his wife Andromache's entreaties, he abandons her and their *nêpios* son to harsh fates in order to efface his shame and win *kleos* (6.429–46, 22.482–99). "Hektor fails to recognize, or chooses to ignore, that his own death will destroy his son also. . . . Surely [Astyanax's] grandparents, his uncles, or someone, for Hektor's sake, would see that Astyanax was well brought up." But, even without the fall of Troy, the reality is otherwise. Achilles too has a son, Neopotlemos, "raised for his sake by others" (19.326–27). For Hektor, the sacrifice of family and city to the pursuit of glory is an aberration, but Socrates' death, like Achilles', may merely complete and make permanent losses and abandonments that have already occurred.[35]

Having chosen death and renown over life-saving escape, Socrates explains to Crito why he believes the ship that brings his final death sentence will arrive a day later than expected:

I dreamed that a beautiful, fair woman [*kalê, eueidês*], clothed in white raiment, came to me and called me and said, "Socrates, on the third day thou wouldst come to fertile Phthia." (*Crito* 44a–b)

The allusion is telling, as Phthia is the fatherland to which Achilles says he may return in three days (9.363, which Socrates quotes here); and Aphrodite's victory in the contest that disrupts Thetis's wedding notwithstanding, Thetis herself is Hera's chief rival for the title *kallistê*, the most beautiful and desirable of goddesses. A few lines later, Thetis tells Achilles of a choice analogous to the one that confronts Socrates: to stay and face certain death at Troy or ignominiously flee (9.410–16). In a parallel passage quoted approvingly by Socrates in the *Apology*, Achilles chooses to stay at Troy to avenge Patroklos's death and win glory, even though Thetis—having just lamented that she will never "receive [her son] won home again [*nostêsanta*] to his country and into the house of Peleus" (18.88–96, 18.441)—tells him that he will die soon after (18.95–96). The combined effect of these allusions is to suggest that Socrates looks forward to his death as a return home to Achilles' divine mother. Indeed, Socrates' imperviousness to Crito's pleas on behalf of Socrates' sons suggests that the reunion has already taken place.[36]

Notes

INTRODUCTION

1. As Bowlby acknowledges, studies of father-daughter incest and child sex abuse reveal similar dynamics in relationships with fathers, who are not primary caregivers: *Secure Base*, 57, 104–7. Cf. Hrdy, *Mothers and Others*, on the critical importance for hominins of "allomothers," who contribute to care. Primary caregivers remain particularly important, then, but responsible care or betrayal by persons in positions of trust, for example priests or military leaders, can have similar effects. On betrayal by commanders as a key factor in post-traumatic stress disorder, see Shay, *Achilles in Vietnam*, 25, cited by Freyd, *Betrayal Trauma*, 62.

2. On generalized competiveness, Slater, *Glory of Hera*, 36–37 (cites Finley, *World of Odysseus*; Huizinga, *Homo Ludens*; and Gouldner, *Enter Plato*). For an analysis of the roots of Homeric competition and violence in father-son conflict, see Wöhrle, *Telemachs Reise*. Leah Himmelhoch's review of it in *Bryn Mawr Classical Review* is very pertinent to this study.

3. The Mundugumor of Papua New Guinea developed remarkably similar aggression-enhancing family patterns, in which father-daughter and mother-son bonds took precedence over marital ones. Mead, *Sex and Temperament*, part 2.

4. Early family psychologists, on whose writings Slater relied, recognized that mothers may demand that children respond to rejection as if it is loving care. Slater took note of maternal "demands that reality be misperceived," but he made little use of concepts like Gregory Bateson's "double bind" in his analysis. Slater, *Glory of Hera*, 49, 53, 83, 346; Bateson et al., "Toward a Theory of Schizophrenia." Bowlby, also influenced by Bateson, made "defensive exclusion of information" about parental hostility or neglect a centerpiece of his theories of mother-infant attachment and its pathologies, in particular the formation of divided working models of parent-child relationships. Bowlby, *Attachment and Loss*, cited in Bretherton, "Origins of Attachment Theory," 767–68; Bretherton and Page, "Shared or Conflicting Working Models?" 551–52.

5. For challenges to uncritical reiterations of 18th- and 19th-century paradigms of patriarchy, misogyny, and seclusion of women in the historiography of classical Athens, see, e.g., Katz, "Ideology and the 'Status of Women,'" 21–43; Patterson, *Family in Greek History*; 3–43; also Pomeroy, *Families in Classical and Hellenistic Greece*, 14–16, 102–3, chaps. 2 and 3.

6. Maternal ambivalence and gender conflict: Slater, *Glory of Hera*, Loraux, *Mothers in Mourning*. Chodorow downplays Slater's emphasis on culturally specific maternal ambivalence in favor of sons' near-universal dependence on mothers but regards the issue of maternal destructiveness as unresolved. She also calls for culturally and historically specific, gendered psychologies such as this revision of Slater's. (Chodorow also cites an example of invoking children's birthrights to stigmatize working mothers.) Chodorow, *Reproduction of Mothering*, 103–8, 180–90; *Feminism and Psychoanalytic Theory*, 1–3 and no. 2, chap. 4 (with Susan Contratto) "The Fantasy of the Perfect Mother," 79–96, and 184–85. On male ambivalence toward women as primarily rooted in sons' near-universal dependence on mothers: Spiro, *Gender Ideology and Psychological Reality*, 151–52, who cites Dinnerstein, *Mermaid and Minotaur*, 59–60,165–72; Hudson and Jacot, *The Way Men Think*, 44–49. Mother-blame: Chodorow and Contratto (above); Caplan and Hall-McCorquodale, "Mother-Blaming in Major Clinical Journals," 345–46. But cf. Bowlby, *Secure Base*, 50, 126, 145; and Sroufe, *Development of the Person*, 17, 50, 53. 82, 118. For nuanced accounts that emphasize both sons' inevitable ambivalence and the effects of mothering, see Nussbaum, *Upheavals of Thought*, 209–12, and Pitkin, *Fortune Is a Woman*, 192–98.

7. On Achilles as "a charismatic warrior whose outstanding strength and prowess are matched by a dangerous, unconventional independent-mindedness," see Alexander, *War that Killed Achilles*, 36, who cites Hammer, "Who Shall Readily Obey?" 4. See also Saxonhouse, *Free Speech and Democracy*, 1–3, 118–120.

8. While the *Iliad*'s unrivalled prestige argues for the reality and durability of these family patterns, correspondences between actual family patterns and those implied in ancient Greek myth and epic necessarily vary. On ancient Greek families, see works by Patterson and Pomeroy cited above; also Golden, *Childhood in Classical Athens*. On the cultural preeminence of the *Iliad* in Greece from about 700 BCE onward: Lendon, *Soldiers and Ghosts*, 36, 65–67, 157–58. On differences between narratives that defensively exclude negative experience of child-caregiver relationships and those that reflect actual experience see, e.g., Cassidy and Kobak, "Avoidance and Its Relation." Psychological bases of "metaphysical beliefs": Nussbaum, *Upheavals of Thought*, 153–54, 193–220.

9. On philosophy's need for psychology and literature, and their importance for political thought and politics, see Nussbaum, *Upheavals of Thought*, 3, 6, 497–99.

CHAPTER ONE

1. Unless otherwise noted, references are to Richmond Lattimore's translations of the *Iliad* and *Odyssey*.

2. Agamemnon raged (*emênie*—verbal form of *mênis*) at Achilles (1.247).

3. On the association of Nestor, Odysseus, and Diomedes with the intellectual virtues of *noos* and *mêtis*, their connection with *nostos* (safe return home), and the contrast between all three and Achilles, see Frame, *Myth of Return*, chaps. 3–5.

4. Clay, *Hesiod's Cosmos*, 29, 132. Zeus's *mêtis* as learning from experience: Muellner, *Anger of Achilles*, 117. After promising to uphold justice, the first god Zeus honors is Styx, guarantor of oaths. *Theogony* 397–402. Also Holway, "Poetry and Political Thought," "Part II: The Justice of Hesiod." Nussbaum traces similar links between psychological development and justice in *Upheavals of Thought*, 212, 214–15.

5. *Theogony*, 392–96. In Hesiod's *Works and Days*, "the goal of human life is neither heroism nor glory, but the drabber ends of work and justice." Clay, *Hesiod's Cosmos*, 139. In the *Theogony*, *timê* "denotes the particular sphere over which a given divinity presides. . . . It is as though the mutually exclusive and perfect 'division of labor' in the divine world precludes" competitiveness over *timê* as "relative social prestige in an individual as recognized by his peers" in human society. Muellner, *Anger of Achilles*, 68.

6. On intimations of persistent threats to Zeus's regime, see Slatkin *Power of Thetis*, 261–62, and Muellner, *Anger of Achilles*, 90–91.

7. "The quarrel between Agamemnon and Achilles really comes down to a single issue: who has the right to *mênis*." "If Achilles is indeed the best of the Achaeans, then Agamemnon has no grounds for *mênis*." Although ultimately "nullified" by the *Iliad*, Agamemnon's claims are potentially legitimate. Muellner, *Anger of Achilles*, 108, 111, 119–22.

8. On the demigod hero's "rival status," which threatens any mortal king—not merely a weak, buffoonish one like Agamemnon—see Redfield, *Nature and Culture*, 93–95.

9. "After Agamemnon has precipitated the flight of the Greek army by his ill-advised test of their morale, Odysseus restores order among the troops (Il. 2.183–332). He snatches up the scepter of Agamemnon, the same scepter whose history the *Iliad* had earlier traced all the way back to Zeus (2.101–8). Quickly and efficiently, Odysseus manages to impose his authority and stops the army's headlong flight." Clay, *Hesiod's Cosmos*, 75, cites Reinhardt, *Die Ilias und ihr Dichter*, 113.

10. Sthenelos's *pateras poth' homoiêi entheo timêi* echoes and inverts Agamemnon's "so another man may shrink back from likening himself to me (*ison emoi phasthai*) and contending against (*homoiôthêmenai antên*) me" (1.187). Cf. Nestor: "never equal" (*ou poth' homoi emmore timêis*) is the king's portion of honor (1.278–79). As Muellner points out, the diction parallels Zeus's threat of *mênis* against Poseidon at 15.163–67. *Anger of Achilles*, 109.

11. Etymology of *Achilles* as he whose *laos* (host of fighting men) has *achos* (grief). Nagy, *Best of the Achaians*, chap. 5, §1f.

12. Foley rightly critiques "a key part of Slater's intrafamilial model . . . the remote and therefore relatively untroubled father-son relationship" because it ignores abundant evidence of "open father-son conflict." "Sex and State," 36. For the mythology that gave us Oedipus, and in which succession struggles pitting mothers and sons against fathers are a perpetual threat, this is a remarkable oversight, the more so

because the family psychologists on whom Slater relies link mother-son liaisons and paternal marginalization to father-son conflict. *Glory of Hera*, 57.

13. On the ways the *Iliad* alludes to or transforms myth into dramatic situations within the epic, see Schein, *Mortal Hero*, 19–29, and Slatkin, *Power of Thetis*, 4–6, both of whom cite Reinhardt, "Judgment of Paris."

14. Aeschylus's Klytemnestra justifies her lethal hatred by citing Agamemnon's penchant for sleeping with every Chryseis at Troy, as well as his sacrifice of their daughter, Iphigenia. *Agamemnon* 1438–44. Early source for Artemis's demand for the sacrifice of Iphigenia: Proclus Summary of the *Cypria* fr. 1.

15. Laura Slatkin's *Power of Thetis* shows how the *Iliad* defines itself and its characters through mythological allusions, notably *Iliad* 1.404, which alludes to a tradition outside the *Iliad* in which Thetis is fated to give birth to a son stronger than his father and who will overthrow his father: Pindar *Odes* 8.29f.; Aeschylus *Prometheus Bound* 908f.; and Apollod. *Lib.* 3.13.5.

16. Muellner argues that Thetis intervenes to avert a *loigos* that would have befallen the divine community as a result of Zeus's *mênis* at their rebellion, not a *loigos* that was about to befall Zeus from the rebellious *mênis* (implied in the *loigon amunai* theme) of Hera and her allies, including Zeus's formidable son, Apollo (see chaps. 2 and 5 this volume). Thetis saves Zeus at a time when he is in no position to inflict his *mênis* on anyone. Muellner also argues that the *Theogony* is a proem, a prefatory narrative, to the *Iliad*. Thetis's use of her prior service to Zeus to secure his support for her son's *mênis* constitutes "the precise link between Achilles' *mênis* and Zeus's that bespeaks the metonymic relationship between the whole *Theogony* and the first line of the *Iliad*." If the mother-backed *mênis* of Achilles incurs the *mênis* of Zeus, however, that suggests a different kind of link between the *Iliad* and *Theogony*. *Anger of Achilles*, 117 n. 48, 118–22.

17. Slatkin paraphrases the discussion of the quid pro quo structure of prayers in Muellner, *Meaning of Homeric EYXOMAI*, 27–28. *Power of Thetis*, 62.

18. Slatkin notes that had Achilles been the son of Zeus and Thetis, he would have been king of the gods and that "the price of Zeus's hegemony is Achilles' death." She goes on to state that his favor to Zeus is being *minunthadios*, but does not explain why acquiescing in his mortality, which secures Zeus's sovereignty, is not enough. *Power of Thetis*, 101–2.

19. Since Thetis can inflict as well as avert destruction (*loigon amunai*) "on a cosmic level," hers is "potentially the greatest threat of all." Slatkin, *Power of Thetis*, 88. While citing Nagy's "Mythological Exemplum" to argue that oral composition militates against ad hoc invention, Muellner notes that the *Iliad*'s inversion of the myth linking Thetis to a "son greater than his father in might" serves to downplay, even as it alludes to, Achilles' Theogonic threat to Zeus. *Anger of Achilles*, 119–20, 118 n. 54, 121–22 (cites Slatkin, *Power of Thetis* and Holway, *Poetry and Political Thought*).

20. Slatkin observes that the principal cause of Thetis's anger is being married to an inferior husband. Her implied *mênis* (at Zeus) is subsumed in Achilles' *mênis* at Agamemnon. *Power of Thetis*, 97–99, 103. Elaborated by Loraux, *Mothers in Mourning*, 49.

21. Many sources identify Dionysos-Zagreos as the offspring of Zeus and Persephone with whom Zeus mated in the form of a snake. A late source depicts Zeus and his rivals, maddened with passion, competing for Persephone, as Zeus and Poseidon competed for Thetis: Nonnus, *Dionysiaca* 5.562–6.168.

22. What Agamemnon "does not know, however, is that the usurpation he fears has in effect already taken place." Alexander, *War That Killed Achilles*, 36; cf. 23–25, 158, 200–201.

23. Cf. Clay's identification of Pandora as Wife and of her "jar and the 'gifts' of Zeus to mankind it contained . . . as a part of her dowry." *Hesiod's Cosmos*, 125.

24. "The rebellion that would have played in heaven will take place on earth." But how or why would it have "played in heaven" is unclear, given that "Agamemnon's strutting of power on earth below . . . is a reminder of the unassailable magnitude of the real thing: the authority of Zeus . . . against which the combined forces of all the other gods cannot contend—this is what it means to be the lord of heaven." Alexander, *War That Killed Achilles*, 29–31.

25. The quarrel among the goddess "about beauty" (*neikos peri kallous*). Proclus Summary of the *Cypria*.

26. On the plan or will of Zeus, see Nagy, *Best of the Achaians*, chap. 11, §11, §12, §14. On the characterization of Aphrodite as an ultimately subordinate daughter of Zeus within the Olympian family in the *Iliad* and *Homeric Hymn to Aphrodite*, in contrast to the *Theogony*'s account of her birth from the severed genitals of Ouranos, see Clay, *Politics of Olympus*, 200 and n. 159. For fuller accounts of Thetis as a daughter in Zeus's house whom Zeus desires, as well as Hera's resentment of Zeus's philandering and her appreciation for Thetis's resistance to her husband's advances, see Lang, "Reverberation and Mythology," 154; Apollod. *Lib.* 3.168; Apol. Rhod. *Argon.* 4.757, 783f.

27. For synthesis and sources for prophecies that Paris would bring about the downfall of Troy, see Graves, *Greek Myths*, 630–32, 637 (§159*f–h*).

28. Scodel relates various extra-Iliadic accounts of the *Dios boulê* to the *Iliad*'s specific purposes. "Achaean Wall," 33–50. Particularly apt here is Clay's contribution to the attempt (as Muellner puts it) to articulate the "unfolding meaning of the succession myth in the *Theogony*, its sequential relationship to the *Iliad* tradition, and ultimately, the relation of both the *Theogony* and the *Iliad* to the social context of their performance." Muellner, *Anger of Achilles*, 54. "With Gaia subdued, Mêtis incorporated, and thus the removal of the threat of succession, the stabilization of the cosmos appears complete." Yet Zeus must supplement these measures with "the generation of the heroes. Through their intercourse with mortals, the gods are able to deflect the more troublesome aspects of generation away from the gods themselves." Hesiod's Pandora, who, in perfect accord with the plans of Zeus, *Dios boulêsi* (*Theogony* 79; cf. 49, 99), both represents (as Wife) and dispenses attractively packaged evils to unsuspecting mortals. "The sending of Pandora and her jar . . . constitute part of Zeus's final dispensation, simultaneously ridding Olympus of noxious forces and foisting them off on mankind." Clay, *Hesiod's Cosmos*, 30, 125 et supra.

29. Hesiod, *Cat. of Women and Eoiae, fr. 68.100–106, Hom. Hymns and Hom.*;
Hyginus *Fables* 81; Apollod. *Lib.* 10.8.; Proclus Summary of the *Cypria* fr. 1; Pausanias *Pausanias Des.* 3.19.9–13.

30. For the *Iliad*'s suppression of Thetis's erotic aspect, see Slatkin, *Power of Thetis*, 31.

CHAPTER TWO

1. Hera, "the only immortal with whom *kouridios* is employed" (15.40), is uniquely designated as Zeus's lawful wife. Lowenstam, *Death of Patroklos*, 15–16.

2. "Parent-child alliances or triangulation . . . involve caregivers who are oriented toward their own whims, needs, and satisfaction at the expense of meeting their children's developmental needs." Jacobvitz, "Reconstructions of Family Relationships," 732. See also Minuchin, *Families and Family Therapy*, 102.

3. "Daughters sensed that their fathers' special interest in them did not develop in response to their own need for parental nurturance, but rather expressed their fathers' needs. In the person of the favorite daughter, the fathers found a wholly dependent being who would serve and flatter them and whom they could control. The favorite daughter also served as a pawn in the marital struggle. By flaunting the special relationship, the fathers revenged themselves upon their wives for real or imagined grievances and kept their wives actively competing for their attention." "At the time, most of the daughters took their fathers' side. It was easy enough to sympathize with the fathers' feelings of deprivation, for most of the daughters themselves felt slighted or neglected by their mothers." The failure of husbands to live up to the idealized images of fathers, daughters' inability to establish marriages based on mutuality and trust—for these and other dynamics of families in which daughters are in incestuous or quasi-incestuous relationships with seductive fathers, see Herman, *Father-Daughter Incest* (hereafter *FDI*), 43–45, 79–83, 97–98, 103, 112–15, 119–22. On the shock of strategic marriage, which represented "an involuntary and radical break in the life of a woman," see Foley, "Sex and State," 31; cf. Slater, *Glory of Hera*, 27.

4. Thetis's acceptance of her "loathed" marriage on this condition. Quintus Smyrnaeus, *Fall of Troy*, 3.580. Attempts to "recapture the specialness that they had felt in the relationships with their fathers," Herman, *FDI*, 103. Highlighting mothers' attempts to recoup their special status as father-favored daughters by rearing hero-sons is one of the ways in which this study revises and extends Slater's *Glory of Hera*, published a decade before Judith Herman and others exposed the prevalence of father-daughter incest and the family dynamics associated with it.

5. Herman's work sparked research on various types of generational boundary dissolution, including seductive mother-son relationships, that exhibit a strong correlation with a maternal history of father-daughter incest or seductiveness. Sroufe and Ward, "Seductive Behavior of Mothers," 1224–28; Sroufe et al., "Generational Boundary Dissolution," 322. As mothers, incest victims did not do to their children "the identical things that were done to them, but rather engaged in culturally dictated female counterparts." Sroufe et al., *Development of the Person*, 115–19. See also

Fullinwider-Bush and Jacobvitz, "Transition to Young Adulthood," 99: "Cross-gender boundary violations [i.e., father-daughter and mother-son] and an emotionally distant marriage resemble the family dynamics typically described by incest victims (Cole & Woolger, 1989). Mothers who, as children, were sexually abused have been observed to engage in a reversal of parent-child roles with their own children (Burkett, 1991)."

6. In classical Athens, "marriage did not involve a change in [a woman's] legal or political status, for wives were as subordinate as daughters. It signaled a change in control: the husband replaced the father . . . as a woman's *kyrios*." Golden, *Children and Childhood*, 48–9.

7. This study takes its place among still rare attempts to determine "how different cultures . . . fit attachment behaviors and relationships into their overall social organization." Bretherton cites ethnographies by Firth (Tikopia) and Bateson and Mead (Bali) as examples of how "a biological system is molded to a particular society's purposes (by fostering specific relationships [with parents or parent-figures] or controlling exploration)." Bretherton, "Origins of Attachment Theory," 770. More relevant to ancient Greece is Mead's ethnography of the Mundugumor, for whom incestuous or quasi-incestuous father-daughter and mother-son relationships substituted for troubled marital ones. Mundugumor "ropes" are "composed of a man, his daughters, [his daughters' sons,] his daughters' sons' daughters; or if the count is begun from a woman, of a woman, her sons, her sons' daughters, her sons' daughters' sons, and so on." Marriages are conflictual; mothers resent special, sometimes actually incestuous, father-daughter relationships; fathers are intensely competitive toward sons favored by mothers who may sleep with them; men and women are in general aggressive, vulnerable to insult, and prone to anger. Hostility to infant care-seeking is the most distinctive feature of Mundugumor mothering. Mead, *Sex and Temperament*, 166–67, 185–86, 204. A critique of critiques of Mead on the Mundugumor: Lipset, "Rereading *Sex and Temperament*," 693–713.

8. "It is certainly significant from the standpoint of the external social context of the myth that the first family in the world is characterized by *echthrê* 'hatred' between father and children rather than the *philotês* 'friendship' that ideally governs family relations in the epic world and in daily life." Muellner, *Anger of Achilles*, 61. For a sampling of recent scholarship on the rise of the polis, see Alexander, *War That Killed Achilles*, 10–11.

9. "None of the informants thought that her parents were happily married; many were well aware that their parents were miserable together." Herman, *FDI*, 80. Fullinwider-Bush and Jacobvitz, "Transition to Young Adulthood," 86–88.

10. Bowen, "overadequate-inadequate reciprocity," in "Family Relationships in Schizophrenia," 153; Lidz, et al. "Intrafamilial Environment," 246; Wynne et al., "Pseudo-Mutuality," 206f. For the integration of attachment theory with family systems theory, in which marriages characterized by "either distance or conflictual . . . interactions" are associated with destructive parent-child alliances, see Jacobvitz, "Cross-Sex and Same-Sex," 41.

11. *Theogony* to *Iliad*: Muellner, *Anger of Achilles*, 95–96.

12. On father-daughter incest, and Freud's "disastrous" abandonment of the seduction theory, Bowlby, *Secure Base*, 57, 104–6, 78. "Most of the research on the effects of cross-gender alliances on children comes from studies of incest victims, cases in which fathers turn to their daughters, instead of their wives, to gratify their need for companionship, affirmation, sex, and nurturing. Females who have experienced intrafamilial sexual abuse during childhood . . . are more likely to engage in boundary disturbances with their children." Jacobvitz, "Cross-Sex and Same-Sex," 44, who cites Burkett, "Parenting Behaviors of Women." Like Thetis, Demeter, and Leto, seductive mothers generally single out one son for special attention. Sroufe et al., *Development of the Person*, 116.

13. On the historicity of female prizes of war, see Alexander, *War That Killed Achilles*, 5. Fathers who are seductive with favored daughters may initiate sexual relationships with their daughters' age mates or friends. Herman, *FDI*, 112.

14. "Mothers' resentment made the daughters feel guilty, but could not entirely extinguish the pleasure they derived from their favored status. Some even exulted in their mothers' mortification: Paula: 'Face it, she was just jealous. The man she loved preferred me!'" But "these competitive feelings often concealed a deeper longing for maternal care and protection. Like the incest victims, many of these women felt that their mothers had in some degree sacrificed them to their fathers. While overtly the mothers resented the special relationship between father and daughter, covertly, the daughters felt, their mothers promoted or at least acquiesced in the relationships." Herman, *FDI*, 83, 114.

15. Herman, *FDI*, 97–98, 114.

16. These daughters' narcissistic orientation is a product of parent-child boundary dissolution, just as the hero-sons' narcissistic orientation is the product of similar family dynamics and relationships with their mothers. In "the kind of personality that Winnicott (1960) describes as 'false self' and Kohut (1977) as 'narcissistic,' the information being blocked off [consists of] signals, arising from both inside and outside the person, that would activate their attachment behavior and that would enable them both to love and to experience being loved." Bowlby, *Secure Base*, 34–35. On both daughters' sense of specialness and the belated realization, on the part of incest victims and daughters of seductive fathers, that fathers have sacrificed the daughters' needs for care—or have simply sacrificed their daughters—to the fathers' needs: Herman, *FDI*, 103, 115. "Eleanor Hill, an incest survivor, describes her stereotypical role as the virgin chosen for sacrifice, a role that gave her an identity and a feeling of specialness: 'In the family myth I am the one to play the "beauty and the sympathetic one." The one who had to hold [my father] together. In primitive tribes, young virgins are sacrificed to angry male gods. In families it is the same.'" Herman, *Trauma and Recovery*, 106–7.

17. In many cases, distant or hostile mother-daughter relationships precede the onset of incest. "In the special alliance with their fathers, many daughters found the sense of being cared for which they craved, and which they obtained from no other source. The attentions of their fathers offered some compensation for what was lacking in their relations with their mothers." The mere presence of a functional mother reduces the likelihood of incest. Herman, *FDI*, 82–83, also 44, 79–82, 103, 112–14.

18. Daughters who have been sexually or emotionally exploited by fathers, and who are seductive with sons, tend to be "hostile, derogating, or derisive" toward their daughters. Sroufe et al., *Development of the Person*, 116. In addition to intense rivalry for fathers' attention, "accounts of incest victims are replete with descriptions of distant, unavailable mothers and with expressions of longing for maternal nurturance." Herman, *FDI*, 44. Comparing *The Homeric Hymn to Demeter* to *The Oresteia*, Foley says "the events of both . . . are triggered by a violent male intrusion into the mother-child bond and the real or metaphorical sacrifice of the daughter Persephone or Iphigenia." Foley, *Homeric Hymn to Demeter*, 116.

19. "My mother's a bitch and a nag. I don't know why Daddy stays with her; she makes his life miserable. Daddy and I really understand each other. If my mother doesn't like it, too bad." Mothers "perceived, correctly, that what bound father and daughter together was in part a shared hostility toward themselves." Herman, *FDI*, 114.

20. Links between mothers' exploitation by their fathers, their seductiveness toward sons, and their hostility toward daughters: Sroufe et al., "Generational Boundary Dissolution," 317; Sroufe et al., *Development of the Person*, 115–17.

21. Slatkin locates the "primary cause" of Thetis's grief (*achos*) and resulting *mênis* in "the wrath of a goddess who is forced to marry a mortal man without compensation" (Loraux's paraphrase). Demeter's *mênis* stems from the forced marriage of Zeus's and Demeter's daughter, Persephone, to Hades, which, Loraux points out, may repeat Demeter's rape (with Zeus's connivance) by Zeus's other brother, Poseidon. Zeus uses all three unions to preserve his dominant position in "the existing hierarchy of divine power." Slatkin, *Power of Thetis*, 97–99. Loraux, *Mothers in Mourning*, 49, 59. On the trauma for a fifteen-year-old daughter of leaving her father's *oikos* for that of her thirty-year-old husband in classical Athens, see also Golden, *Children and Childhood in Classical Athens*, 49.

22. Sophocles, *Tereus*, fr. 524, Nauck; as quoted by Hans Licht, *Sexual Life in Ancient Greece*, (Barnes and Noble, 1963, 39–40); in turn quoted by Slater, *Glory of Hera*, 27, and Foley, "Sex and State," 31.

23. Foley, *Homeric Hymn to Demeter* 284–86.

24. Remarkably, both Foley and Slater view the relationship between Iphigenia and the father who orders her sacrifice to save face in Euripides' *Iphigenia at Aulis* as tender and loving, disagreeing only about whether such father-daughter bonds were rare (Slater) or common—exacerbating the trauma of betrayal when daughters are sold like commodities by their fathers via strategic marriages (Foley). Slater, *Glory of Hera*, 26–27, 169; Foley, "Sex and State," 31.

25. The daughter's "contradictory identities, a debased and an exalted self, cannot integrate." She "cannot develop a cohesive self-image with moderate virtues and tolerable faults. In the abusive environment, moderation and tolerance are unknown. Rather, the victim's self-representations remain rigid, exaggerated, and split. In the most extreme situations, these disparate self-representations form the nucleus of dissociated alter personalities." Herman, *Trauma and Recovery*, 106.

26. Husbands are seen as inadequate compared to idealized fathers; daughters devalue mothers, attempt to recapture specialness of relationship with fathers, and

continue relationships with idealized, seductive fathers: Herman, *FDI*, 122, 79, 103, 120. Father-favored daughters' husbands tend to be seductive with daughters, just as father-favored daughters tend to be seductive with sons. Jacobvitz, "Transmission of Mother-Child Boundary Disturbances," 516. Lidz et al., "Intrafamilial Environment."

27. Herman, *FDI*, 124–25; 32–33, 152–53, 231; Herman, *Trauma and Recovery*, 114, who cites Kaufman and Zigler, "Do Abused Children Become Abusive?" who actually answer with a measured affirmative. Cf. also Egeland et al., "Breaking the Cycle," 1086. But "early experience is not destiny." Various factors can break the "cycle of mistreatment." Sroufe et al., *Development of the Person*, 118, 240.

28. Herman, *FDI*, 48–49. Chodorow, *Reproduction of Mothering*, ix–xii, 106–8; Chodorow, *Feminism and Psychoanalytic Theory*, 4–5.

29. When "the child's attachment behavior is the very thing being rejected," this is a prime cause of segregation of information in manifest and suppressed working models. Solomon and George, *Attachment Disorganization*, 12. In "narcissistic parentification" the "child determines that it is better to identify with an illusion of invulnerable greatness than to identify with a devalued and seemingly worthless true self." Wells, "Object Relations Therapy," 119. Cf. Nussbaum, who cites Winnicott and Bowlby on anxious, perfectionist mothering and the child's narcissism and shame versus delight in his or her care-seeking, human self. *Upheavals of Thought*, 193–97, 212–19. On "narcissistic self-enhancement" as a response to a situation in which "bids for proximity and support . . . typically result in a negative outcome (inattention, rejection, anger, disdain, abuse) for showing vulnerability or need," see Mikulincer et al., "Attachment-Related Defensive Processes," 296, 300, 302.

30. Bateson, "Toward a Theory," 256–57. Bowlby inspired by Bateson and other family systems theorists: Bretherton and Page, "Shared or Conflicting Working Models?" 551. Similarity of Bowlby's account of a child's response to maternal rebuff and the "double-bind" situation described by Bateson: Main and Stadtman, "Infant Response to Rejection." On children's responses to mothers who are "angry, inexpressive, and disliking of physical contact with the infant" and "pressures by parents . . . to ensure that their children develop and maintain a wholly favourable picture of them," Bowlby, *Secure Base*, 55, 104–6.

31. Citing writings of Bateson, Lidz, and Wynne on schizophrenia, Slater characterizes Hera as a "'schizophregenic mother'" who "demands that reality be misperceived," although this is not a central element of his analysis. *Glory of Hera*, 346. On the importance of attention to father-daughter incest (by Herman and others), "both to its unrecognized high incidence and to its pathogenic effects," including divided working models, on child-victims, see Bowlby, *Secure Base*, 104–6. Herman's critique of the patriarchal bias of family psychology and notion of the "schizophregenic" mother: *FDI*, 32, 152. Recent studies of the co-causality of genetics and harmful family dynamics in depression and schizophrenia: Sroufe et al., *Development of the Person*, 237–38.

32. "If the attachment figure has acknowledged the infant's needs for comfort and protection while simultaneously respecting the infant's need for independent exploration of the environment, the child is likely to develop an internal working model of self as valued and reliable. Conversely, if the parent has frequently rejected the

infant's bids for comfort or for exploration, the child is likely to construct an internal working model of self as unworthy or incompetent." Bretherton, "Origins of Attachment Theory," 767. "Betrayal by a trusted caregiver is the core factor in determining amnesia for a trauma." Freyd, *Betrayal Trauma*, 62.

33. "If the power to *loigon amunai* is bivalent—if the one who wields it cannot only avert destruction but also bring it on—then the threat posed by Thetis, who could *loigon amunai* on a cosmic level, is potentially the greatest of all." Slatkin, *Power of Thetis*, 88. When the child experiences the parent as frightening, "the child is compelled both to approach and withdraw from the same figure." In such situations, Bowlby proposed that both anxiety (fear) and anger are segregated because their display would likely alienate the attachment figure still further." Solomon and George, *Attachment Disorganization*, 12–13; Mikulincer et al., "Attachment-Related Defensive Processes," 298.

34. Précis of Bowlby, *Loss*, in Bretherton, "Origins of Attachment Theory," 87. Bowlby, *Secure Base*, 101, 102. In addition to gross abuse and neglect, situations that are "subtle and hidden, but common," such as mothers' reliance on sons to meet their needs while neglecting sons' nurture, are a frequently overlooked cause of the formation of divided working models. Bowlby, *Secure Base*, 107–8.

35. "Emotional responses" such as anger "may be directed away from the person who caused them to third persons or to the self." Bretherton, "Origins of Attachment Theory," 768. "It is better to be a sinner in a world ruled by God than to live in a world ruled by the Devil." Fairbairn, *Psychoanalytic Studies*, 65–67, quoted in Nussbaum, *Upheavals of Thought*, 215–17. Bowlby recounts how an abused girl redirected her anger "away from her mother and toward something which, or someone who could not retaliate. As a child it was dolls, as an adult crockery, and her baby's pram, but never quite the baby herself." Bowlby, *Secure Base*, 87. Although she denies the intergenerational transmission of abuse, Herman presents a similar account of the psychology of abused children: splitting, idealized parent, bad child, displacement of anger "far from its dangerous source . . . to discharge it unfairly on those who did not provoke it," resulting in "self-condemnation." *Trauma and Recovery*, 96, 104–7, 114.

36. Although these father-son dynamics are explored by the family psychologists on whom Slater relies, he expressly discounts them with regard to classical Athenian society. *Glory of Hera*, 57–59.

37. On lack of maturation as a characteristic of heroes nourished by divine *kourotrophos* mothers, see Sinos, *Achilles*, 13, 22–24.

38. In narcissism born of mother-son incest, "the enormous guilt related to perceived oedipal transgressions leads these patients to fear retaliation from an enraged, vindictive, and castrating father at any moment." Gabbard and Twemlow, "The Role of Mother-Son Incest."

39. Cf. Alexander, *War That Killed Achilles*, 29: "Achilles will assert his birthright—not as the lord of heaven but as the best of the Achaeans. Stronger than all his father's generation . . . he will operate beyond the reach of the conventional moral code of their society."

40. "The word *loigos*, 'devastation,' and the expression *aeikea loigon amunai*, 'to ward off unseemly *loigos*,' are contextually restricted in epic to the devastation that

is the result of *mênis*." If *mênis* is rooted in the proneness to dishonor instilled by heroic parenting, it makes sense that it is associated with heroic epic and its subject, *klea andrôn*, but not the *Theogony*, and its subjects, *theon genos*, the "birth of the gods"—and of cosmic *themis*. Also, honor in the *Theogony* has a different meaning and is less associated with conflict than it is in heroic epic. Muellner, *Anger of Achilles*, 117 (cites Nagy *Best of the Achaians*, 73–76); *mênis* and epic vs. Theogony: 95–96, 68 n. 39.

CHAPTER THREE

1. The myths related here are versions or composites taken from a number of sources. Since the *Iliad* is one of the earliest surviving works of Greek poetry, many of these sources are later than Homer's epic. They may nonetheless summarize lost epics or retell orally transmitted myths that may be contemporaneous with or precede our text of the *Iliad*. Myths constantly evolve, so later elaborations can bring out logic implicit in earlier ones. What is clear is that the *Iliad* exists within a vast mythological matrix, even though it is often impossible to tell with certainty whether a particular version of a myth that we know from another source was known to Homer and his audience. Slatkin, *Power of Thetis*, ix–xvi, 2–6.

2. Apollod. *Lib.* 3.12.6 along with numerous other versions cited in tr. note 14.

3. In one form of parent-child boundary dissolution, a psychologically controlling parent tells the child, in effect, "If you are not what I need you to be, you do not exist for me." Ogden (1979) quoted in Kerig, *Implications of Parent-Child Boundary Dissolution*, 12.

4. On the combination of inflated views of self with "splitting defenses—that is, attempts to protect desirable aspects of the self by detaching them from the undesirable aspects" that are projected onto others, see Mikulincer et al., "Attachment-Related Defensive Processes," 302–3.

5. The child may idealize a rejecting parent "as a means of reducing negative affects that would be associated with reflection about the true nature of the relationship" and "to reduce the child's sense of alienation from the parent in a manner similar to what Anna Freud (1966) termed 'identification with the aggressor.'" Cassidy and Kobak, "Avoidance," 310.

6. Peleus here represents a paradigm case of anxious-ambivalent attachment—clinging to a rejecting caregiver—that is often manifest as early as the first year of life and carried over into marital relationships. Bowlby, "Secure Base," 126–27. McCarthy and Taylor, "Avoidant/Ambivalent Attachment," 465. Macfie, "Intergenerational Transmission," 55. Combining attachment and family systems theory, Byng-Hall describes a "distance conflict" in which one spouse "is ambivalent and clings while the other is avoidant and distances himself or herself from any emotional demands." Byng-Hall "Relieving Parentified Children's Burdens," 380.

7. Quite apart from the mother's need to recoup her favored status through her son, the father's selection of a mate like his (rejecting) mother can result in his son experiencing similar maternal rejection. "A boy who is in a role reversal with his mother

may grow up to marry a woman who has an internal working model of the family similar to his. This woman may then repeat with their son (but not their daughter) in the next generation her husband's role reversal with his mother." Macfie, "Intergenerational Transmission," 55.

8. Wells and Jones, "Object Relations Therapy," 118–19. On the importance of the context of care, including "adult support in childhood or current support," for breaking the "cycle of mistreatment," see Sroufe et al., *Development of the Person*, 118.

9. Kohut describes the son's oscillating views of the narcissistic mother-son relationship in these terms: "I am perfect" (i.e., an extension of the mother—like Phokos, or Achilles), or "You are perfect and I am part of you" (Peleus and Thetis, or Aiakos and Psamathe). Kohut, *Analysis of the Self*, 26–27.

10. Graves, *Greek Myths*, 81, who cites Antonius Liberalis, *Transformations*, 38; and Tzetzes, *On Lycophron*, 175, 901.

11. Apollod. *Lib*. 3.13.6; Apol. Rhod. *Argon*. 4.757f. (and scholiast on 4.816); scholiast on Lycophron 178; Statius, *Achilleid* 1.134f. Abandonment and threats of abandonment cause "segregated systems" of information and divided working models. Solomon and George, *Attachment Disorganization*, 12. Alexander interprets these as "desperate tactics deployed by Thetis to rescue her mortal offspring from his mortal fate." Alexander, *War That Killed Achilles*, 91–92.

12. Apol. Rhod. *Argon*. 4.872–78. Thetis's angry response, which encompasses the son as well as the interfering mortal parent, illustrates the consequences of perceiving and responding to abuse: abrupt cessation of care-giving behaviors on which the child's physical and psychological well-being depend. The myth illustrates Freyd's theory (based on Bowlby's) that "information blockage" regarding abuse (which often involves an alternative, rationalizing account of reality by perpetrators and other family members) functions not (only) to avoid psychological pain, but to suppress responses to abuse that might provoke anger or abandonment. Freyd, *Betrayal Trauma*, 69, 71. For other versions, see translator's note on Apollod. *Lib*. 3.13.6.

13. See also Meleager story. A nearly identical story is told by Plutarch, in his *On Isis and Osiris* (*Moralia* IV?), of the goddess Isis burning away the mortal parts of Dictys of Byblos, son of Queen Astarte, and being likewise interrupted before completing the process. *Hymn Dem*., 335–36, 240–41 in Hesiod, *Hom. Hymns and Hom*.; cf. *Iliad* 24.58–60.

14. Mirroring the attitudes Herman observes in incestuous fathers, divine mothers view themselves as "aloof from moral rules of ordinary people" whom they regard as "lesser beings" while they are subject to a "higher law." Herman, *FDI*, 231. Although Foley notes that Demeter, angered by mortal presumption, throws Demophoon to the ground, leaving him gasping, as dying heroes do in epic, and she draws parallels between this incident and Demeter's placing Demophoon in fire to actual rites in which children were exposed to weed out those undeserving of nurture, such actions play no part in Foley's account of female psychology or sons' psychological development. Following Chodorow, Foley argues mothers are liable to treat daughters *but not sons* as extensions of themselves, regarding boys as separate and different from themselves, fostering their independence and autonomy through identification with their

fathers or fathers' roles. Demeter's unusual mothering practices, and the carnage that, according to Demeter's prophecy, will strew Demophoon's path to unending honor, appear dire only to the uninitiated: foolish mortals—or scholars—who are unaware that Demophoon is a paradigmatic initiate in Demeter's Eleusinian Mysteries. Foley, *Homeric Hymn to Demeter*, 48–52; 113–22; 243f. Foley references Chodorow's essay in the same volume. Loraux, *Mothers in Mourning*, 53–54, notes Metaneira's "serious mistake of interpretation when she prematurely started to mourn a child whom Demeter was saving from the life of mortals" and emphasizes the protectiveness of mothers toward sons whom the male-governed state claims for military use. But she silently follows Slater in locating a highly *ambivalent* mother-son relationship at the center of Greek myth, epic, and drama.

    15. Foley, *Homeric Hymn to Demeter*, 231–300.

    16. Foley, *Homeric Hymn to Demeter*, 262–74.

    17. Main, "Predicting Rejection of Her Infant," 212.

    18. On the presentation of Thetis and Demeter as *kourotrophos*, see Slatkin, *Power of Thetis*, 7, 26–27, 40–41 (incl. notes 26 and 27). Slatkin notes that Thetis's nurture and protection of Achilles are predicated on and even hasten her son's imminent, heroic death and that goddesses who protect their mortal sons from death diminish their heroic stature. *Power of Thetis*, 44–45.

    19. Bowlby's ideas of defensive exclusion of information and the construction of divided working models are similar to Frankel's on identification with the aggressor: "Chronic identification with the aggressor can lead to a situation in which the aggressor's beliefs take the place of one's own and one's beliefs are no longer drawn from one's own experience. One's narrative about one's own life is not derived from personal experience but from someone else's story." Frankel, "Exploring Ferenczi's Concept," 114.

    20. Mothers who were themselves deprived of care and who look to their children to mother them are liable to become impatient and angry when the child "fails to oblige and starts crying, demanding care and attention." Bowlby, *Secure Base*, 86. The mother of Winnicott's perfectionist patient, B, "required perfection of herself, and interpreted any neediness on the part of the infant as a signal that she had not achieved the desired perfection (which she saw as commanded by a quasi-paternal idealized husband)." For her, a perfect feeding was one in which B did not cry or demand to be fed. B's mother "understood perfection as a kind of death of the child, in which he would have nothing more to demand." Winnicott, *Holding and Interpretation*, 10, 95–97, 123, 163, 172; quoted in Nussbaum, *Upheavals of Thought*, 193–98.

    21. Cf. 18.436–38. Thetis's reminiscence gives us a "glimpse of Thetis as *kourotrophos*, nurturer of the plant-like *kouros*, Achilles." Sinos, *Achilles, Patroklos*, 24. Thetis's account of rearing Achilles, together with myths to which the *Iliad* alludes, corresponds to narratives of rejected children. "Subjects with high idealization claimed . . . an idyllic past with nearly perfect parents. However, careful reading of [interviews] revealed either a lack of specific examples to substantiate these generalizations or actual contradictory indications of lack of support or rejection of the child by the parent. . . . The defensive nature of this idealization has been underscored by the finding of a strong correlation between the subject's idealization of the parent"

[for example, by bestowing the epithet *kourotrophos* on Thetis?] and "rejection by that parent in childhood." Main and Goldwyn, "Predicting Rejection." Cassidy and Kobak, "Avoidance," 310.

22. Hainsworth and other commentators note a possible allusion to Achilles' vulnerable spot in Paris's wounding of Diomedes with an arrow in the foot (11.369f.), in Kirk, *The Iliad*, 3:267. See also Mackie, "Achilles in Fire."

23. Daughters who are victims of paternal seduction or incest are elevated by fathers to a "special position." They may glory in their erotic triumph over their mothers while realizing that they are robbed of a nurturing family that would foster development to adulthood. Herman, *FDI*, 79–81, 83, 86, 97–98, 103, 122. There is an extensive debate over why Demeter interrupts her search for her daughter to immortalize Demophoon. Clay links the humiliation and betrayal of a forced, strategic marriage to the fashioning of a hero-son by a divine mother: Demeter plans to avenge Zeus's betrayal of her and their daughter by fashioning an immortal son who will topple Zeus from power. Like the son of Thetis, Demophoon is a potential threat to Zeus. Clay, *Politics of Olympus*, 222–29. On tales of Demeter's rapes by Zeus and Poseidon, see Foley, *Homeric Hymn to Demeter*, 125; and Lowenstam, *Death of Patroklos*, 59.

24. Clay notes that Leto's persona in *Hom. Hymn Apol.* is defined by contrast to Hera's. This paramour of Zeus (whom Clay identifies as "husband to Leto") "exemplifies the conduct appropriate to the consort of Zeus, conduct characterized by quiet concord rather than rivalry and opposition." Clay, *Politics of Olympus*, 22, 69–70. The hymn's portrayal of Leto mimics the thinking of daughters of incestuous or seductive fathers: ignoring fathers' contribution to marital discord (Zeus's philandering), in which daughters' themselves play a part, as well as fathers' sacrifice of daughters' needs to their own, daughters view themselves, in contrast to fathers' wives, as the kind of spouse that beleaguered, idealized fathers deserve. Herman, *FDI*, 114, etc.

25. *Hymn Apol.*, 1–14, 89–130, 315–16, in Hesiod, *Hom. Hymns and Hom.* Apollod. *Lib.* 1.4.1, 3.5.6 and n. 1. Alternatively, Apollo is angered: *Iliad* 24.602–17.

CHAPTER FOUR

1. The account of catharsis presented here builds upon those of René Girard and Walter Burkert rather than that of Aristotle, but it differs from the former in tracing the violence problem in ancient Greek societies to cultural rather than biological evolution. This leads to differing claims about what is denied and purged. Girard, *Violence and the Sacred*, 2–4, 17–19.

2. See, for example, Muellner, on the contrast between Agamemnon's sacrifice of the *laos* "for whom he is responsible," which "undermine[s] the basis of his own authority," and Achilles' kingly care for them. *Anger of Achilles*, 103–4, 117. For links to Achilles' "relationship of identity and antagonism with Apollo that pervades the *Iliad*," see Nagy, *Best of the Achaians*, 103 n. 22. For Alexander, Achilles here demonstrates instinctive, genuine leadership and elsewhere, for example, "real leadership." *War That Killed Achilles*, 23–25, 158, 200–201.

3. Clay's translation: "Those who dispense justice (*dikaspoloi*) and who uphold the Ordinances (*themistas*) of Zeus." *Hesiod's Cosmos*, 73.

4. Hammer claims that "Homer" uses the quarrel to critique not just Agamemnon but supposed "Dark Age" norms of authority based on fear, superior might, and inherited authority, "upon which Agamemnon premises his leadership." But the *Iliad* portrays Agamemnon as, like his forbears, an egregious violator of paternal and kingly norms. Supposedly atypical in this regard, he is a child-sacrificing father, a people-sacrificing king. So the notion that he exemplifies norms of kingship, traditional or otherwise, is problematic to say the least. Similarly, the *Iliad* portrays Achilles as, supposedly, uniquely willing to acknowledge and call Agamemnon to account for blatant violations of traditional norms, not as articulating new ones. The Achaians should not "readily obey" Agamemnon because he grossly violates traditional reciprocity between king and people—and between a leader who is *primus inter pares* and the friends who help to avenge a sleight to his honor. At least in the quarrel, Achilles' critique of Agamemnon and his fellow Achaians is not the vehicle for a novel "political" conception of authority. What might be novel is a narrative in which a hero critiques a leader who flouts fundamental norms, while the hero accuses his fellows of (unlike him) ignoring the leader's failure to fulfill the traditional kingly responsibilities on which their ready obedience should be based—but even this may be traditional. "Who Shall Readily Obey?" 3–7. Pitt-Rivers, "Honour and Social Status," 21-22f.

5. Early source for sacrifice of Iphigenia: Proclus, Summary of the *Cypria*. For history of the speculation that Agamemnon alludes to Kalchas's advice to sacrifice Iphigenia, see Kirk, *Iliad*, on 1.108. For Achilles and Apollo as rivals for the same *timê*, see Nagy, *Best of the Achaeans*, 150.

6. In "the strategy of 'splitting' . . . the individual splits his or her ambivalent feelings between two relationships, keeping one positive and close, and projecting negative feelings to the second relationship." Jacobvitz et al., "Cross-Sex and Same-Sex," 42, who cite Juni, "Triangulation as Splitting."

7. The metaphor of the scepter that will no longer flourish is particularly significant in light of Sinos's location of Achilles in a class of vegetal heroes, tied to *kourotrophos* goddesses throughout their interminable youths, and whose normal cycles of vegetal growth to maturation are cut short due to the peculiar circumstances of their births. *Achilles, Patroklos*, 13f.

8. "Enormous guilt related to perceived oedipal transgressions leads" sons whose mothers are seductive toward them "to fear retaliation from an enraged, vindictive, and castrating father at any moment." Gabbard, "Role of Mother-Son Incest," 71f.

9. Slater, *Glory of Hera*, 29–33, 193, 198, 200, 338–39.

10. Agamemnon's sacrifice of his men is well-suited as a vehicle to evoke the "betrayal trauma" of child-sacrifice. Jonathan Shay cites Agamemnon's betrayal of *themis* in the *Iliad* as an example of betrayal by superiors, which may have been the leading cause of post-traumatic stress disorder among returning Vietnam veterans. *Achilles in Vietnam*, 25; cited by Freyd, *Betrayal Trauma*, 62.

11. For projection in an attachment framework, see Mikulincer et al., "Attachment-Related Defensive Processes" 303–4.

12. Avoidant (as opposed to securely attached) individuals erroneously attribute to others "traits taken from their unwanted selves." Mikulincer et al., "Attachment-Related Defensive Processes," 303–4.

13. Hammer accepts at face value Achilles' assertion that "the only people Agamemnon still has authority over, the only people who will submit to Agamemnon's leadership, are 'nonentities (*outidanoisin*),' those who no longer speak or act." "Who Shall Readily Obey?" 4–6.

14. *Iliad* 18.437–38. On Thetis as "*kourotrophos*, nurturer of the plant-like *kouros*, Achilles," see Sinos, *Achilles, Patroklos*, 24. On the derivation of *kouros* from *koros* (shoot [of a plant]) and its connection to *kourotrophos*, and Thetis's characterization of Achilles as *phuton hôs* (like a shoot) at 18.57 and 18.438, see Nagy, *Best of the Achaians*, §11 n. 5 and n. 6.

15. For Hammer, Agamemnon's glaring shortcomings are less significant than the traditional concepts of kingly authority that he supposedly embodies. (Kingly virtues of responsible care and *noos*, which might inspire ready obedience, are left out of the account.) Achilles, by contrast, introduces new conceptions of political authority and excellence appropriate to the emerging *polis*. "Who Shall Readily Obey?" 3–4; cited by Alexander, *War That Killed Achilles*, 237 n. 20.

16. "The tragic figure of Oedipus becomes the original *katharma*" (scapegoat victim; used as a synonym for *pharmakos*). Where once there was an altar on which the victim was sacrificed, "now there is an amphitheater and a stage on which the fate of the *katharma*, played out by an actor, will purge the spectators of their passions and provoke a new *katharsis*, both individual and collective. This *katharsis* will restore the health and well-being of the community." Girard, *Violence and the Sacred*, 290–91; cf. 303 and 76–77; see also Burkert, *Homo Necans*, 35, 38, 124–26; Burkert, *Structure and History*, 65–66; and Burkert, *Oedipus*, 82–84.

17. For a parallel discussion of Achilles as a sacrificial victim who takes the pain of the Achaians on himself, see Sinos, *Achilles, Patroklos*, 66–67. On a child's redirection of anger "away from her mother and toward something which, or someone who could not retaliate," see Bowlby, *Secure Base*, 87.

18. By scapegoating Agamemnon, the *Iliad* and myth place him at the center of an amnesia that preserves attachments to traumatically abusive caregivers. Cf. Freyd, "Betrayal Trauma," 317–19.

19. In the course of arguing that epic and comic as well as tragic catharsis, and the purgation of anger as well as pity and fear, are Aristotelian, Janko quotes a scholiast on *Iliad* 1.1, who explains that "'Homer begins his epic with the word 'wrath,' in order that, as a result of this emotion, the relevant part of the soul may be purified [*apokathareusei*] and he may make the hearers more attentive to . . . the poem and accustom us to endure our *pathê* nobly." Janko, "From Catharsis," 350.

20. On the ways that tragic catharsis may enhance moral clarity and "a character's correct understanding of his situation as a human being," see Nussbaum, *Fragility of Goodness*, 45, 388–91; and essays by Janko, Nehemas, and Rorty, in Rorty, *Essays on Aristotle's Poetics*.

CHAPTER FIVE

1. *Theogony* 392–400. Zeus "promised that those who joined his side would be allowed to keep the honor they held previously; and whoever had been without honor or privilege under Cronus would receive both, as appropriate, *he themis estin*"—and in accord with *dikê.* Clay, *Hesiod's Cosmos*, 29, 132. On Zeus's *mêtis* as "anticipating what would happen on the basis of what had happened and learning from others' experience," see Muellner, *Anger of Achilles*, 117.

2. For the *mênis* of Thetis, see chapters 1, 2, 4, 7, and 8, this volume.

3. On Apollo as Zeus's loyal son and defender from the beginning and Apollo's threat to Zeus and *themis* as a malicious rumor concocted by Hera, see Clay, *Politics of Olympus*, 74. On the omission of Apollo's name from the list of conspirators and allusion to his participation by referring to his and Poseidon's punishment for the crime, see Lang, "Reverberation and Mythology," 148, 150–51. Cf. Apollod. *Lib.* 2.5.9 n. 3: "Homer does not explain why Apollo and Poseidon took service with Laomedon, but his Scholiast on Hom. *Il.* 21.444, in agreement with Tzetzes, Scholiast on *Lycophron 34*, says that their service was a punishment inflicted on them by Zeus for a conspiracy into which some of the gods had entered for the purpose of putting him, the supreme god, in bonds. The conspiracy is mentioned by Hom. *Il.* 1.399ff., who names Poseidon, Hera, and Athena, but not Apollo, among the conspirators." In a parallel incident, Apollo's light sentence of servitude to a mortal for opposing Zeus is the result of Leto's intercession: "Apollo would have been cast by Zeus into Tartarus" because he was angry with Zeus for thunderbolting his son "but Leto interceded for him, and he became bondman to a mortal." *Cat. of Women and Eoiae* fr. 91, in Hesiod, *Hom. Hymns*; cf. Apollod. *Lib.* 3.10.4; Diod. 4.71. Cf. also Muellner, who sees the binding episode as lacking the intergenerational threat of mother and son versus father. *Anger of Achilles*, 119–20.

4. This does not explain why Poseidon receives the same light sentence, and we do not know the punishments meted out to the other conspirators, though none reside in Tartaros. Since Hera presumably gets the upper hand by guile, perhaps her punishment is similar to the one Zeus recounts in 15.14–33. When she deceives him with regard to his son, Herakles, Zeus tortures her and hurls from Olympus any god who comes to her defense.

5. *Iliad* 5.650–51, 7.452f., 21.450–57. Apollod. *Lib.* 2.5.9 and notes.

6. *Hymn Apol.* 334–62, Hesiod, *Hom. Hymns and Hom.*

7. This premise underlies Alexander's contentions that Achilles was free to return home; that his tragic flaw or mistake was his failure to make good on his threat to leave; that the *charis* he sought by sacrificing himself for Agamemnon was unimportant to him or his mother; and that the war was meaningless to Achilles. *War That Killed Achilles*, 101–6, 224–25. The competitive son's yearning for a paternal model mirrors the competitive daughter's yearning for maternal nurture. Herman, *FDI*, 114.

8. Cf. Mead's description of the "big men" of the Mundugumor, who assert their superiority to enemies by giving them lavish feasts that they cannot reciprocate. They are "aggressive, gluttons for power and prestige, [take] far more than their share of

the women of the community and . . . neighboring tribes." They "fear no one and are arrogant and secure enough to betray whom they like with impunity." *Sex and Temperament*, 175–76. On Homeric *basileis* as anthropologists' "big men," see Gottschall, *Rape of Troy*, 23, 76, 177.

9. Herman, *FDI*, 47.

10. While attachment researchers have observed in troubled families many of the features that Bateson and his colleagues hypothesized as causes of schizophrenia, one that is most relevant here, "the absence of anyone in the family, such as a strong and insightful father, who can intervene in the relationship between the mother and child and support the child in the face of the contradictions involved," has not been investigated empirically. Bateson et al., "Toward a Theory," 256. The operation of such a factor is however consistent with recent research, which emphasizes the importance of fathers' indirect (e.g., via their roles in marital conflict or harmony and in overall family functioning) as well as direct effect on children in family systems. See Lamb, *Role of the Father*, 7; Cummings et al., "Fathers in Family Context," 196–221; and DeKlyen et al., "Fathering and Early Onset," 17.

11. Apollod. *Epitome*, 3.5–9 (in vol. 2 of Apollod. *Lib.*); Apollod. *Lib.* 3.10.8–9, with Frazer's notes.

12. The Mundugumor fight their own miniature Trojan Wars over women and their possessions. "Whether she is the wife or is the daughter of another man," a girl will run away to an agreed-upon spot where her new husband and his supporters have gathered to defend her from her enraged male relatives. "She carries with her . . . the sacred flute, which otherwise her angry male relatives will try to keep from her. Her relatives pursue her, and a battle is fought, varying in bitterness according to the chances of a return payment and in proportion to her father's or brother's [or husband's] possessiveness about her. About one-third of Mundugumor marriages begin in this violent fashion." Mead, *Sex and Temperament*, 178, 206, 197–98. Gottschall employs sociobiology to characterize violent contests for Helen and Briseis as, at bottom, Darwinian competition among prolifically procreating males for females. *Rape of Troy*, 44, 59, 62, 84.

13. Digamous, trigamous: Hesiod, *Cat. of Women and Eoiae* fr. 67 (Stesichorus), in *Hom. Hymns and Hom.*, discussed by Davies in "Judgment of Paris," 57–58. Sroufe et al. found that mothers who had been incest victims were liable to be seductive with a son. *Development of the Person*, 115–19.

CHAPTER SIX

1. There is a large literature on "role-reversal" and "parentification"—in which children's needs are sacrificed to parents'—but remarkably little on the specific types analyzed here. Parents' use of children to meet narcissistic needs—to assuage shame and humiliation and to validate parental claims of superiority to ordinary (i.e., attachment-oriented) human beings—is under-researched. This is so even though Bowlby understands Kohut's narcissistic personality and Winnicott's "false self" in terms of the suppression of information that would activate attachment behaviors,

which can result from inversion of mother-child relationships. Bowlby, *Secure Base*, 18, 31–37, 50–52. Cf. Sroufe and Ward, "Seductive Behaviors of Mothers;" Bellow, "Conceptual and Clinical Dilemmas," 47; Wells and Jones, "Object Relations Therapy," 117–31.

2. Slater observes that "the misogynistic heroes of Greek myth can rarely achieve any of their goals without extensive feminine assistance," *Glory of Hera*, 44.

3. For Hera as eponymous mother of heroes, see Householder and Nagy, "Greek," 770–71.

4. *Threpsasa*, from *trephô*, identifies Thetis as *kourotrophos*. Sinos, *Achilles, Patroklos*, 22–24. "Defining Thetis through a selective presentation of her mythology, the *Iliad* makes explicit, emphatic use of her attributes as a nurturing mother—a *kourotrophos*—and protector. . . . Her maternal, protective power [is linked to theme of] the vulnerability of even the greatest of the heroes, . . . semidivine Achilles." Slatkin, *Power of Thetis*, 7, 40–41, and n. 27, who cites Sinos regarding *kourotrophos* goddesses: *Achilles, Patroklos*, 22–24 (Thetis/Achilles), and 13–15 (Demeter/Demophoon). See also Nagy, *Best of the Achaeans*, §11 n. 5, who also cites Sinos; Clader, *Helen*, 75–77; Vidal-Naquet, "Le chasseur noir," 947–49; and Detienne, "*L'olivier*," 302, esp. n. 7. For *Kourotrophos* goddess and right of first sacrifice, see Clay, *Hesiod's Cosmos*, 140, cf. 133, 137.

5. On the prolonged youth and short life expectancy of favored sons nurtured by *kourotrophos* goddesses, see Sinos, *Achilles, Patroklos*, 13.

6. For "bitch-faced" for *kunôpidos* (18.396), see Slatkin, *Power of Thetis*, 57.

7. Cf. Schein, *Mortal Hero*; Slatkin, *Power of Thetis*, 33–39; and Alexander, *War That Killed Achilles*, 14, 154–57. All point to the *Iliad*'s emphasis on Achilles' mortality, his kinship with mortals, and Thetis's kinship with their grieving mothers. Achilles and Thetis are indeed representative of human beings who devalue, deny, and project their humanity—in the specific, fundamental senses of the term described by Bowlby and his followers—onto others, whom they abandon or kill.

8. Sroufe et al., *Development of the Person*, 248; also Sroufe, "Attachment and Development," 361, and the many sources he cites.

9. On "narcissistic parentification" in which the child is "the parent's idealized self-projection," see Jurkovic, "Destructive Parentification," 245–46; and Wells and Jones, "Object Relations Therapy," 118–19.

10. While fantasy (or Kleinian phantasy), splitting, and projection play varying roles in different elaborations of object-relations theory from Fairbairn to Klein to Winnicott and beyond, quality of care—as in Winnicott's famous formulation, "good-enough mothering"—is posited by all as the critical factor in the success or failure of children's efforts to overcome internal splits of self and object. Comparisons and contrasts with ideas of Winnicott, Fairbairn, and Klein, as well as Kohut and Kernberg, are strewn throughout Bowlby's *A Secure Base*. Bowlby attributes differences between his and Klein's ideas about mourning to his "prospective" method, which starts with observing how normal children and adults respond to loss, in contrast to the retrospective method of Klein and others, who make "inferences about earlier phases of psychological development based on observations made during the analysis of older, and emotionally disturbed, subjects." *Secure Base*, 31–32.

11. A gross reversal of *themis*, a parent's sacrifice of a child's needs to his or her own, must remain hidden and unacknowledged. Jurkovic, "Destructive Parentification," 239. For this reason, a child's awareness that his or her needs are being sacrificed must be blocked. Bowlby, *Secure Base*, 101–2, 109.

12. "The avoidant person's motto seems to be 'I would rather handle stresses and distress myself than be humiliated or thrown off guard by having someone reject my bids for help or protection.' Intrapsychically, avoidant defenses involve three main self-protective maneuvers. The first is to block awareness of, or cognitive access to, any emotion, thought, image, fantasy, or memory that might activate the attachment system and cause a wish or desire to seek help or support from an unresponsive attachment figure. A second protective maneuver is to maintain an exaggerated sense of self-worth and entitlement while warding off any emotion, thought, image, fantasy, or memory that implies personal weakness, imperfection, vulnerability, or need. This makes it less likely that a person will be tempted to rely on others for comfort, protection, or support. Along with this strategy comes the third: devaluing others and looking down on them. By means of what social psychologists call downward social comparison, a person can view him- or herself as better, stronger, and wiser than others, and hence as not needing anyone else's love or assistance." Mikulincer et al., "Attachment-Related Defensive Processes," 300.

13. Hektor prays to Zeus that his son will surpass him in *biê*, rule Troy, and bring home blooded spoils of victory to "delight the heart of his mother" (*chareiê de phrena mêtêr*; 6.476–81).

14. On splitting, projecting onto others parts of the self traumatized by narcissistic parents' rejection, and inflicting trauma on those others, see Wells and Jones, "Object Relations Therapy," 118–19.

15. Mothers' envious ambivalence toward sons who reflect glory on them is a major theme of Slater's *Glory of Hera*, but in the *Iliad* it is fathers and father-figures who envy glorious sons. Slater claimed that Athenian families differed from modern, dysfunctional ones in this respect. "The father did not compete with his son within the family . . . Greek males could genuinely love their sons, and, indeed, young boys in general, without these relationships being incapacitated by rivalry." *Glory of Hera*, 57–58. In exchange for his allowing her to sack Troy, Hera offers Zeus the three cities dearest to her heart, Diomedes' Argos, Odysseus's Ithaka, and Agamemnon's Mycenae, as targets for revenge (4.451–53).

16. When "bids for proximity and support fail to achieve a positive interpersonal result (closeness, love, comfort), and instead typically result in a negative outcome (inattention, rejection, anger, disdain, abuse) for showing vulnerability or need, . . . reliance on an attachment figure, and involvement in a dependent or interdependent relationship more generally, is construed as frustrating, demeaning, and painful. Under these conditions, a person may decide, consciously or unconsciously, to rely on him- or herself—becoming what Bowlby (1969/1982) called compulsively self-reliant, and what others have called dismissive of attachment or simply avoidant (of intimacy, closeness, and interdependence)." Mikulincer et al., "Attachment-Related Defensive Processes," 296.

17. Narcissistic parentification demands that "the child . . . sacrifice of the true self for the sake of relational maintenance." Wells and Jones, "Object Relations Therapy," 119.

18. On this reading, the divine mother's anger at mortal presumption in myth is *mênis*. Cf. Slatkin on why Thetis's *mênis* and unmatched power to wreak revenge remain implicit in the *Iliad*. *Power of Thetis*, 96–98.

19. Muellner, *Anger of Achilles*, 106 and 8, 26, 37, 116–17 n. 48, and 126 n. 67. Cf. Nagy, *Best of the Achaians*, 73–76.

20. Thetis's *mênis* "displaced . . . from a mother to her son." Loraux, *Mothers in Mourning*, 49. Thetis's *mênis* "absorbed in the actual wrath of her son." Slatkin, *Power of Thetis*, 103. On *mênis* as indiscriminate, Zeus and Thetis as "enforcers of the social order," and Theogonic versus epic *mênis*, see Muellner, *Anger of Achilles*, 8, 121, 126, 96.

21. See Edmunds, *Homeric Nêpios*, 52, on the fundamental distinction between mother-oriented heroes like Achilles and father-oriented ones like Diomedes and Odysseus. Cf. Mead's discussion of "misfits" among the Mundugumor, without whom the society would disintegrate. These include men who favor intelligence over force and openly cooperate with their fellows, and women who lovingly care for infants and openly accommodate the wishes of others. *Sex and Temperament*, 212–17.

22. In contrast to Zeus of the *Theogony*, who learns from the mistakes of his predecessors, Agamemnon makes the same mistake twice and does not learn from his own immediately preceding experience. Muellner, *Anger of Achilles*, 117.

23. Diomedes cannot remember his father, who died at Thebes when he was little, but he knows stories of his deeds. Athena, his father's protector as well, infuses Diomedes with his father's strength when Diomedes is wounded (6.222–24, 5.116–27).

24. See Clay, *Wrath of Athena*, 81f., 96f., for Homer's elaborate characterization of Odysseus in the *Odyssey* in opposition to two heroes of *biê*, Herakles and Achilles.

25. On Nestor's, Odysseus's, Diomedes', and Antilochos's association with *noos*, *mêtis*, and *nostos*, see Frame, *Myth of Return*, 83–85, and chaps. 3–5.

26. Cf. Clay, *Wrath of Athena*, 43–53, and an explanation of the cessation of Athena's wrath, 214f. Muellner argues for "an analogy between the armor given to Peleus, the armor given to Achilles, and the everlasting glory conferred upon Achilles by the epic tradition, *kleos aphthiton*," all of which are "'immortal' compensations for death." *Anger of Achilles*, 166; cites Nagy, *Best of the Achaians*, 178–89, esp. sec. 8 n. 1.

27. See Muellner, *Anger of Achilles*, 92–93 and 109–11 on the staged learning process that culminates in Zeus's ingestion of Mêtis, though Muellner tends to see Zeus's rule as based on superior force and cunning rather than the experience-based intelligence, or kingly *mêtis*, that would give his rule legitimacy. Cf. Clay, *Wrath of Athena*, 184–85; and Clay, *Hesiod's Cosmos*, 29, 84, and 132.

CHAPTER SEVEN

1. "Clear generational boundaries are characterized by a hierarchy in which parents nurture their children and assume executive roles within the family. In families

with dissolved generational boundaries, the hierarchical relation between the parent and child subsystems is lost." Shaffer and Sroufe, "Boundary Dissolution," 70.

2. Clay, *Hesiod's Cosmos*, 112, notes the conflict with the plan of Zeus at *Iliad* 1.5 and that Zeus purposefully goads Hera into a violent response so he can "appear to give in to his bloody-minded wife . . . while . . . getting his own way."

3. Apollod. *Lib*. 3.13.08 and n. 1. Slatkin recognizes that "Hephaistos's repayment of what he owes Thetis equips her son for destruction and brings him closer to it," but not that the *kourotrophos* mother sacrifices her son's needs for nurture to her own for vindication. *Power of Thetis*, 40–41, 44–45.

4. "Betrayal trauma is also consistent with difficulties with trust, either in the form of too great a willingness to trust or no ability to trust, also common results of child abuse." Brown and Finkelhor, 1986, cited in Freyd, "Betrayal Trauma," 319–20.

CHAPTER EIGHT

1. Cf. Girard on Sophocles' Oedipus, who "is indeed the responsible party, so responsible that he frees the community from all accountability." Taking responsibility for the community's ills may be a part of the victim's role. *Violence and the Sacred*, 77. While noting striking parallels between Sophocles' *Oedipus the King* and the *Iliad*, Griffith denies that either Agamemnon or Achilles plays a scapegoat's role in a cathartic, sacrificial narrative like those analyzed by Burkert and Girard. "Oedipus Pharmakos?" 109. See Hrdy, *Mothers and Others*, for recent developments in ethology that support the thesis presented here.

2. Achilles' realization of the meaning of his loss fits Nussbaum's description of *pathei mathos* in *Fragility of Goodness*, 44–46. Wilson, *"Pathei Mathos* of Achilles," discussed in Lee, *Fathers and Sons*, 189–90; also Else, *Homer and the Homeric Problem*, 44. On misinterpretations of Achilles' supposed critique of the heroic ethos, see Wofford, *Choice of Achilles*, 96, 425; also Whetter, review of *Pity of Achilles*, 235–36.

3. Clay notes the contrast between the proem of the *Iliad*, in which "the wrath of Achilles is blamed for the destruction of countless Greeks," and that of the *Odyssey*, in which the protagonist is absolved of responsibility for the deaths of his companions, even though "in the *Odyssey* itself, Eurylochus places the sole blame on Odysseus for the loss of men in the Cyclops's cave." *Wrath of Athena*, 37–38.

4. On determining who is responsible (*aitios*) for grief (*achos*) as a prelude to *mênis*, see Slatkin, *Power of Thetis*, 85–98, 97–103. Nagy elaborates Palmer's etymology of *Achilles* as "[one] whose *laos* (host of fighting men) has *akhos* (grief)." *Best of the Achaians*, §5 1.6. On "emotional development" as "part of our reasoning capacity as political creatures," and "strong reasons to promote the conditions of emotional well-being in a political culture," see Nussbaum, *Upheavals of Thought*, 3; and epilogue, this volume.

5. On Achilles as "the great leader the Achaeans never had," see Alexander, *War That Killed Achilles*, 23–25, 158, 200–201. "Paragon of leadership." Shay, *Odysseus in America*, 241. In proposing that the funeral games over which Achilles presides

model new conceptions of community, authority, and excellence appropriate to the emerging *polis*, Hammer (on whom Alexander relies) cites numerous authorities who view Achilles as a model king in that context. "'Who Shall Readily Obey?'" 3 n. 16. Yet in the realistic genre of heroic epic, not just Agamemnon but Achilles, Thetis, and even Zeus violate Theogonic *themis*. In the *Theogony*, Zeus is elected king. His authority is both earned and (for good reason) readily obeyed. Although Whitman sees Achilles in the funeral games as having "returned to society as its master, quiet-voiced, a little aloof, but just and generous," he also notes that "only after abandoning all human hope does he at last, in the scene with Priam"—which concerns a different funeral—"achieve his greatest communion with humanity." *Homer and the Heroic Tradition*, 215, 205.

6. The word "*nêpios*" ('deluded, foolish'), is employed when future disaster is implicit." Lowenstam, *Death of Patroklos*, 39, 112. The exchange between Achilles and Patroklos in book 16 echoes that of Thetis and Achilles in book 1, but Achilles "puts Patroclus in the subordinate role of the helpless child petitioning her mother (Achilles), who stands aloof from her child's highly emotional state." Although Thetis seems compassionate while Achilles is distant and cruel, Thetis, in virtue of her divinity, may be less compassionate than she seems. Ledbetter, "Achilles' Self-Address," 484–85, 490 n. 20.

7. The repetition of "Tell me, do not hide it in your mind, and so we shall both know" (*exauda, mê keuthe noôi, hina eidomen amphô*; 16.19, 1.363) and "groaning / sighing heavily [Patroklos / Achilles] answered" (*baru stenachôn prosephês*; 16.20, 1.364) "not only evokes the former scene between Achilles and Thetis, but it also reverses the role played by Achilles; instead of the child seeking comfort, he is put into the role of the parent, or more precisely, the role of his mother." Ledbetter, "Achilles' Self-Address," 483.

8. Loraux, following Slatkin, argues that Homer has "displaced the wrath from a mother [Thetis] to her son" so that Thetis's *mênis* is "absorbed" in Achilles'. Both authors take the wrath of Thetis at face value. It is "the wrath of a goddess who is forced to marry a mortal man without compensation; the grief of Thetis mourning a son who is about to die; the grief-wrath of Thetis, who knows that 'the price of Zeus' hegemony is Achilles' death' and who forces Zeus to give in because he knows she knows." *Mothers in Mourning*, 49; quotes Slatkin, *Wrath of Thetis*, 103. But Thetis is compensated, by Zeus, for her marriage in a way that requires her son's early death and the sacrifice of his *nostos*.

9. Muellner argues that giving Patroklos a chance at glory by warding off devastation from the Achaians is an act of friendship. *Anger of Achilles*, 158–59.

10. "The ability to *loigon amunai* (or *amunein*) within the *Iliad* is shared exclusively by Achilles, Apollo, and Zeus." Slatkin, *Power of Thetis*, 65; cites Nagy, *Best of the Achaeans*, 74–78. Here it extends to Patroklos as an extension of Achilles; cf. also Diomedes: 16.75.

11. Loraux assigns the view of Thetis presented here to the "completely imaginary . . . tradition of the 'race of women'—which the *andres* rouse when they want to feel both terror and fascination." Yet as a paradigmatic, son-sacrificing mother of heroes,

Thetis is in fact "originally guilty of what . . . makes her cry." *Mothers in Mourning*, 55–56. One myth calls in question Achilles' mother's claim to superiority. Cheiron started the rumor that she was Thetis to glorify his friend, Peleus: Schol. Apollon. Rhod. *Argon.* 4.816.

12. Epitomized by the fatal antagonism between Achilles and Apollo, "the hero's ritual antagonism with a divinity can find its epic expression in his aspiration to get the same *timê* as his divine counterpart." Nagy, *Best of the Achaeans*, 150.

13. The final repetition of "speak out, do not hide it" (*exauda, mê keuthe*; 18.74; cf. 16.19 and 1.363) is addressed by Thetis to Achilles, who "sighed heavily" (*baru stenachonti*; 18.70; cf. *baru stenachôn*; 1.364 and 16.20).

14. On Achilles' attempt to have both long life and glory, see Lowenstam, *Death of Patroklos*, 109–10, and n. 8.

15. Nagy, *Best of the Achaians*, 33.

16. On nakedness and its association (for Winnicott's Mr. B) with shame at human need and vulnerability; also on shame, self-repudiation, and violence, see Nussbaum, *Upheavals of Thought*, 196, 346–47.

17. Cf. the trick with which Apollo beguiled him (*dolôi d' ar' ethelgen Apollôn*; 21.604).

18. Favored sons of seductive mothers have "a paranoid tendency to anticipate imminent betrayal." They "often feel that their special role *vis-à-vis* mother is a precarious one contingent on doing her bidding." Gabbard, "Role of Mother-Son Incest," 71–72.

19. Cf. 9.344: "He has deceived me [*apatêse*] and taken from my hands my prize of honour."

20. "Achilles' favor to Zeus consists in his being *minunthadios*, whereby Zeus's sovereignty is guaranteed." Otherwise, "Achilles would have been not the greatest of the heroes, but the ruler of the universe." "The price of Zeus's hegemony is Achilles' death." Slatkin, *Power of Thetis*, 101–2.

21. Mackie, "Achilles in Fire," 330–37. Cauldron: 21.362.

22. On the long history of soldiers' reluctance to kill, see Grossman, *On Killing*.

23. Lowenstam, *Death of Patroklos*, 109–10, 123–24.

24. Achilles is contemptuous of Hektor's survival strategy, but it works, for him and his city: "Hektor would not drive his attack beyond the wall's shelter / but would come forth only so far as the Skaian gates and the oak tree" (9.353–54). Hektor rejects Poulydamas's counsel to return to their unbeatable defensive strategy after the death of Patroklos brings Achilles back into the fighting (18.246–313).

25. "Direct intervention in the human domain does not suit Zeus's style of rule since he acts among mortals only through intermediaries." Thus Apollo's *mênis* at Agamemnon, modulating into Achilles', stands in for Zeus's *mênis* in book 1 of the *Iliad*. Achilles himself "draws a delicate and precise parallel between Zeus and Thetis as enforcers of the social order in which Achilles has the *mênis* and Zeus seconds it." Yet there is "a more antagonistic and competitive model of the relationship between Zeus and Achilles than the *Iliad* permits on its surface. . . . The *Iliad* does not suppress the fatally dangerous aspect of Achilles' superiority: it displaces it from Achilles to

Patroklos, just as it displaces [the role of] Achilles' (and, for that matter, Patroklos's) divine antagonist from Zeus to Apollo." Thus it displaces Zeus's *mênis* at Achilles to Apollo's at Patroklos. Muellner, *Anger of Achilles*, 102–3, 121–22.

26. See Lowenstam's remarkable demonstration of how Patroklos's status as a *nêpios* and *therapôn*; his wearing of Achilles' armor; his being struck a stunning blow by Apollo that precedes the lethal blow; the wrapping of his thigh bones in fat at his funeral; and a number of other motifs mark Patroklos as a substitute victim for Achilles—albeit one whose sacrifice fails to avert Achilles' own. *Death of Patroklos*, 39, 112, 127–29, 157–59, 165, 168–69, 176.

27. "*Mênis* is . . . a continuing expression of the reign of Zeus which emerges in the traditions that culminate in the *Theogony* of Hesiod," but "neither the word *mênis* nor the proper use of the term is conceivable until the *Theogony* is complete." Even as Muellner explicates the *Iliad*'s seeming legitimation of Achilles' *mênis* by equating it with Zeus's, he maps this alternative equation, in which Achilles' *mênis* provokes Zeus's, coinciding with it only when Achilles turns his *mênis* on himself. "For a hero to have *mênis* without incurring it at the same time, Zeus must conspire with him rather than against him." Muellner, *Anger of Achilles*, 26, 94, 120–22. Devious-devising Zeus can conspire with and against a hero at the same time.

28. Muellner, *Anger of Achilles*, 121–22. Cf. the *mênis* of Zeus against mankind in the *Cypria* and *Erga*. Scodel, "Achaean Wall," 82. Cf. Loraux, *Mothers in Mourning*, 52, for a maternal *mênis* that kills only sons, as a revenge on the father/husband.

29. In addition to divine "caprice and whim," Clay recognizes the gods' ruthless protection of their own prerogatives as alternatives to divine support for Theogonic *themis* and *dikê* among men, in the *Iliad* and the *Odyssey* alike. *Wrath of Athena*, 219f., esp. 229–30 and 238–39, with the scholarship she cites.

30. This explanation for the associations among paternal absence, the vulnerability of *nêpia tekna* to disaster, and sons who are *nêpios* complements Edmunds, *Homeric Nêpios*, 28–29: "All instances of *nêpios* children in the *Iliad* are associated with the absence of fathers and the presence of mothers who cannot help them. . . . The third contextual element . . . is the fact or imminence or possibility of doom or destruction."

EPILOGUE

1. This chapter is based on a similarly titled article in *Political Theory* 22, 4 (1994). Unless otherwise noted, all translations of the Platonic dialogues are from *Plato: The Collected Dialogues*.

2. In democratic Athens, as in other "agonistic societies," litigation based on competing legitimacy claims provided a means to engage in rather than resolve ongoing, feud-like contests for honor and dominance. Cohen, *Law, Violence, and Community*, chaps. 4–6, and 163. On Plato's use of the contrast between clever, smooth-talking Odysseus and guileless, truth-telling Achilles to compare rhetorically adept sophists with the truth-seeking philosopher, Socrates, see Barrett, "Plato's 'Apology,'" 15f.

3. For a useful, if overly skeptical discussion of purported examples of justice as the resolution of conflict in the *Oresteia* and other works, see Cohen, "Theodicy of

Aeschylus." On the succession myth in relation to Solon and Aeschylus, see Holway, "Poetry and Political Thought," 367, which cites Solmsen, *Hesiod and Aeschylus*, 107f.

4. For discussions of Socrates' appropriation of Achilles as a model that hew closely to Socrates' self-presentation as a true friend of Athens who speaks truth without dissembling, attacks corruption, and fearlessly stands by his post—while purging, moralizing, and appropriating the *Iliad*'s heroic ethos for philosophy—see Euben, *Tragedy of Political Theory*, 219–25; also Saxonhouse, *Free Speech and Democracy*, cited below, and Zuckert, *Plato's Philosophers*, 256, 815.

5. Cf. how Achilles honors the king of Eëtion, whom he killed, and renounces the queen who is his prize for the deed (6.414–20).

6. Leo Strauss and his devotees have been especially attentive to Socrates' invocation of Achilles: Strauss, "On Plato's *Apology*," 41, 44, 47, 55; Bloom, *Closing of the American Mind*, 66, 274, 280, 281; and Bloom, "Interpretive Essay," 358. For overdrawn contrasts between Socrates and Achilles, see Greenberg's otherwise rewarding "Socrates' Choice," 45–82, 73–74, 79; and West, *Plato's* Apology, 151–52, 154–56, 159. On the emergence of the *polis* in eighth-century Greece, see Martin, *Ancient Greece*, 60–61: and Alexander, *War That Killed Achilles*, 35–36.

7. Adkins, *Merit and Responsibility*; Dodds, *Greeks and the Irrational*, chap. 2. But cf. Long, "Morals and Values," 121–39; and Dickie, "*Dikê* as a Moral Term," 91–101. Here as elsewhere, gods inspire mortals to actions that are consonant with mortals' characters. Gods represent aspects of motivation in "overdetermined" or polyvalent human actions. Dodds, *Greeks and the Irrational*, 7–13. For an overview of Homeric gods, see Schein, *Mortal Hero*, 45–67. For valuable but also problematic revisions of Dodds's shame/guilt dichotomy with regard to Achilles and Socrates, see Hammer, "The *Iliad* as Ethical Thinking," 203–4; and Saxonhouse, *Free Speech and Democracy*, 66–75.

8. As in Socrates' account, so in the *Iliad*: Apollo enforces the distinction between gods and mortals. He beats down heroes when they threaten to become "greater than human." *Iliad* 5.440–42, 16.786–88. (Marsayas, to whom Alcibiades compares Socrates in the *Symposium* [215b], was flayed alive by Apollo for challenging the god to a contest in flute-playing.) But for power (*kratos*) or heroic might (*biê*) that challenge divine prerogatives, Socrates substitutes wisdom. Morgan, *Platonic Piety*, 22.

9. *Apol.* 40a, discussed by Brann, "The Offense of Socrates," 1–2. Critics who deny an association between Homeric *dikê* and justice notwithstanding, Lattimore's translation of *dikaspoloi* as those who "administer the justice of Zeus" is borne out by 19.180–81, where Agamemnon finally acknowledges that his treatment of Achilles was not just (*dikaios*). Long, "Morals and Values," 25–26.

10. *Meno* 95a. Plato anticipates Freud's discovery that "unlawful desires" (*paranomoi/anomoi epithumioi*)—for example, to kill fathers and have intercourse with mothers—while hidden from us in waking life, reveal themselves in dreams. *Rep.* 571a–572b, 573d. Cf. *Rep.* 359d–360b.

11. Cf. the teachings of Socrates' mentor, Diotima: wisdom is communing with the divine, in which are united beauty (*to kalon*), goodness (*to agathon*), and wisdom (*sophia*). (Cf. *Apol.* 21d: Socrates seeks knowledge of what is *kalon k'agathon*.)

Diotima implies that the gods are wise because, being good and beautiful themselves, they are in constant communion with these qualities (*Sym.* 201d–212a). The lover of wisdom, beauty, and goodness is midway between mortal and immortal: although he does not possess these qualities, he is intelligent enough to seek after them (*Sym.* 202e–204b). On Socrates as *pharmakos*, see Morgan, *Platonic Piety*, 204 n. 19. On sacrificial victimage as a path to immortality, see Carpenter, *Folktale, Fiction, and Saga*, 112–14, 122–23.

12. On Apollo's participation in the rebellion, suppressed in *Iliad* 1.399, see chap. 5, this volume. For Plato's attack on Hesiod and on the succession myth in particular in *Republic* 2.376–383, see Belfiore, "'Lies Unlike the Truth,'" 51 f.

13. West, *Plato's* Apology, 129. Cf. the heroic combats that demonstrate Achilles' superiority to mere mortals. Even the formulation "He is wise who, like Socrates, realizes his ignorance" leaves Socrates superior to all other reputedly wise men since they believe themselves wise (*Apol.* 21a–23). On Socrates' implicit claims to demigod status, see Clay, "Socrates' Mulishness," 53–60. On the philosopher's need to identify proper initiates, the "most promising, beautiful or noble (*kaloi*) members of the new generation," youths "with the potential to realize his vision," "in whom to sow [his] seeds" and "'plant' his conception of the best life, the philosophic life," see Zuckert, *Plato's Philosophers*, 199–201.

14. The "human aspiration to divine status" animating Socratic and Platonic philosophy. Morgan, *Platonic Piety*, esp. 8, 21–31, 81–99. In the *Symposium*, Plato's Socrates ultimately rejects both Alcibiades' discourse on love for a particular person (Socrates) and Aristophanes' comic encomium of love between particular persons. Nussbaum, *Fragility of Goodness*, 172–73. On Diotima's and Socrates' repudiation of "earthly need and longing" as "mortal rubbish," see Nussbaum, *Upheavals of Thought*, 495–99, 681–83. Nichols' argument that the *Phaedus* and *Lysis* move beyond the *Symposium's* nonreciprocal eros to establish the importance of "friendship as a reciprocal human relationship, rooted in need" is interesting in light of attachment theory's understanding of "narcissistic self-enhancement." This defense, in which "a person can view him- or herself as better, stronger, and wiser than others, and hence as not needing anyone else's love or assistance," serves to preclude what the person fears will be demeaning or painful experience of dependent or interdependent relationships. Mikulincer et al., "Attachment-Related Defensive Processes," 296, 300, 303.

15. Foley styles Demeter's mothering of Demophoon as a model for the goddess's future relation to initiates—as a symbolic killer, nurse, and "mitigator of death." Foley, *Homeric Hymn to Demeter*, 114. On Diotima as, most likely, a fictional character, see Zuckert, *Plato's Philosophers*, 190 and n. 21.

16. *Sym.* 212e. For Socrates' rivalry with Anytus as Alcibiades' lover, see Littman, "Loves of Alcibiades," 263–76. On "paternal jealousy" as a possible motive of Socrates' accusers, see Strauss, *Fathers and Sons*, 199, 350 n.37; discussed by Saxonhouse, *Freedom of Speech*, 103.

17. Cf. 33c–34b and Socrates' claim that if he had corrupted the young, their fathers would have complained. The jury knew perfectly well "that the chief accuser Anytus considered himself to be just such a parent." Brann, "Offense of Socrates,"

12. Xenophon's Socrates traces Anytus's hostility to Socrates' suggestion that the tanner—and Athenian general—not confine his son's education to preparation for his own servile (*doulopretei*) occupation, but rather to entrust him to a worthy teacher like Socrates. Xen. *Apol.* 29–30.

18. On Socrates' humility in the *Crito*, see West, *Plato's* Apology, 171; Brann, "Offense of Socrates," 1–21, 15, 17–18; and Saxonhouse, "Philosophy of the Particular," 292–97. Also cf. Weiss, who argues that Socrates feigns a hyper-respectful attitude toward the laws for the benefit of Crito, who is not ready for a truer revelation. *Socrates Dissatisfied*, 85f. Cf. the reversal, in *Iliad* 24, of Achilles' initial defiance of paternal and kingly authority.

19. On Socrates' execution as the price of victory in his contest with his accusers, see Greenberg, "Socrates' Choice," 68–72, 76–77, 81.

20. In the *Apology*, Plato deliberately shows us a Socrates who "once at least, was truly dangerous" to the laws of Athens. Brann, "Offense of Socrates," 20–21.

21. "When death comes to a man, his mortal part, it seems, dies, but the immortal part goes away unharmed and undestroyed . . . the soul is immortal and imperishable [*athanaton kai anôlethron*]." *Phaedo* 106. Because of their exceptional purity, Socrates imagines, philosophers will not only escape punishment, they will live without bodies in a pure and beautiful abode. *Phaedo* 114b–c.

22. Socrates implies that his habitual exposures of the incompetence of Athens' leaders and educators *are* provoked—by their hubris in laying claim to a wisdom that is "more than human." *Apol.* 20e; cf. 23b, 29a.

23. In the *Phaedo* (66c–e), Socrates blames the body for passions, desires, and fears that prevent the philosopher from beholding the truth. Only with death and consequent separation from the body is wisdom possible.

24. For Saxonhouse, Socrates is "the open, democratic man who without acknowledging boundaries sees all as equal, interrogating rich and poor alike." "Socratic *parrhesia* in its capacity of revealing denies the division between public and private, what is shared and what is hidden; one's innermost thoughts are revealed and opened in the practice of free speech. There is no realm of hierarchy—divine or human." 123, 105–6, 110–11. While acknowledging Socrates' "antidemocratic sentiments," Euben seeks "to complicate the picture of Socrates as antidemocratic" by asking "whether the real friend may be the seeming enemy." *Corrupting Youth*, 204–6f. Nussbaum, drawing on some of the same psychological works cited here, links the Platonic rejection of ordinary humanity to "an illiberal perfectionist politics, a politics that respects the choices of citizens only insofar as they come up to an externally imposed moral mark." *Upheavals of Thought*, 497–99, 681–83.

25. See Stone, *Trial of Socrates*, especially chap. 9. Leo Strauss and his students have tended to declare Socrates guilty as charged because philosophy is inherently subversive, but not in any way unjust or mistaken. Strauss, "On Plato's *Apology*," 41, 44, 47. Plato's "true *Apology* of Socrates," the *Republic*, "tacitly admits the truth of the charges" against him. Categorically superior to the many, Socrates teaches young men to "despise" Athens, its laws, and its "ignorant" jurors. Although Socrates is innocent of injustice, the uninitiated cannot see this. "There must be a revolution in men's understanding of justice for just deeds to be recognized as such." Bloom, "In-

terpretive Essay," 307–12; and Bloom, *Closing of the American Mind*, 275–76. See also Brann, "Offense of Socrates," 12–13, 19–21; West, *Plato's* Apology, 71; and cf. Mara, *Socrates' Discursive Democracy*, 228. For a summary of these debates, which continue into the present, as well as for an example of this tendency, see Saxonhouse, *Free Speech and Democracy*, 102–11. On the "intense guilt" for injuries to fathers associated with narcissistic mother-son dyads, see Rothstein, "Oedipal Conflicts," 189–99; and Gabbard, "Role of Mother-Son Incest," 333.

26. Like Stone, Munn attributes the antipathy of Socrates' accusers to his arrogance and rejection of popular sovereignty. Munn, *School of History*, 286–91.

27. For a similar comedy of philosophic innocence, in which the friendly attempts of Plato and his pupil Dion to educate Dionysius II (including a "practical lesson" involving military force) "so that he might become a king worthy of is office" are misinterpreted by the tyrant as a clever plot to usurp his throne, see Plato's *Seventh Letter* 333b–c, 334a, 334d–e, 345c–346a, 350b–352a; cf. 324e–325c.

28. On irreconcilable conflicts and incommensurable goods, see Redfield, *Nature and Culture*, 93–95, 166, 219–20; Nussbaum, *Fragility of Goodness*, 25f., 39–42, 51f., 89–104; Euben, *Tragedy of Political Theory*, 36, 233, 235f.

29. A key component of both emotional maturation and of the *mêtis* and *dikê* of theogonic Zeus, this form of respect is highly discriminating. (Hesiod employs *aidôs* and related terms [*Theog.* 92, *WD,* 200] but it is his dramatization in the *Theogony* of respect for others' rights to which I refer here.) This basic respect differs from *aidôs* construed either as indiscriminate respect for authority and community norms, or as shame, "which restrains behavior" by "sensitivity to the judgmental gaze of others and to the historical and social setting in which one lives." Saxonhouse opposes this *aidôs* (which she also attributes to Diomedes in the *Iliad*) both to Socratic free speech and to Socrates' and Achilles' supposed redefinitions of shame. Rather than basing shame on a sense of *dikê*, which Saxonhouse sees as "derived from the customs and the traditions of the community," Achilles and Socrates root shame in "their own private judgments about how justice is to be served." Saxonhouse, *Free Speech and Democracy*, 1–3, 7, 70–71, 118–20. Cf. Nussbaum: "without emotional development, a part of our reasoning capacity as political creatures will be missing." *Upheavals of Thought*, 3.

30. As West points out, Socrates faults not only men like Anytus, who believe in the competence of any Athenian gentleman to teach virtue, but sophists as well for "mindless acceptance of tradition and common opinion." *Plato's* Apology, 102.

31. Achilles calls his fellow Achaians "nonentities" for putting up with Agamemnon's unjust treatment. He must say exactly what seems best to him, regardless of Agamemnon's threats or his friends' wishes. He detests that man "who hides one thing in the depths of his heart and speaks forth another." *Iliad* 1.76–91, 1.231–39, 9.309–14; cf. *Apol.* 32a–e, 36b–c; and *Crito* 46b. Saxonhouse, for example, views Socrates as both "impervious to the gaze of others" and "complete and invulnerable himself." He is completely transparent, having "nothing to hide from others." "No barrier hides any parts of Socrates while allowing other parts to reveal themselves. There is no secret Socrates." Saxonhouse, *Free Speech and Democracy*, 75, 123.

See also, n. 24, above, and Euben, *Tragedy of Political Theory*, and Zuckert, *Plato's Philosophers*, n. 4, above.

32. *Rep.* 571–75, 571b. Just as "Achilles is perfection" and therefore rightly the master of other men (an arresting political theory), so "no one wants Socrates to be ruled by inferior men." Bloom, *Closing of the American Mind*, 265; cf. 274–75, 282, 283, 290. For a contrasting view, see Arist. *Pol.* 1276b 20–30, 1277b 10–30, 1318b–1319a.

33. Clay, *Hesiod's Cosmos*, 73–74.

34. For Socrates' boast that he has triumphed over Anytus in a contest for "whichever one of us has wrought the more beneficial and noble deeds for all time"—accompanied by a reference to Anytus's occupation as "servile" and a claim to superior judgment in the matter of the education of his son, see Xen. *Apol.* 29–30.

35. Edmunds, *Homeric Nêpios*, 31–32. Cf. Euben: "Socrates mentions his sons and so reaffirms his mortality and identity as a member of a community situated in time and space." *Tragedy of Political Theory*, 228–29.

36. "The dream means, obviously, that on the third day Socrates' soul, after death, will find its way home." Grube, *Trial and Death of Socrates*, 44. Quoted by Kramer, who situates the dream in this wider network of allusions centered on "Thetis, beautiful and fair." Kramer, "Socrates' Dream," 193–97.

Selected Bibliography

Adkins, Arthur. *Merit and Responsibility: A Study in Greek Values.* Oxford University Press, 1960.

Aeschylus. *Prometheus Bound, with an English Translation by Herbert Weir Smyth.* Harvard University Press, 1926.

Ainsworth, Mary D. Salter. *Infancy in Uganda: Infant Care and the Growth of Love.* Johns Hopkins University Press, 1967.

———. *Patterns of Attachment.* Lawrence Erlbaum Associates, 1978.

Alexander, Caroline. *The War That Killed Achilles: The True Story of Homer's* Iliad *and the Trojan War.* Viking, 2009.

Apollodorus. *The Library, with an English Translation by Sir James George Frazer, F. B. A., F. R. S. in 2 Volumes.* Harvard University Press, 1921.

Apollonius Rhodius. *Argonautica.* Edited and translated by R. C. Seaton. Harvard University Press, 1912. Gutenberg electronic edition edited, proofed, and prepared by Douglas B. Killings, 1997.

Aristotle. *The Complete Works of Aristotle: The Revised Oxford Translation, Jonathan Barnes,* ed. Princeton University Press, 1984.

Arthur, Marylin. "Politics and Pomegranates: An Interpretation of the Homeric Hymn to Demeter." *Arethusa* 10, no. 1 (Spring 1977): 7–48.

Austin, Norman. *Helen of Troy and Her Shameless Phantom.* Cornell University Press, 1994.

Bacciagaluppi, Marco. "The Relevance of Attachment Research to Psychoanalysis and Analytic Social Psychology." *Journal of the American Academy of Psychoanalysis* 22, no. 3 (1994): 465–79.

Barrett, James. "Plato's 'Apology': Philosophy, Rhetoric, and the World of Myth." *Classical World* 95, no. 1 (2001): 3–30.

Bateson, Gregory et al. "Toward a Theory of Schizophrenia." *Behavioral Science* 1, no. 4 (1956): 251–64.

Becvar, Dorothy Stroh, and Raphael J. Becvar. *Family Therapy.* 6th ed. Pearson Allyn and Bacon, 2006.

Belfiore, Elizabeth. "'Lies Unlike the Truth': Plato on Hesiod, *Theogony* 27." *Transactions of the American Philological Association* 115 (1985): 47–57.

Bellow, Shana M. et al. "Conceptual and Clinical Dilemmas in Defining and Assessing Role Reversal in Young Child-Caregiver Relationships." In *Implications of Parent-Child Boundary Dissolution*, edited by Patricia K. Kerig, 43–66. Haworth Press, 2005.

Bennett, C. Susanne. "Attachment Theory and Research Applied to the Conceptualization and Treatment of Pathological Narcissism." *Clinical Social Work* 34, no. 1 (March 2006): 45–60.

Bloom, Allan. *The Closing of the American Mind: How Higher Education Has Failed Democracy and Impoverished the Souls of Today's Students*. Simon and Schuster, 1987.

———. "Interpretive Essay." In *The Republic of Plato*, 307–12. Basic Books, 1968.

Blum, Harold. "The Role of Identification in the Resolution of Trauma." *Psychoanalytic Quarterly* 56 (1987): 609–71.

Boszormenyi-Nagy, Ivan et al. *Invisible Loyalties: Reciprocity in Intergenerational Family Therapy*. Harper & Row, 1973.

Bowen, Murray. "Family Relationships in Schizophrenia." In *Schizophrenia: An Integrated Approach*, edited by Alfred Auerback. Ronald Press, 1959.

Bowlby, John. *Attachment and Loss*. Basic Books, 1969–1980.

———. *Maternal Care and Mental Health*. World Health Organization, 1952.

———. *A Secure Base: Parent-Child Attachment and Healthy Human Development*. Basic Books, 1988.

Bowlby, John et al. *Child Care and the Growth of Love*. Penguin Books, 1965.

Brabeck, Mary M. *Practicing Feminist Ethics in Psychology*. 1st ed. Psychology of Women Book Series. American Psychological Association, 2000.

Brann, Eva. "The Offense of Socrates: A Rereading of Plato's *Apology*." *Interpretation* 7, no. 2 (May 1978): 1–2.

Bretherton, Inge. "The Origins of Attachment Theory: John Bowlby and Mary Ainsworth." *Developmental Psychology* 28 (1992): 759–75.

Bretherton, Inge, and Timothy F. Page. "Shared or Conflicting Working Models? Relationships in Post-Divorce Families Seen through the Eyes of Mothers and Their Preschool Children." *Children, Development and Psychopathology* 16 (2004): 551–75.

Burkert, Walter. "Greek Tragedy and Sacrificial Ritual." *Greek, Roman and Byzantine Studies* 7 (1966): 87–121.

———. *Homo Necans*. Translated by Peter Bing. University of California Press, 1983. First published 1972 by De Gruyter.

———. *Oedipus, Oracles, and Meaning: From Sophocles to Umberto Eco*. University of Toronto, 1991.

———. *Structure and History in Greek Mythology and Ritual*. University of California Press, 1979.

Burkett, L. P. "Parenting Behaviors of Women Who Were Sexually Abused as Children in Their Families of Origin." *Family Process* 30 (1991): 421–34.

Byng-Hall, John. "Creating a Secure Family Base: Some Implications of Attachment Theory for Family Therapy." *Family Process* 34 (1995): 45–58.

———. "Relieving Parentified Children's Burdens in Families with Insecure Attachment Patterns." *Family Process* 41, no. 3 (2002): 375–88.

Cairns, Douglas. *Aidos: The Psychology and Ethics of Honour and Shame in Ancient Greek Literature.* Oxford University Press, 1993.

Caplan, Paula J., and Ian Hall-McCorquodale. "Mother-Blaming in Major Clinical Journals." *American Journal of Orthopsychiatry* 55, no. 3 (1985): 345–53.

Carlson, E. A., L. A. Sroufe, and B. Egeland. "The Construction of Experience: A Longitudinal Study of Representation and Behavior." *Child Development* 75, no. 1 (2004): 66–83.

Carpenter, Rhys. *Folktale, Fiction, and Saga in the Homeric Epics.* University of California Press, 1956, 112–14, 122–23.

Cassidy, Jude, and R. Rogers Kobak. "Avoidance and Its Relation to Other Defensive Processes." In *Clinical Implications of Attachment*, edited by J. Belsky and T. Nezworski, 300–23. Lawrence Erlbaum Associates, 1988.

Chase, Nancy D., ed. *Burdened Children: Theory, Research, and Treatment of Parentification.* Sage Publications, 1999.

Chodorow, Nancy. "Family Structure and Feminine Personality." In *The Homeric Hymn to Demeter*, by Helene P. Foley, 243–66. Princeton University Press, 1994. First published 1974 by Stanford University Press.

———. *Femininities, Masculinities, Sexualities.* University Press of Kentucky, 1994.

———. *Feminism and Psychoanalytic Theory.* Yale University Press, 1989.

———. "Mothering, Object-relations, and the Female Oedipal Configuration." *Feminist Studies* 4, no. 1 (1978): 137–58.

———. *The Reproduction of Mothering: Psychoanalysis and the Sociology of Gender, with a New Preface.* University of California Press, 1978/1999.

Clader, Linda Lee. *Helen: The Evolution from Divine to Heroic in Greek Epic Tradition.* Brill, 1976.

Clarkin, John F., Elsa Marziali, and Heather Munroe-Blum. *Borderline Personality Disorder.* Guilford Press, 1992.

Clay, Diskin. "Socrates' Mulishness and Heroism," *Phronesis* 17 (1972): 53–60.

Clay, Jenny Strauss. *Hesiod's Cosmos.* Cambridge University Press, 2003.

———. *The Politics of Olympus.* Princeton University Press, 1989.

———. Review of *The Anger of Achilles: Mênis in Greek Epic*, by Leonard Muellner. *American Journal of Philology* 118, no. 4 (1977): 631–34.

———. *The Wrath of Athena.* Princeton University Press, 1983.

Cohen, David. *Law, Violence, and Community in Classical Athens.* Cambridge University Press, 1995.

———. "The Theodicy of Aeschylus: Justice and Tyranny in the 'Oresteia.'" *Greece and Rome*, 2nd ser., vol. 33, no. 2 (October 1986): 129–41.

Collins, Christopher. *Authority Figures.* Rowman & Littlefield, 1996.

Cosmides, L. "The Logic of Social Exchange: Has Natural Selection Shaped How Humans Reason? Studies with the Wason Selection Task." *Cognition* 31 (1989): 187–276.

Cosmides, L., and J. Tooby. "Cognitive Adaptations for Social Exchange." In *The Adapted Mind: Evolutionary Psychology and the Generation of Culture*, edited by J. H. Barkow, L. Cosmides, and J. Tooby, 163–228. Oxford University Press, 1992.

Crotty, Kevin. *The Poetics of Supplication*. Cornell University Press, 1994.

Cummings, E. Mark et al. "Fathers in Family Context: Effects of Marital Quality and Marital Conflict." In *The Role of the Father in Child Development*, edited by Michael E. Lamb, 4th ed., 196–221. John Wiley & Sons, 2004.

Daston, Lorraine, and Fernando Vidal. *The Moral Authority of Nature*. University of Chicago Press, 2004.

Davies, M. "The Judgment of Paris and *Iliad* XXIV." *Journal of Hellenic Studies* 101 (1981): 56–62.

Davies, P. T., G. T. Harold, M. C. Goeke-Morey, and M. E. Cummings. "Child Emotional Security and Interparental Conflict." *Monographs of the Society for Research in Child Development* 67, no. 3 (2002).

DeKlyen, Michelle et al. "Fathering and Early Onset Conduct Problems: Positive and Negative Parenting, Father-Son Attachment, and the Marital Context." *Clinical Child and Family Psychology Review* 1, no. 1 (1998): 3–21.

Detienne, Marcel. *Dionysos Slain*. Johns Hopkins University Press, 1979.

———. "*L'olivier: Un mythe politico-religieux*." In *Problèmes de la Terre en Grèece ancienne*, edited by M. I. Finley, 293–306. Mouton, 1973.

Dickie, Matthew, "*Dikê* as a Moral Term in Homer and Hesiod," *Classical Philology* 73 (1978): 91–101.

Dinnerstein, Dorothy. *The Mermaid and the Minotaur: Sexual Arrangements and the Human Malaise*. Other Press, 1999.

Diodorus of Sicily, translated by C. H. Oldfather et al. Loeb 279, 303, 340, 375, 377, 384, 389, 390, 399, 409, 422–23. Harvard University Press and W. Heinemann, 1933–1967.

Dodds, E. R. *The Greeks and the Irrational*. University of California Press, 1951.

Edmunds, Susan T. *Homeric Nêpios*. Garland, 1990.

Egeland, Byron et al. "Breaking the Cycle of Abuse." *Child Development* 59, no. 4 (August 1988): 1080–88.

———. "*The Developmental Consequences of Different Patterns of Maltreatment*." *Child Abuse and Neglect* 7, no. 4 (1983): 459–69.

Elicker, J., M. Englund, and L. A. Sroufe. "Predicting Peer Competence and Peer Relationships in Childhood from Early Parent-Child Relationships." In *Family-Peer Relationships: Modes of Linkage*, edited by R. D. Parke, and G. W. Ladd, 77–106. Lawrence Erlbaum Associates, 1992.

Else, Gerald. *Homer and the Homeric Problem*. University of Cincinnati Press, 1965.

Euben, J. Peter. *Corrupting Youth: Political Education, Democratic Culture, and Political Theory*. Princeton University Press, 1997.

———. *Platonic Noise*. Princeton University Press, 2003.

———. *The Tragedy of Political Theory: The Road Not Taken*. Princeton University Press, 1990.

Fairbairn, Gavin and Susan. *Integrating Special Children*. Avebury, 1992.

Fairbairn, W. R. D. *Psychoanalytic Studies of the Personality*. Tavistock/Routledge, 1952.

Fairbairn, W. R. D. et al. *From Instinct to Self*. Jason Aronson, 1994.

Fenik, Bernard. *Typical Battle Scenes in the Iliad*. F. Steiner, 1968.

Finley, Moses I. *The World of Odysseus*. Viking Press, 1978.

Fish, M., J. Belsky, and L. Youngblade. "Developmental Antecedents and Measurement of Intergenerational Boundary Violation in a Non-clinical Sample." *Journal of Family Psychology* 4, no. 3 (1991): 278–97.

Foley, Helene P. *Female Acts in Greek Tragedy*. Princeton University Press, 2001.

———. *The Homeric Hymn to Demeter*. Princeton University Press, 1994.

———. *Ritual Irony*. Ithaca, NY: Cornell University Press, 1985.

———. "Sex and State in Ancient Greece." Review of *The Glory of Hera: Greek Mythology and the Greek Family*, by Philip E. Slater. *Diacritics* 5, no. 4 (Winter 1975): 31–36.

Frame, Douglas. *The Myth of Return in Early Greek Epic*. Yale University Press, 1978.

Frankel, Jay. "Exploring Ferenczi's Concept of Identification with the Aggressor: Its Role in Trauma, Everyday Life, and the Therapeutic Relationship." *Psychoanalytic Dialogues* 12, no. 1 (2002): 101–39.

Freud, Anna, and Dorothy Burlingham. *The Ego and the Mechanisms of Defense*. International Universities Press, 1967.

———. *Introduction to Psychoanalysis*. International Universities Press, 1974.

———. *Normality and Pathology in Childhood*. International Universities Press, 1965.

———. *Psychoanalytic Psychology of Normal Development, 1970–1980*. International Universities Press, 1981.

———. *War and Children*. Greenwood Press, 1973.

Freyd, Jennifer. *Betrayal Trauma*. Harvard University Press, 1996.

———. "Betrayal Trauma: Traumatic Amnesia as an Adaptive Response to Childhood Abuse." *Ethics & Behavior* 4, no. 4 (1994): 307–29.

Fullinwider-Bush, Nell, and Deborah B. Jacobvitz. "The Transition to Young Adulthood: Generational Boundary Dissolution and Female Identity Development." *Family Process* 32 (1993): 87–103.

Gabbard G. O., and S. W. Twemlow. "The Role of Mother-Son Incest in the Pathogenesis of Narcissistic Personality Disorder." *Journal of the American Psychoanalytic Association* 42, no. 1 (1994): 171–89.

Gantz, Timothy. *Early Greek Myth: A Guide to Literary and Artistic Sources*. Johns Hopkins University Press, 1993.

Girard, René. *Violence and the Sacred*. Johns Hopkins University Press, 1977.

Golden, Mark. *Childhood in Classical Athens*. Johns Hopkins University Press, 1990.

Gottman, John M., and Clifford I. Notarius. "Marital Research in the 20th Century and a Research Agenda for the 21st Century." *Family Process* 41 (2002): 159–97.

Gottschall, Jonathan. *The Rape of Troy: Emotion, Violence, and the World of Homer*. Cambridge University Press, 2008.

Gouldner, Alvin. *Enter Plato: Classical Greece and the Origins of Social Theory*. Harper & Row, 1971.

Graves, Robert. *The Greek Myths.* Penguin Books, 1992.

Greenberg, N. A. "Socrates' Choice in the *Crito.*" *Harvard Studies in Classical Philology* 70 (1965)

Griffith, R. Drew. "Oedipus Pharmakos? Alleged Scapegoating in Sophocles' 'Oedipus the King.'" *Phoenix* 47, no. 2 (1993): 95–114.

Grossman, Dave. *On Killing: The Psychological Cost of Learning to Kill in War and Society.* Little, Brown, 1995. Rev. ed., 2009.

Grotstein, J. S., and D. B. Rinsley, eds. *Fairbairn and the Origins of Object Relations.* Guilford Press, 1994.

Grube, G. M. A. *The Trial and Death of Socrates.* 2nd ed. Hackett, 1975.

Guttman, Herta A. "The Epigenesis of the Family System as a Context for Individual Development." *Family Process* 41, no. 3 (2002): 533–45.

Haaken, Janice. "Sex Differences and Narcissistic Disorders." *American Journal of Psychoanalysis* 43, no. 4 (1983): 315.

Haaken, Janice, and Sharon Lamb. "The Politics of Child Sexual Abuse Research." *Society* 37, no. 4 (May 2000): 7–14.

Hammer, Dean. "The *Iliad* as Ethical Thinking: Politics, Pity, and the Operation of Esteem." *Arethusa* 35 (2002): 203–35.

———. *The Iliad as Politics.* Oklahoma Series in Classical Culture, vol. 28. Norman: University of Oklahoma Press, 2002.

———. "'Who Shall Readily Obey?': Authority and Politics in the *Iliad.*" *Phoenix* 51, no. 1 (Spring 1997): 1–24.

Harrison, Simon. Review of *The Mundugumor: From the Field Notes of Margaret Mead and Reo Fortune,* by Nancy McDowell. *Oceania* (June 1995): 362–63.

Hazen, Nancy et al. "Antecedents of Boundary Disturbances in Families with Young Children: Intergenerational Transmission and Parent-Infant Caregiving Patterns." In *Implications of Parent-Child Boundary Dissolution for Developmental Psychopathology: "Who Is the Parent and Who Is the Child?"* edited by Patricia K. Kerig, 85–110. Haworth Press, 2005.

Herman, Judith L. *Trauma and Recovery: The Aftermath of Violence—From Domestic Abuse to Political Terror.* Rev. ed. Basic Books, 1997.

Herman, Judith L., and Lisa Hirschman. *Father-Daughter Incest.* Harvard University Press, 1981/2000.

Herman, Judith L. et al. "Childhood Trauma in Borderline Personality Disorder." *American Journal of Psychiatry* 146, no. 4 (1989): 490–95.

Hesiod. *The Homeric Hymns and Homerica, with an English Translation by Hugh G. Evelyn-White, M. A.* Cambridge, MA: Harvard University Press and W. Heinemann, 1914.

———. *Works of Hesiod and the Homeric Hymns.* Edited by Daryl Hine. University of Chicago Press, 2005.

Himmelhoch, Leah. Review of Georg Wöhrle, *Telemachs Reise: Väter und Söhne in Ilias und Odysee. Bryn Mawr Classical Review* 2000.

Holway, Richard. "Achilles, Socrates, and Democracy." *Political Theory* 22, no. 4 (1994): 561–90.

―――. "Poetry and Political Thought in Archaic Greece: The *Iliad*, the *Theogony*, and the Rise of the Polis." Ph.D. diss. University of California, Berkeley. 1989.

Homer. Iliad, *Book Nine*. Edited with introduction and commentary by Jasper Griffin. Oxford University Press, 1995.

―――. *The Iliad*. Translated by Richmond Lattimore. University of Chicago Press, 1951.

―――. *The Odyssey of Homer*. Translated by Richmond Lattimore. Harper & Row, 1967.

Householder, F. W., and Gregory Nagy. "Greek." *Current Trends in Linguistics* 9 (1972): 735–816.

Hrdy, Sarah Blaffer. *Mothers and Others: The Evolutionary Origins of Mutual Understanding*. Harvard University Press, 2009.

Hudson, Liam, and Bernadine Jacot. *The Way Men Think: Intellect, Intimacy, and the Erotic Imagination*. Yale University Press, 1993.

Hughes, Dennis D. *Human Sacrifice in Ancient Greece*. Routledge, 1991.

Huizinga, Johan. *Homo Ludens: A Study of the Play-Element in Culture*. Routledge, 1980.

Ingalls, Wayne. "Demography and Dowries: Perspectives on Female Infanticide in Classical Greece." *Phoenix* 56, no. 3/4 (2002): 246–54.

Irwin, Elizabeth. *Solon and Early Greek Poetry*. Cambridge University Press, 2005.

Jacobs, Janet Liebman. "Victimized Daughters: Sexual Violence and the Empathic Female Self." *Signs: Journal of Women in Culture and Society* 19, no. 11 (1993): 126–45.

Jacobvitz, Deborah B., and Nell F. Bush. "Reconstructions of Family Relationships: Parent-Child Alliances, Personal Distress, and Self-Esteem." *Developmental Psychology* 32, no. 4 (1996): 732–43.

Jacobvitz, Deborah B., and Nancy Hazen. "Developmental Pathways from Infant Disorganization to Childhood Peer Relationships." In *Attachment Disorganization*, edited by Judith Solomon and Carol George, 127–59. Guilford Press, 1999.

Jacobvitz, Deborah B. et al. "Cross-Sex and Same-Sex Family Alliances: Immediate and Long-Term Effects on Sons and Daughters." In *Burdened Children: Theory, Research, and Treatment of Parentification*, edited by Nancy D. Chase, 34–55. Sage Publications, 1999.

Jacobvitz, Deborah B. et al. "The Transmission of Mother-Child Boundary Disturbances across Three Generations." *Development and Psychopathology* 3 (1991): 513–27.

Janko, Richard. "From Catharsis to the Aristotelian Mean." In *Essays on Aristotle's Poetics*, edited by Amelie O. Rorty, 341–58. Princeton University Press, 1992.

Jantzen, Grace M. *Foundations of Violence*. Routledge, 2004.

Jones, R. A., and M. Wells. "An Empirical Study of Parentification and Personality." *American Journal of Family Therapy* 24 (1996): 145–52.

Juni, S. "Triangulation as Splitting in the Service of Ambivalence." *Current Psychology: Research & Reviews* 14 (1995): 91–111.

Jurkovic, Gregory J. "Destructive Parentification in Families: Causes and Consequences." In *Family Psychopathology*, edited by L. L'Abate. Guilford Press, 1998.

———. *Lost Childhoods: The Plight of the Parentified Child.* Brunner/Mazel, 1997.

Katz, Marilyn. "Ideology and 'The Status of Women' in Ancient Greece." In *Women in Antiquity: New Assessments,* edited by Richard Hawley and Barbara Levick, 21–43. Routledge, 1995.

Kauffman, Jeffrey. *Loss of the Assumptive World.* Brunner-Routledge, 2002.

Kaufman, Joan, and Edward Zigler. "Do Abused Children Become Abusive Parents?" *American Journal of Orthopsychiatry* 57, no. 2 (1987): 186–92.

Kerényi, Karl, and James Hillman. *The Gods of the Greeks.* Grove Press, 1960.

———. *Oedipus Variations.* Spring Publications, 1991.

Kerig, Patricia A., ed. *Implications of Parent-Child Boundary Dissolution for Developmental Psychopathology: "Who Is the Parent and Who Is the Child?"* Haworth Press, 2006.

Kernberg, Otto F. *Aggression in Personality Disorders and Perversions.* Yale University Press, 1992.

———. *Borderline Conditions and Pathological Narcissism.* Jason Aronson, 1975.

———. *Love Relations.* Yale University Press, 1995.

———. *Psychodynamic Psychotherapy of Borderline Patients.* Basic Books, 1989.

———. *Severe Personality Disorders.* Yale University Press, 1984.

Kim, J. *The Pity of Achilles: Oral Style and the Unity of the Iliad.* Greek Studies: Interdisciplinary Approaches. Rowman & Littlefield, 2000.

Kimerling, Rachel, Paige Ouimette, and Jessica Wolfe. *Gender and PTSD.* Guilford Press, 2002.

Kirk, G. S. *The Iliad: A Commentary.* Cambridge University Press, 1985–1993.

Kitts, Margo. *Sanctified Violence in Homeric Society: Oath-Making Rituals and Narratives in the Iliad.* Cambridge University Press, 2005.

Klever, Paul. "Marital Fusion and Differentiation" in Murray Bowen and Peter Titelman, eds., *Clinical Applications of Bowen Family Systems Theory,* 119-146. Haworth Press, 1998.

Kochanska, Grazyna. "Mutually Responsive Orientation between Mothers and Their Young Children: A Context for the Early Development of Conscience." *Current Directions in Psychological Science* 11, no. 6 (December 2002): 191–95.

Koenig, Linda J. *From Child Sexual Abuse to Adult Sexual Risk.* 1st ed. American Psychological Association, 2004.

Kohut, Heinz. *The Analysis of the Self.* International Universities Press, 1971.

———. *The Curve of Life.* Edited by Geoffrey Cocks. University of Chicago Press, 1994.

———. *The Restoration of the Self.* International Universities Press, 1977.

———. "Two Analyses of Mr. Z." *International Journal of Psychoanalysis* 60, no. 1 (1979): 3–27.

Kohut, Heinz, and Arnold Goldberg. *The Psychology of the Self.* International Universities Press, 1978.

Kohut, Heinz, and Charles B. Strozier. *Self Psychology and the Humanities.* W. W. Norton, 1985.

Kohut, Heinz et al. *The Kohut Seminars on Self Psychology and Psychotherapy with Adolescents and Young Adults.* W. W. Norton, 1987.

Kramer, Scott. "Socrates' Dream: Crito 44a-b." *Classical Journal* 83, no. 3 (1988):193–97.

Kretchmar, Molly D., and Deborah B. Jacobvitz. "Observing Mother-Child Relationships across Generations: Boundary Patterns, Attachment, and the Transmission of Caregiving." *Family Process* 41, no. 3 (2002): 351–74.

Lamb, Michael E. *The Role of the Father in Child Development.* 4th ed. J. Wiley, 2004.

Lang, Mabel L. "Reverberation and Mythology in the *Iliad*." In *Approaches to Homer*, edited by Carl A. Rubino and Cynthia W. Shelmerdine, 140–64. University of Texas Press, 1983.

Lasch, Christopher. *The Culture of Narcissism.* W. W. Norton, 1979.

Ledbetter, Grace M. "Achilles' Self-Address: *Iliad* 16.7–19." *American Journal of Philology* 114, no. 4 (Winter 1993): 481–91.

Lee, M. Owen. *Fathers and Sons in Virgil's Aeneid: Tum Genitor Natum.* State University of New York Press, 1979.

Lendon, Jon E. *Soldiers and Ghosts: A History of Battle in Classical Antiquity.* Yale University Press, 2005.

Leon, Kim et al. "Representations of Parent Alliances in Children's Family Drawings." *Social Development* 16, no. 3 (2007): 25–44.

Lidz, Theodore, and Stephen Fleck. *Schizophrenia and the Family.* International Universities Press, 1985.

Lidz, Theodore et al. "The Intrafamilial Environment of Schizophrenic Patients: II. Marital Schism and Marital Skew." *American Journal of Psychiatry* 114 (1957): 241–48.

Lipset, David. "Rereading *Sex and Temperament*: Margaret Mead's Sepik Triptych and Its Ethnographic Critics." *Anthropological Quarterly* 76, no. 4 (2003): 693–713.

Littman, Robert J. "The Loves of Alcibiades." *Transactions of the American Philological Association* 101 (1970): 263–76.

Long, Anthony. "Morals and Values in Homer" *Journal of Hellenic Studies* 90 (1970): 121–39.

Loraux, Nicole. *Mothers in Mourning.* Translated by Corinne Pache. Cornell University Press, 1998; Originally published as *Les mères en deuil.* Editions de Seuil. 1990, 1990, and 1988.

———. *The Mourning Voice.* Cornell University Press, 2002.

———. *Tragic Ways of Killing a Woman.* Harvard University Press, 1987.

Lowenstam, Steven. *The Death of Patroklos.* Königstein: Anton Hain, 1981.

MacCary, W. Thomas. *Childlike Achilles.* Columbia University Press, 1982.

Macfie, J. et al. "The Effect of Father-Toddler and Mother-Toddler Role Reversal on the Development of Behavior Problems in Kindergarten." *Social Development* 14 (2005): 514–31.

———. "Intergenerational Transmission of Role Reversal between Parent and Child: Dyadic and Family System Internal Working Models." *Attachment and Human Development* 7 (2005): 51–65.

Mackie, C. J. "Achilles in Fire." *Classical Quarterly, New Series* 48, no. 2 (1998): 329–38.

Main, Mary, and Ruth Goldwyn. "Predicting Rejection of Her Infant from Mother's Representation of Her Own Experience: Implications for the Abused-Abusing Intergenerational Cycle." *Child Abuse & Neglect* 8, no. 2 (1984): 203–17.

Main, Mary, and Jackolyn Stadtman. "Infant Response to Rejection of Physical Contact by the Mother." *Journal of the American Academy of Child Psychiatry* 20, no. 2 (1981): 292–307.

Mara, Gerald M. *Socrates' Discursive Democracy*. State University of New York Press, 1997.

Martin, Richard P. "Hesiod, Odysseus, and the Instruction of Princes." *Transactions of the American Philological Association* 114 (1984): 29–48.

———. *The Language of Heroes*. Cornell University Press, 1989.

Martin, Thomas R. *Ancient Greece: From Prehistoric to Hellenistic Times*. Yale University Press, 1996.

Marvin, R. S., and R. B. Stewart. "A Family System Framework for the Study of Attachment." In *Attachment beyond the Preschool Years*, edited by M. T. Greenberg, D. Cicchetti, and M. Cummings, 51–86. University of Chicago Press, 1990.

McCarthy, Gerard, and Alan Taylor. "Avoidant/Ambivalent Attachment Style as a Mediator between Abusive Childhood Experiences and Adult Relationship Difficulties." *Journal of Child Psychology and Psychiatry and Allied Disciplines* 40, no. 3 (1999): 465–77.

McDowell, Nancy. *The Mundugumor: From the Field Notes of Margaret Mead and Reo Fortune*. Smithsonian Institution Press, 1991.

Mead, Margaret. *Sex and Temperament in Three Primitive Societies*. Morrow, 1935/1963.

Michell, Gillian. "The Reproduction of Narcissism." *Women & Therapy* 7, no. 4 (1988).

Miklowitz, David J. "The Role of Family Systems in Severe and Recurrent Psychiatric Disorders: A Developmental Psychopathology View." *Development and Psychopathology* 16 (2004): 667–88.

Mikulincer, Mario, Phillip R. Shaver, Jude Cassidy, and Ety Berant. "Attachment-Related Defensive Processes." In *Attachment Theory and Research in Clinical Work with Adults*, edited by Joseph H. Obegi and Ety Berant, 293–327. Guilford Press, 2009.

Miller, Alice. *Prisoners of Childhood*. Basic Books, 1981.

Minuchin, Salvador. *Families and Family Therapy*. Harvard University Press, 1974.

Morgan, Michael L. *Platonic Piety*. Yale University Press, 1990.

Muellner, Leonard C. *The Anger of Achilles: Mênis in Greek Epic*. Cornell University Press, 1996.

———. *The Meaning of Homeric EYXOMAI through Its Formulas*. Innsbrucker Beitrèage zur Sprachwissenschaft. Bd. 13. Inst. f. Sprachwissenschaft d. University Innsbruck, 1976.

Naas, Michael. *Turning: From Persuasion to Philosophy*. Humanities Press, 1995.

Nagler, Michael N. *Spontaneity and Tradition in the Iliad*. University of California Press, 1974.

Nagy, Gregory. *The Best of the Achaeans*. Johns Hopkins University Press, 1979.
———. *Comparative Studies in Greek and Indic Meter*. Harvard University Press, 1974.
———. *Greek Mythology and Poetics*. Cornell University Press, 1990.
———. "Mythological Exemplum in Homer." In *Innovations of Antiquity*, edited by R. Hexter and D. Selden, 311–31. Routledge, 1992.
———. *Pindar's Homer*. Johns Hopkins University Press, 1990.
Nichols, Mary P. *Socrates on Friendship and Community: Reflections on Plato's Symposium, Phaedrus, and Lysis*. Cambridge University Press, 2010.
Nichols, Michael P., and Richard C. Schwartz. *Family Therapy*. Allyn and Bacon, 1998.
Nonnos. *Dionysiaca, Volume 1, Books 1–15, with an English Translation by W. H. D. Rouse*. Harvard University Press, 2004.
Nussbaum, Martha C. *The Fragility of Goodness*. Cambridge University Press, 1986.
———. *Upheavals of Thought: The Intelligence of Emotions*. Cambridge University Press, 2001.
O'Brien, Joan V. *The Transformation of Hera*. Rowman & Littlefield, 1993.
Ogden, Daniel. "Crooked Speech: The Genesis of the Spartan Rhetra." *Journal of Hellenic Studies* 114 (1994): 85–102.
Paris, Joel. *Borderline Personality Disorder*. American Psychiatric Press, 1993.
Parke, R. D. "Development in the Family." *Annual Review of Psychology* 55 (2004): 365–99.
———. *Fatherhood*. Harvard University Press, 1996.
Parke, R. D., and Raymond Buriel. "Socialization in the Family: Ethnic and Ecological Perspectives." In *Handbook of Child Psychology*, edited by William Damon and Richard M. Lerner, vol. 3 of *Social, Emotional, and Personality Development*, edited by Nancy Eisenberg. John Wiley & Sons, 2006.
Patterson, Cynthia B. *The Family in Greek History*. Harvard University Press, 1998.
Pausanias. *Pausanias Description of Greece with an English Translation by W. H. S. Jones, Litt.D., and H. A. Ormerod, M. A., in 4 Volumes*. William Heinemann, 1918.
Peck, S. D. "Measuring Sensitivity Moment-by-Moment: A Microanalytic Look at the Transmission of Attachment." *Attachment and Human Development* 5 (2003): 38–63.
Peristiany, J. G. *Honour and Shame: The Values of Mediterranean Society*. University of Chicago Press, 1977.
———, ed. *Mediterranean Family Structures*. Cambridge University Press, 1976.
Peristiany, J. G., and Julian Pitt-Rivers, eds. *Honor and Grace in Anthropology*. Cambridge University Press, 1992.
Pindar. *The Odes of Pindar including the Principal Fragments with an Introduction and an English Translation by Sir John Sandys, Litt. D., F. B. A.* Harvard University Press, 1937.
Pitkin, Hanna Fenichel. *Fortune Is a Woman: Gender and Politics in the Thought of Niccolo Machiavelli*. University of Chicago Press, 1999.

Pitt-Rivers, Julian. "Honour and Social Status." In *Honour and Shame: The Values of Mediterranean Society*, edited by J. G. Peristiany, 21–77. University of Chicago Press, 1977.

Plato. *The Collected Dialogues of Plato Including the Letters*. Edited by Edith Hamilton and Huntington Cairns. Princeton University Press, 1961.

Pomeroy, Sarah B. *Families in Classical and Hellenistic Greece: Representations and Realities*. Oxford University Press, 1997.

Proclus. Summary of the *Cypria* in Proclus's *Summary of the Epic Cycle, Omitting the Telegony*. Translated by Gregory Nagy. http://www.stoa.org.

Pucci, Pietro. *Odysseus Polutropos*. Cornell University Press, 1987.

Quintus Smyrnaeus. *The Fall of Troy*. Translated by A. S. Way. Internet Classics Archive.

Raaflaub, Kurt, and Hans Wees, eds. *A Companion to the Archaic Greek World*. Blackwell, 2006.

Rabel, Robert J. "Apollo as a Model for Achilles in the *Iliad*," *American Journal of Philology* 111, no. 4 (1990): 429–40.

Redfield, James M. *Nature and Culture in the Iliad*. University of Chicago Press, 1975.

Reinhardt, Karl. "The Judgment of Paris." In *Homer: German Scholarship in Translation*, edited by G. M. Wright and P. V. Jones, 170–91. Oxford University Press, 1997.

———. *Die Ilias und ihr Dichter*. Göttingen: Vandenhoeck und Ruprecht, 1961.

Richardson, N. J. *The Homeric Hymn to Demeter*. Oxford University Press, 1974.

Ricks, Margaret H. "The Social Transmission of Parental Behavior: Attachment across Generations." In *Monographs of the Society for Research in Child Development* 50, no. 1/2 (1985): 211–27.

Rorty, Amelie O., ed. *Essays on Aristotle's Poetics*. Princeton University Press, 1992.

Rothstein, A. "Oedipal Conflicts in Narcissistic Personality Disorders." *International Journal of Psychoanalysis* 60, no. 2 (1979): 189–99.

Sandler, J. "Countertransference and Role-Responsiveness." *International Review of Psychoanalysis* 3 (1976): 43–47.

Satter, Beryl. "The Sexual Abuse Paradigm in Historical Perspective: Passivity and Emotion in Mid-Twentieth-Century America." *Journal of the History of Sexuality* 12, no. 3 (July 2003): 424–64.

Saxonhouse, Arlene W. *Free Speech and Democracy in Ancient Athens*. Cambridge University Press, 2008.

———. "The Philosophy of the Particular and the Universality of the City: Socrates' Education of Euthyphro," *Political Theory* 16 (1988): 281–99.

Schein, Seth L. *The Mortal Hero: An Introduction to Homer's Iliad*. University of California Press, 1984.

Scodel, Ruth. "The Achaean Wall and the Myth of Destruction." *Harvard Studies in Classical Philology* 86 (1982): 33–50.

Segal, Charles. *Singers, Heroes, and Gods in the Odyssey*. Cornell University Press, 1994.

———. *The Theme of the Mutilation of the Corpse in the Iliad*. Leiden: Brill, 1971.

Shaffer, Anne, and L. Alan Sroufe. "Boundary Dissolution in the Family System: The Developmental and Adaptational Implications of Generational Boundary Dissolution, Findings from a Prospective, Longitudinal Study." *Journal of Emotional Abuse* 5, no. 2/3 (2005): 67–84.

Shay, Jonathan. *Achilles in Vietnam: Combat Trauma and the Undoing of Character.* Atheneum, 1994.

———. *Odysseus in America: Combat Trauma and the Trials of Homecoming.* Scribner, 2002.

Shields, Ann, and Dante Cicchetti. "Parental Maltreatment and Emotion Dysregulation as Risk Factors for Bullying and Victimization in Middle Childhood." *Journal of Clinical Child Psychology* 30, no. 3 (2001): 349–63.

Sinos, Dale S. *Achilles, Patroklos and the Meaning of Philos in the Iliad.* Institut für Sprachwissenschaft der Universität Innsbruck, 1980.

Slater, Philip. *The Glory of Hera: Greek Mythology and the Greek Family.* Beacon Press, 1968 (repr. Princeton University Press 1992).

Slatkin, Laura. "Genre and Generation in the Odyssey." *Metis* 1, no. 2 (1986): 259–68.

———. *The Power of Thetis: Allusion and Interpretation in the Iliad.* University of California Press, 1991.

Snodgrass, Anthony. *Archaic Greece.* University of California Press, 1980.

Solmsen, Friedrich. *Hesiod and Aeschylus.* Cornell University Press, 1995.

Solomon, Judith, and Carol George, eds. *Attachment Disorganization.* Guilford Press, 1999.

Spiro, Melford E. *Gender Ideology and Psychological Reality: An Essay on Cultural Reproduction.* Yale University Press, 1997.

Sroufe, L. Alan. "Attachment and Development: A Prospective, Longitudinal Study from Birth to Adulthood." *Attachment & Human Development* 7, no. 4 (2005): 349–67.

Sroufe, L. Alan, and Mary J. Ward. "Seductive Behavior of Mothers of Toddlers: Occurrence, Correlates, and Family Origins." *Child Development* 51, no. 4 (December 1980): 1222–29.

Sroufe, L. Alan et al. *The Development of the Person: The Minnesota Study of Risk and Adaptation from Birth to Adulthood.* Guilford Press, 2005.

Sroufe, L. Alan et al. "Generational Boundary Dissolution between Mothers and Their Preschool Children: A Relationship Systems Approach." *Child Development* 56, no. 2 (April 1985): 317–25.

Statius, *Thebaid, Achilleid.* J. H. Mozley, tr. Harvard University Press, 1928.

Stevens, P. T. "The Judgment of Paris." Review of *Euripides and the Judgment of Paris*, by T. C. W. Stinton. *Classical Review* 16 (December 1966): 290–91.

Stone, I. F. *The Trial of Socrates.* Little, Brown, 1988.

Strauss, Barry. *Fathers and Sons in Athens: Ideology and Society in the Era of the Peloponnesian War.* Princeton University Press, 1993.

Strauss, Leo, "On Plato's *Apology of Socrates* and *Crito.*" Originally published in 1976. Reprinted in *Leo Strauss: Studies in Platonic Political Philosophy*, edited by Thomas L. Pangle, 38–66. University of Chicago Press, 1983.

Terr, Lenore. "What Happens to Early Memories of Trauma? A Study of Twenty Children under Age Five at the Time of Documented Traumatic Events." *Journal of the American Academy of Child and Adolescent Psychiatry* 27, no. 1 (1988): 96–104.

———. *Unchained Memories: True Stories of Traumatic Memories, Lost and Found.* Basic Books, 1994.

Thomas, Carol G., and Craig Conant. *Citadel to City-State: The Transformation of Greece, 1200 B.C.E.* Bloomington: Indiana University Press, 1999.

Troy, M., and L. A. Sroufe. "Victimization among Preschoolers: Role of Attachment Relationship History." *Journal of the American Academy of Child and Adolescent Psychiatry* 26 (1987): 166–72.

Tuzin, Donald F. Review of *The Mundugumor: From the Field Notes of Margaret Mead and Reo Fortune*, by Nancy McDowell. *Ethnohistory* 40, no. 3 (Summer 1993): 505–10.

Van Brock, N. "*Substitution rituelle.*" *Revue Hittite et Asianique* 65 (1959): 117–46.

Van Nortwick, Thomas. *Somewhere I Have Never Travelled: The Second Self and the Hero's Journey in Ancient Epic.* Oxford University Press, 1992.

Vidal-Naquet, P. "Le chasseur noir et l'origine de l'éphébie athénienne." *Annales: Economies, Sociétés, Civilisations*, (1968) 947–64.

Walcot, P. "The Judgement of Paris." *Greece & Rome*, 2nd ser., vol. 24, no. 1 (April 1977): 31–39.

Weil, Simone. *The Iliad; or, the Poem of Force.* Pendle Hill, 1976.

Weiss, Roslyn. *Socrates Dissatisfied: An Analysis of Plato's Crito.* Oxford University Press, 1998.

———. *The Socratic Paradox and Its Enemies.* University of Chicago Press, 2006.

Wells, Marolyn, and Rebecca Jones. "Relationships among Childhood Parentification, Splitting, and Dissociation: Preliminary Findings." *American Journal of Family Therapy* 26 (1998): 331–34.

———. "Object Relations Therapy for Individuals with Narcissistic and Masochistic Parentification Styles." In *Burdened Children*, edited by Nancy D. Chase. 117–31. Sage Publications, 1999.

West, Thomas G. *Plato's* Apology of Socrates: *An Interpretation, with a New Translation.* Cornell University Press, 1979.

Whetter, K. S., review of *The Pity of Achilles: Oral Style and the Unity of the Iliad* by Jinyo Kim. Rowman and Littlefield, 2000. *Classical Review* 52, no. 2 (2002): 235–36.

Whitley, James. *The Archaeology of Ancient Greece.* Cambridge University Press, 2001.

Whitman, Cedric H. *Homer and the Heroic Tradition.* W. W. Norton, 1965.

Willcock, Malcolm M. *A Commentary on Homer's Iliad.* St. Martin's Press, 1970.

———. *A Companion to the Iliad: Based on the Translation of Richmond Lattimore.* University of Chicago Press, 1976.

———. *The Iliad of Homer, Books XIII–XXIV.* St. Martin's Press, 1984.

Wilson, Donna. *Ransom, Revenge, and Heroic Identity in the Iliad.* Cambridge University Press, 2002.

Wilson, John R. "Eris in Euripides." *Greece & Rome* 26, no. 1 (December 1966): 7–20.

Wilson, P. C. "The *Pathei Mathos* of Achilles." *Transactions of the American Philological Association* 69 (1938): 557–74.

Winnicott, D. W. *The Child, the Family and the Outside World*. Penguin Books, 1969.

———. *The Family and Individual Development*. Tavistock/Routledge, 1989.

———. *Holding and Interpretation: Fragment of an Analysis*. Grove Press, 1986.

———. *Maturational Processes and the Facilitating Environment*. International Universities Press, 1965.

———. *Mother and Child*. Basic Books, 1957.

Winnicott, D. W. et al. *Home Is Where We Start From*. W. W. Norton, 1986.

———. *Deprivation and Delinquency*. Tavistock/Methuen, 1984.

Wofford, Susanne. *The Choice of Achilles: The Ideology of Figure in the Epic*. Stanford University Press, 1992.

Wöhrle, Georg. *Telemachs Reise: Väter und Söhne in Ilias und Odysee oder ein Beitrag zur Erforschung der Männlichkeitsideologie in der Homerischen Welt*. Vandenhoeck & Ruprecht, 1999.

Wood, Beatrice, ed. "Attachment and Family Systems." *Family Process* 41, no. 3 (2002).

Wright, G. M., and P. V. Jones. *Homer: German Scholarship in Translation*. Oxford University Press, 1997.

Wright, John Henry. *Essays on the Iliad*. Bloomington: Indiana University Press, 1978.

Wynne, Lyman C. "Communication Disorders and the Quest for Relatedness in Families of Schizophrenics." *American Journal of Psychoanalysis* 30, no. 2 (1970): 100–114.

Wynne, Lyman C. et al. "Genotype-Environment Interaction in the Schizophrenia Spectrum: Genetic Liability and Global Family Ratings in the Finnish Adoption Study." *Family Process* 45, no. 4 (2006): 419–34.

———. "Pseudo-Mutuality in the Family Relations of Schizophrenics." *Psychiatry* 21, no. 2 (1958): 205–20.

Xenophon. *Xenophon in Seven Volumes. Memorabilia, Oeconomicus, Symposium, and Apology*. E. C. Marchant and O. J. Todd, trs. Harvard University Press, 1979.

Zuckert, Catherine H. *Plato's Philosophers: The Coherence of the Dialogues*. University of Chicago Press, 2009.

Index

24, 64, 83, 85, 91, 98, 107, 118–19, 121, 123, 171; as husband, 17–18, 93–94; insecurity of, 12, 15, 39, 64, 66, 68, 72, 83; and marriage/concubinage arrangements, 8–9, 14–15, 17–18, 30, 34, 36, 39–41, 58, 92–93, 95–97; motivations of, 12, 32; Odysseus and, 125–27; and peace attempt, 131–36; as prototype for Socrates' accusers, 182; quarrel of, 3, 7–26, 45, 61–77, 83, 91–96, 177–78; as scapegoat, 75–77, 117, 120, 154; Thetis's and Achilles' sacrifices for, 86–89; transgressions/mistakes of, 7–8, 12–14, 17–18, 64, 66, 71, 76, 85, 170, 173, 181–82; Zeus and, 23–24, 81
aggression, 1–2, 154,
aidôs (shame, respect), 228n29. *See also* shame
Aigisthos, 172–73
Aineias, 100, 162
Ainsworth, Mary, xiii
aitios (blameworthy, responsible for), 156, 162, 163, 165, 167, 172–73, 175; and *mênis*, 221n4
Alcibiades, 186–87
Alexander, Caroline, 200n7, 203n22, 203n24, 209n39, 211n11, 213n2, 216n7, 221n5
alkê (courage), 143
alter egos, Achilles', 155–70
Amyntor, 16–17, 45, 69, 81
anger: daughters', 3, 38, 41, 81, 85; divine mother's, 1, 54, 57, 116, 119, 120, 122, 133, 137, 151; Hera's, 17, 23–4, 28, 30, 59, 80, 89, 109, 150; and honor, 46; maternal, 123, 131, 142–150, 174; at parents/caregivers, 77–78, 87, 106, 116; paternal, 46, 172; purgation of, 154–56; redirection of, 2, 3, 5, 31, 33, 41, 44, 61, 78, 79, 106, 116, 145, 157, 167; Thetis's, 20, 107, 108, 115, 150; wives', 116, 148. *See also mênis*

Antilochos, 127
anxiety, maturation and, 131, 137–38, 147
Anytus, 179–80, 184, 189, 190, 193–95
apatê (deception), 134
Aphrodite, 14, 22–25, 35–36, 80, 82, 98, 100, 103, 129, 137, 139, 173
Apollo, 8, 11, 14, 22, 46, 47, 59–60, 64, 88–90, 95, 100, 128, 159–60, 162, 163, 170, 171, 179–82, 184–86
Archilochos, 4, 179
Aristotle, 78
Artemis, 60, 66
Asklepios, 89, 95
Atê, 141
atê (madness/delusion/folly), 134–35, 138, 140–41, 144–46
Athena, 8, 18, 22–23, 35, 72, 86, 88, 123, 128, 129, 133, 138–39, 144, 146–48, 150, 153, 161, 162, 166, 169, 181, 220n23
Athens, political culture of, 177–97
attachment, xiii, 1, 27, 34, 42–3, 68, 75, 110, 162, 199n4, 205n7, 205n9, 206n16, 208n29, 208n32, 209nn33–35, 210n4, 210n6, 211n11, 214n11, 215n12, 215n18, 217n10, 217n1, 218n7, 219n12, 219n16. *See also* divided working models of child and parent/caregiver, defensive exclusion of information, defensive processes, narcissistic self-enhancement, working models of child and parent/caregiver
authority: of Agamemnon, 9, 82–83, 85, 120, 132–34, 151; kingly, 7, 12, 27, 120, 132, 214n4; paternal, 7, 27, 80, 132; of Zeus, 10, 81, 84
autonomy, 194–95
avoidant defenses, 219n12, 219n16

Bateson, Gregory, 42, 45, 199n4
biê (might), 12, 14, 147
blame. *See aitios*
Bloom, Allan, 192, 227n25